VILLAINS & VIRTUES
BOOK I

THRONE
IN THE
DARK

A.K. CAGGIANO

ISBN: 9798844640414

Throne in the Dark is a work of fiction. Names, characters, places, and incidents either are the product of the author's imagination or are used fictitiously. Any resemblance to actual persons, living or dead, events, or locales is entirely coincidental, and would, frankly, be pretty damn wild, don't you think?

Cover Art by Anna Mariya Georgieva

First printing 2022 by A. K. Caggiano

For more, please visit:
http://www.akcaggiano.com

ALSO BY A. K. CAGGIANO

STANDALONE NOVELS:
The Korinniad - An ancient Greek romcom
She's All Thaumaturgy - A sword and sorcery romcom
The Association - A supernatural murder mystery

VACANCY
A CONTEMPORARY (SUB)URBAN FANTASY TRILOGY:
Book One: The Weary Traveler
Book Two: The Wayward Deed
Book Three: The Willful Inheritor

VILLAINS & VIRTUES
A FANTASY ROMCOM TRILOGY:
Book One: Throne in the Dark
Book Two: Summoned to the Wilds
Book Three: Eclipse of the Crown

FOR MORE, PLEASE VISIT:
WWW.AKCAGGIANO.COM

For anyone who hasn't yet had enough of silly love stories

Contents

CHAPTER 1 - SUPREME EVIL AND WHAT IT ENTAILS....................1

CHAPTER 2 - A DISSERTATION ON INTENT AND ITS USEFULNESS...13

CHAPTER 3 - THE EBBING SANITARIUM OF MAL-SOMETHING-OR-OTHER...23

CHAPTER 4 - HEAVY IS THE HEAD THAT WEARS THE CROWN OF BUREAUCRACY...34

CHAPTER 5 - SACRIFICIAL DESIGNATIONS...........................41

CHAPTER 6 - THE ROAD TO THE ABYSS ISN'T PAVED WITH GOOD INTENTIONS OR REALLY ANYTHING, PAVEMENT HASN'T BEEN INVENTED YET..52

CHAPTER 7 - THE TRANSITIVE PROPERTIES OF BLOOD AND CURSES...59

CHAPTER 8 - BETTER THE DEMON YOU KNOW THAN THE WOLF YOU DON'T..67

CHAPTER 9 - THE FABRICA OF SWAMP ALCHEMISTS..............79

CHAPTER 10 - ALL THAT IS GOLD DOES NOT GLITTER, BUT IT IS USUALLY MALLEABLE...90

CHAPTER 11 - ALCHEMICALLY SIGNIFICANT SUCCESSES AND FAILURES...97

CHAPTER 12 - TO LOATHE, HINDER, AND OBEY.....................106

CHAPTER 13 - HOW TO FORCE COMPANIONSHIP AND MANIPULATE EVIL..119

CHAPTER 14 - KAREE ON, MAYK MARY, ADOOR TROOLY..129

CHAPTER 15 - UNHOLY OFFERINGS.....................................139

CHAPTER 16 - THE CORRELATION BETWEEN THE BUSTINESS OF GODDESSES AND THE FORTUNE OF THEIR FOLLOWERS...151

CHAPTER 17 - IDENTIFYING ARCANA AND ITS USES...........164

CHAPTER 18 - TRADE DEALS, TARIFFS, AND TRANSLOCATION...172

CHAPTER 19 - A VERY GOOD THIEF AND A VERY BAD VILLAIN..181

CHAPTER 20 - FEAR AND LONGING IN THE HAUNTED FOREST..193

CHAPTER 21 - ESSENTIAL KNOTS FOR CAPTURE AND RELEASE...203

CHAPTER 22 - NEGOTIATION TACTICS FOR FOREIGN AND DOMESTIC SOIL...215

CHAPTER 23 - A REBUTTAL TO THE USEFULNESS OF INTENT 224

CHAPTER 24 - A MAN THAT STUDIES REVENGE, KEEPS HIS OWN WOUNDS GREEN..230

CHAPTER 25 - ON THE DANGERS OF LIBRARIANS 242

CHAPTER 26 - THE PRIMEVAL ARCANA OF CURSING........249

CHAPTER 27 - THE PRACTICAL EFFECTS OF SLOWLY ADMINISTERED POISON..259

CHAPTER 28 - IN KNOWING NOTHING, LIFE IS MOST DELIGHTFUL, OR AT LEAST TOLERABLE.................................271

CHAPTER 29 - THE MANY FACETS OF TEMPERAMENT........281

CHAPTER 30 - A FEW DROPPED EAVES....................................287

CHAPTER 31 - THE FUTILITY OF FINDING HUMOR IN EVERY CHAPTER OF A ROMANTIC COMEDY..................................295

CHAPTER 32 - A LESSON IN VILLAINY......................................303

CHAPTER 33 - BALL GOWNS AND BLOOD MAGES.................310

CHAPTER 34 - A MORALITY PLAY IN ONE ACT 322

CHAPTER 35 - THROWN IN THE DARK.....................................336

CHAPTER 1
SUPREME EVIL AND WHAT IT ENTAILS

The discourse surrounding the most superlatively evil being to have ever blighted the realm of Eiren is complex and has already been written about in many thick and pedantic tomes. While the argument has been made for a number of villains to ascend to the coveted spot of Supreme Evil, notably Everild the Necromancer, Scorlisha Baneblade of the Mounted Beasts, The Plague Bringer Norasthmus, and Dave from Next Door Who Insists on Doing Yard Work at Dawn, there are also a number of names which remain unspoken by the populace of Eiren, for merely their utterance alone is said to corrupt. These are the demons, servants of the dark gods who are sealed in the Abyss, and while valiant scholars and the devoutly holy are compelled to study these beings so that their attempts to rise to power may be thwarted, infernal names are only traded in hushed whispers for fear of summoning them.

If only summoning a demon were so easy.

Damien Maleficus Bloodthorne fell into a heap, nearly drained, dagger clattering to the floor at his side. So viscous it was nearly black, blood pooled around him. It crawled slowly away from his worn, muscled body in the shaft of hazy light that cleaved through the chamber's single window many stories above. He steadied himself, hand slick against the stone floor, breath coming ragged but full. Peering between black strands of sweat-drenched hair, his violet eyes bore into it, the amalgamation of years of study and expedition reduced to a small pile of components atop a single piece of inkarnaught ore no larger than a gold coin. With the last of his infernal arcana, he dragged a finger in his own gore, trailing crimson across the floor as he drew the sigil he had designed, and waited.

Silence blew through the chamber, sweeping over Damien's pallid skin. The slices across his chest and arms burned with the frigid air but gave up no more blood—there was nothing left to give, unless his thinning patience counted. He grit his teeth, refusing to accept another failure. This attempt included not just his strongest spell and his own noxscura-flooded blood, but sand from the shores of the Everdarque, dew from the ash tree that grew in the middle of the Maroon Sea, and a feather of the last known fire roc. If it did not succeed, nothing would.

The inkarnaught ore sparked to life all at once. Damien's blood seeped away from him, drawn through the grooves of the cobblestones toward the ore in the chamber's center. The shaft filled with a sanguine aura as the inkarnaught absorbed what he offered it, and then it rose of its own accord from the ground. Swelling with power, it filled the freezing room with the heat of brimstone and infernal fire, and even in his anemic state, Damien pushed himself to stand in its presence.

With two long strides, he crossed to the chamber's center, sallow skin bathed in scarlet as he reached bloodied, scarred arms out. The talisman descended to rest in his palms—in its *master's* palms—eager and alive as it thumped with the same beat that pounded in his own chest.

"My life's work," said Damien, lips curling at the corners and thin, black brows narrowing. "It is finally complete." He was twenty-seven.

Climbing many stories of railing-less, stone steps out of the depths of a cold and unforgiving earth is difficult enough, and after draining oneself of nearly all of one's lifeblood, it would be nigh impossible for even an adept mage of most arcane arts, but Damien compelled not fire nor earth nor even the arcana of something as trivial as luck—none of those so-called gifts bestowed by the gods. Damien was a blood mage, not blessed but cursed by his infernal heritage, though he saw no evidence of misfortune provided he did not look too hard, and blood mages were not merely gifted arcana but had it flowing through their very veins. This, and he was spurred on by one fact: *he had finally done it.*

Many times, he had climbed out of that dark chasm—a pit he had constructed to contain and coalesce his too-often tempestuous powers—with only bitter failure. There was sometimes progress, though more often frustration with how close he came to his own death with little to show for it. But this—he ran his thumb over the newly smooth inkarnaught ore, no longer unrefined earth and a pile of components but now an enchanted talisman—*this* was what success felt like. And it felt…wobbly.

Damien ascended the last step out of the chasm and staggered, reaching out to grip the archway that would lead back into the halls of Bloodthorne Keep, but his fingers slipped. He sucked in a breath, the world falling out from beneath him, vision tunneling, and then darkness.

No, not darkness. *Noxscura.*

Damien was standing straight again, hand gripping the archway as if he had never missed. He focused on a sconce, a skeletal hand clutching a thick, black candle, to keep the corridor from spinning, and he filled his lungs with the warmer air of the keep. He hadn't summoned the noxscura, but it came anyway. He didn't like that, but seeing as he hadn't plunged a hundred feet downward into the pit at his back, he pushed the unease at his magic working autonomously away, and with it went a second, deeper unease, one he couldn't quite place.

Damien was rarely, if ever, vulnerable in such a way. Expending so much arcana and leaving himself drained was never an option save for in crafting the talisman, and that weakness must have been the kindling for the sudden disquiet in his gut. He simply needed to heal.

The many cuts he had made along his chest and arms were still fresh, and though they had stopped weeping, remained open. He placed a hand over his ribs where the largest gash sliced through taut skin, and he mustered a pulse of magic. It prickled painfully, worse than when the cuts had been made, sewing itself closed along half of its length. If there had been fewer wounds, and he hadn't been so arcanely spent, his body's innate ability as a blood mage to mend itself would have taken care of things on its own, but as it was, this mess needed more skilled attention. It would all be easy enough to heal for someone else, someone who had spent their life studying the curative arts and was blessed by some god, but Damien had little time or use for most medicinal magic. Instead, he had dedicated his life to a different kind of arcana, the kind that enchanted and compelled, and he finally had the talisman to justify his many years of toil.

Damien swept through Bloodthorne Keep to the makeshift temple he had established in one of the castle's wings that also served as an infirmary. It was useful to have healers on hand when one was so overzealous with a dagger, and the object of devotion didn't matter. There were plenty of dark gods to choose from, twenty-five to be exact, and since they were all locked in the Abyss, they didn't much mind which of them got the most attention—or, no one heard their complaints, if they did.

When he arrived in his bloodied state, a lamia priest wordlessly slithered over to tend to his wounds. The lamia, with their serpent lower halves and human torsos, made some of the best healers, and Damien assumed it had something to do with the fact they shed their own skin twice a year. It wasn't pleasant to find a sloughed-off and slippery chunk of scales in the hall, especially by accident with one's foot in the middle of the night, but it was a small cost for their services.

Renewed with his flesh fully healed, the only scar remaining the one across his face that no magic would mend, Damien left the temple for his private chambers. There, he stripped, doused himself in frigid water to fully come back into his senses, and washed off the drying rivulets of blood. Donning black, leather armor, he didn't allow himself a second look in the mirror tucked into the corner of his bedchamber once he confirmed he was acceptable enough for the throne room.

By the time he emerged into the main keep, word had spread— second only to their healing abilities was a lamia's skill at gossip. The damage he had done to himself coupled with the lack of a sour mood when he arrived in their wing had them buzzing, or rather hissing, and the others who served in the keep, goblins and draekins mostly, were trading guttural whispers as they darted out of his way. As he stalked the main hall, headed for the throne room, the tiny form of Gril appeared from the shadows to fall in with Damien as if he had been walking beside him all along.

Reaching only Damien's hip, Gril, like most of the draekins who served in the keep, could be easy to miss, especially as nearly all of them insisted on wearing black, hooded cloaks that often made them indistinguishable from the dark stone floors. His tail, however, jutted out from beneath the trailing fabric, mossy green and a dead giveaway. Today, it was wagging.

"Is it true, Master Bloodthorne?" the little figure croaked from his side, turning up his scaled snout, a jagged underbite grinning from beneath his hood.

Damien confirmed only with a smirk, but did not stop—to stop would mean to think, and even with healing and bathing, that odd feeling at his success had not lifted but instead settled more firmly in his chest. It would be better if he simply told his father of his accomplishment before...well, he wasn't quite sure before *what*, exactly, but there was something niggling at him, something à bit like

4

the noxscura, that made him want to hesitate. He ignored it.

Gril made a small noise in response, a clicking in the back of his throat unique to draekins. Though he couldn't reproduce it himself, Damien had learned many years ago that that particular sound translated to either "excellent" or "potatoes." The tail wagging suggested the former, though Gril was quite enthusiastic about root vegetables as well.

The throne room of Bloodthorne Keep was a monument to superfluousness, but it instilled fear in lesser creatures. Impossibly tall, it was lit only by well-placed windows, filled with blue glass to illuminate infernal sigils carved into the shining obsidian overhead. At the back of the long room, the largest window was set high up on the wall, round with silver webbing and aligned with the static moon, Lo, to cast a twilit haze down over the chamber.

Swathed in this amethyst light, the room was long, and footsteps echoed out into it, announcing anyone who would dare enter. Damien crossed the black marble to the dais in the room's center, pausing for only a moment to gaze on the orb that hovered there, so like the second moon, Ero, that waxed and waned as it crossed the sky. Untouchable to all in the keep and even the city beyond, the orb was the reason the place could exist at all, protected from forces that would see Bloodthorne Keep and its city of Aszath Koth razed to the ground in some holy crusade by those in the realm to the south. Damien gave it a reverent nod, eyes tracking over the symbol on it, a crescent with the shape of a dove—no, just a bird—in flight atop it, and continued on to the throne itself.

Towering in black marble, the seat would dwarf any but the keep's true lord, Damien's father. Damien cast his eyes up its length, admiring how the stone's veins ran crimson against the black, how it rose up to the tattered banners above, how the peak extended with many tendrils, reaching out to grasp and choke and kill. He never dared consider taking it.

A figure two heads taller than even Damien stepped down from the dais the throne sat upon. It said nothing, heavy robes trailing behind, head bent but horns protruding from under its hood to look down on him. Damien clenched a fist around the talisman, its rhythm thrumming through his body familiarly, as if it had always been a part of him and ready to carry out its fated deed.

Then the thought suddenly struck him: should he have put it in a nice box first, or even an embroidered pouch? Something commissioned to protect it but also venerate the importance of—no, it was too late now, and there was no use in pondering what he had possibly missed, just like there was no use in pondering why his initial discomfort had wormed its way from his gut to his chest to invade his entire being.

The hulking, horned figure stepped aside to allow Damien to pass, and the blood mage alighted the dais to drop to one knee before the throne, the talisman still clenched as he bowed his head. "Father, I come with news."

There was a rumble, a sound like far-off thunder that sent tremors through the chamber, and then the voice of Zagadoth the Tempestuous, Demonic Lord of the Infernal Plane, tore into the throne room of Bloodthorne Keep. "Huh? Who's—oh, well, hey there, kiddo! Haven't seen you in half a moon! Where you been?"

Damien lifted his head, a lock of black hair falling into his view. From afar, the throne appeared empty, but this close, one could see a roughly cut shard of crystal propped up in its center and the eye that blinked back from the smoothest surface of the gem, groggy. Apparently, Zagadoth the Tempestuous had been taking a nap.

"Executing the ritual. It was long and arduous," said Damien, turning the talisman over in his hand compulsively. His eyes flicked to it then back up to the crystal that housed his father's existence. "And it is finally done."

"It?" His father's baritone mused quietly. "You don't mean—"

"Bloodthorne's Talisman of Enthrallment is complete."

The eye in the crystal widened, its slice of a pupil honing in on the ore held aloft in Damien's hand. "Kiddo! That's just swell!" The voice of Zagadoth the Tempestuous was said to have once brought entire cities to its knees, and even now as it roared into the throne room with wholly enthusiastic words, Damien could feel the centuries of awe it had inspired. "I knew you could do it! Oh, champ, you gotta let me see that thing."

Damien rose and brought the talisman close to the blinking eye. Holding it between two fingers, it seemed unimpressive, the size of a simple, gold coin and colored a red so deep it was nearly black, but the aura it gave off was a powerful, twisting, nauseating thing. His father, a demon with infernal power unimaginable, was one of the few who could truly sense all that it was, even while his body was locked away in an unreachable pocket of existence. His iris flickered with Abyssal fire when the talisman came close. "I never doubted you for a second, but this is really something. You sure outdid yourself."

Damien lifted the bit of magicked ore to his own face then. Bloodthorne's Talisman of Enthrallment was a long-pondered dream, or nightmare, dependent upon which end of it one found oneself.

Even more potent than he had intended, a simple touch by any other being would cause it to be absorbed immediately. Filled with rare and powerful components, unparalleled enchantments, and his own, infernal blood, Damien could command the creature who would become the talisman's vessel absolutely with or without their knowledge—they only had to hear the word.

To have complete control over a creature, enthrallment, was almost unheard of in such a way. Short bursts of coercion and suggestions that a target may or may not follow were possible through spells Damien had learned, and slightly longer bouts of enthrallment were only possible by creatures with the ability inborn, though Damien wasn't interested in dying and being resurrected for that. It was only the holy and unholy orders that had something similar to what he held, but that spell required a broken vessel to continuously ingest a concoction to keep it up, it rendered the target dull and changed, and was easy enough to thwart if its source could be found.

Bloodthorne's Talisman of Enthrallment was exceptional in its existence in that it allowed the vessel to keep its true mind and was unexpellable save for with that creature's death. As long as he could keep his vessel alive, he could control it completely, in theory, while allowing it to retain its memories, its personality, everything to make it seem as if nothing were controlling it at all. And a creature that could be controlled wholly should be easy enough to keep alive until Damien's desires were brought to fruition.

"You're gonna have your pops outta this crystal in no time!" Zagadoth's voice broke Damien of his wonder at what he'd done, a reminder of what he still had yet to do: break his father out of his crystalline confinement. Zagadoth the Tempestuous had been imprisoned for twenty-three years, nearly Damien's entire life, and it had taken Damien just as long to master his inborn abilities, ascend as an adept blood mage, and craft the only tool that could free his father and carry out revenge upon the bastard who had imprisoned him.

"Of course." He closed his fist around the talisman again, snuffing out its dull glow. "I'll leave for that wretched city immediately."

"Whoa, wait, wait, Damien, you gotta slow down. At least take the night to sleep off creating that thing." The eye blinked and softened, looking him over. "You sure are in a rush, huh? You okay there, bud?"

Glancing briefly to the towering form that was Valsevrus, the minotaur who attended the throne room and the crystalline shard his father was trapped within, and then down to the draekin Gril behind him, Damien cleared his throat. "Yes. Definitely. I'm fine."

"Son, let's go for a walk." Zagadoth had always been perceptive. Irritatingly so.

Valsevrus hustled up the stairs with a snort, grabbing the shard of occlusion crystal and carrying it so it was level with Damien's head. They crossed the throne room, boots and hooves scuffing into the long room's silence, Gril waddling behind studiously. Through an archway, they stepped out onto the uncovered, elevated walk that circled Bloodthorne Keep, a low parapet at their side. Below, the city of Aszath Koth was laid out, encircled by the Infernal Mountains casting their dark miasma over all.

"Damien," Zagadoth began, "I know what I'm asking of you is...a lot."

"This is what I was born to do, who I was meant to be, and I've made a vow—"

"Let me finish, kiddo." His father's voice dropped to a quiet but firm tone, one he used infrequently. "You *are* the only one who can free me from this crystal, Damien, but getting trapped in this thing was my doing, and heaping my break from it onto your shoulders was no small request, especially as early as I did. The vow of a child, it doesn't mean *nothing*, but children shouldn't be held to the promises they made. I know you're grown now, by human standards,"—at this he cleared his throat—"you can make your own decisions, and you've never wavered in your dedication to freeing me, but I want you to know I'm not blind to the work you've already put into this or the risk you'll be taking to break the occlusion crystal that bastard Archibald trapped my body within."

Valsevrus and Gril both hacked phlegm in the back of their throats. Damien eyed them, and they halted their instinct to spit at the name of Archibald Lumier, the so-called king of the realm of Eiren and a mage by heritage in his own right, if a disgraceful one. Years ago, Zagadoth had asked those in the keep to stop spitting when the hateful man's name was used, and the floors were better for it— draekin saliva was especially acidic.

When it was clear both had swallowed, Damien cast his gaze over the tilted, dark peaks and shadowed streets of Aszath Koth, just outside of the reach of Eiren and its insufferably beloved ruler. As the son of a demon, it was the only place that had ever been his home and could ever be.

"The talisman will turn that pompous monarch into my puppet." Damien grinned, imagining it, not even all that disappointed he wouldn't have to torture him. "Archibald Lumier will be all too eager to reverse his own divine binds and set you free."

Zagadoth mused a quiet sound, something between hesitancy and approval. "I am also not blind to the power you've acquired, son. The progeny of demons and humans have always been spoken of as formidable, and you've proven that, but there is a cost to infernal arcana."

A sigh wanted to rake through Damien and grumble out, overburdened and childish, but he held it back.

"You are exploitable, Damien," Zagadoth said with a harshness that suggested he knew exactly the reaction Damien wanted to have. "The darkness that runs in your veins, the noxscura, is meant to be carried and wielded by a demon—"

"And my humanity makes me weak," Damien concluded for him, jaw clenching on the last word.

"Your humanity makes you unique," the demon lord's voice corrected. "Insusceptible to binds, unlike your foolish father, and capable of withstanding the divine, but you are not infallible, not incapable of becoming lost to it."

Damien stepped away from Valsevrus holding the shard and to the edge of the parapet. Below, the long, stone side of Bloodthorne Keep plummeted into darkness, the pull of it tugging at that odd, hesitant feeling still prickling at his skin from the inside. "I appreciate your faith in me," he grumbled.

"You know I have never doubted you for a moment." Valsevrus stepped up just behind Damien to hold the crystal near his ear. "It is *your* faith that mustn't waver. You must have something to hold onto, a way to remain grounded in yourself and know who you are."

Damien's mouth opened, but no words came out, and he snapped it back shut. Irritating, as always, but his father was right. Noxscura was sometimes a *problem*. Dark and all-encompassing, it left him vulnerable to a select few, holy people with too much power, the nox-touched, and his own temperament, the thought of which made him want to choke the life out of something.

But instead, he blew out a breath and nodded, the corners of his lips lifting. "I do have something to hold onto. I named the talisman after myself, didn't I? I've faith in my abilities: you will be free."

"Well, thank the depths of the Abyss, kid, because I have got to get the fuck out of this crystal." Zagadoth's husky laughter carried out over the parapet and echoed down into the city. Somewhere in Aszath Koth a goblin involuntarily emptied his bladder. Voice returning to its brazen tone, Zagadoth sighed in a contented if wistful way. "It's too bad I'll be mostly outta commission on the trip—I'd really like to see you in action."

"That, actually, is where my concern lies." Damien turned away from the edge of the walkway and continued on, palming the enchanted ore and squinting out at the Infernal Mountains and their smoky haze. "This talisman gives off an aura I'm unsure can be masked. I know I must take your shard to be fused with the rest of the occlusion crystal in Eirengaard before you can be released, but to be carrying two such powerful, infernal objects past the mountains and across the realm seems…challenging."

His jaw ground at the thought of the ridiculous, white-clad buffoons of Eiren's holy order who patrolled the roads and cities. Their ranks were made up of mages blessed by any number of their gods, wielding simple enough to quell holy magic, but sometimes they were led by the descendant of a dominion, the virtuous counterpart to a demon. Though very few were as direct a descendant as Damien was—apparently dominions held some moral high ground by infrequently leaving the celestial plane to dabble with humans on earth—divine mages were not to be trifled with. Thankfully, most were so far removed they were simply divine mages in name only, the children of the children of the children of dominions, and serving in Eiren with royal titles rather than in militaristic roles, but on occasion, an aristocratic family would produce an extremely adept magic user. And running into one of those would be unpleasant.

"There won't be much juice left in this baby once it's outta the keep, you know that, so it'll take someone keenly aware to detect it, I reckon." The shard of Zagadoth's prison was fueled by the chaotic, infernal energy that swam beneath Bloodthorne Keep. An expenditure of Damien's arcana and a drop of his blood would allow his father to communicate through it for brief moments once he left Aszath Koth, but not forever. Though none of that accounted for the talisman. "Isn't there a cloak of Abyssal shielding or maybe a mask of damned souls or something at the Sanctum? You could pick some sort of buffer up there and darkness knows what else is in that place that might come in handy."

Damien tipped his head. The Ebon Sanctum Mallor indeed housed some of the most potent, accursed objects in existence, and it was only a short detour on the way out of the city.

"And you're gonna visit The Brotherhood before you leave, right?"

"Oh, uh, well?" His voice hitched. "I don't know if I'll really have time. I mean, especially if I go to the Sanctum, and—"

"They're my most loyal subjects outside of the keep, kiddo."

Damien scratched at the back of his head with the talisman, and it thumped against his skull. "Yeah, I know. They're always saying."

Valsevrus stopped and turned toward Damien, Zagadoth's eye in the crystal meeting his. "Look, bud, I know they're a lot, but we gotta throw them a bone every once in a while. They're the reason this shard of your pop's prison got back to Aszath Koth at all after Archibald's attack. Also, they're, like, *right* at the city gates, so I doubt you'll be able to avoid them."

Eyes darting away, he sighed. "Sure, yeah, I'll try."

"Damien,"—Zagadoth's voice hardened—"you won't try: you'll do it."

Standing a little straighter, he nodded.

"But you're gonna sleep first, kiddo. You look exhausted. You know what I always say: even the wicked—"

"—need to rest."

The sky had gone the slightest bit darker, threatening clouds rolling overhead and blotting out what little light dared shine on Aszath Koth. Damien was weary, limbs heavy before he had begun to travel and mind filled with complications before they arose, but it all fell away with a drop of rain plucking at his shoulder. The Sanctum first—that, at the very least, would be a simple infiltration for the morning, once the storm cleared.

His gaze trailed to the pass through the mountains where he knew the gates of the city let out. Beyond, there was the tiniest pinprick of light, even in the darkness of night, where the moons shined differently on the very farthest reaches of Eiren and Archibald's realm.

"Anything else on your mind, kiddo?"

Damien shook his head before even contemplating the possibility. "I won't let you down, Father."

"Aw, champ, I know you won't. Hey, Valsevrus, give Damien a hug for me, all right?"

The minotaur's arms dutifully came around Damien all at once, and he stiffened under the furry embrace. Hands slapped down onto his back much harder than would have been preferred after the bloodletting ritual, but he managed to stay upright, lucky so close to the edge of the wall. The malodorous scent off the minotaur filled his nostrils as he was pulled into his chest, and he held his breath.

"Come on, Gril," called Zagadoth's voice, muffled in Valsevrus's fist, "get in on this."

The draekin waddled over, throwing spindly, scaled arms around Damien's legs, perhaps even tighter than the minotaur, his claws sinking in. Damien was unsure if it was either creature's lack of practice or simply their nature that made them so dreadful at embracing, but a very distant memory from childhood told him it shouldn't feel like this.

"Thanks, guys," Damien mumbled, pulling away, and they finally released him. Valsevrus brought the crystal back into his eyeline. "And thanks, Dad."

What lay beyond the borders of Aszath Koth was worthy of his wariness, but the city itself, the inky blackness of its streets and the trials inside the Ebon Sanctum Mallor, held nothing for Damien to fear. He was born of this place, even if his human heritage made him starkly different from nearly all the other beings that inhabited it.

But there was one creature that trolled Aszath Koth's alleys that night, one from beyond the Infernal Mountain's pass, that he couldn't have counted on, and that creature would prove to test Damien's resolution more than any darkness ever could.

CHAPTER 2
A DISSERTATION ON INTENT AND ITS USEFULNESS

Like the unfixed moon, Ero, the influence of evil had waxed and waned over the realm's many thousands of years of existence under whatever name the aristocracy gave it at the time. In most recent years, the mass of land in question was called Eiren, and goodness had clenched an authoritative fist around its throat, choking the evil out until only the last gasps of goblin dens and giant spiders remained. There was, of course, always a *little* evil around, but that was what worshiping the gods and those who served them was for, after all: protection.

The first crusades had begun with a divine mage called Ignatius Lumier, the direct descendant of a dominion, some seventy years prior. Ignatius followed the god Osurehm, as his father was a dominion in his service. Despite presiding over the season of summer and the entirety of the concept of honor, Osurehm was still a lesser-known god at the time for reasons that were almost entirely titularly-based, but, to be fair, most gods were lesser known when the pantheon was stuffed with one hundred and forty-two of them, not to mention the fact most had such silly names. However, two decades of rooting out the worst of the necromancers and dragons had afforded both Ignatius and Osurehm notoriety, the love of the people, and a crown that really only worked for Ignatius since he had the head. For Osurehm, a very large and very opulent temple was built, which is almost as good as a crown, and some say is even better.

The crown was inherited by Ignatius's son, Auberon, also touched with divine arcana and a zest for destroying evil. Osurehm kept the temple since gods live a lot longer than men, for eternity it can be argued, if not measured, and the people came to the conclusion that he should have probably been worshiped in place of Tarwethen, the previously most-worshipped deity on the pantheon, all along. Tarwethen, the god of winter and wealth, had risen in renown in a slightly similar way a century or two prior when another divinely-blessed mage had crusaded against an infestation of fire rocs. Since neither god seemed to have anything to say about the switch, as was the norm since the gods stopped visiting earth and communicating directly with its creatures after The Expulsion ten or twenty thousand years prior, Osurehm ended up sticking.

Like his father, Auberon's adeptness with the Holy Light of Osurehm made him beloved by the masses who were thrilled with his efficiency at wiping out evil. That is, until he met an early and tragic end at the hands of a demon.

Auberon left behind a son, Archibald Lumier, coronated on his fifteenth birthday, a short week after his venerated father's death. Youth didn't delay Archibald's adoption of the family businesses of both ruling and exorcising, and his divine powers were said to be stronger than his father and grandfather combined. Whether it truly was strength or simply the efficiency of the divine mages who came before him, in three short years, the good king hunted the last slivers of evil to the farthest reaches of Eiren, and it slunk back into the shadowy places, the uninhabitable quags and desolate karsts and forsaken wastes. There, evil was left to fester beyond where the Holy Knights of Osurehm patrolled, and Archibald maintained his oath to the people of Eiren for nearly four decades that for as long as he reigned, darkness would have no place in Eiren.

But evil still wormed its way into the realm, though its face was often unexpected, a truth some of its inhabitants knew all too intimately.

Amma supposed it was morning though the sun never rose on Aszath Koth. Vapors off the mountain range and rumors of an infernal miasma sought to keep the city shrouded in a constant haze, but that was just as well—she didn't want to be seen here anyway as humans had no place in the city of monstrous beasts.

Body stiff, Amma unwrapped her arms from about her knees and eased the tattered cloth she'd hidden behind to the side. The storm from the previous night had ended, and she actually managed a smile as she slipped off the barrel she'd curled up on for the night. Things might be looking up.

Landing right down in a murky, grey puddle, a shock of cold drove up through her body, followed by a wave of nausea from the smell. On second thought, upward may have been a too-lofty direction for things to look. Perhaps things were actually, well...*parallel* to the day before. At least she had been lucky enough to hide herself away overnight and stay relatively dry until now. An inn would have been better, but the keeper of the only one she could find was a creature with long, spindly limbs, big batwings for ears, and skin tinged green—a goblin, she thought, though she had never seen one before. He offered her a room for half off with a shifty smile, but from what Amma understood, goblins sometimes ate humans. Half off sure sounded good unless it was one's limbs.

Amma adjusted her cloak's hood as low as was practical and tugged a sagging cowl up over her mouth and nose. Together, they worked to obscure her face and block out the stench of the city, but she feared her identity, the human part of it at least, still wasn't well hidden. She had only seen perhaps two other humans since crossing the unpatrolled gates through the mountain pass into Aszath Koth. One had donned a crimson robe, head shaved to a scarred-up scalp with purple circles under his eyes. He had gripped a thick tome in bony hands as he hissed out a ceaseless string of nonsense words and wandered about. The other had been a woman selling pelts that didn't smell properly skinned. She hollered about the end times between sales pitches. "Annihilation is nigh!" she shouted in a creaking, leathery voice. "The harbinger of night eternal and civility's destruction lurks at the corners of the realm, biding its time until the hallowed son releases it to reign again! Buy two rabbit skins, get a chipmunk pelt for free!" Spattered with the dried blood of what Amma hoped was her occupation as a furrier, her dark hair was in wild knots, and her layers of clothing had likely never seen a wash.

But nearly three weeks into her journey, Amma feared she wasn't faring much better, and try as she might to accept it, the ickiness was getting to her. Not something she would have otherwise chosen to wear, at least the over-sized tunic had been a crisp, clean linen when she donned it, but now it was stained with mud and sweat and even a little blood. The breeches, which had to have the waist secured with an extra tie and the excess length stuffed into the tops of borrowed boots, were torn up one leg and sagging quite uncomfortably. Amma chastised herself silently yet again for not bringing needle and thread to at least patch things up. Perry would not want these clothes back regardless, even though she would be relieved when she could finally return them to him.

She only had to accomplish this first, but *this* was no simple thing. Traveling alone had been dangerous, and leaving home had been complex, but none of it would compare to what waited for her today. So close to her goal she could almost smell it, if it smelled of urine and rot and perhaps spiced pork, she took a regrettably deep breath and crept to the alley's end to peek out into the street.

Aszath Koth was already alive with a handful of creatures going about their dark deeds, selling stolen goods, completing illicit chores, getting breakfast. Amma winced at the pang in her own stomach, pushing it aside to focus on finding the mysterious temple. The route to what she sought, which roads to follow and which cities to pass through to find the gates to Aszath Koth, had been in a restricted book at the Grand Athenaeum, but the book did not include a business address for the exact building she needed—that was, apparently, too proprietary. Some kind of direction through the city, at least, would have been nice, but for that, she would need to ask a friendly face— one that didn't offer to take her there themselves for a lewd price.

Gripping the hilt of the dagger she kept holstered about her thigh, concealed under the excess of her tunic and her cloak, she slipped out onto the street and, fighting against everything she'd been taught, hunched her shoulders and kept her head down. It was easy enough in early morning to blend—even the monstrous creatures in Aszath Koth seemed bleary-eyed and malcontent to start the day—and she marched herself deeper into the city.

Meandering around a divot filled with murky rainwater, a pair of scaled, child-height creatures waddled in the opposite direction, chatting in clicks and garbles. Unlike most of the other beings she scampered past, these two were short and squat and perhaps less dangerous, so she tugged down her cowl to offer them a cautious grin. One simply glared back, dark eyes beading, and the other showed her all of its jagged teeth at once, set into a long, reptilian snout. When it bit at the air beside her, she jumped, and both creatures devolved into throaty laughter.

Amma pulled her cowl back up and hurried away, taking a blind right down another cobbled street. Only a hairless man walked the road. He had pointed ears like an elf though the similarities stopped there, blue-skinned, yellow-eyed, and fang-toothed. Amma averted her gaze and scurried with a purpose in the opposite direction.

Of course she would find no friendliness here: the city had once been ruled by a demon, summoned to earth by those who were undoubtedly vile and nefarious. Though that demon had been thwarted by King Archibald over two decades ago, Aszath Koth remained a bastion for the dark and deceitful. Amma had been too young for memories when the demon had marched on Eiren's capital, but just the thought of it made her shiver. Her home, luckily, had remained out of evil's path, and when she had been to Eirengaard years later, she had been fortuitous to never see any fallout from the demon's attack on their realm.

Digging into the small satchel on her hip, Amma pulled out the last of her salted meat and took stock of where she had ended up. The cobbled road was wide enough for a cart, its buildings almost normal looking without scaled or furry creatures wandering around, though they were being held up questionably, leaning a bit too far to one side with windows that didn't properly latch. Without signs or barrels of goods, or rather, *bads*, outside, she assumed she'd come upon residences.

Ripping off a piece of the dried beef and working hard to chew at the sinewy leftover, she cast her gaze up to the spires of a fortification that loomed over the rest of the squat city many blocks off. It was ostentatious enough to be the temple she sought, though from where she stood, there was no sign to clarify. Not that a sign would necessarily help: the few she'd seen had been a mix of images, a language she didn't know, and a smattering of poorly spelled words in the common tongue, Key. She was smart enough to figure out an image of what she thought originally was a pipe, a sideways squiggle with a star in the center, and the word "bred" meant *bakery*, and another word "smyf" accompanied with a crude burnished blade meant *armory*, but she didn't see the symbol for the temple that had been in the book in the Grand Athenaeum anywhere.

At a loss, she began to make her way toward where the castle-like building loomed, glad to be taking herself farther from the increasingly busy main road. With the absence of many voices, vendors, and carts, there was a new sound, though, a dismal baying. When she glanced around for its source, she noted that none of the other creatures ambling out of their homes paid the noise any attention, not even commenting that it pierced the ears irritatingly or that it sounded pained.

Concerned for whatever could be crying like that, and interminably distractable when her nerves were high, Amma followed the noise to a sleepy set of narrow roads and then around the corner of a patchwork building with a thatched roof. The noise stopped, and she thought she lost whatever had been howling until she noted a form in the shadows ahead, squat down beside a bundle of fur.

The figure was much larger than the little, squirming creature, and Amma's heart leapt into her throat, mind pinging back to the dark-omen-spouting woman and her pelts. A hand reached out,

17

gripped the furry bundle by the scruff of its neck, and lifted it from the muddied ground. Four little paws and a tail, black as midnight, dangled from the large hand, and it squeaked out a pitiful meow. Amma could not move though she wanted to both flee and intervene, but there was nothing she could do, the flash of red was too quick, and it was over in an instant.

She threw a hand over her mouth to stifle the gasp that came out sharp and loud anyway. Eyes snapped to her from the shadows and held her in their gaze. The figure set the creature back down, but it wasn't limp as Amma expected. Instead, it stretched its skinny legs and chirped with a vigor it didn't have moments prior before darting off down the alley and deeper into the shadows. Without taking its gaze from her, the figure stood up out of the darkness.

Amma took an instinctive step back though she was already at the far end of the alley. Tall but not as hulking as some of the aberrant beings she had seen earlier, and pale but not ghostly like the mad priest at the city gates, what stood before her was a seemingly normal, human man, only the third she had seen in Aszath Koth. Though with his head tipped down, glaring at her from under a furrowed, dark brow and swathed entirely in black from his cloak to his boots, he certainly looked as menacing as any of the monsters around.

Then he whipped away to leave through the opposite end of the alley.

"Wait!"

He stopped.

Gods, what in the bright goodness was she doing? Just because he was human, and just because he helped that cat, did *not* mean he was going to be kind.

Into the quiet of the alley, his voice swept over her, smooth but with a commanding bite as he glanced back over his shoulder. "Well?"

Amma snapped back into herself, dipping her own head with narrowed eyes, trying to make her shoulders as wide as possible and dropping her voice as low as it dared go. "Tell me where the Ebony Sanatorium of Malcontent can be found."

His eyes darted skyward for a moment and then back to her. "The what?"

She cleared her throat, hacking up more husk into it, and she even took a step forward though she shook. "The Sanatorium of Ebony Malicious, uh, wait—the Mal Sanctum, er…Ebon—"

"The Ebon Sanctum Mallor?"

"That's it!" Amma pointed at him, voice lilting up high as she grinned. "Ugh, everything around here sounds like that, all ominous and creepy, I don't know how you keep the names straight." She swallowed back the nervous giggle that bubbled up out of her, crossing her arms tight over her chest.

The man turned back to her fully, tipping his head to one side. Amma's heart sped up, but she held her ground as he began to close the distance between them with a few long strides. Closer now, she could see the color of his eyes even in the gloam, a striking violet, stark against the shadows in the alley and blackness of his hair, messy and pushed back on one side though it still fell in his face. "What do *you*,"—and that *you* was not complimentary—"want with the Sanctum?"

She squeezed her hands into fists. "That is, uh, none of your business, buddy."

The corner of his mouth twitched. "Buddy?"

Amma's stomach dropped to the bottom of her borrowed-without-asking boots. Still, she didn't move. "You heard me," she managed to eke out, then added, "jerk," for good measure, though she immediately regretted it.

To both her relief and horror, he only smirked, eyes flitting down the length of her. As he raised a hand to a clean-shaven jaw in thought, she saw a slice of red across his palm.

"Oh, no, you're bleeding." Amma's concern overrode her faux bravado, dropping the stance, the voice, the everything when faced with someone else's problem.

He pulled his hand away from his chin, cocking a brow at the cut. "So, I am." When he flipped his hand to flex his fingers, she could see the mark better, and it was deep.

"That looks painful." She dug into her hip pouch and found the handkerchief she had used to tie up dried fruit when she first set out three weeks prior. "Let me help."

He curled his lip, surveying his palm once more. "It will heal shortly."

Amma shook her head, scrunching up her nose, and stepped right up to him to wrap the handkerchief over the slice, tying a simple knot at the back of his hand.

His eyes widened at the sudden appearance of the cloth—Amma had always been nimble-fingered and too quick for others to track, let alone stop when she was determined to do something she thought was for someone else's good. She grinned up at him, recognizing the surprise and taking it as a compliment.

So close, she could see a long scar drawn over his face in raised, silver skin, running down his forehead, over the bridge of a long and pointed nose, just missing his violet eye, and ending mid cheek. There was no bandaging that, it was old and permanent, but it did very little to mar his looks which, now that Amma was really looking, made her own face suddenly go very warm. She made herself take a hefty step back and pulled up her cowl.

"Now." She lowered her voice again, and his eyes snapped up to hers as if she had some command over him. "I did a favor for you, so repay me. Where is the...sanctum of dark, evil stuff?"

A frigid breeze blew down the alley, picking up his cloak and hair. It swept over Amma, catching her hood and pushing it back. Not quick enough, she fumbled to conceal the messy nest her wheat-colored hair had become, mumbling a minced oath.

The man finally dropped his arm, balling his newly wrapped hand into a fist. "I *will* do you a favor."

Amma almost fled at the darkness in his voice, visceral and cutting right to the center of her, but then he went on and gave her very exact directions, complete with landmarks, and much better than those inside any of the Grand Athenaeum's books. When he was finished, she thanked him sincerely, and with one last, long stare, he whipped around and was gone.

She hummed to herself as she turned for the route he had told her, "I guess he was kind after all."

Except, the man Amma had met was *not* kind, and after following his directions through Aszath Koth and ending up right back at the city's entry gates, no Sanctum in sight, Amma very much wanted to tell him just how not-kind she thought he was. Under normal circumstances, she never would. In fact, in all of Amma's twenty-five years she had almost never told anyone they were "not kind" or any other variation thereupon. But this journey had been grueling, and even Amma's patience could be taxed to the point she might say something nasty.

But then her mother's words flitted through her head, as they often did when she felt anger well up in her heart. *Blame not one's failings on cruelty when ignorance is the much more likely cause*, or, more simply, most of the time people weren't mean, they were just dumb. Amma would have settled, then, on telling him she thought he was very, *very* dumb.

However, as fate and plot would have it, Amma found an elderly woman selling prickly berries on a street corner who looked human enough, though the point to her ears suggested an elven bloodline, and an offer of gold bought her better directions. By the time Amma found the Sanctum, it was late evening, she had finished off the fruit, and despite cutting the inside of her mouth twice and wasting the entire day on the wrong, meandering route, her mood had righted itself. A brighter mood was, after all, a much easier way to exist in the world, whether it was kind back to one or not.

The Ebon Sanctum Mallor was exactly as its name advised, made up of slick, black stones and altogether terrifying. Set away from the city, one had to pass through many twisting, narrow alleys to be let out at its northwestern corner, traverse a desolate and craggy moor, and follow a winding, disused footpath that crossed through once-palatial ruins. There, the Sanctum stood tall and narrow, nestled into a small orchard of gnarled kalsephrus trees that had died long ago but somehow continued to grow. Necrotic energy did that sometimes, and while Amma was not magically inclined herself, she had read quite a lot about arcana in preparation for her trip. No amount of reading could have prepared her, though, to feel it humming through the very air as she approached.

She reached out for one of the trees. Kalsephrus were rare enough that she'd only ever read about them, but that's what these had to be. Even undead, they had the mottled, flaky bark and twisty branches from the illustrations in her horticultural texts. But as her hand touched the trunk, it pulsed back at her, and her mind was suddenly clouded with a vision of the same tree blooming with sapphire leaves that glittered like glass under the sun centuries earlier.

Amma gasped, pulling back. The books would need to be updated: apparently undead kalsepherus could use latent arcana to send messages. It was by no means the only tree that did so, but she was surprised to meet a second species in her lifetime that could.

She shook her head, pat her dagger, and tightened the strap of her hip pouch. Amma had made it this far, and it had been no easy feat. What she sought was only a little farther inside, but everything she had read about the dark and cruel temple jumbled together in her mind. The place was cursed and built on the remains of a wronged people whose stories were lost to time. That made it perfect for housing evil artifacts, but it also made it perfect for killing those who would take them. But Amma only wanted one, an ancient scroll, and despite her query's inherent evil, her intentions were good, and that had to count for something.

As the perpetual twilight of the city and its surrounding lands shifted ever so slightly to dimmer twilight, she stepped up to the black void of the Sanctum's entry. It required an offering, and though the text in the Grand Athenaeum was vague, she felt she knew what it

21

might want.

Grabbing the hilt of her dagger, she looked for the sigil that would allow entry, finding it easily as blood was already smeared across it. It didn't drip, but in the last of the evening's light, it gave off a faint shimmer. She shifted her eyes over to the void and carefully stuck her hand through. Swallowed up into darkness, it felt neither hot nor cold, and when she pulled it back, it remained unblemished. So, the door was already opened then—lucky—and Amma stepped through.

The Ebon Sanctum Mallor was quite dissimilar to how it was described on the inside. Sure, the walls dripped a green ooze, the origin of which was undefinable, and disembodied wails swept down corridors that split off and moved around on their own, and there was even a moment when Amma thought she had been run through by a sword that turned out to just be an illusion meant to send her screaming back the way she'd come, but there were absolutely no traps.

The Sanctum was, supposedly, known for its clever and nigh impossible to survive snares, and she had expected to spend hours or even days disarming them, but every means of certain death had easy ways to be traversed. The pit full of vipers appeared fed and happy, a mended and steady bridge over top, and the room of statues that had once clearly been alive was filled with bases instead of full figures, crumbled stone, and an odd arm gripping a sword here and there.

She hurried along, not wanting to dawdle for fear of her good luck running out, until finally Amma came upon the sigil from the book marking the room she needed. The Scroll of the Army of the Undead was only a few short steps away, and it would finally be hers.

Except someone else—and a familiar someone at that—was already picking it up.

CHAPTER 3
THE EBBING SANITARIUM OF MAL-SOMETHING-OR-OTHER

hy not? thought Damien as he picked up The Scroll of the Army of the Undead. It was here, and he'd already come all this way, made a blood offering to open the door, disarmed each perilous trap, and answered all three riddles of the ghoulish spirit that guarded the inner chamber. The Sanctum was full of odd, nefarious objects, and along with Skrimger's Amorphous Earthen Illusion and the Sack of Obfuscare, a scroll that could unleash the literal Abyss could come in handy, so he slipped it into the inner pocket of his cloak alongside the enthrallment talisman. Now, if only he could locate a stronger shielding pouch than the one he'd found, one strong enough to mask said talisman like his father had suggested.

Damien picked up on the presence just before it made itself known. Movement from the chamber's entrance and a sharp inhale that belonged to something living gave itself away a second later. He threw his arm to the side, called out Chthonic words, and blindly cast a binding spell in the sound's direction. He expected it to ping off the Sanctum's walls and disperse when it missed—of those daring and skilled enough to enter the Ebon Sanctum Mallor, a raider or thief could dodge such a simple spell, and a mage would shield themselves from it with little effort, but in either case the intruder would reveal what they were, and then he could properly do away with them. Damien was very surprised then when the spell hit its target dead on.

There was a shriek as his arcana struck and then a thump as a body collapsed to the floor, the sound echoing out into the Sanctum that was meant to be empty. Damien turned to see the bandit at the chamber's entrance, a small, lumpy shadow, though not as small as a draekin or goblin. His binds of necrotic energy had wrapped themselves around it completely, head to toe, and under the arcane glow of the sapphire stones lining the Sanctum's walls, the tendrils glistened as the form tried fruitlessly to wriggle free.

Unlucky, he supposed, for this novice to show up when he, an adept blood mage, had decided to raid the place. Then again, perhaps this was the luckiest they were ever going to get: following on his heels was surely the only way they'd survived thus far, especially if they couldn't dodge a poorly-aimed, base bind that didn't even require his blood to cast.

He took his time striding over to the body, considering how to handle it as they managed to squirm over onto their shoulder in a valiant if futile attempt at escape. He would likely just leave them—in a few hours the spell would wear off, and they could stumble out the way they'd come—but it would be helpful to know if there were more coming behind. A party of adventuring imbeciles, especially one he may have run into before, wouldn't take kindly to their sorry excuse for a scout being bound up, and he wanted to be out of Aszath Koth by nightfall, not wasting his time and arcana clearing a path back into the city.

Coming to stand over his captive, hands clasped behind him, he used a boot to roll them from their side onto their back. A tendril of the bind was pressed over their mouth so that their cries were muffled, but when their eyes, big and bright and blue, fell on him, Damien started. "You?"

He glanced down the length of her, bound tightly in his spell, clearly female, then crouched to yank her hood back and reveal that wheat-colored hair. So, it was the same girl from the streets. He peered out of the chamber to the long corridor and listened, but he could hear nothing else save for the panicked breaths she was taking through her nose. She'd been alone in Aszath Koth that morning, and there was no reason to think she'd made friends since, though he was sure she'd tried and failed miserably.

"What are you doing here?" Damien frowned down at her. "You should already be on the other side of the mountain pass by now."

The girl mumbled against the bind and craned her neck. He sliced down through the single, arcane tendril with a finger, dispelling it.

She sucked in a huge breath, round eyes unblinking as they stared up into his, and then finally whimpered, "You gave me bad directions on purpose?"

Damien's mouth fell open, thrown. "Y-yes?"

24

She scrunched up her nose in the same way she had in the alley, all petulant and insistent, and the freckles spattered across her cheeks tightened. "That's not very nice."

Nice? Did she have any idea where she was? Damien scoffed. "Well, I'm not very nice."

Breathing hard and casting a wary gaze over all of him, she gave him *that* look, the one of profound fear that he had seen hundreds of times before, but never on a face so…well, to borrow a word, so nice.

He ground his jaw, crushing the thought between his teeth. "This time, I will be clear." Damien swept a hand over her to dispel the bind completely. As the tendrils melted away into nothingness and she scrambled to sit up, he leaned in close, face inches from hers. "Go home."

She didn't attempt to run despite being free, staring back at him like a wild prey animal caught in a thorny copse.

"Do you understand?"

She gave him the briefest of nods, her eyes never leaving his, lips parted and trembling. Still crouching before her, Damien knew he should have backed off if he really wanted her to flee—she was little more than a rabbit in an open field while he bared down on her like that—but a question hammered at the back of his mind, anchoring them both to the floor of the Sanctum. *Why did you help me?* It begged to be asked, though he kept his lips drawn into a tight line, only able to stare back, trapping her there without binds.

And then he felt it, the tiniest tug at his side. His brow cocked, and the realization flashed on her face that he had discovered her nimble fingers—those same ones that had tied the cloth around his hand so swiftly—had found their way into his cloak pocket. Ah, so she was just a dirty, little thief after all. Good enough to pull one over on him temporarily, but no one was truly good enough to get away with that in the long run.

Damien grinned. "What do you think you're do—"

She shrieked, her face changed, the fear draining out of it and replaced by a shock of pain.

Then it was Damien's turn to have what little color there was in his face drain away. He grabbed onto the arm she was cradling that had been in his cloak pocket, turning her palm upward. Bloodthorne's Talisman of Enthrallment was in her hand though she didn't clutch it. The inkarnaught ore was already embedding itself, pulsing crimson as it burrowed down into her skin.

She screamed, kicking against the floor to pull away, but Damien held her still by the wrist, shifting onto his knees and making a grab

25

for the talisman with his free hand. His fingers just grazed the stone's smooth surface before it disappeared completely, leaving only a crimson glow in her palm, skin unmarred.

He unsheathed the dagger hidden in the bracer of his other arm, squeezing her wrist that much tighter. "Stay still," he growled, jerking her forward and measuring to be sure he could properly cut it out, hovering the blade's tip over her palm.

"Oh, my gods, no!" Her shrieking finally formed proper words, and she grabbed onto his dagger-wielding hand. "Please, don't stab me!"

He grit his teeth, pushing her frantic voice out of his head and pressing the blade to her palm, her attempt to throw him off no match for his own strength. Her skin yielded, soft and pliable, but he didn't draw blood. It should have been easy, he had sliced through his own palm, his arm, his chest, hundreds of times, but he couldn't press any harder. And then the glow of the talisman faded.

He flipped the dagger so the blade was no longer threatening and yanked up her sleeve. The crimson light was traveling up the length of her arm. It was lost at her elbow where her clothing bunched up, but he knew where it was headed.

Damien snatched the cowl off of her, exposing her head and neck as she protested. Then he grabbed the wide collar of her too-big tunic and yanked it down. At this, her grip on his arm tightened enough to remind him it was still there at all.

"What do you think you're doing?" She threw his words back at him, her voice dropping from an ear-splitting shriek to an incensed growl. But he didn't have to explain, they both could see the glimmer of red light shooting across her skin to the center of her chest where it halted. Both of their gazes flicked to the dagger, still in his hand, then up to each other. The girl blanched, shaking her head, voice falling to one that was small and weak, "Please, don't."

The crimson light intensified, and she screamed again, curling into herself. Her grip on him weakened, face going slack as she stared straight through him, then her eyes crossed, and she fell backward into a heap, unconscious.

Damien still had a hold of her arm, no longer tense in his grasp. He wiggled it, and her hand flopped to the side, totally lax. Dropping her arm, he chucked the dagger across the stone floor in his vexation, grabbing her shoulders to shake her back awake. Her head only lolled to the side, the glow disappearing entirely.

That was it. The talisman had been absorbed, and it was gone.

"Fuck."

Damien stared up at the carvings on the walls of the Sanctum but instead saw a lifetime of studying the arcane, trekking across perilous lands, gathering precious components, learning near-impossible magics, all flashing away. Bloodthorne's Talisman of Enthrallment had been so ludicrously powerful that it begged to be absorbed, so it should have been no surprise it had latched onto the first being that wasn't Damien to touch it. And now it was utterly wasted.

Though perhaps it wasn't.

"*Sanguinisui*, wake up."

The girl sat up so quickly she cracked her forehead right against his. He jerked back, and she wavered again but remained conscious. "What happened?"

"What happened?" he growled, rubbing at his head. "*You* happened."

Pawing at her temple and then her chest, her voice was breathy. "Where are—who are you?"

Damien grunted, rolling his eyes. "Right, it's meant to be forgotten. *Sanguinisui*, fetch my dagger."

She jumped to her feet, eyes falling right on the blade as she went for it, picking it up with no hesitation and returning it to where he knelt, hilt first.

Damien was the one to hesitate then before taking it, looking her over as she stood there, bent at the waist and offering the weapon he'd nearly used to end her life. There was emptiness in her eyes, that spark he'd seen before in the alley gone, the will to live when he'd had her under the binding spell wiped away. When he took the dagger and resheathed it in his arm bracer, he shook his head—of course the talisman worked, but it was almost unnerving to see how well.

"Um." She blinked, looking around the room with a renewed liveliness. "Who did you say you—oh, you're that man from the alley? The nice one who—oh, no, *you* gave me bad directions."

Well, that had been a quick pivot away from *nice*. It was better that way—she needn't get the wrong idea. "Brilliant. Remember anything else?"

"You were going to...to kill..." She swallowed, taking a step back as he stood to his full height before her. Limbs stiffened at her sides, eyes darting to his hands as if looking for the weapon she couldn't remember just giving back to him.

"And do you know why?"

She shook her head, small and tight, frozen under his glare.

So, it had worked as intended: she had no memory of the talisman, and no awareness she'd just completed a task he had

27

ordered. She would only know if he told her, which was perhaps also worth testing out. "You tried to steal from me, an object that became a part of you, and now you're my thrall."

She searched the ground for an answer, but appeared to come up blank.

"*Sanguinisui*, remember."

Fear and horror broke out on her face as the memory came back, clawing at her own chest. "Oh, gods! What was that thing? What did you do to me?"

"Me?" He snorted. "You're the thief, blindly sticking your hand in a man's pocket, and—" Then it dawned on Damien like the brightness of Ero reflecting back the static moon Lo: she hadn't done this blindly at all. It was no mistake they had met that morning; she'd even tried to get close to him in the alley, but he had been smarter then. If only he'd kept his guard up.

Damien grabbed the front of her tunic and yanked her to him. "Who are you?" he spat. "And who's behind this?"

She gasped, gripping onto his arm. Significantly shorter, her toes scuffed the floor as he held her aloft, face drawn back into that pitiful, terrified look again, but this time it only made him furious, and he shook her.

"Tell me! Do you belong to Eirengaard's holy order? A Knight of Osurehm? Have they really sunk so low as to recruit little girls? Or did Shadowhart send you? Is this what he thinks of me? That I would fall for this?" He scanned her quickly—calling her a little girl wasn't really fair, she was just hiding a woman's body under ill-fitting clothes—then he scoffed. "I knew I should have killed that bastard last time I had the chance."

"I don't know what you're talking about," she stuttered out, her nails digging into the leather of his bracer.

"There's no need to keep playing, you've succeeded." The admittance was thick and disgusting on his tongue. "But no one's coming to help you now, are they? Don't repay your disloyal master by staying silent."

She whined in the back of her throat, feet still kicking. "Please, I don't understand."

Damien rolled his eyes. Of course, a good spy wouldn't tell him unless she was forced, and he was a master of coercive torture, but he had a much easier way of getting to the truth now by her own doing. "*Sanguinisui*, tell me why you are here and who sent you after me."

Her grip on his arm loosened, and her legs went lax. "I'm here for the Scroll of the Army of the Undead. You had it, I wanted it, I tried to take it from you. No one sent me, I came on my own, and I have no idea who you are, I swear it by Sestoth. Please, don't hurt me, I didn't mean to take that stone." She choked on the last of her words, eyes glassy. "I'm sorry."

Damien winced. The words he had designed to elicit complete obedience out of the talisman's vessel worked perhaps even better than any truth spell. The ore had been imbued with even more potent components, his own blood chiefly among them, to evoke his will. And here she was, *apologizing*. No one had ever apologized under any truth spell he had cast. And why should she even be sorry? He was the one holding her captive, and the only way to get the talisman out of her was to—"Shit."

He set her feet flush with the ground, but didn't release her, glancing off into the darkness of the Sanctum to think. She was telling the truth; it really had been an accident. "And now I have to kill you."

When she squeaked out a questioning sound, he cast his gaze back onto her face. Nothing about her read spy, he could see that now, except that she absolutely did not fit the description of a hardened guard or rogue assassin. Under the dirt and a bruise across one temple, she had rounded cheeks and a pointed, slip of a chin, but she wasn't as young as he'd originally thought, not with a body like that, eyes that somehow looked right into the depth of him, and full lips that were suddenly quivering.

"What are you doing?"

She moved her mouth, but no words came out. Tears, however, did streak down her face. And there were a lot of them.

"Are you crying? Oh, dark gods, stop that."

"I can't," she squealed, breathing in raggedly. "You said you're going to kill me, so it's just happening."

"Well, if you'd like to live a bit longer, you better bloody well *try*."

She swallowed, succeeding for a moment, and then devolved into a sobbing mess.

Damien released her fully, scoffing in disgust, and she sank to the ground in a heap. He paced to the entrance of the chamber, rubbing his temples and trying to block out her wailing. Killing her would, of course, solve both of his problems: the only way to get the talisman back so it could be embedded in its intended target was through her death, and, even more compelling, if she were dead, he wouldn't have to listen to her keening any longer.

Yet he hadn't even been able to cut into her palm when the talisman had first been absorbed, and cutting into palms was *easy*, especially for a blood mage, of all beings. It's what blood mages *did*. They killed too, also a relatively easy task, and yet the hesitance welling up in him was making just the thought difficult. Too similar to the feeling that had seeded itself into his gut the evening before, his disinclination to simply run her through and be done with it was odd and heavy and as unwelcome as it was unshakable.

Damien was certainly evil, nothing born of a demon could be any less, and yet...

That was the way he had designed the talisman—to only be shucked out of its vessel through death. It was a failsafe so no other adept mage or enterprising host could pry it out. In fact, everything about the talisman was meant to keep it inside, how it made itself be forgotten, how it attached itself inconspicuously, how it changed to become a part of its host so as to be difficult to trace. Even now as the woman sat on the ground of the Ebon Sanctum Mallor and blubbered, Bloodthorne's Talisman of Enthrallment gave off no telltale glow on her skin, and its infernal presence had been snuffed completely out.

Damien whipped back around and strode across the room to stand over her. "You've blocked its aura."

Her blue eyes were rimmed red and puffy when she glanced up from her hands.

"The talisman is no longer so loud. It's not even pulsing at all." She sniffled.

Damien paced, rubbing his smooth jaw. "This could...this could work. I could take the most direct route, stay in town instead of the wilderness every night, even get right into the palace." He stopped, looking down at her again and snorted out a laugh. "Perhaps you're a more useful shield than anything else I would have found in here."

As the thought continued to bloom in his mind, she composed herself, likely easier since he wasn't threatening to kill her any longer. She wiped at her face, clearing away some of the dirt with her tears. She wouldn't even be terrible to look at, all things considered, on the trip.

"For now, you may remain alive to accompany me to Eirengaard. Just keep your mouth shut, and, by all that is grim and unholy, will you stop with the tears and get up off the floor?"

She bit her lip and inhaled sharply, words coming out fast and wavering with the desire to continue crying. "Can you please just tell me what's going on? What was that pink, glowy thing, and why is it inside me?"

He pinched the long bridge of his nose. "That *red* thing is inside you because you very cleverly decided to touch it. You are now the exclusive vessel of Bloodthorne's Talisman of Enthrallment. Congratulations."

"I don't know what that means." Her breathing had gone erratic once again, and she was in danger of hyperventilating.

"It means I can do this: *sanguinisui*, stand up and calm down."

She hopped to her feet, then looked around, bewildered. That, at least, seemed to dry up the well. "You made me do that," she whispered. "That...that is a dark use of magic."

"You're in the Ebon Sanctum Mallor on the outskirts of Aszath Koth, seeking out the Scroll of the Army of the Undead, so I'm not sure what you expected, but you're not the talisman's intended target, so I don't intend to use it for much else." He pointed at her. "Unless you force my hand."

She blinked back at him, voice stilling. "Your hand. It's already healed?"

Damien looked down at his palm, the one he had sliced that morning to cast the only healing spell he knew for that pitiful, little creature in the alley. That had been just before she'd first happened upon him and decided to help him. *Blech.* "Of course it's healed. I told you it would."

"But that was so fast." Suddenly, her hands were on his, holding and spreading out his palm as she looked closely at it, the terror gone from her face, his order to calm down making her bold. "You used magic to do this? You're a...a healer?"

Damien watched her thumbs as they smoothed over the place the cut had been, her fingertips on the back of his hand, holding him there with a touch so gentle it sent shivers up his arm. He ripped his hand away from her and shook his head.

"A mage?" She was getting there, but much too slowly.

"A blood mage."

Damien waited to see if she might pass out again, but consciousness didn't waver over her features, they only creased in thought. There were so few actual blood mages that anything could be said of them and be accepted as truth, the prevailing belief that they were inherently evil beings, Abyssbent on destroying the realm—a bit of gossip that happened to be entirely accurate.

"You're a demon?"

And that was the other bit of gossip, but it was only half true.

Damien looked her form over, remaining calm by his command. She was no spy for some higher order, just a common street thief—a dirty, little thing that no one would believe even if she did mouth off to some Holy Knight of Osurehm. And if she would be stuck with him for the time being, she may as well know the truth if for no other reason than to understand the danger in trying his patience. "My father is Zagadoth the Tempestuous, Ninth Lord of the Infernal Darkness and Abyssal Tyrant of the Sanguine Throne. As his son, I, Damien Maleficus Bloodthorne, have inherited and honed the arcane abilities of bloodcraft and am, indeed, half demon."

"What?"

He heaved a sigh. Unlike the talisman, his origin was rarely absorbed on the first go. "My father is Zagadoth the—"

"No, I heard you, it's just..." The woman's shoulders relaxed, and she tipped her head to the side. "You don't have any horns."

Damien's mouth opened, but not even a scoff came out. She really should have been terrified to know she stood across from a being with enough infernal arcana flowing through him to open a rift right to the infernal plane and show her, yet it was exactly that power that had made her so complacent. "Horns? Infernal blood and noxscura itself flows through my veins. Blood mages don't wear their heritage like half elves with their pointy ears and questionable affinity for trees. It's just within us, lurking right below the human shell."

"What's wrong with liking trees?"

"Nothing, that's not...listen,"—Damien rubbed his hand over his thigh, trying to wipe away the lingering feeling of her offensively soft touch—"I am corruption made corporeal, a nightmare in human flesh, the Abyss brought topside, all right?"

Her blue eyes roved over his face, down to his chest and back up. "Yeah, but you don't look anything like a demon. You're not red or hooved, and you're not that much bigger than anyone else. You just look like...a boy."

Damien's nostrils flared, and he welled up to yell, then swallowed it back. He might have preferred her crying to this new nonchalance, and considered briefly ordering her back into terror via the enchanted word, but that might have invalidated the point. Malice would be easy to prove if he grabbed her by the throat and slammed her against the wall, or took her to her knees with a broken wrist, but throwing his own tantrum would prove nothing except that he was human, at least by half.

Instead, he closed the space between them and loomed over her. "Have you ever seen a demon?"

"Well, no, thank Osurehm." There was nervous laughter in her voice.

"Then how could you possibly know they don't also look like boys—er, men?"

She narrowed her eyes at him, dubious.

"Regardless, I am quite a bit bigger than you." He bared down slightly. "So, what I say goes, and I say, I am half demon." The talisman would help as well, but he left that unspoken.

She nodded, swallowing. "Okay. That's fair."

"Is it? Is it *fair*?" He glowered over her a moment longer until she gave him a single nod then swept away, headed back for the entrance to leave. "Come, we've a long way to go, and night is surely falling." There were no steps behind him, and when he glanced back, she was still just standing there, staring after him. "What?"

"Nothing," she squeaked out and scurried up behind him. "I just thought you would…um…have a tail."

Damien could not even dignify that with a response. He simply turned and continued on. It was definitely going to be a bloody long trip.

CHAPTER 4
HEAVY IS THE HEAD THAT WEARS THE CROWN OF BUREAUCRACY

A blood mage. By Osurehm, Amma was following *a blood mage* right out of the Ebon Sanctum Mallor and back toward the monstrous city of Aszath Koth. She thought they were only legends, as removed from the world as direct descendants of dominions were, and that no one could truly be born of a demon and exist on earth rather than on the infernal plane.

Existence was broken into six planes, everyone knew, even Amma who paid little attention in theology. Planes were actually not arranged in any kind of order, they all existed at the same time in all of space, on top of, inside, and around one another, but if they *were* stacked up, as so often they were depicted in art, Empyrea would be at the top. The home of the one hundred and seventeen gods of light and love, Empyrea had no means of ingress or egress. It had not always been that way, but after The Expulsion, the gods had seen fit to abstain from earthly interaction. Below Empyrea would lay the celestial plane, home of the dominions and servants of the gods from which exit could be achieved by mortal summoning. Dominions were largely considered good, and when they walked the earth their deeds were also typically kind, but pissing one off was not recommended.

There would then be some disagreement on whether earth or the Everdarque came next, an argument of absolutely zero consequence as, again, the planes were not layered in any way. However, the plane of mortal beings, on which Amma had resided her whole existence, was more frequently considered just below the celestial plane, likely because those who made up the charts felt a sort of affinity to being placed as high and close to godliness as possible themselves. The center of the imaginary layers was usually followed by the fae realm of the Everdarque, home to immortal beings whose magic only flourished within their plane, so if one could avoid ever going there, one was safe from the dangers spoken of fae. Though there were some who would claim the Everdarque didn't exist at all and was only a fairytale—that is, a made-up tale told by the very creatures who supposedly did not exist.

But there was no argument that below all of these was the infernal plane, home of the demons and their ilk. Like the dominions of the celestial plane, demons could only leave when they were summoned, which was a mad and difficult thing to do, but obviously, if someone like Damien existed, it could be done. Finally, below every other plane, lay the Abyss at the deepest level of level-less existence. The Abyss was known only as a hollow pit of nothing forever, into which the twenty-five dark gods had been cast during The Expulsion where they remained imprisoned and could never escape.

Though almost no one ever crossed planes, their existence was confirmed by the reality of magic. All arcana was a gift, Amma knew, even the darkest kinds, from planes beyond vision and reach, but none of it manifested directly from earth. Of course, she had seen and experienced magic, and she knew all too well that evil certainly existed, but this man, this Damien Mal-whatever-thorn, claimed to be one of the most feared and powerful beings in and out of the realm. And he was, what, a glum and self-absorbed twenty-something, living up in the Infernal Mountains and prowling the dirty streets of Aszath Koth to heal wounded kittens?

She had so many questions, and all of them should have struck fear right into her soul, but her heart didn't pound like she knew it should, and she wasn't sweating half as much as she expected, all of which likely had something to do with that word he'd used on her in a language she didn't know and the two significantly more infuriating ones in Key: *calm down.* Never had anyone actually calmed down when ordered to, she was sure of it, and yet there she was, feeling calm.

Amma glanced skyward when they passed out of the Sanctum. There were two moons over Eiren, one called Lo that remained static, shining brightly every night, and a second called Ero that waxed and waned while arcing through the sky every twenty-eight days. They were named after a pair of goddesses who were said to be linked in deep friendship but broken by The Expulsion. Lo currently resided in Empyrea, and was a stalwart beacon of consistent goodness, but Ero had fallen, one of the Abyss-cast, and in retribution, her namesake moon would blot out Lo's whenever it got the chance. There was, of course, an astronomical element to that, and Amma's schooling may well have covered it, but she hadn't paid attention—a thing she currently regretted as she could remember only one thing: the moons had a distinct influence on magic in Eiren. She knew how the seasons affected the natural world and how fickle magical things could be, and she was especially aware how the twain of the two took very special care, but never had she been under a spell, and perhaps if she'd paid more attention, she could figure out how to...not be.

Her shoulders sagged. No, that wasn't likely—Amma might have been familiar with the tiniest sliver of magic, but she couldn't cast it, and even if she could, she'd be no match for a blood mage.

Amma's eyes fell onto the back of him in the moonlight, a slightly darker shadow against the dusk of the way ahead. Perhaps she could just bolt—he wasn't even paying attention—but she only knew one way back into town, the way they were going, and the empty outskirts of Aszath Koth were even more frightening in the dark. The kalsephrus trees looked like gnarled, clawed hands, reaching out to grab her, and the ruins ahead loomed against the sky like giants that might enjoy munching on humans.

"So, this is where you live?" she asked, keeping her voice quiet as she remained as close to him as she dared.

"What?" The man called Damien glanced over his shoulder. "No. Well, not right *here*."

"But in Aszath Koth? There aren't a lot of other humans there."

"I told you, I'm not human."

"But you look like one." Her eyes darted from the long shadow of one ruin to another, searching for anything hidden within. "And all the lizard people and the goblins don't really seem to like humans much. It must be lonely."

He scoffed, picking up his pace.

"Do you have a family, or—" Amma gasped at a sound out in the orchard behind them.

Damien did not react. "You're beginning to feel fear again?"

Before she could respond, a shifting in the nearby brush made her wince and fall still with terror. "What was that?"

"Interesting." He looked her over, turning to walk backward and watch her as he went. "Well, let's try something else then, hmm? *Sanguinisui*, follow me, and don't speak."

Amma's feet moved on their own, propelling her forward whether she wanted to or not. The skin of her neck itched and words in her throat were immediately strangled back, a rush of anxiety flooding her at even the thought of speaking, yet the intense desire to do so fighting back. The sensation was nothing short of terrible.

He waited a moment, and when she said nothing, turned away and kept going. Amma was compelled to follow right after. Through the ruins, there were plenty of other sourceless noises and figures flickering in the twilight at the corners of her eyes, but her reactions remained silent and her feet never stopped as they trekked back to the city.

When they reached the edges of Aszath Koth, Amma wished she had her cowl and hood still to pull up, but they'd been left abandoned in the Sanctum. Damien, however, walked around with his own hood back, shoulders set and taking long strides she had to jog to keep up with as if they were not entering a city full of monsters.

He was swathed in a long, black cloak though, and the rest of his clothing was black as well, the leather armor strapped over his torso, the bracers around his forearms, his boots, even his tunic and pants, so he at least looked the part of menacing human. She was an abundance of color in comparison with her own tawny breeches and over-sized, once-white-now-stained tunic, belted at the waist with a green sash, and her light hair pulled into a knot at the back of her head. Cloakless now, it was more difficult to blend in, and even in the darkness of late evening, the creatures still lurking about took notice.

Whether the arcane urge not to speak was beginning to wane or not, the practical influence of the city did well to keep her mouth shut. When the streets had widened with heavier foot traffic, Amma hurried to stay behind Damien more out of fear of everything else rather than compulsion. Eyes on his back, she continued forward until a scaled tendril swept down through the air and cut her off.

Amma opened her mouth, but the yelp that was instinctive to what appeared to be a giant snake falling before her was strangled in her throat. Her feet attempted to continue forward, taking her closer to it as her eyes cast up the length of the thick appendage, serpentine and scaled in dismal yellow and a color that would have been turquoise if it hadn't been mud-caked.

At the side of the road, the tendril was connected to a vaguely human torso that was leaning up against a building's post. Clad in a tattered vest, the pallid skin beneath was marked with brighter patches of scales, including a spattering across the noseless but otherwise human face. The half-human creature lurched off the post and toward her with a smile she was sure wasn't nearly as friendly as it purported to be.

Amma averted her gaze, feet still moving, and focused on the way forward, but the tail was just in front of her, and then it was behind her too, and in a moment its full length was wrapped around her waist. She grabbed onto the scaled hide, as much for balance as for an attempt to escape, feet scuffing as she again opened her mouth to scream. Nothing came out as she was dragged away from the road.

Then there was a sizzle in the air and a snap. A long gash tore through the serpent tail just below Amma's hands, spattering hot, thick blood. She stumbled back as the squeeze around her middle relented, even her sounds of disgust silenced as she held out arms sprayed with blood. Her aggressor, however, was not silent, letting out a howl, eyes flashing angrily at her as if she had somehow injured him.

A hand wrapped around Amma's arm, jerking her backward over the now-lax tail. "What are you doing?" Damien's voice spat.

She pointed to herself and then to the snake man who hissed back in response, lunging forward.

"No," Damien said to him, almost bored. He gave Amma a shake. "This is mine."

The creature cut his next hiss off short when his eyes fell on the blood mage. He recoiled, pulling his tail in, the cut along it still oozing.

Damien swept away from him and continued on as if he had not just cast a spell that sliced through a stranger in the middle of a busy street. The act had garnered a few looks, but no interference by any kind of authority or even any other villagers. "*Sanguinisui*, you may speak again since it seems useful for the time being. Do not get yourself eaten," he said, still dragging her by the arm.

Mouth dry, she managed to croak out, "How is that up to me?"

"Just don't. The talisman will likely end up inside whatever devours you, and a lamia would be exponentially more difficult to travel with. Stop trailing behind and stay beside me for darkness's sake."

"Thanks for your concern," she mumbled, though not quiet enough. He cast her a withering look then finally released her. Of course he didn't truly care, he only needed her for smuggling, but at least now she could let him know if she were about to be devoured by another beast.

Rubbing her arms, she tried to wipe away some of the blood. "I can't believe you just attacked that snake-man, and no one stopped you."

Damien chuckled then, a low sound that climbed up her spine and made her straighten. "Right, well, I'm sort of the lord around here. I tend to do what I want."

Then it was Amma's turn to scoff, his words making her forget the blood, the danger, and even her predicament. "Oh, of course you do," she muttered.

"What was that?" His voice pressed in on her, suddenly close as he leaned near.

Her stomach clenched, and she bit her lip, staring forward and avoiding the angry gaze she could feel boring into the top of her head. She knew men just like him, and it didn't matter if they called themselves evil or not, they were all the same. She swallowed, injecting as much sweetness as she could into her voice. "Did you say we were going to Eirengaard?"

The man's eyes finally turned back to the street. "Yes."

That was the capital city of the realm. Massive and sprawling, she had visited on plenty of occasions, and it was much more lawful than this place. His actions wouldn't be tolerated there. In fact, his entire existence probably wouldn't. "You won't be able to do whatever you want when you're in the realm, you know. What are you going for exactly?"

Damien huffed. "You don't need to worry about that, you won't be around for it."

Amma drew in a sharp breath, heart hitching—he still intended to kill her as he had threatened in the Sanctum. Her eyes flicked to his cloak and where she knew he was harboring the Scroll of the Army of the Undead. If nothing else, the travel southward would give her an opportunity to get her hands on that as she waited for the most apt moment to flee.

Night had fallen, torches and glowing stones from the taverns and shops along the main road lighting the way. Damien seemed to have no desire to stop, but Amma was exhausted. Her body ached, stomach panged, and her mind was so overfull she could scarcely think of much else. Damien never veered off the main road though, taking them the way she had become familiar with, past the market as it was being closed up, and along the steady incline that would lead to the city's exit and then the gates through the mountain pass, likely much less safe in the dark. It was only when she recognized the way out of the city ahead that he finally came to a stop.

Damien stood in the middle of the street, Amma at his side, glancing up at him and then nervously at the those who diverted their own paths to give him space. She would have liked to at least crowd him out of the way of the others, even if they were scaled and fanged, but he was unbothered by the obstruction he'd created. He looked down a connecting road and exhaled hoarsely. "I need you to tell me something."

Amma tipped her head, waiting.

When he glanced back, his face had changed, the pinch to his brow still there but in contemplation rather than annoyance. "You weren't sent here to thwart me, and I hadn't answered your query when you did this." He held up his hand where the cut she had wrapped once was. Both the handkerchief and wound were gone. "So, why?"

"Um, you were bleeding?"

"Yes, obviously, but *why*?" Narrowing his eyes, something flashed in them, a deep bewilderment from their stunningly violet color.

Amma thought on this for a very long moment, much longer than the answer she was about to give warranted, but it was a question she hadn't pondered, not in regard to what he was asking nor to much else she did. "Well, I suppose for the same reason you gave me those bad directions."

"Because you're just a bastard sometimes?"

She clicked her tongue. "Okay, maybe not that. I guess I should have said for the same reason you helped that cat."

Damien wrinkled his nose. "You thought I was pathetic?"

Amma shook her head. "Because it just seemed like the right thing to do."

"Of course you'd say something like that." Hands on his hips, Damien grunted. "We've a stop to make before heading out of town." He turned, leading her away from the path out of Aszath Koth. She began to follow when he whipped back to her, halting them both once again. "We have a rat problem."

"Rats?"

"In the city. Cats are helpful in controlling vermin that would otherwise spread disease, so…" He gestured vaguely to the street.

"Oh, so healing that kitten was just your way of helping your city." She grinned and nodded, understanding.

"Well, not…" That pinched annoyance came back into his face, and he rolled his eyes. "I suppose."

CHAPTER 5
SACRIFICIAL DESIGNATIONS

A squat building of dark stone was positioned near the gates of Aszath Koth proper. It stood on a corner, its entry angled toward the intersection of the main road and another that boasted a tavern with chamber pots that only needed to be shared with one other room. The choice was purposeful, making it hard to miss for those entering the city.

Amma had given it a wide berth a day prior when she first saw it. The angled door at its front was flanked with columns, each topped with a statue of a winged beast positioned as if they might dive off and attack, and above the door hung a banner, black with a red, embroidered circle styled to look like it was wearing horns and dripping blood. Amma could not read the language that was painted on a sign propped up beside the door, but she didn't feel she needed to in order to know to stay away.

Damien, of course, led her straight to it.

The door, a wet-looking wood with iron bars across the small window in its center, was pulled shut unlike how the building had stood during the day, wide open with an unwelcoming void of an entrance. She fidgeted at Damien's side as he raised a fist to knock. "*Sanguinisui*, say nothing of the talisman." As he rapped twice on the door, the magic he spoke invaded her, sending a terrible chill through her brain like biting into something frozen.

There was a scuffle from beyond the door, and then a low, baying voice that requested, "After hours pass phrase?"

Damien spoke words similar to the one he used to enchant her, the sibilant tones giving her a second chill.

There was quiet, and then the voice rose up again. "That was last moon's pass phrase. We need this moon's pass phrase."

Damien rolled his eyes, thought a moment, then offered up another foreign utterance that crawled up Amma's spine like frigid fingertips.

"Sir, this is the Infernal Brotherhood of The Tempest. Applications for admittance to the fold are taken every—"

"It's me, you fool, The Tempest's son." The sharpness of Damien's voice cut off the drone of the other, and an eye peeked out between the bars of the door's window.

There was a scuffing against the wood, a worried curse, and then the door was thrust open. "Master Bloodthorne!"

Amma had seen the man who stood in the void of the building's entrance before. With a set of ornate vestments, a shaved head, and eyes rimmed in purple blotches, the priest was hard to forget, though now instead of murmuring to himself and ambling through the streets, he had an arm thrown out, head bowed, welcoming the two of them into the building. Amma did *not* want to go inside.

"Apologies, apologies," the priest wailed, bowing even lower and shuffling out of the way, the symbol he wore, the same from the banner, swaying heavily about his neck on a thick chain. Damien stepped past him, and Amma hesitated but followed, still compelled against her wishes.

Cave-like, the building's small entry was dark and narrow. When the door behind them shut with a creaking rattle, its echo climbed up the walls, and they were plunged into pitch black.

"We are honored by the shadow of your presence," the priest's voice filled up the space as sounds of him skulking about reverberated around them. "Anything you request, anything you desire, it shall be yours."

Damien groaned. "Some light would be nice."

"Of course!" There was a bang and then a bright burst in Amma's face from which she and Damien both recoiled. Above the sudden light, the priest was grinning, exposing every last one of his teeth, tinged with the nauseating glow off a ball of arcane green flames held in his palm. "To what are we to give unholy gratitude for the dark delight of your visit, Master?" When he bowed again, the irritated nicks on his scalp from a messy shave were illuminated.

Damien's eyes flicked over to Amma, and for once the disgusted curl to his lip wasn't meant for her. "The, uh, prophecy is to be fulfilled."

"Truly, Master?" The priest's head popped back up, pale eyes glazing over.

Damien shrugged a shoulder. "Sure."

"Infernal powers, we weren't planning on such a celebration, but we still have the altar up from Belracht, and we're sure to have an appropriate blade in the ceremonial drawer." His smile stretched impossibly wide over his bony skull as he gestured to Amma with the magicked flame. "*And* we just got a new, dragon-shaped gravy boat, but it's never been used, so it should make a lovely collection vessel for the blood from the virgin you've brought to sacrifice."

Sweat broke out on the back of Amma's neck, gaze shooting up to Damien. He cocked a brow at her, half a smirk on his face, then he shook his head. "Mmm, we'll see how the night progresses. I might not want to waste her—she's a...minion."

"Well, a minion of The Tempest's son is a minion of The Brotherhood. Come, come, we want to see you, to celebrate the fulfillment of the prophecy!" He held his lit palm out to illuminate an archway. With a hearty sigh, Damien stepped through, and Amma was compelled to follow despite every fiber of her being wanting to bolt in the other direction.

The rest of the building opened up into a chamber with a bit of light from candles gathered in waxy pools in the center of long, wooden tables. Others in robes were crowded around the globs of light, working at parchment with nubs of charcoal or holding cloth close to their faces and stitching. The flames danced in the reflection of each bald head, some even human, though there were others too who didn't need shaving, covered instead in scales or thick green hide, and one who looked like he would have fared much better if he'd been covered in fur but every inch of him was smooth and pink.

When Damien entered, they each dropped what they were doing, heads turning in unison, realization spreading across their faces like a wave. "Master Bloodthorne," rose up from the crowd in one, awestruck voice, and then in a flurry of squealing benches, they all fell to the ground, supplicant on their knees, heads down. Their host even followed suit, and the two were left standing there in the silence of three dozen faces planted firmly against the floorboards.

Damien squeezed his eyes shut, groaning quietly in the back of his throat, then he seemed to remember Amma was there, straightening as he cast a glance at her, something like unease passing over his features but replaced too quickly with disdain to be sure. "Yes, hello, get up."

Following the order as if they had enthrallment talismans embedded in them, each robed being scrambled to their feet, practically vibrating with excitement at whatever would be asked of them next.

"The prophecy," the priest who had bade them entry announced, "Master Bloodthorne embarks upon its fulfillment!"

"The prophecy!" they all cheered in unison, and then there was a frenzy. Robed members skittered around, rearranging tables and benches, grabbing brooms and sweeping the room's center, carrying in and out baskets and crates from shadowy spaces off the main room. One of the members had bundled up the fabric they'd been working on, and Amma could see a nearly-completed, soft doll, red, horned, and it, indeed, had five appendages. She *knew* it: demons did have tails.

As everyone else moved around them, Amma actually found herself inching closer to Damien until she bumped his arm, and like she'd been shocked, she pulled back into herself. "It won't work," she hissed quickly.

"The prophecy? Well, it was given by the oracle, but I've been having my own doubts—wait, that isn't what you mean, is it?"

One of the figures crossed the chamber with an overfilled armful of unlit candles, and another followed, picking up each as it fell and inspecting the dents left in the wax.

"Sacrificing me." She swallowed, the words coming out quavering as she wondered if the argument would stick. "I'm not...*qualified*, not like he said. If you kill me like this, it'll be a waste of everyone's work."

"You're either brazen or clever but hopefully not both. Either way, sacrificing you *would* be a waste." Damien chuckled, and the sound made her sick despite the relief that she apparently wouldn't be drained of her blood that night. "Pay no mind to The Brotherhood—they just say things like that because it's what they think they ought to do. Summoning takes a life, but they haven't done that for about seventy years, and I don't think these specific members have really ever sacrificed anyone, virgin or otherwise."

Someone scurried by carrying a stack of parchment with crude drawings in messy ink, flashing them both an unblinking smile. Amma hadn't really encountered anything like them before, though they reminded her slightly of those who belonged to a temple. "What, um...what *are* they?"

Damien thought a moment. "They're a sort of excessively zealous consortium who have unorthodox views."

"You have a cult?" Amma's voice was squeaky even as she tried to keep it low.

"No, no, this is their own thing, not mine. Big fans of my father, really, I just drop by in his stead on occasion."

Amma watched the ruckus, robed figures bumping into one another, dropping things, knocking heads as they picked them up, scurrying about. *Summoning*, Damien said, and fans of his *father*. These...these were the vile, nefarious cultists who had summoned a demon from the infernal plane to wreak havoc on earth?

A cultist hustled up to them out of the frenzy. He dropped to a knee, thrusting a tray over his shaved head. Amma stepped back from the sudden movement, but when she saw the two goblets filled with a maroon liquid and a plate of flattened pastries, her eyes went wide with hunger. Damien picked up one of the sweets and gestured to the rest of the plate. "They're actually quite good."

Amma grabbed one and stuffed it in her mouth. Whether he meant to kill her or not, she didn't intend to die hungry. The pastry was divine, but her mouth instantly dried up, and she reached for a goblet.

"Ah, ah." Damien snatched her hand, then waved off the cultist. "Don't drink the wine unless you'd like to end up a mindless devotee like them."

As the members of The Brotherhood finished their tasks, Amma noted how they grinned, each in the same stilted and unnerving way. With the middle of the chamber now cleared, another cultist carried in a roll of crimson fabric that she began to unfurl at Damien's feet, walking backward with a smile and beckoning them to follow across it.

Amma leaned in, her voice a whisper. "You mean they're prisoners?"

Damien began to walk the length of fabric to the back of the chamber, and she kept up. "Of course not, but no one comes to The Brotherhood unwilling to forget some terrible misdeed or tragic upbringing or what have you. The wine's enchanted to help clear their minds of, you know...guilt or shame or fear or whatever it is humans feel, and those pendants they're wearing keep them complacent and manageable."

There was a high-backed chair sitting alone at the end of the fabric they'd just pointlessly walked on to get from one end of the chamber to the other. Damien looked it over then dropped down with a huff, nothing like how someone called *master* might, and sat there disinterested, elbows on the armrests and knees splayed out.

In the dim glow of the room, his eyes skimmed up Amma's form slowly, her body flushing under the baggy clothes as she became too aware of herself. "On second thought, maybe you ought to have a

45

taste. It may make you easier to deal with. Tell me, have you some horrible memory to expunge or a desire to abscond from your responsibilities?" His gaze reached her face, and it was as if he were looking right through her, seeing the horrible truth of those things written out on her insides.

But Amma shook her head. Things were dire enough—she didn't need to be mindless atop it all.

Damien's gaze didn't relent, but he did move, leaning forward and taking her by the arm. Her heart shot up into her throat, and she put her hands out to stay upright, but he only tugged her a few inches toward him and out of the way of a cultist scurrying up behind her.

With a flourish, the cultist sat a simpler chair at Damien's side and encouraged Amma to sit. She perched on the edge when he released her, thankful to both be out of his direct line of sight and not sitting on his lap where she'd momentarily and embarrassingly thought she'd end up.

Two more cultists rolled back the crimson fabric and removed it from the chamber. "Can they leave anytime they want?"

He shrugged, gesturing to a podium in the room's corner, atop it a small statue of a bat-like creature carved from red stone. It gave off a gentle glow. "Maybe if that relic ever gets shattered."

Arcana was being used to possess them. Dark arcana. Amma clicked her tongue, offended on their behalf.

Damien casually rested an elbow on the chair's arm closest to her, chin in his hand, and she stiffened, afraid to move even as he came close. His eyes were unfeeling pits of violet as he murmured, "They're castoffs and ne'er-do-wells. They were empty and hollow from whatever tragedy befell them—if they left, where would they even go? Brother Eternal Crud has given them purpose." He pointed to the man who had answered the door, standing atop an upturned crate in the room's corner and directing the others.

"Eternal Crud?"

"The cult's been around a long time, so they're really scrounging the bottom of the epithet barrel, I will admit."

"Master Bloodthorne!" Brother Eternal Crud threw out his hands and crossed to the center of the now-empty room. The rest of the cultists fell into silence, watching from the wings of the chamber with long stares and smiles that didn't reach their purple-rimmed, unblinking eyes. "Allow us to offer a gift for your travels."

Damien shifted to sit a bit straighter, his imposing demeanor likewise shifting with something like disquiet. "Oh, no, you really need not do that."

46

"Please, Master, we must!"

The other cultists joined in the beseeching, and Damien slunk right back down into the chair. "Fine." He rolled his head back, and his clear annoyance gave Amma the tiniest bit of amusement. "Get comfortable," he droned. "I never know how bloody long these things are going to take."

Amma did sit back then, watching as the other cultists filled in around Brother Eternal Crud in the center of the room. They took their places like this had been planned long ago, and in unison pulled up their hoods. At the same moment, nearly all the candles in the room were snuffed out, and Amma gasped. In the dark beside her, Damien laughed at what she could only assume was her expense.

The shadows of the cultists moved under the glow of a window on the ceiling letting in silvery moonlight, the billowing sleeves of their robes sweeping behind as they, well, what was it they were doing? Dancing, Amma supposed, and singing too, though there was no true melody or difference in pitch, just a monotone chant buzzing in a strange language. Brother Eternal Crud crouched in the center, his hand roving over the ground and leaving a line of something powdery and white.

Then he stood, hands raised above him so that his sleeves fell down, exposing arms as thin and pale as bones. His voice rose above the others, calling up enchanted words into the high ceiling of the temple. Amma pinched her knees together and worried the hem of her tunic, the room feeling colder, shadows growing on the walls. The other cultists were moving quicker now, their voices harsher. Amma glanced over to Damien who could not have looked more disinterested if he had been asleep.

Then a cultist tripped, sailing over the tail that jutted out from under the robe of one of their shorter brothers. This began an unending ripple of cultists piling up over the hems of their robes, eyesight obscured by their hoods as they rushed forward in their dance. Amma covered her mouth, sitting forward. Damien only groaned as the last of them finally fell flat on his face.

"Apologies, Master!" called Brother Eternal Crud as he rushed to get the others to their feet. "Once more, this time with feeling. To your places, and we will begin again from one—"

"No, no!" Damien brought his hands together with a sound that echoed loudly into the room and made the others halt, half on the ground, half mid-rush to their starting spots. "That was marvelous. Really brilliant. Well done."

He hadn't sounded particularly convincing, but Amma raised her hands and politely clapped for emphasis, giving them a smile.

Brother Eternal Crud took a deep breath and nodded. "You humble us, Master. Now, the summoning!"

Amma's heart sped up, hands gripping the seat on either side of her. Damien had said a life was required for summoning.

The cultists scattered again and revealed that the brother had been drawing a symbol in chalk in the room's center. Four other cultists came to kneel around the circle, and Brother Eternal Crud stood at the apex. He chanted a few dark words, and they were repeated back to him by the rest of the room, a sound that, unlike the hollow droning of the previous chant, was imbued with a new fervor.

As they filled the chamber with their invigorated calls, one of the four tossed a handful of something that looked like dirt into the center of the symbol. With a red flash, the dirt let off smoke when it scattered across the floor. The second cultist followed suit with a splash of something dark brown that congealed and oscillated around the dirt. The third lifted a candle, and when she tossed it in, it lit the other components so that a blaze crackled in the center of the floor.

Amma's skin went cold as a ripple passed over her, a sourceless breeze thick with magic. She drew in a ragged breath, unable to blink as she watched the fourth cultist reveal what he held. He raised a live rat by its tail, the thing squeaking shrilly as he swung it in, and it cried out, immediately gobbled by the flames.

Amma let out a sad, little whimper and looked to Damien. He glared back, face firmly reading, *And what would you like me to do about it?* Well, at least it hadn't been her flung into the fire.

The flames grew under Brother Eternal Crud's words as he pulled his hands up through the air, and the others joined in until their voices crescendoed. Arcana swept around the room, the fire licking upward in a swirling pillar. There was a crack, and a fissure drew itself within the pillar's center, partially obscured by the dancing flames but a deeply dark color, rivulets of undulating silver flowing within. A shadow poked itself out of the fissure's edge, claws gripping the side of a hole that had been drawn right down through existence, and from it climbed a creature with impossibly long limbs and a set of pointed horns.

Amma swallowed, pressing back into the chair and pulling her knees up. She may have never seen a demon before, but she knew what was said about them, and this thing—this thing with *horns*—had to be one, being summoned right out of the infernal plane.

Then all at once, the flames doused themselves, plunging the chamber into darkness again. The fissure was exposed for only an instant, strands of silver glowing as they ebbed over one another, and Amma had the totally out-of-place thought that it was the most beautiful thing she had ever seen in her life. And then it snapped itself shut, and Amma's ears popped. She pressed her mouth up against her knees to muffle a terrified squeal. After a moment in total darkness, there was movement and then a clatter. A cultist whispered something, and another answered, and finally several candles sprung back to life, slowly filling the chamber with light.

The flickering flames fell over the new form in the room's center, and Amma did not dare even blink for fear the demon would use the opportunity to possess her soul. She watched as it was illuminated, twisted horns jutting off of a bony skull, sharp claws dangling at the ends of arms too long for its body, and wings with leathery skin pulled taught between knobby joints.

"Kaz, is that you?" Damien had leaned forward, elbows on his knees, squinting.

"Master Bloodthorne," the thing screeched out in a voice that was as much water as it was rot. "I have been called into your service!" It began forward on legs that bent the wrong way and ended in talons, a tail flicking behind it, just as Amma had known it would, and as it finally crossed the room to fall to a knee and bow before Damien, Amma actually sat forward as well. The thing, terrible as it was, was also only about a foot and a half tall.

Damien rubbed his smooth chin. "I thought you were dead."

It gazed back up on him with bulbous, black eyes, a strange, strangled smile spreading over its crooked jaw, two jagged teeth on one side poking out. "I was. I have been reborn to serve you once again. It is my duty as an imp of the infernal plane to return to earth when summoned to serve The Tempestuous bloodline."

"Ah, I see. And you've, uh…you've got wings this time."

The imp blinked, twisting about to try and see its back. It spun in place until it grew dizzy and stumbled to a stop. It shook its head and squeezed its fists, and the wings flapped just a bit. "Apologies, Master, but they don't work yet."

"Noted." Damien sat back. "Well, welcome back. Again."

"My lord and master," the imp cried out, dropping into another deep bow, "declare your will."

Damien glanced out at the waiting, rapturous faces of The Brotherhood. "Right. Well, if that's all, then I suppose we're off."

"Master Bloodthorne, night falls!" Brother Eternal Crud scurried up to the chair. "Surely you will want to set out in the morning?"

Being adored and catered to apparently exhausted a person, and after only a bit more prodding, Damien relented to The Brotherhood's offer of accommodations. Amma didn't like the idea of staying in the place, but when she was given a small, private room, one that didn't leak or cost her a literal arm and leg and came complete with a cot and even more food, she forgot her own objections.

But when Damien stepped into the room behind her and shut the door, she whipped toward him and backed away. Very little good ever came from men doing that.

"I didn't say anything about the talisman." She did her best to keep her voice even, but it cracked with her nerves at being shut in alone with him.

"And you won't. *Sanguinisui*, do not leave this room, do not hurt yourself or anyone else, and do not speak to anyone."

Amma's chest thumped, and her vision blurred as her body went rigid. When she came back into herself, Damien was already leaving the room. She opened her mouth, but nothing came out. Apparently he was part of the anyone she couldn't speak to.

But he stopped on the threshold even without her calling to him, turning slightly over his shoulder. "And do not drink the wine, that was only an ill-humored joke—I don't require any additional compliance from you."

When he left and the door latched, she went right to the tray of food, stuffing her mouth without hesitation. As she chewed, she lifted the goblet, taking a sniff of the pungent stuff, then carried it to the chamber pot and dumped it out before returning to finish off the prickly berries and gnaw the cheese down to its rind.

Amma fell onto the cot then, eyes already heavy. Everything was a disaster. She had no scroll, was trapped under the roof of a cult of demon worshipers, and had been cursed to follow the orders of a blood mage. She had tempted fate, it seemed, or rather the god of fate, when she wondered if things could get worse, and somehow they actually had. Perhaps if she'd remembered that god's name, she would have fared better.

Closing her eyes, images of The Brotherhood's display and the appearance of that horrible, little imp played behind her lids. She whined and tried to knock them away with thoughts of home, but then guilt and shame and fear and all of those uncomfortable, human feelings flooded her veins until she relented to the visions of the city streets of Aszath Koth, the oozing insides of the Sanctum, the slippery feel of the spell that had bound her when she had been discovered, and then Damien.

Son of a demon, wielder of bloodcraft, and set to fulfill some apparent prophecy with an entire, dark religion behind it. That was no small ask, and the way he looked each time they called him "master," well, that was actually a little funny. Amma chuckled to herself—if he were one of those jerks who just did whatever he wanted, then he deserved at least a little discomfort. But then again, jerks who did whatever they wanted typically *liked* being called "master."

Before Amma could extrapolate much from that thought, the vision of that fissure slipped into her mind, the way the silvery streams ran over one another so beautifully. It should have been horrifying, but of everything that had happened in the last few hours, that was the vision that calmed her enough to allow sleep to finally take her.

CHAPTER 6
THE ROAD TO THE ABYSS ISN'T PAVED WITH GOOD INTENTIONS OR REALLY ANYTHING, PAVEMENT HASN'T BEEN INVENTED YET

Damien gazed out at the way ahead and into the pass through the Infernal Mountains. They weren't really *that* infernal, the mountains, they were of this plane just as much as Ashrein Ridge was, an extension that ran down into Eiren proper, but the entire range didn't come into being until The Expulsion when some god punched or kicked or slapped some other god so hard that the range just popped up into existence. Damien couldn't remember if Nontigpechi had been the attacker or the defender, but as the god of night and deception, he had been deemed evil and locked away in the Abyss, and that, of course, had not helped the landscape's reputation.

The resulting mountains did have infernal energy to them—the strike had been so fierce that it made the *slightest* tear between earth and the infernal plane—but that only made conducting business with demons and other native creatures a bit easier. It also produced a hazy miasma that turned out to have a purely aesthetic value. It was *not* just like strolling into another plane of existence though, like so many believed, but stories told by those who'd never even seen the place seemed to hold much more weight than those told firsthand.

The mountain pass serpentined at a slight decline, crumbling cliffside all along it, hemmed in and dark. The miasma of the Infernal Mountains still blotted out the sun though it was morning, he could tell, from the way the light was a slightly different shade of muddy grey. That and The Brotherhood's horn to welcome the dawn had been blown what felt like only an hour after he'd finally fallen asleep, jolting him back awake.

The night had been restless, like many nights as of late, but this one was especially irritating, and all because of *her*. He peered over his shoulder at the blonde thing sitting astride her mount. At the very least, she looked to be settling in on the knoggelvi which was better than her staring at the creature, horrified and like she might be sick—not that he cared about her comfort, things would just be marginally easier if she cooperated. Though, it had been rather amusing to see her reaction to the Abyssally-enchanted beast.

Knoggelvi were almost like horses, athletic, fast, and four-legged with a mane and tail of stringy, black hair, but their bodies were covered in a rough hide, their eyes were like fire with roving, red irises nestled into a skeletal head, and of course they breathed out the shadows of terrors past. Another result of The Expulsion, they had once been arcanely adept wild horses that roamed the plains that existed before the Infernal Mountains were thrust into being, and that little tear warped their arcana—for the better, Damien thought.

The woman had to be commanded with the Chthonic word to climb astride one which had also been entertaining since she wasn't quite tall enough to get up without a boost. One of the cultists eventually stepped in to offer their back. That had ruined Damien's fun at watching her struggle but relieved the knoggelvi who was marking his displeasure by scuffing a hoof in the dirt and snorting out an inky blackness that sounded faintly like the wailing of burn victims. When she was finally astride, the beast wasn't much happier, but it wouldn't defy Damien's will, and he wasn't going to have the woman walk—that would be too time consuming and perhaps needlessly cruel.

Damien ground his jaw at the thought of needless cruelty. It shouldn't bother him, it never really did before. It certainly didn't when Kaz, the imp who now sat before him atop his knoggelvi's head, had his "accident" nearly a decade prior, tumbling off the parapet of Bloodthorne Keep before his body was smart enough to grow itself wings. But imps were so terrible it almost seemed a mercy to put them out of their misery. It was certainly a mercy to everyone else. Eternal servitude and groveling and praise just felt like a waste of a life, and even as he looked at the back of the imp's head now, perched between the knoggelvi's ears, he considered slitting his throat and freeing him of his renewed existence.

But then Kaz glanced back at him with that weird smile on his crooked jaw, crinkles around his watery, irisless eyes, and Damien shook himself of the plan. It would have been too messy anyway—imp blood was sticky and viscous, and it stained even black clothing—and Damien wasn't eager to do things that were messy: he carved into himself enough already.

"I am honored to be fulfilling the prophecy with you, Master Bloodthorne," Kaz groveled in his weathered, rotting voice.

Damien acknowledged him with a slight lift to his chin. That would be the prophecy that he, son of Zagadoth the Tempestuous, would return the demon lord to power. Brother Eternal Crud had attempted to recite it at the onset of their journey that morning in the dinge of the stables behind the temple, but Damien stopped him. He already knew it by heart, he had heard it and read it and dreamed about it since his father had been taken away from him twenty-three years prior. The Denonfy Oracle had been consulted by a constituency of Zagadoth's best, surviving lieutenants and the leaders of The Brotherhood, on how to free him from his crystalline prison, and were told:

When the day is night, and the corners of the realm have fallen into rot, the hallowed son shall release the Harbinger of Destruction upon earth once again. Only by the spilling of the descendants' blood may It rise, and by the spilling of the heart of the earth's blood to beseech the gods may It fall.

The problem was just that it felt a bit…off. Damien had no idea how he was meant to make the corners of the realm rot—he didn't even know where the corners of an amorphously-shaped landmass were—and when he went on his own as a teen to visit the Denonfy Oracle himself for clarification, they had been just as vague. Vaguery was, of course, how an oracle stayed in business, but it was no less frustrating.

What he did know was that he was meant to be doing this alone, not even with an imp to assist, and certainly not with some human trailing behind him. The prophecy said the hallowed son, not the hallowed son, the Abyss's most annoying servant, and some girl who got herself in the way, but then again, now was no time to start putting complete stock in the words of a diviner even if everyone else already had. The fervor of the others' belief was almost contagious, but it was a lot easier to put one's full faith in a prophecy when one wasn't meant to be its fulfiller.

Damien had considered, briefly, speaking with his father that morning, but decided there was no point telling Zagadoth he'd fucked up already, not before he gave himself a chance to fix things. He left the occlusion crystal shard safely tied up within the only pouch of shrouding he'd been able to scrounge from the Sanctum. It wasn't particularly strong, but with the talisman buried inside the woman, the infernal aura of his father's prison wasn't as much to hide, and it would weaken once they passed out of the Infernal Mountains anyway. Zagadoth would then only be reachable when Damien chose to expend the arcana and blood to call him forth, and with the most recent turn of events, that certainly wasn't happening anytime soon.

"So, what's this prophecy you're fulfilling?" The woman's voice was quiet, grazing the back of Damien's head with the breeze that swept through a break in the mountain pass.

"It's none of your concern." Damien did not look back at her.

"I feel like it sort of is," she said with a pinched quietness he wasn't sure if he were supposed to hear or not, but then she raised her voice and injected some sweetness into it that made him squirm. "Does it have to do with Eirengaard?"

"No," he replied, which wasn't exactly a lie, but it wasn't exactly the truth either.

"Then why are we headed there?"

"Because we must," he answered with finality.

But she clearly didn't understand the conversation was over. "For something other than the prophecy?"

Before he could retort, Kaz leaned out around him and snarled back at her. "Do not pester Master Bloodthorne with inane questions and mindless prattle!"

Damien didn't need to see the girl to know she had been offended by that; it was clear in the small, vexed noise she made.

"Master," said Kaz, turning fully to him and balancing between the knoggelvi's pointed ears, "why are we dragging this harlot along behind us?"

"Harlot?" Her voice was barely more than a breath as she repeated the word like it had never been spoken in her presence before.

Kaz hissed, baring all his crooked teeth then looked back to Damien, composed once again.

"She is...integral to my machinations." The imp didn't need to know the details of this particular screw up.

"Surely there are warm bodies all across the realm, Master. Why tote *this* prostitute the entire journey?"

"I'm not a prostitute!" she chirped. "Tell him I'm not a prostitute."

Kaz hopped up onto Damien's shoulder, talons digging into his leather armor. Damien would have knocked him right off if the imp didn't just as quickly propel onto the rump of the knoggelvi. "You will address Master Bloodthorne only as Master or My Lord, wench!"

"Well, *my* name is Amma." There was a quiver to her voice as she struggled to retain the last bit of her poise. "Can you please use that instead of insults?"

"Never, you filthy whore!"

Damien's temple twitched at the imp's screeching. "Kaz, that's enough. I would prefer less bickering, regardless of her profession."

"But I'm *not* a prostitute." Her voice was pivoting from offended to a full-on whine, and Damien had a brief vision of just tossing her and the imp right off the mountain before blowing out a long sigh.

He glanced back at her, sitting astride the knoggelvi in baggy clothes and wearing a look like she might cry, neither particularly attractive. "Clearly you are not—you're nowhere near as virtuous as a prostitute, are you?"

"What's that supposed to mean?"

"You're a thief—you don't fairly exchange services for coin."

"I..." her voice trailed off into a squeak.

"The strumpet should still address you properly and with respect!" Kaz's talons were beginning to irritate the knoggelvi as he stomped on its rump. "She dares make demands of you and does not even bother to call you master!"

"She does not need to call me master." He glared back out at the road ahead, cold and empty. "In fact, she does not need to speak to me at all."

"Ah, you see!" Kaz snickered in a watery, annoyingly satisfied way. "The harlot should keep her mouth shut. No more stupid questions and no more pestering Master Bloodthorne." As the imp scrambled up Damien's back, he winced, and then Kaz propelled himself off his shoulder and landed on the neck of the knoggelvi again with a useless flap of his wings. The girl clicked her tongue, but remained otherwise silent. "But, my lord, that does not explain why she is with us at all on so important a mission. Is she for eating? Sacrificing? She doesn't seem very useful."

Damien peered over the imp's head. Craggy earth rose up on either side of the pathway, and just ahead, two curved, stone columns were set into the mountainside. Massive and towering, the crescent shapes marked the border of the lands wholly under the control of Aszath Koth. The mountain's miasma was weaker, and beyond those gates it would quickly dissolve. "She is useful," said Damien absently, feeling the change in the air.

Kaz grumbled, taking another look at her by peering around Damien. "You said she's a thief?"

"Not a very good one."

"Is she also a mage?"

Damien could only assume not; she'd given no hint she used arcana nor radiated any magical aura, something Damien could typically feel. "No."

He scrunched up the snub of his nose. "An assassin?"

"No."

"Certainly not a warrior."

"I thought we weren't supposed to ask Master Bloodthorne anymore stupid questions?" she quipped.

Damien nearly smirked at the mockery in her voice, but held it back. The way she'd said *Master Bloodthorne* tickling him, perhaps in a way it ought not have. "She is a shield," he told the imp pointedly before the two could truly begin sniping at one another again.

Kaz's eyes narrowed, glancing down at the knoggelvi's mane, confused. The woman knew the truth about her own predicament, that she was accidentally enthralled by the talisman, and the imp knew the intention of their journey south was to release a demon, but there was no good reason that either of the two needed to have the entire picture, so he went on in a way he assumed would satisfy.

"The talisman I will use to fulfill the prophecy is being shielded by her presence. She will mask the aura of our descent to Eirengaard and leave us unbothered by the Holy Order of Osurehm."

"Ah!" Kaz perked up, something like a smile on his horrible, little mouth. "You are a genius, Master Bloodthorne."

Damien's insides twisted in a way that was unfortunately becoming more familiar.

"But what will we do with her when we get to Eirengaard?"

The crescent markers were looming right before them now, their pointed tops many stories overhead, taller than Damien remembered. His last journey out of Aszath Koth had taken him north of the city to the frozen dunes, and before that, he had gone west and across the Maroon Sea. It had been at least a year, he supposed, since he traveled this way, and much longer since he had gone due south. South lay Eiren proper, predominantly human rather than beast, where dominions and the gods they served were worshiped rather than the gods locked in the Abyss and their demon disciples, where darkness was shunned and light reigned supreme. As the road pitched down ahead, he could already see a patch of sunshine shimmering across it.

"He's going to kill me."

For a moment, Damien wasn't sure she had said the words or if they were only in his own head. He had not known her very long, but her voice was unlike what he had become used to, flatter and resigned. But Kaz's reaction told him the woman had spoken aloud.

"Truly, Master?" The imp clacked his claws against one another, grinning from batwing ear to batwing ear. "You'll be slitting this one's throat when we reach the realm's capital?"

Damien's brows lifted, and he sat straighter. "Yes."

"Excellent!" Kaz spun around triumphant, and Damien was glad to no longer be under the imp's eye.

Once they passed through the gate, Damien glanced over his shoulder. The girl, Amma, she had said was her name, was staring down at her hands as she pulled them gently through the mane of the knoggelvi. Carefully, she was undoing a knot, her brow knitted with focus, corners of her mouth turned down. Her fingers worked with delicate precision, and it was as if he could feel them then on his own hand all over again.

Damien snapped back around. On the gate's other side, the path continued southward, but there was a divergence off of it to the east as well. Another breeze swept over them, this one a bit warmer. "This way."

As he tugged on the knoggelvi's reins and they headed for the easterly path, Kaz looked back at him. "Forgive me, Master, but unless the cities have gotten up and moved since my death, I believe Eirengaard is directly south of Aszath Koth, is it not?"

"It is," he sighed, annoyed at the imp's memory. "We must make a small detour first." It helped that going east would also allow Damien to give the half-abandoned city of Briarwyke the widest berth. With its desecrated temple and tainted memories, it could be avoided on the southern road as well, but it was perhaps too dangerous to chance getting even that close.

"But, Master, the prophecy! The demon lord awaits, and—"

"I said," warned Damien, eyeing the creature with contempt, "we must make a small detour. Surely your master should not be questioned."

Kaz shrunk back on himself, bowing and settling down.

Damien glanced back once again. She was looking up now, big eyes filled with a hundred questions when they found his. Rather than let her ask any of them, he whipped back around and led them down the easterly road, diverting off the most direct route to the capital of Eiren and away from his destiny.

CHAPTER 7
THE TRANSITIVE PROPERTIES OF BLOOD AND CURSES

As much as Amma had disliked Aszath Koth, the swamp may have actually been worse. It at least smelled quite a bit worse. There was a lurching suck of a sound as the grotesque creature she rode pulled its hoof out of a puddle of muck and stepped back up onto the raised path of soft earth that wound deeper into the bog. Even the weird, evil horse-thing didn't seem to like it, not that its reaction to her sitting astride it suggested it liked much at all.

They had traveled steeply downward for a few hours once they had passed out of the mountains, sunshine glowing down on Amma for the first time in days and managing to raise her spirits just that much. But then they kept going, and the road they traveled, notably not the one she'd taken to get to Aszath Koth, narrowed and grew soggy, and the sky clouded over once again. This may be Eiren, but it was no place she had ever been.

Amma had attempted to ask a few more questions, but Damien, or rather, Master Bloodthorne as that horrible, little monster insisted he be called, offered only one-word answers in a needlessly harsh tone. The quiet had given her time to consider things, her mind less clouded than the night before. Running seemed possible for a short while after they had left the city, but without the scroll that, as far as she knew, was still tucked into the blood mage's pocket, the entire ordeal she had gone through would be for naught.

And this thing that was inside her, the talisman, what would it do? If she was far enough from the mage, perhaps he couldn't control her, but she was unwilling to count on that so soon. Instead, she would need to bide her time, test the range of that stupid talisman, and find a way to get her hands on the scroll. He would keep her alive until at least Eirengaard, and the capital was still perhaps a week or two's journey south if the main road was taken, though she had no idea where this detour would lead.

As time waned on the road, so did the effect of Damien's grouchiness and the cloud that had hung over Amma at the mention of the impending, murderous deed he was meant to carry out. When she had finally untangled the knots from her knoggelvi's mane in a section large enough to begin braiding, she finally asked, "Where are we?"

"Tarfail Quag." Well, that had been two words, and that was a little better than one.

"The quag?" The imp called Kaz stuck out his forked tongue. Even a creature from the infernal plane hated the place. At least he and Amma had that in common. "This will be slow going."

The trees were bare, standing like lightning-struck trunks at awkward angles out of the murky water at either side of the path—more kalsepherus, but some bald cypress too, their roots climbing up out of the bog to form knees good for basking reptiles and long-necked cranes. From their leafless branches, a greying moss hung and swayed even in the stagnant air. Amma glanced up at the sky between the scraggly boughs, clouded over and grey, and then everything was blotted out as something wet plopped onto her face.

Amma shrieked and slapped at her eyes, making contact with a rubbery, slick mass stuck to her skin. Her vision returned to one eye as she pried at the slimy blob, and with a snap, whatever had landed on her came free. Pain seared through her face, and a splatter of blood rained down onto the knoggelvi's thick hide before her.

Kaz's worn and gurgly voice was already falling into hysterical laughter as Amma rubbed at her eye to free it of the thick mucus that had pooled there. In her hand, through her blurred vision, she began to make out what had fallen on her face, a thick band of what looked like snot, yellowed with a wisp of something crimson swirling across its middle.

"Probinum leech," Damien's voice droned as he pulled his mount alongside hers. "They feed on blood."

"Ew!" Amma flicked her hand to toss the blobby parasite away, but it held fast. Her fingers twitched as a pulse thrummed through her, and the line of crimson in its translucent body thickened. Panicked, Amma swung her arm up and down, but it remained stuck, and Kaz devolved into even harder laughter.

Damien leaned across her mount and snatched her flailing arm.

The knoggelvi shifted, and the two were bumped up against one another, Amma nearly losing her balance as she continued to panic, but Damien held her still. Through her clearing vision, Amma could see the dagger unsheathed in his other hand, then she felt the cool metal slide between the leech and her palm.

She gasped at the sting, but it wasn't the knife's edge that slid into her skin, just the suckers of the leech being pried off. It held fast for a painful moment and then was catapulted off of her to land in the sludge of the swamp with a splat.

A line of pin pricks ran down Amma's palm, blood oozing up from them. She whined and rubbed it off against her breeches, then gasped, touching her face. Her vision had almost entirely come back, but her eyes still stung, and she could only imagine what had happened to her skin there. "What do I do? Does it look bad?"

As Amma's sight cleared, she realized she was looking back at a man with a scar across his face much worse than what any leech's sucking could do to her own. He scoffed, "You will recover."

Kaz was, of course, still laughing. He had dropped off the knoggelvi's head and fallen to the ground, rolling just to the edge of the water. As he lay there in the mud, a tendril slipped out and crawled toward one of his spindly legs. Amma had been glaring down at the rotten, little imp, but as she saw its doom crawling toward it, she opened her mouth to warn him.

Damien put up his hand to stop her. He stared down at the imp still wholly engaged with what he thought had been hilarious, and a smirk crawled up the side of his face just as the tendril crawled up from the water to wrap around the imp's leg.

Kaz shot himself up from the ground, splattering mud everywhere as he tried to beat his wings. The tendril strained to hold him down, pulling him toward the thick, murky water. "Master!" he crowed, clawing at the air. Damien's knoggelvi cantered a few steps backward.

"Yes, Kaz?" he asked, blinking down at the imp.

Kaz screeched, reaching out for him.

Amma's sight now restored, she watched Damien watch Kaz, the blood mage's boredom and the imp's utter panic in vast contrast. The imp's wings, still new and awkward, beat hard but uselessly, and the tendril pulled taut, a mound cresting the water as it tried to drag him in. There was a flash of smoke and dim light as Kaz moved his hands about, trying and failing to cast. "Please, Master, my powers are still unrestored since my resurrection!"

Damien nodded, tilting his head thoughtfully. "I see."

The imp was suddenly jerked down an extra foot, slamming into the ground. He screeched again then valiantly tried to fly once more.

Amma's heart beat a little harder. "Aren't you going to help him?"

"You think I should?" Damien turned to her, brow cocked as if the suggestion were a brand-new idea he'd never considered.

Kaz was making all sorts of panicked noises now, and the head of something with a toothy maw was surfacing in the bog.

"Yes, of course."

Damien shrugged. "I think he ought to learn to fend for himself. He used to be able to."

Amma frowned, and then she huffed—so, it was up to her then. She threw a leg over the knoggelvi and slid off its back to the ground with a wet thump.

Damien's voice was thick with boredom. "What do you think you are doing?"

But Amma ignored him, stalking up to the imp who was so panicked he actually rerouted himself to fly toward her. Amma hesitated, looking at the mound in the water, considering pulling out her dagger, but not wanting to reveal to Damien that she had it. Instead, she stomped down on the tendril with the heel of her boot and jumped back.

The tension on Kaz was released, and he slammed into Amma, knocking her backward into the mud. There was a splash from the swampy waters, and the tendril retreated beneath the surface leaving a trail of bloody muck on the path.

Kaz's clawed hands were wrapped tight around Amma's neck, and she choked out a cough beneath them. Then he retreated just as suddenly, stumbling backward and half-hopping, half-flying to land back atop Damien's knoggelvi. "Filthy trollop," Kaz growled, hunkering down low and eyeing her.

"You're welcome." Amma pulled herself up from the ground and shook out her arms. The swamp's smell was significantly more intense now that she was covered in it.

Damien was still astride his knoggelvi, his face hard to read past a quiet disinterest. "Are the two of you finished?"

Amma stared back at him, too shocked at his lack of concern to even be angry.

"Back on the knoggelvi," he said, jerking his head toward the horse-like creature. "We've still much of the swamp to cover."

She snorted, crossing her arms and opening her mouth, but there was a sound out in the distance, the low baying of an animal, that made her tense up. "What was that?"

Damien tipped his head, listening. "Wolf."

Another howl answered the first, this one closer.

"No, excuse me: *were*wolf."

Amma gasped, standing straighter and whipping around. There wasn't anything moving out amongst the low laying fog and the murky water, nothing two-legged anyway. When she looked back to Damien still up on his knoggelvi, he was grinning from one side of his mouth. "Oh, very funny," she said, "but a pack of wolves is frightening enough—you don't need to pretend there are monsters out here."

"You think there aren't werewolves in Tarfail Quag?" He tipped his head. "Or you think there aren't werewolves anywhere because you don't believe they exist?"

Uncomfortably, Amma shifted her weight to her other foot. There were many strange things in the world, wonderful and terrible both, but of monsters she had only heard stories, actually seeing very little until she'd made it to Aszath Koth. Of course, she was standing before a blood mage, the supposed son of a demon, and it hadn't occurred to her those were real until a day ago either. "I've never seen one," she said hesitantly.

He looked her up and down. "And I suppose you've never seen a vampire, so those must not exist either."

She snorted at him, but when his face didn't change into another knowing smirk, she hurried up to her knoggelvi and grabbed a hold of the reins. It took a few steps away from her just as she tried to jump upon it, and she stumbled.

"Hurry up," said Damien as he urged his mount to continue on, trotting away from her. "If you fall behind, you'll most certainly be eaten. Or worse."

She glared after him, then put a valiant if failed effort into climbing back astride. She'd always thought she'd been a fine rider, but never had to mount something so tall from the ground. Amma led it by the reins to a bent cypress tree, stepped up, and then with a clench to her stomach and a huge swing of her leg, lunged over and up. The knoggelvi grunted, pawing at the soft earth and then took off under her to catch up with its companion, failing though it tried to jostle her right back off.

As they traveled on, the clouds darkened overhead, threatening rain, but the air only thickened with stagnancy and stench. Kaz had fallen into silence, hunched over on the head of the knoggelvi, but Tarfail Quag more than made up for it with new sounds the deeper they went. Frogs and crickets sang, interrupted by the random splash of creatures retreating into the waters. And then there were the howls, maybe closer, maybe not, but each made goosebumps erupt over Amma's skin. Damien seemed significantly less concerned, so she reasoned they must not be that much of a threat. Surely, they were only regular, sharp-fanged, pack-hunting wolves.

Amma flexed her fingers and glanced down at the hand the leech had attached to. It no longer hurt unless she moved her thumb a certain way. Then she poked at her face. There was a twinge of pain beneath her eye, and the skin felt puffy. When she glanced at Damien, he could have been watching her, but he looked away quickly if so. "Thank you," she eventually said in a quiet voice.

Damien's long nose crinkled, and his lip turned up. "Thank you?" he said mostly to himself as he glared out at the path ahead then over to her like she was as disgusting as she actually felt. "For what exactly?"

She held up her hand, showing him her palm marked by the leech.

"Well, that's my blood in there now too, in the talisman," he clarified, clearing his throat. "Don't want the quag getting a taste for me."

An owl hooted from overhead, and Amma flinched, worrying the knoggelvi's reins in tight fists. "Once, when I was little, a dog bit me. I just wanted to play with him, he looked so cute, you know? He was one of those small ones with the curly tails, and he wore this little bell. But he did *not* feel the same way about me and went for my ankles. He knocked me down then bit into my elbow and started shaking his head and wouldn't let go." She swallowed, blinking out into the spindly trees, the shadows in the fog looking like they were moving. "I remember my mother screaming, and there was a lot of blood."

Damien didn't look at her, but his back stiffened.

"I still have some scars on my legs and my arm. I've been afraid of dogs ever since." At that, there was another howl, this one decidedly closer.

"Why are you telling me this?"

"Why?" Amma blinked, thinking that it was a good distraction, then laughed nervously. "Oh, what you said about the swamp getting a taste for you? That dog always hated me, like he wanted my blood or something."

"It should have been put down."

Amma's eyes widened. "Oh, no, it was my fault, I should have known better. But they wouldn't have ever done that to him anyway, he was—" She stopped herself, clamping her mouth shut. No, she couldn't say that. "He belonged to someone important."

Damien narrowed his eyes and grunted.

There was another sound out in the swamp, this one Amma was entirely unable to identify but terrified her nonetheless. "Do you want to see?" She didn't give him the opportunity to say no, pulling back the too-big sleeve of her tunic to reveal her elbow. She brushed away the drying mud up along her arm to uncover the silvery white marks.

He glanced momentarily at her then away again, mumbling something under his breath about heroism.

Amma bit her lip, dropping her arm back down and the sleeve with it. That may not have worked out how she'd wanted. A twig snapped nearby, and her stomach clenched as she grabbed up the reins again, and went on nervously, "So, how did you get yours?"

The mage scrunched his face again, and the scar scrunched with it. He was annoyed, but she couldn't help herself; she needed a distraction from the sounds creeping ever closer.

"Do you remember my saying that you needn't speak to me?"

She huffed. "Yes, but you didn't say I *can't*."

"I would like to clarify my meaning then."

Amma twisted up her lips, annoyed but mostly frightened by yet another too-close splash. She fidgeted, looking around and humming to herself instead, but it came out as a whine.

"A formidable foe."

Amma turned to him, waiting for more with an encouraging smile.

He rolled his eyes, voice a grumble. "I misjudged a situation and placed trust where I should not have, I suppose a bit like you and the dog, but this was a wholly different kind of beast, one capable of premeditation." He raised a hand to touch his nose but pulled it away before making contact. The scar ran down the length of his face diagonally, missing his eye so perfectly it almost seemed to be done with intention and not just luck.

"I'm sorry someone did that to you," she said with a gentle hesitation, watching his face convulse like she'd insulted him. She went on, quicker, thinking of his hand and how unmarred it had been so quickly after cutting it. "Why do you have it though? Don't you heal right away?"

"Well, I do in almost every instance unless the wound is severe, and I'm incapacitated, but there are also certain magics that—" He snapped his head toward her, jaw hardening. The look he gave struck her to her core, and she felt trapped in it, just like in the Sanctum.

Then he frowned and broke their gaze. "Infernal darkness, you are clever, aren't you?"

Amma had no idea what he meant. "I have no idea—"

"*Sanguinisui*, ask no more about this."

Amma's breath caught as her words were cut off. Her throat burned as she swallowed back the rest of what she had to say. Rendered magically mute once again, all she could do was pout and turn her unfortunate focus back on the noises bubbling up out of the swamp.

CHAPTER 8
BETTER THE DEMON YOU KNOW
THAN THE WOLF YOU DON'T

The swamp that was Tarfail Quag was always just a little bit worse each time Damien visited it, and after a lifetime spent in Aszath Koth, that was saying something. Hours had passed in cursedly wonderful silence after Kaz had been reminded of his place and the girl had been arcanely ordered quiet. He was coming to learn that if his orders through the talisman were given with no specific end, they would wear off, and he could feel the magic wane, a good thing to learn before using it on King Archibald. But once he could feel his enthrallment come to an end on his last command, she remained silent.

She was frowning again as well, though her eyes were stuck open wide, that bright blue searching the ever-darkening swamp. He shouldn't have been as annoyed as he was, and truly he wasn't sure at exactly what was annoying him, but he was bloody annoyed nonetheless, and the swamp with its incessant smells and noises wasn't helpful. Why Anomalous Craven chose to make his home in such a place was beyond him, but the man better make himself useful when they finally reached their destination in the depth of the bog.

The Brotherhood had laden them with an abundance of food before they left Aszath Koth, but evening was falling, and they would need to rest. Anomalous's tower was too far off to reach before dark, and Damien realized he should have accounted for slower travel with a begrudging group in tow, but hadn't. For all that the quag was during the day, traveling at night could be dangerous if a wrong turn drove a knoggelvi off the path. Thick muck could mean drowning, and the things within the waters were an even worse way to meet one's end.

Damien began to keep an eye out for an acceptable place to make camp for the night. There was little to choose from on the narrow path between the low-lying wetlands. He hadn't planned for this, not any of it, but especially not making an extraneous trip across Tarfail Quag. He glared over at the cause of it all, sitting there looking forlorn, her hands still working at the knoggelvi's snarled mane. Well, it wasn't *entirely* her fault, he supposed. He could have secured the talisman better, sheathed it somehow, before blindly dropping such a powerful thing in his cloak pocket. Not that her hand belonged in there, but—

There was a sound deep in the swamp, different than the rest, sticking out of the cacophony of insects and birds and then sinking back in. The others didn't notice it, Kaz still sulking and the girl...also sulking. But what right did she have to be sulking? Because what, he had made her stop talking for a short while? She was the one who had tried to suss out his weaknesses disguised as interest in him. And to think, he had almost been idiotic enough to let slip his vulnerability to beings who could manipulate noxscura.

Damien sat straighter, scanning the line of trunks jutting up through the fog and shaking off the memory of the dagger cutting across his face years ago. There was something out amongst the trees and the wetness, and not the simple bog beasts that had been trailing them or the curious crocodiles who lazily floated at the surface of the waters. Neither truly dared make them prey, it would be a loss for them, but this thing that was tracking them—and those were measured steps he could now hear, matching the knoggelvi's gait— this thing was braver. Or stupider, it would all depend.

"Stop." Damien kept his voice low, but both knoggelvi responded. The woman and Kaz perked up as Damien dismounted. His boots sank into the soft ground, silent as he took a few steps along the road ahead of them. They'd been followed long enough that the thing knew their movements, but with their subtle alteration, it too stopped. The foulness of the swamp masked its smell, and the fog was too thick to spot what Damien suspected might be amongst it. Sending Kaz a few paces ahead, alone, might draw it out, but treating him like bait would just make him sulkier. And for reasons Damien couldn't possibly understand, it would probably upset the girl too, so Damien closed his eyes and muttered Chthonic to arcanely feel the world around him instead.

There were many living things out in the swamp that depended on blood. First was his own, constant and familiar, a baseline for his arcane senses. Then his, well…his party, he supposed, two knoggelvi and the imp, all infernal and marginally close to the aura he gave off, tinged with brimstone and eternal death and flickers of the chaotic noxscura deep within them, tainting them to be divergent from all other beings. And then there was her too, significantly different than the others, but not so different than himself. Those were the human parts they had in common.

Human blood had a way about it that was almost curious. It moved along and explored whatever space it was in, cautious but eager. Her blood was hitching in its veins with a nervous tick as her heart pumped it too quickly in her chest. He lingered a second longer than necessary on the odd sanctuary of her presence amongst all the infernal ones, so like his own but not, then pulled away when he remembered he had more important things to concern himself with.

Reptiles, mostly, the slow, viscous march of their blood heavy out in the humid, buzzing swamp. There were many, but they were mostly dormant. A few smaller, fuzzy things that called this place home, their erratic heartbeats a flurry, and birds too, equally scattered and nervous amongst the trees. And then he felt it, the other blood, and it was *wrong*.

Damien focused as he slipped the dagger from his bracer. He risked pushing his spell over the creature ahead of them to confirm his suspicion—magically imbued creatures often knew when they were being sought out, and if they were good enough trackers, could follow the spell to its source. Even though the arcana in this beast was more like a curse, it felt his prodding all the same, and it did not like it. The feeling was mutual.

The werewolf propelled itself over a fallen log, barreling down the path toward them, kicking up mud and parting the fog as its long strides brought it upon them in seconds. It was a wretched, skinny thing, but its reach was absurdly long as it swiped. All fangs and claws and matted hair along sinewy limbs, it snapped hungry jaws, sailing toward Damien.

But he was faster—blood mages always were if they already magically knew their query—and he wrapped his fingers around the blade of his dagger. The bite of the metal stung, hot wetness welling up in his palm, and then he ripped his hand through the air.

The slice he drew materialized, his blood sharpening into its own, crimson blade, and it cut up through the air between him and the werewolf. The beast couldn't correct course, already leaping toward him, and the magicked blade found its target, slicing right through its open jaws and severing up through its head. A gurgling whimper, unbecoming of a beast so big, sounded into the marshy quiet that had fallen around them, and the body toppled to the ground, its own blood—that blood that was so wrong—spilling out on the wet earth just at Damien's feet.

Werewolves were unlike most other creatures, born human and changed by an infectious curse, notably not infernal, but wrongly considered to be a result of demonic possession anyway. Bloodcraft sometimes allowed the wielder to manipulate their target, but the cursed parts of any being were often too erratic for something like that. Thankfully, cutting into most anything's head was usually enough to kill it, and Damien's well-aimed spell coupled with the werewolf's own reckless lunge made quick work out of the beast. He would never admit it aloud, but luck had been on his side.

He raised his hand to survey the cut he'd inflicted on himself. Beneath the wet crimson that glimmered in the low light, it was already healing. Careful not to touch any of the blood with his open wound, he knelt beside the fallen creature. This much closer, he saw that it was quite large even if it had little mass to its bony limbs and chest. He dipped a finger into its blood, the last thrum of life draining away. Nasty, infectious stuff. The eyes on the severed, upper half of its head were so human, a deep, rich brown, nestled into patchy, matted fur on a face neither human nor animal and creased with anger and pain, not a fate he wanted for himself. It had been a mercy kill, surely, but there was little chance this was the only one.

Damien swept around and strode back to his mount. He scanned the swamp again as he climbed astride, not expending another spell to feel for more creatures—he knew what he was looking for this time— and then his eyes fell on her.

Her face was drawn into a mixture of terror and awe. That was appropriate for what he'd just done, he supposed, but she still hadn't seen what he could truly do, not yet. "Holy gods," she whispered.

"Infernal darkness," he corrected, then urged his knoggelvi on. "This is no place to stop. We—"

A splash in the muck to their side cut him off, and a howl cut up through the swamp. They smelled the fallen, surely, and his display had failed to turn them away. So, they *were* that stupid then.

"Go."

The knoggelvi took off down the mucky path as werewolves burst forth from the dense fog at their sides. Damien didn't bother to count them for tearing down: the knoggelvi were faster and, judging by their pursuers' withering mass, would have more stamina too. As long as they could stay astride, they would outrun them.

But of course the girl was already struggling with that, not to mention shrieking. He watched her grip the reins, white knuckled, as she bounced against the knoggelvi's back. Between her tiny frame and lack of armor, she barely had enough weight to keep herself in place as it galloped. Damien groaned in the back of his throat, unable to reach out and push her down, but she managed to dip her head low and hang on.

Then Damien was slapped in the side of the face by leathery skin and bony wings. He grabbed at the imp who had lost his grip on the stallion's head, holding him out by the nape of his neck. Fleetingly considering just letting go, Damien instead jerked the squirming Kaz down against the knoggelvi's neck and wrapped him up in the reins to keep him in place.

The knoggelvi leapt, and even Damien found himself lifted off the beast's back at such a speed. They cleared a river of swampy water, splattering mud upward as they landed, behind them the calls of wolves and the sound of many paws splashing in pursuit.

The path ahead widened, and Damien thought for a moment they might be relieved as he spied a ramshackle hut, but the new space only proved to reveal another wolf standing just in the way, the building clearly abandoned. Damien reopened the wound on his hand with his dagger, familiar now with the cursed blood in the beasts, but called up a new spell. A crackle of black and violet burst all around the werewolf as it attempted to charge, slamming into the arcane wall of magic instead. He again tightened his fist, and the spell coalesced around the beast, strangling it just as their knoggelvi parted to pass by on either side.

The girl shrieked again as her mount changed course, the werewolf's cries muzzled by the spell that finished it off. She threw her arms around the knoggelvi's sinewy neck, sliding to the side, but remained atop it. At this rate, they would make it to their destination half a day sooner if they could keep pace. But they would also need to stay astride.

Another beast broke onto the path from the bog, cutting off the other knoggelvi, snapping at its hooves. It kicked instinctively at the werewolf, connecting with its head and knocking it back with a sickening crack of bone and a whimper. The knoggelvi stumbled then reared back, coming to a too-quick halt.

Damien whipped around to see the girl slide off backward and land in the mud as the knoggelvi regained itself and sped off again. Free of a rider, not to mention one it despised, it galloped on, past even Damien as he pulled his own mount's reins, choking Kaz who was tangled up in them. The beast below him did not want to stop, and so Damien flung himself from its back with a curse, slapping it to continue on after the other.

Werewolves were feral things, but had the ability to reason—hopefully they would decide the knoggelvi would be easier targets and be led away, and if their mounts kept speed, they could outrun them. If Kaz survived, he could find them later, but that was not for Damien to worry about now—he needed his focus and energy here instead. Because of *her*.

"Bloody Abyss," he swore, assessing the path as the sounds of squelching mud beneath hooves disappeared. Werewolves hunted in packs, he had killed two, and the knoggelvi had fatally injured a third. That could have been the lot of them, but they'd already had a fair share of luck so far, and Damien was devout to no god, including luck's deity.

The girl rolled onto her side. At least she hadn't knocked herself unconscious in her fall off the mount, but then she groaned into the silence left behind, the swamp creatures scattering at the pack's attack. A splash from the wetlands signaled that something heard her moaning, and another, violent splash told him it was headed their way.

"Fuck," Damien swore again, closing the space and standing over where she was pulling herself up out of the mud. There was a glint and a shadow beyond the trees, and then another of the pack stepped out onto the path, rising up onto two feet. Tall and sinewy, the creature was just as wrong as the others, but this one was bigger. Body like an animal with stringy muscles and legs that bent backward, its too-long limbs reached out, amalgam of a human and canine face twisted and snarling. It came to a stop yards away, assessing them and smelling the air, likely less confident all on its own.

The girl scrambled to her knees, dazed, but much too slowly for Damien. He dragged her up by the arm and put her right on her feet. When she finally saw the towering form of the werewolf, jaws quivering over elongated fangs, she reached backward, grabbing his side and pressing herself against him. The terror she'd reserved for him once was redirected now, though he supposed a blood mage was the better option when werewolf was the other; a blood mage was easier to reason with, if he were feeling like it. Usually.

As the girl clung onto him, Damien stood a little straighter and unsheathed his dagger. He dug it into the healing cut once again, the pain barely registering. He sheathed the dagger on his bracer and pressed both hands together then flung them out. Like cuts made material, blades of blood sliced through the air just as the werewolf lunged for them. The creature redirected, caught mid jump like the first, and earned deep, oozing wounds all down his back, falling out of the air and skidding into the mud right at their feet.

"Oh, gross," she whispered, and her words broke Damien of any gallant feeling that might have been creeping up his sides along with her tightening grip.

Then the thing lifted its head even as blood poured from it and snarled.

"Run," he commanded her, and she complied as if he had used the talisman's magic. The two flew off down the soggy path, the knoggelvi long gone. Winding through the fog and puddles of muck, neither were quiet, and sounds out in the bog let them know they hadn't lost the rest of the pack yet. Following the makeshift road, there was a small row of seemingly abandoned huts ahead. Dilapidated, they were cover at the very least.

Damien was much faster than she, so he slowed, grabbed her wrist, and jerked her into one of the makeshift cabins. Its door was lying flat across the entrance, and as they crossed it, it broke beneath them with a wet squelch.

Inside, the cabin was just one room and quite dark, but there was old furniture within, a table, a knocked over chair, a sagging cot, and a big box of a closet-sized larder that was still intact. The larder's door squeaked as he wrenched it open and dragged her inside, pulling it to behind them and shutting out stray moonlight.

Her breathing filled up the tiny space, too fast and too loud. Damien was slightly winded from the run and expense of arcane energy, but the flood of fear she'd no doubt experienced was not helping her to catch her own breath. He looked down at the top of her head in the cramped larder, the color to her hair light enough to be seen in the dark. Her chest heaved against him, and he briefly and embarrassingly thought what a disappointment it would be to not survive this.

"Quiet," he said as low as he could, trying to listen against the wood for the sounds outside in the swamp. They were so covered in mud and muck that the werewolves might not be able to sniff them out, but all the noise she was making would waste the stench they were coated in.

She shook her head, taking another ragged, too-loud breath. "Those are werewolves," she coughed out.

"Well, I did say," he murmured back.

73

"And you just…" She tilted her head up, and even in the dark he could see the blue of her wide, roving eyes. "You killed them."

Damien glanced away from her and down to his palm. A sliver of light through a break in the wooden wall fell across the cut, healing again, though slower than he would have liked. "Of course I did," he whispered. "Now, shut your mouth, or they'll find us."

She pressed her lips together, chest still heaving, then as if she couldn't help herself, spat out, "But you're a blood mage. Why are we even hiding?"

"Everyone has their limits," he growled. "Killing them *and* looking out for you is a much bigger chore."

"I thought you wanted me dead."

"I want the talisman." He leaned over to squint out into the swamp through the slit in the wood, pushing her out of the way though there wasn't really anywhere for her to go in the cramped larder.

She had fully caught her breath, and used the opportunity to sigh as if she were being put out, voice low and annoyed. "And if I get eaten by one of them, it'll be harder for you to sneak into Eirengaard with a werewolf, right?"

Damien ground his jaw. Yes, she was correct about that—what else did she want from him? And where did she get off being so snarky and petulant, especially at a time like this?

He scowled back at her, vision adjusted to the darkness. She had mud splattered across her nose, but it didn't blight the soft curve of her cheek nor did the cut over her lips mar their fullness, and the strands of hair that had come loose from where it was tied back were somehow framing her round face in a pleasing way despite being such a mess. He looked down the length of her, hidden beneath a tunic that was too big, but it wasn't difficult to imagine what was there.

"On second thought, if they get their claws on you, I doubt you'll be eaten." He let her mind ponder the suggestion as he searched for their pursuers through the break in the wood once more, then clarified, "I'm not particularly interested in rooting out their den to retrieve you and the talisman, so you should really quiet down unless you think you'd enjoy being mated with the surviving pack."

At that, she inhaled sharply. Damien waited for her next pithy response, but none came. He glanced back to see her eyes glazing over. Well, that had worked at making her shut up, but his stomach turned in a way that told him he perhaps shouldn't have said something so crude.

When a shadow passed over the sliver of light coming in through

74

the crack in the wall, she squealed in horror and pressed into the larder's corner. No, he definitely should not have said that.

The werewolf stalking outside made an angry, questioning sound, and another answered it with a snarl. She gasped again, and all Damien could do was throw a hand over her mouth. She struggled against it, grabbing his wrist just like in the Sanctum when he had been ready to strangle her for being an assassin. Her breaths came even faster now that she'd been silenced. If he let go, she would probably scream, and they would be found instantly.

There were at least two outside, possibly more, and commanding her with the talisman might not be worth the expenditure of magic if he didn't know exactly what he would be up against.

"Shh," he hissed, leaning closer, but her struggle persisted, and she scuffed a foot against the wall. Strange, scaring her was apparently not the way to get what he wanted despite that it usually worked on others. He couldn't shout either, that would bring the werewolves right to them. Well, that was him, out of ideas. Except, of course, something even more disgraceful.

Damien wrapped his free arm around her back and yanked her away from the wall so she could no longer kick it. Pulling her up against him, he dipped his head beside her ear. "I will not allow anything to happen to you," he said, leveling something like comfort into his voice, "but you must be quiet now. Please."

She took one deep breath through her nose and held it, her chest expanding against his in the tight embrace. For a tense moment, the two remained still and silent, her small body warm and fitting to his own, easy to hold now that she was no longer thrashing. As completely useless as he knew it would be, Damien still pleaded silently to every dark entity he knew that he would be able to release her as soon as possible.

She breathed out against his hand, her grip on his wrist unclenching, and she managed a nod.

Her eyes were still full of fear, but not for him. For him, there was something else, but he couldn't quite place it. He slid his hand from her mouth, and she remained quiet. "Good girl."

Damien loosened his grip, and she stepped back in the tiny space, her warmth and touch gone as she stared at the ground. His pleas had been answered, and he should have been relieved, yet he wondered if just another moment or two would have been for the best, solely to prolong her obedience, of course.

Damien's throat was hoarse as he tried to keep it quiet, "Now, wait here."

Creeping out of the larder, he could easily see there were no other creatures in the hut, but he knew they had circled around to its front. Dagger in hand, he pushed the larder's door to behind him and stepped out onto the soft wood of the floor, but when he took another step, there was a crack, and his boot broke through a board.

There was a scuffle outside and a howl, and at the space where the hut's door had been, the sinewy form of a werewolf blotted out the moonlight. It was drooling, its eyes flashing with excitement as they fell on him. Damien cast immediately at the thing, throwing a line of blood that solidified into blades just as a second werewolf attempted to pile in behind the first. The magicked blades slashed into the beast's chest full force as it was trapped in the doorway, and it fell with a gurgling cry.

The second thoughtlessly clamored over the body of the first, pouncing at Damien. He jumped away, and it slammed into the corner of the larder, the girl inside crying out. Damien whistled sharply to pull the wolf's attention back to him, and it pounced right into another conjuring of the same spell despite just witnessing his companion fall to identical arcana, hunger likely making it doubly stupid.

The first wolf raised back up, gore dripping from the wounds along its ribcage, and the second remained standing though wobbled. Damien squeezed his self-inflicted wound at the sight of all that cursed blood, and instead called out in Chthonic to what little blood was left inside the two. Their bodies lurched toward him and one another, already weak, wounds gushing as they were moved under his spell.

He'd managed to get them right beside one another and released a last spray of his own blood that turned solid and sharp in midair. The two fell simultaneously, gone with a pair of agonizing howls. "Of all fucking things," he groused, willing his palm to heal faster as he eyed the cursed blood sprayed all over the cabin.

But then a shadow rose up from behind where the most recent defeated lay. The largest of the werewolves, the one he had already cut up and left for dead on the road, slammed a clawed, paw-like hand onto each side of the doorway, blocking off the light and baying into the hut. Damien grabbed at his collar, but hesitated a second too long before he could take the dagger's blade to his own chest and open a new wound.

The werewolf sprung the length of the hut and was on him in an instant. The wall came up against Damien's back with a crack, the monstrous beast crushing him into the rotting wood, and then it broke, the two falling out into the marshy ground of the swamp.

The weight of the beast was shocking, baring down on Damien and snapping saliva-covered jaws in his face. A hot droplet of blood dripped down onto his cheek. Cursed blood, blood that shouldn't mingle with his own. Damien knew what it was like to lose himself to something he couldn't control—he refused to be the victim of a curse that did the same. Cutting himself now would be too risky, and burying his dagger into the beast was absolutely out of the question on the off chance the curse tainted his blade.

He thrust an elbow up under the werewolf's neck to hold its jaws at bay, frothy, putrid slobber dripping onto his nose. It bit at the air an inch from his face, and the two sank into the wet earth with a squelch. Damien tightened his cut hand into a fist to protect the wound from the curse. Muscles aching as he struggled under the beast, he sheathed his dagger on his bracer and began to focus the energy for a spell that didn't rely on his blood, something weaker that he could only hope would work enough to get himself out from under the thing and then release the Abyss on it.

But it screamed before he even cast, a long, painful noise that pierced his ears and cut right into his gut. The animalistic man threw its head back, baying to the sky, and with a last, strangled cry, collapsed wholly atop Damien, dead.

He lay still beneath it, all he could do with its heft atop him and his own paralyzing surprise. Then he saw a shadow moving behind the body, tensing at the possibility of yet another werewolf, but it was only her.

She was standing there, wide-eyed, hand hovering near the back of the beast, seemingly unable to move. Damien shifted the body to the side with a huff and slid out from under the heavy thing. A hilt was sticking out from just under the werewolf's shoulder. A black ooze bubbled out around the impalement, and its skin was already cracking, the fur burning away as if she had cast some spell through the weapon when she plunged it in.

Damien glared at her, still unmoving, eyes focused on the fallen beast: she had given off no arcane aura at all, and yet—he wrenched the weapon out of the werewolf's back, and as it came, the cursed blood burnt itself off, leaving the blade perfectly clean.

"Silver," he said with a huff. "You had silver on you this whole time, woman?"

She blinked, looking at him like he had just appeared, then shrugged.

"By the basest beasts, with all the talking you do, how did *this* not come up?" He turned the weapon over, admiring it. It was small, a

77

better fit for her hand than his own, but masterfully crafted. With a good weight, the handle and hilt were intricately hammered and poured to resemble bark with a twisting vine running up it and delicate leaves jutting off. It would have been quite expensive, perhaps exorbitantly so, if she had actually paid for the thing. "Impressive plunder. I suppose you actually are a capable enough thief."

"I didn't—" She cut herself off with a swallow.

He waited for her to go on and plead her innocence, what all thieves were wont to do, but when she didn't, he sucked his teeth. "I shouldn't return this to you lest you try and slit my throat with it, but it seems you've decided to use it to prolong my life instead, so." He flipped the hilt toward her, and offered the dagger up.

She hesitated, then in one quick movement grabbed it back, and he watched as she sheathed it in a holster on her thigh hidden behind the tear in her breeches.

He kicked at the body beside them. "Still, strange choice. You were almost free of me."

"And alone in this swamp with them," she said, glancing around at the near blackness of a falling night.

"Fair point." Damien ran a hand through his hair and swept it back out of his face. "And I suppose some gratitude is in order, so thank you...you."

"My name's Amma."

"Yes, I know," he snapped then blew out a long breath. "Thank you, Amma."

CHAPTER 9
THE FABRICA OF SWAMP ALCHEMISTS

K az proved himself useful enough to bring the knoggelvi back
to them after an hour or so, shockingly uneaten if spent, and
Damien identified the driest hut to bed down in. The
Brotherhood had supplied them with blankets that remained tied
along the sides of the knoggelvi, and they stopped for the night.
Damien rationed out some cheese and bread to Amma, and
considered confiscating her dagger while she ate, but ultimately
decided not to renege on his word—that would, perhaps, set a bad
precedent, and while he was decidedly discourteous, he wasn't
dishonest. Not when it counted, anyway.

Damien did, however, bind her to the spot and order her to do no
harm nor to run in the night by way of the talisman's Chthonic word.
She might have aided in keeping him alive, but she wasn't
trustworthy by a long shot, and he needed his sleep. With an imp
around who required very little rest himself and could keep watch
with heightened senses, Damien was looking forward to lying down
but was unprepared for how fitful the night would be.

Like at The Brotherhood's temple but worse, Damien was restless
until he fell into a vivid and exhausting dream of releasing demons,
stabbing men and wolves, drowning in muck, and perhaps most
upsettingly, being pressed up against a woman. That last element
wouldn't have been so terrible had he been with someone who could
satisfy that desire, or even on his own, but when he woke in the
middle of the night he was simply frustrated, especially with the
suspected source lying so close. Amma was curled up into a ball
against the opposing wall, her face soft under the shaft of moonlight

that streamed in through the hut's lone window, and now it was annoying him in a whole new way.

After a few more hours of attempting to sleep, Damien got himself up before the sun rose, ordered Kaz to wake the girl—a mistake as the imp did it by pelting her with stones and starting her off prickly first thing in the morning—and the three were off again, decidedly less enthusiastic than the day before. Likely still rattled, neither Amma nor Kaz spoke much, which was perfectly fine with him, but then evening began to fall and Kaz's reincarnated mind finally put the pieces of their detour together upon seeing a tower atop a hill in the distance.

"Oh, no, Master, not him." Kaz turned back, a wretched little frown on his face.

Feigning ignorance, Damien tilted his head. "What qualms do you have with Anomalous?"

"Well, he doesn't think I exist, for starters."

Damien snorted, oddly mirthful, and a grin threatened the corners of his mouth. "Oh, yes, I had forgotten about that." He hadn't.

The tower rose up from the fog, a muddled amalgamation of stones and wooden boards and metal plates. It leaned slightly to the left, perhaps a little more intensely than when Damien had last visited, but an ever-sinking swamp will do that to buildings.

Near the tower's top, a ring of spikes jutted out perpendicularly from a walkway that encircled it, a bevy of crows resting there, calling out to one another above the constant buzz in the swamp, and at the very peak, a pole extended skyward, longer than last time, the place where an addition had been welded clear even from this distance as if Anomalous had reattached it a few times after failed attempts. Damien twisted his lips at the thought of the man clambering up the side in some dangerous, metal rig and being nearly impaled multiple times just to gain a few more feet of height, but then a flash of light from one of the tower's windows followed by a puff of green smoke told him the man hadn't managed to accidentally off himself yet.

As they ascended the hill to the tower, there was a scurrying in the brambly bushes, and a crocodile climbed out from under them covered in a strange contraption. When it opened its mouth and hissed, Amma yelped, pulling on her knoggelvi's reins, but the beast didn't respond, only glaring back at her.

The crocodile cut them both off, swinging around, and the contraption on its back sprung outward, many metal legs jutting off of it to plant into the wet ground and extend, pushing the reptile up onto

80

its back feet. Long jaws now level with the knoggelvi's head, it craned them open.

"Who's that, who's there?" called a frazzled, quick voice from deep in the creature's gullet.

"A traveler in need of assistance," said Damien, eyeing the black box dangling from the back of the crocodile's throat.

"Bloodthorne!" The voice practically jumped with glee. "Come in, come in, there's always room for you here."

The crocodile snapped its jaws shut and was cranked back down to the earth from the strangely-jointed, metal legs, and then scurried back away into the bushes. Damien glanced over at Amma, her mouth falling open.

"You're friends with that thing?" she asked.

"*Friends* is a strong word." Damien bade his knoggelvi up the path to the tower.

"I didn't even know they could speak." She was looking after where it had gone, but the crocodile was camouflaged already in the tall grasses.

He chuckled, but of course she wouldn't recognize alchemical contraptions when she saw them. "They don't."

At the tower, they dismounted, and before Damien could prepare Amma, the door, a rusty-hinged slab of metal, burst open, and there stood a giant of a man absolutely covered from head to toe in soot.

Anomalous threw thick arms out, grinning a row of bright, white teeth from his otherwise blackened facade, but Damien leaned back just enough to avoid the man's embrace. "Ah. Have you seen yourself?"

Anomalous glanced down, then back up. "Have you seen *your*self?"

When Damien looked down at the mud-streaked and bloodied armor he wore, the man took the opportunity and embraced him in that back-breaking, too-tight, awkward way that Damien would never return—a thing Anomalous consistently found hysterical. Damien was no small man himself, but Anomalous was massive. That happened when one's ancestry was riddled with giants and goliaths and a mammoth or two, and there was no avoiding his touch if that's what he intended.

"And who's this?"

Released and able to breathe again, Damien slapped his own chest, soot puffing up. Amma squeaked from the back of her throat as Anomalous reached out and took her hand, tiny in his colossal palm.

"Welcome to Craven Tower," he said in his rushed way,

shoulders hunched as he leaned down to shake. Her whole body rippled with the movement, and then she actually coughed out a laugh and smiled back at him. "I am Anomalous Craven, alchemist. And you are?" He was already pulling her into the building.

She glanced back at Damien warily as she was led inside. "Um, I'm Amma."

"Am*ma*. Am-ma," he repeated, playing with the cadence of the name despite there being very little to work with, then rubbed her hand between both of his. "Hmm, well, nice skin you have."

When he let her go, Amma looked down at her hand, covered in soot, then up at Damien who only shrugged at her bewildered expression and followed inside.

The entry space was crammed with crates and parts that had been dragged in and abandoned. Damien took a long step over the axle to a cart, hands behind his back. Everything was useful, according to Anomalous, just maybe not right now, so it was hoarded wherever was convenient, or not, and when one did not have many guests, an entryway served a greater purpose as a storehouse.

"Come with me, quickly, I've something to show you!" He waded ahead of them down a tunnel that was carved out of more hoarded goods, perfect for his size and no bigger. "You'll never guess what I've got up on the slab, oh, it will be such a surprise!"

"Is it a man?" Damien asked, leaning away from a cracked lantern that hung off a fishing rod jammed between the wheel of a cart and a cast iron pan.

"How did you know?" Anomalous was hurrying ahead of them and disappeared into the next room.

Damien cocked a brow at Amma who was keeping close at his side in the cramped walkway. "It is literally *always* a man," he whispered from the side of his mouth.

Amma giggled, a bright if quiet sound as she picked her way around a bolt of silky fabric that jutted out. Damien grinned, then saw Kaz trailing behind them, arms crossed, his sour expression going even sourer, and Damien corrected into a frown.

The room beyond the entry hall was a round space also crammed with objects, but the stairs that ran along the outer wall at a curve and took them upward were mostly clear. Anomalous was already halfway up them, and they followed, fewer of his precious goods as they climbed, and then finally freed themselves of the clutter on the next level. Here, there was a makeshift kitchen, a fireplace, a set of comfortable, if soggy-looking seats, and something bubbling away on the hearth and scenting the air with spices. The space was familiar to

Damien, cozy even, but Anomalous continued on, upward. The next level was all books and papers and spilled ink. Damien lingered a moment, but knew there was no sense to be made of the mess, and finally they climbed up to the lab.

There was the rhythmic plunking of water, the incessant chirp of a cricket, and a skitter from somewhere unseen when they entered, all playing out over a constant hum. A huge, round space bathed in a green light emanating from glass jars strung up around the room, it was not so crammed with junk that it could not be traversed, but to say the room was not its own kind of mess would be a lie. Equipment that Damien did not care to think on for very long lined a wall, metal and strange and cobbled together dangerously, some sparking, others giving off groaning sounds like lost souls were trapped inside. Another curved wall held shelves, a few even straight, and were strewn with jars and cages and jugs. Much larger tubes were set on the ground, one filled with a yellow liquid in which something floated, animal-like, eyes closed and fetal. Finally, the curved roof on one side was made up of glass, and beyond it, clouds rolled in the darkening sky.

Though it was familiar enough to Damien, seeing Amma observe the lab for the first time with big, blue eyes that took it all in with a sense of wonder and horror tied together too tightly to ever be separated, reminded him of how impressive it was. Then her eyes fell on the table just in the room's center and the gore laid across it, and he thought she might pass out. He grabbed the back of her tunic just as she wavered on her feet and kept her aloft.

Anomalous didn't even notice, of course, wholly absorbed in whatever it was he had been saying their entire ascent despite being too far ahead of them to be properly understood. He was prattling on about veins, very specifically thicknesses, ways to connect them, and how he had discovered a new method that proved to be quite successful in fusing a swamp rabbit with a crane. "Didn't ultimately survive," he said with a sigh that had a sort of finality to it, "but for those seven and a half minutes we had a jumping, flying abomination that I could have really wreaked some havoc with. Called him Vinny. He's buried out back with the rest now."

"What is this place?" Amma finally asked, voice breathy as she got her bearings back.

Damien released her tunic, and she managed to stay upright. "Anomalous calls it a laboratory," he said, gesturing to the man. "He does alchemy here. It's a bit like magic, but with a lot of unnecessary steps."

"That is, as always, completely and utterly incorrect, my friend, and yet close enough an explanation. And this," said Anomalous, striding up to the table and running his hands along the long edge to loom over the pieces laid across it, "this is my great experiment."

It was, of course, just an assortment of body parts, and not even enough for an entire being at that. There was an arm, torso, multiple pieces of both legs, nearly a whole head, and many organs, though Damien couldn't differentiate a spleen from a liver if he needed to—piercing either brought pain, and it was really impaling the heart that ended things quickest. The smell was off putting to say the least.

Amma wobbled again, pressing a hand to her stomach.

Then there was a plunking on the windows, and Anomalous stood straight, clapping. "Oh, good, the hag is back!" He bustled over and cranked a lever to open one of the glass panes inward.

Outside, a woven basket the size of a cart was hanging from a long cord on a pulley, and in it sat Mudryth, a woman, or at least something like one. "You wouldn't believe the haul I got today, Louie!" She stood and stepped forward, perching a bare foot on the thin edge of the window sill and hoisting herself from the basket. Climbing inside with a sack over her shoulder, her long, spindly limbs were spider-like as she stepped down from the height that should have been much harder for her to traverse. With dark, wild hair that frizzed out in all directions, streaked with a shock of silver from her left temple, and ashy, greying skin, she may well have been part insect. "Oh, we have company? And look at yourself!"

"Bah!" Anomalous waved at her, making grabby hands for the bag she had just slung onto the ground with a wet squelch. It looked too heavy for her slim frame to carry, but then she was as tall as Anomalous, and, well, she wasn't exactly human, Damien knew.

"Well, don't you look absolutely dreadful," Mudryth gave Damien a black-toothed grin from across the room but didn't rush to embrace him like Anomalous always did, something he appreciated. "Hey, not yet!" Before the alchemist could reach the bag, the woman whipped her apron off and attacked his face, rubbing hard all over and into his hair. Soot puffed up and coated the closest machinery, but when she pulled back, she revealed a shock of ginger curls, ears a bit too big, even for Anomalous's head, and a smattering of freckles on pale skin. "I'll sort these, you clean yourself up."

"Anomalous, I was actually hoping we could speak," Damien interjected.

"Of course, of course, come with me." The alchemist headed back to the stairs.

Damien turned to Amma whose eyes had gone wide, hesitating on the Chthonic word, and then not using it. "Do not cause any trouble,"—then to Kaz—"Watch over her."

The imp, who had found a way to sulk twice as hard in the interim, finally grinned. "Of course, Master."

Damien followed Anomalous to his office below where the man proceeded to scramble around for several minutes in the stacks, professing he had something for Damien, but ultimately coming up empty. Promising to find the mystery gift later, he took him out onto a walkway suspended between the tower and another stone building at the back. This building jutted off the tower with no support below it, but thick cords ran from the tower's top to the stones at its corners, slightly offsetting the whole structure's ever-increasing lean. New to Damien, it could have been magic that held it up, but Anomalous was never that practical. He had likely worked for moons and moons with numbers and odd, little letters, done hours of brutal handiwork all on his own, and suffered gobs of failure to get it right.

Open to the elements, a swampy breeze blew over them while they crossed the bridge. Above, the window Mudryth had climbed through was cranked shut with a slam, and Damien looked up, but couldn't see within. He thought of Amma there, knowing she would be fine with the hag and the imp and the disembodied human parts even if she would likely disagree. But if she managed to work herself up into hysterics again, he supposed he understood how to calm her down. It would be a chore, of course, to summon the restraint, but if he had to wrap his arms around her—

"So, some terrible, hopeless thing has brought you all the way out to my corner of Tarfail, eh? I can't imagine this is just a social call, not trailing a stranger along with you." Anomalous had pushed on the door into the building, opening upward.

"Terrible, yes, but hopefully not hopeless." The two entered into a dining hall of sorts, or it had been at one time, though it was turned on its side. That had been a window they climbed through, he realized, not a door, and the wooden floor ran the length of the wall many stories upward. Before them up the back wall were doors turned on their side, and a stairway had been cobbled together with old planks from carts that had been lost in the swamp to access each one, the rooms turned to form storied levels rather than a number of rooms along a hall. "Nice addition."

"You like it? I lifted it off a ruin in the Wastes and brought it back with the spider." Anomalous climbed into the bottom-most doorway.

"The Accursed Wastes?" Damien followed, ducking down and climbing through the doorway turned on its side. "You've got to be careful out there, Anomalous, even in that big, metal contraption. Shadowhart thinks he owns everything and everyone who wanders into his territory."

"Bah!" Anomalous threw his hands up, waving the warning away.

Inside, the room was tall and long, though not terribly wide. The furniture was lined up in a row along the floor-wall and sconces had been hammered into the wall-ceiling, flicking on with flames when Anomalous pressed a button that had been welded beside the door. The action looked a lot like magic, if only the alchemist believed in that kind of thing.

"So?" Anomalous began pulling off his soot-covered clothing and dropping them as he walked to a wardrobe at the room's back.

Damien focused on admiring a painting still hung on the wall that had become the floor. The flaking canvas depicted The Expulsion in a classical style. It was massive, and if Damien counted, he assumed all one hundred and forty-two gods may well have been illustrated upon it, frozen in the final moment before the one hundred and seventeen gods of goodness and light thrust the remaining twenty-five dark gods to the Abyss to be locked away for eternity. The "good" gods would then ascend to Empyrea, never to show themselves directly to earth-dwelling creatures again.

In the painting's corners there were demons and dominions both, enjoying their last moments on earth before similarly being sealed in the infernal and celestial planes, the only hope of escape through summoning. His father wouldn't be amongst them, Zagadoth hadn't been around way back then, but if he had, Damien was sure he would know every detail of the event thrice over. Instead, the tale of The Expulsion was passed on second and third and fourth hand until it had become something of a legendary spectacle that he was unsure really happened quite the way it was often told.

"Damien?" Anomalous's voice broke him of his long stare at the painting.

Where to start, he wondered, taking a deep breath, then delivered the news that he had finally done it, he had completed the talisman he'd been working on for years, and his father would soon be released.

The alchemist was incredulous and supportive even if he never wholly understood what it meant—Zagadoth being a demon, his spirit trapped within a crystal. No one had spirits, least of all demons who didn't even exist to begin with, and people couldn't be trapped in crystals. Damien was just an orphan in Anomalous's eyes as they'd met well after all the unpleasantness.

"It all has a deeper explanation," Anomalous would often say of crystals and magic and demons, "I just haven't figured it out yet. But I am so happy that the thing you believe in is happening according to your perception." That was Anomalous, the most supportive non-believer there was.

But for all the man's obsession with alchemy and disbelief of the arcane arts, he was at least marginally perceptive. "But that's not exactly why you're here."

"Ah, no." Damien sighed, taking the fresh, wet linen Anomalous had offered him from a basin that ran clean water with the twist of a lever built into the wall. Aszath Koth's keep had something almost identical, but it ran on magic instead of the not-magical arcana Anomalous insisted this was. "It's the girl."

"Of course it is! Who is she?"

"Oh, I don't know, some little pickpocket who got lost in Aszath Koth," he said flippantly, rubbing the muck and blood and dried werewolf drool from his face. "And she's making me kill her."

Anomalous made a surprised noise. "Kill her yet you don't know her? But what if she's one of those Holy Knights you're always going on about? Or a lost princess? Maybe even the daughter of an ancient demon you're meant to make more half-demon babies with?" This he said with a kind of mocking derision, but Damien knew it was probably his favorite theory—one couldn't be an alchemist and not an idealist and perhaps a romantic too. That was the whole point of trying to make a person, he supposed—it was difficult to find a companion out in the swamps, one who was still alive and in one piece anyway.

"No, she's definitely not a blood mage. There are so few of us, and I would recognize her from the Grand Order of Dread meetings anyway," Damien mumbled, stripping off his leather armor to evaluate what had happened to his tunic.

"I suppose she wouldn't be; she doesn't seem the type."

He was right, but Damien didn't want to dwell on the increasingly obvious evidence she might be…*good*. Instead, he explained how he had crafted Bloodthorne's Talisman of Enthrallment to remain in its vessel until their death, leaving out the arcane way the curse worked because Anomalous wouldn't believe in it anyway. The talisman had found its way inside Amma, and Damien told him he would very much prefer it not be there.

By the end of his explanation, he'd gotten all of his armor off in a pile and had finished scrubbing the mud from his limbs and face, feeling outwardly much better if also inwardly much worse at the prospect of things. "So, I am hoping that you, Anomalous Craven, with all of your alchemy and tools and knowledge, can possibly get the talisman out of her."

"You want *me* to kill the girl?" He had changed into a blindingly white tunic himself and ran up to Damien. "I don't exactly have much use for most of her parts, but—"

"No, Anomalous, that's just it. Magic, *my* magic anyway, cannot do this, so I'd like to see if your alchemy can remove the thing without killing her."

"You're telling me your blood magery-whatsit can't just shunt it out?"

"The talisman isn't meant to be…shunted."

"A challenge then, and alchemy to the rescue!" Anomalous scurried his massive frame back to the door.

"Wait," Damien called, stopping the man short. "I have one more request, a smaller if odder one. I'd really rather not let on what you're doing. Not to the girl or Kaz."

"Who?"

Damien chuckled. "The figment of my imagination?"

"Oh, yes, the *imp*. I thought you stopped believing in those things when you grew up, but I suppose not." This he said with a weary sigh. Damien had known him going on fifteen years, over half of his own life, and while he had gone from skinny adolescent lost in the swamp with a questionable understanding of his own arcana to adept blood mage in that time, Anomalous barely had changed at all—still a man rooted firmly in his own beliefs albeit surprisingly capable. "But the girl, she doesn't know you've got to kill her to get it out?"

"No, she knows that."

"Then unless she wants to be dead, why should it be a secret from her? It's much easier for your patient to cooperate if they know what's going on. Well, mostly. Second easiest to already being dead."

Damien rocked his head from side to side. It wasn't that simple, and for all the complexity that Anomalous did understand, this would be too much. Damien did not admit, in his internal debate, that it was more likely he himself could not actually explain the distressing feeling he got at the prospect of telling her he actually might not exactly want her quite so dead after all, so instead he offered up something that was only half true. "I don't want to get her hopes up that she might survive, you know? It's much better if she's just resigned to dying."

"Right!" Anomalous threw his hands up as if it couldn't be more obvious. "Awful thoughtful of you, really."

Damien scrunched up his nose. "Don't say that, it's just…prudent."

"Prudent," he repeated with a laugh and hurried to the door. "Of course, that too, not that any of it matters because alchemy will solve all your problems!"

"Wait!" Damien stood from the chair. "One more thing."

"Oh, all right, but quickly—I am just itching to start this experiment, and there are so many measurements and calculations and—"

"I'm sure you're excited," said Damien, pinching his nose, "but perhaps you ought to put on some pants first."

CHAPTER 10
ALL THAT IS GOLD DOES NOT GLITTER, BUT IT IS USUALLY MALLEABLE

Amma stared at the woman, all elbows and knees as she hefted the bag up onto a stained table. It landed with a juiciness, burlap at one time but dyed a rusty, red color at its bottom from years of use, a few patches sewn onto its sides and a new tear forming at the thickest part of it where something wet and dark poked out.

"Excuse Louie, he gets so wrapped up in his work he forgets his manners," she said with a scratchy lilt, shrugging bony shoulders that stuck up through the fabric of her dress. "He'd forget his pants too if someone didn't remind him, elements bless the giant bastard! But he's really just a big, ole sweet thing." She cackled then—actually cackled—head thrown back and hair wild.

"He called you a hag," said Amma, the words coming out before she could stop them.

"Oh, sure, but that's what I am!" She turned to her fully and spread her arms out as a black shadow sizzled up from her feet to climb around her body, envelop her wholly, and then disappear to reveal a face of sunken, withered skin, red eyes, and pure horror. Amma's scream caught in her throat as she covered her mouth, but the visage was gone as soon as it appeared, and the woman was left cackling some more. "Swamp witch, some fellas call me—ladies are always witches when they don't understand us—but hag is the, uh, what's Louie call it? The *technical* term. You can call me Mudryth if you're comfier with that."

Kaz snorted from the corner, and he skittered up on a shelf beside a bubbling jar.

"And you," said Mudryth, pointing to the imp. "Unlike Louie, I

90

believe in arcane nasties since I am one, so don't cause any trouble. Now, what's your name, sweetie?"

"Amma," she ventured, throat hoarse.

"Well, Amma, come on over here and give us a hand."

Carefully making her way across the laboratory, arms pinched in so she didn't touch anything, Amma stepped up to the table, the smell off of the bag a mix of saltiness and sour copper as Mudryth reached into it.

"Ah, here we are!" The hag pulled a thick limb from inside, revealing a bloody, human arm and a limp hand sans its pinky finger, and waved it at Amma. "Guess I can give you one instead!"

Amma didn't know why she moved to take the thing—it was instinctual when someone tried to hand one something, even a severed limb, she supposed—but into her waiting palms was plopped the arm, heavier than she imagined, but just as wet and sticky as she feared.

"Couldn't get the full set," Mudryth was saying as she dug back into the bag. "Croc must have got the rest of him, but just look at that bicep! Louie will love that."

Amma's hands trembled under both the weight and the gore of the thing, and all she could do was glance back up at the woman, or hag, or witch, mouth agape.

"Go on, put it on the slab. We've almost completed this one, just need to find the last parts, and I think that's as good as we're gonna get as far as arms go."

Amma glanced back over her shoulder where the amalgam of a corpse was laid out. With a heavy breath, she went over and set the arm where it belonged in accordance with what was already there, trying very hard to not look at the rest of it, but found herself intrigued by the frost forming on the edges of the metal slab and the sizzle off the arm she had just placed down. She turned back, stiff and unblinking to where Mudryth was hunched over the bag and pulling out more severed pieces of people.

"Oh, and looky at this!" Mudryth unraveled a swath of fabric, a splotch of something skin-like falling off of it and back into the bag. "This should fit you. Much better than that baggy, dirty thing you got on."

Amma looked down at herself, just as dirty as what Mudryth held up but not nearly as covered in gore.

"I'll clean this up, and maybe we'll even find some more pieces your size since it looks like some other little lady bit it out here." She held up a pendant on a chain covered in blood then pocketed it.

"Come on, now, help me sort."

Like her actions were separate from her mind, Amma finally went over and pulled out an indiscriminate body part from the squelchy bag. She swallowed hard, her stomach flipping over, hand shaking as she held whatever she had by a patch of long hair.

Trying her best to keep the vomit down that wanted to push up through her throat, she slapped a hand over her mouth. Mudryth saw her struggle, snapped her fingers, and a bucket from across the room flew into her hands. She shoved it at Amma who immediately filled it up with the day's meals.

There was the cruel, grizzly laughter of Kaz again from up on the shelves as Amma spit and wiped her mouth on her sleeve. "Sorry," she croaked out, throat burning with bile.

Mudryth glared up at Kaz and then hocked at toe at him, shutting him up when it pelted him right in the face. "Well, sweetie, that's not what I was expecting in the least." Mudryth took the bucket from her, squishing up her face as she poked her nose down to Amma's. "You did come here with Damien, didn't you?"

Amma nodded, rubbing her stomach. She wanted to clarify it wasn't by choice, but was too afraid more than just words would come out.

"He almost never brings someone along, just once actually, and she was—well, not much like you, though her stomach was just as weak, but her tongue was a lot sharper. I guess we can't all be comfortable with anatomy puzzles, can we? Here, check these pockets instead."

The pile of clothes resting at the table's other end were like a gift to Amma, and she went for them despite all of their questionable stains. "I can fix this," she said, holding up a man's tunic that would be very nice if it weren't torn completely up its front like, well, she didn't want to imagine how it got that way. "Do you have needle and thread?"

Mudryth fetched her a surprisingly clean kit of sewing things, and Amma set to work. This was, at the very least, better than being chased by werewolves or huddled up on the floor of an abandoned, foul-smelling cabin in the swamp, and embroidery was a good way to keep her hands busy, her mother always said.

When her stomach settled a bit, she eyed Kaz who was focused on an orb he'd taken off the shelf and was peering deeply into, finally distracted. "Mudryth," she asked, voice low, "does Damien come here often?"

"Yeah, regular-like. Couple times a year maybe? He and Louie couldn't be more different, but sometimes people bond when they save each other from drowning in muck, ya know?"

Amma's eyes flicked to Kaz, still absorbed with the things on the shelf. She prodded for more. "Oh? Who saved who?"

"Hear them tell it, you'd never know. Damien was such a skinny, little thing back then, but I still have to rescue Louie every now and again when he wades too deep. Now they get one another out of jams all the time. See, thing is, Louie doesn't believe in magic, which is funny considering, ya know, I've been his best friend for almost thirty years, and Damien doesn't really believe much in alchemy, but sometimes it just works out when one of 'em's stuck. Louie wanted to make a storm in a box a few years ago, but it just kept getting too wet, and then it'd blow up. Damien conjured him up a spell that does the trick and set it into that machine over there." She gestured with the point of her elbow to a big box of a thing covered in dials and levers. "Louie insists it's actually alchemy, he just doesn't fully understand it—not yet anyway! Won't let him use necromancy though. It'd be a whole lot easier if he did, of course, but Louie's too determined to make a real man, whatever that means, not some undead or a walking skeleton or what have you."

Amma jabbed herself with the needle at that, a mistake she almost never made, and stuck her finger in her mouth before pulling it right back out at the memory of touching dead people parts and, well...everything else. Her stomach turned over. "Damien does necromancy?"

Mudryth shrugged. "Louie won't indulge in it, so I'm not exactly sure, but demon spawn are full of surprises. But you already know all about that, don't you?"

As the hag cackled some more, Amma only smiled warily. "Actually, I haven't known him that long, but you seem to be...friends?"

"Something like that, but he's a tough bone to break." As she said this, there was a snap from inside the bag, and her eyes lit up as she mumbled about a perfect fit. "Now, tell me, which do you like better for the man we're making?"

Amma looked up from piecing the tunic back together. In each hand, Mudryth was holding up the severed heads of what looked like swamp eels. Amma squinted, then gasped when she realized they weren't eels at all. "Well, if I were him, I guess I'd appreciate that one a little longer—I mean, more."

Mudryth cackled again. "Yeah, I think this one's better too, might make up for one leg being a few inches shorter than the other." She hummed to herself as she went to the slab with an armful of the best pieces she'd found.

Amma focused again on the tunic, coming across something hard in the breast pocket. She pulled out a wooden trinket, and though it was covered in muck, recognized it immediately. It had been carved to look like a bear, jointed at the head and its middle so it could be bent forward to bow, otherwise in the shape of a cylinder and only a few inches long, but it wasn't the shape she recognized, it was the wood itself.

Amma hadn't seen liathau since leaving home, but the feel of it in her hands was unmistakable, and she squeezed the trinket, a spark of happiness in her chest and a vision of the orchard passing through her mind.

"I think that just about does it!" Mudryth clapped her hands together, standing over the table where what looked like a full person was laid out, just in parts. "Now, I need to check on my stew, but I'll be back in two shakes of a croc's tail." The woman swept off to the stairway, and Amma was left alone in the room save for one possibly-imaginary imp and a person who was actually a lot of people and none at all at the same time.

Amma carefully placed the tunic down and wandered over to the body. It was pretty well proportioned, and now that it had a whole head, it looked more human as well, though the face was bloated and the features hard to make out. Drowning, she assumed, swallowing back another roil of nausea.

As she worried the liathau wood trinket in her palm, she skimmed the rest of the corpse and noticed its missing little finger. She placed the trinket there in its stead, practically a perfect fit, and chuckled. That was better than throwing up, at least.

Amma wandered away from the table wrapping her arms around her middle. Not accounting for all the gore, the rest of the room was terribly interesting if totally incomprehensible. There were tools of questionable use, but many of them gleamed cleanly unlike the tables covered in body parts. There were also jars and bottles set into glass-covered cabinets with brightly colored liquids and suspended objects, some once—or maybe still—alive, and others shimmering like enchanted things.

Amma stopped before a box made up of glass, edges perfect and sealed, its contents roving constantly despite not being moved. There was a blobby goop inside that shimmered like liquid sunshine, and it was speckled with flecks of something silver, like a starry, golden sky. It reminded her, vaguely, of the ribbons of silver she had seen in that fissure to the infernal plane.

As she peered into it, she thought of the night before, staring out through the hut's small window at the cloudy sky, not a star in sight, the sounds of the swamp all around. After Damien had ordered her to stay put, she was compelled to do just that, but when sleep took her, she woke right back up after slipping into a werewolf-filled nightmare. Then she found herself half dreaming, reliving the chase, the fear when the monster broke through the larder she was huddled in, and the decision to stab a living creature while knowing it could be the last thing she ever did.

Damien had vocalized exactly what went through her mind seconds before acting—if she had just let him be mauled, she would have been free of the blood mage. Amma didn't really understand most magic, but unlike Anomalous, she believed in it—she was the victim of it, after all—but she had enough sense to know that if Damien were dead, the enthrallment on her would most likely follow suit. Yet when she saw him struggling under the werewolf, she felt compelled and not by way of some arcane force. It was ridiculous, really, but that was always her compulsion, to help, even if, like Damien, the person she was helping might not really deserve it.

Amma had always followed the impulses that would endear her to others. It was an impulse to smile and agree and go along with just about anything so long as it made everyone else happy. But this impulse, to risk murdering a man cursed to be a monster in order to save another man who was not cursed but just chose to be a monster instead, had been reckless and stupid, but it was, for perhaps the first time, a decision made wholly in her own interest. In that brief, perilous moment, she wanted to keep him alive, and though now she had no idea why, it was simply the thing she desperately needed at the time.

She truly hadn't even expected him to acknowledge she had helped, let alone thank her, but as she stared at the tiny golden ocean made of stars in an impossibly clear box in the alchemist's lab, Amma couldn't shake the thought that somehow saving Damien was for once not a thing she was meant to do, not her duty, not her conscience, not an act honoring a vow to another, but just something she felt like doing. And for once that choice didn't seem so bad, or, if it were, maybe that was okay?

No, that was as ridiculous a thought as thinking Damien wasn't a complete jerk. He was unkind and cruel and a blood mage for Osurehm's sake, and even if he acted as though he were human to her for a moment while they were holed up in that larder, when his touch had been gentle and his words soft, it meant nothing. Amma whipped away from the box, sure that it was some enchanted thing and putting all of those stupid thoughts in her head.

There was a click from across the room, and Amma looked up to see Kaz fluttering near a tall shelf. He had picked up a container and was eyeing her from across the room. Kaz grinned, those bottom teeth sticking out, and he extended his clawed hands out over the floor. "You shouldn't have touched that," he said, and let go of the jar.

CHAPTER 11
ALCHEMICALLY SIGNIFICANT
SUCCESSES AND FAILURES

Amma dove across the laboratory, catching the jar Kaz had lobbed just before it smashed into the floor. The magenta liquid inside sloshed, coating the glass, but the bottle remained intact. "Stop that!" she shouted up at the imp, scrambling to her feet.

"No, *you* stop that." Kaz flitted across the room to where the gently humming machine loomed and yanked down on a lever. There was a whirring as the air crackled.

Amma shrieked, abandoning the bottle on the slab holding the amalgam of a corpse as she bolted to the machine. She gripped the lever and tugged with all her might to switch it back off. The static in the air died down, and the whirring came to a slow halt.

Another jar sailed through the laboratory, and Amma was running after it without another thought, catching it before it smashed into a glass case filled with many more breakable things. "Kaz, no, please!" She clutched the jar to her chest and dove in front of another, the glass to this one thick enough to not smash when it hit the ground, rolling across the floor and under the slab. Amma chased after it and collected all of Kaz's projectiles on the frosty surface.

"I'm not doing anything. In fact, I, Master Bloodthorne's loyal servant, am trying to stop you, the current bane of his existence, from causing all this trouble!" He flicked his tail across a set of tools, knocking them to the ground with a clatter.

"But I saved your life," she grumbled, hurrying to pick up the sharpened tools and trying to set them back as they were.

At that, Kaz made a noise she couldn't place, an angry sort of squawk, and flapped his wings a little harder, a fine time for him to learn to fly just out of reach as he sailed past her. When she turned, he was holding up the glass box of golden ocean stars she had been so drawn to moments before.

"Don't," she pleaded, scurrying beneath where he hovered.

Kaz tipped the small chest before his face, darting away from her and over to the slab. "Can this really be? It's so pretty," he said, a terrible smile curling up over his pointed teeth. "No wonder you just wanted to see what was inside."

"Kaz, please!" She jumped for him, but he was too high, hovering above and fiddling with the box's latch.

Amma climbed up on the table, maneuvering around the things he'd thrown as well as bits of body, a knee, some intestine, a chunk of spine, and she reached for Kaz, but the imp had finally figured out the latch.

Amma jumped, knocking him out of the air, but it was too late. The sunshiney goo plopped out as Amma tackled Kaz into the humming machine, catching a lever in their descent, the table tipping over in her wake. The corpse pieces slid off and toppled to the floor, jars shattered and contents spilled, and the golden, silver-speckled goo landed atop the whole pile, spreading out in a thin layer over everything.

Amma gasped, pushing herself off the imp and crawling over to the mess. She looked for anything she might save, but the goop was quick to cover it all. There was an intensifying hum from behind her, a sizzle of sparks shooting through the air, and the whole laboratory lit up as a bolt of lightning shot out from the machine and struck the pile. Everything went blindingly white, and the air was sucked from the room.

Floating. Amma was floating in nothingness, and then, slowly, little golden specks formed all around her. One hundred and forty-two little golden specks, if she had been able to count them, but the vision cleared too quickly, and then she was just sitting on the floor of the laboratory again, blinking the stars out of her eyes to see the terrible mess did, in fact, still exist.

"Look what you did!" shrieked Kaz. "Look what she did!"

Amma turned from her spot on the floor to see Damien and Anomalous standing just at the top of the stairs, Mudryth craning her neck up over the landing a few steps below them.

The alchemist was first to shout, hands on his face as he ran into the room and to the machine, switching it back off, but Amma couldn't look away from the shock on Damien's face and how it shifted into ire so swiftly. Even without his armor and cloak, he was an imposing figure, and when he strode over, she thought he might kill her right there, but instead he only wrenched her off the floor.

"Get away from there," he growled, pulling her back from the expanding ooze. She stumbled, his hand still tight on her upper arm as he assessed the situation. "What did you do?"

Amma stammered, blinking up at him. "I didn't mean...the table...and the box." She pointed, and the imp quickly chucked the glass container across the room, clasping his claws behind his back.

Mudryth caught the box with her elongated reach before it landed in the pond of melting gold at their feet, growing at an abnormal rate, much more goo now than could have been originally inside the container. Mudryth's form went dark as shadows crawled up her limbs from the floor, and her eyes brightened until they glowed white.

Damien gave Amma a shove backward, telling her to stay out of the way. The ooze had covered the things that fell beneath it, and they bobbed up to the surface, a set of bottles each containing some strange liquid, the shattered pieces of another, chunks of human, the trinket of liathau wood, and then they were sucked into the goo, disappearing as the blob continued to grow until it hit the edge of the shadows Mudryth had called up from the ground, containing it.

Anomalous scurried up to the edge of Mudryth's shadow, peering over and into the pool. "I never knew this could expand its mass in such a way."

"Where did you get this?" Damien carefully circled the barrier, and the ooze began to climb up the foggy walls the hag had built.

"I can't exactly remember!" Anomalous sounded as if he were delivering absolutely positive news to the room, throwing his hands up with a broad smile. "I fell through this hole in the quag a few moons back and got it from one of those underground fellas, you know? They're strikingly handsome but *weird*. They called it something...something strange."

"It didn't happen to be luxerna, did it?" Damien's brow was dark and heavy with concern.

"No, no, it was...I think...god goo! Right, yes, the goo of the gods, he said it was. The gods aren't real, of course, so I just assumed I'd have to play with it to figure out what it really is, but I did sort of forget I even had it. This is absolutely fascinating!"

Damien rolled his eyes, and began to mutter in his sibilant language. The expanding puddle quivered and shrank back in on itself. "It's got a will," he said with a sort of disgusted look on his face. "Something in there is alive. Has it always been like that?"

"I don't know!" Anomalous was positively beaming. "It's much too big for the box now. Muddie, you think you can shift it over to one of the cells?"

The hag said nothing, eyes glowing a brilliant white, but the shadows moved like a fog over the laboratory floor, and the viscous, golden puddle inside sloshed over itself as it went. Anomalous swung open the door to a transparent tube, and the goo was ushered inside and dumped off. The hag breathed in with a horrible, rasping sound, and the shadows collected themselves in one, long rope that she sucked into her mouth and snapped her teeth shut on the very last bit of, eyes losing their glow as the door swung shut with a pop.

Even larger than Anomalous, the cylinder filled with the bright ooze, rising up to nearly its top before settling, and the alchemist smooshed his nose up against the glass. "Simply riveting!" Beside him, Mudryth came back into herself, gathering up a roll of parchment that she handed over to Anomalous and he immediately began to scribble on. The two stood under the glow the strange goop was now giving off, trading excited theories about what might come of all this.

Damien, however, turned back to Amma, quiet fury on his clenched jaw. She shook her head, backing up from him and bumping into the case she'd saved previously, managing to only shift it a bit. Then Damien's eyes flicked across the room to where the imp was huddled in a corner. Kaz's tiny hand shot out, pointing at Amma, and she gasped in betrayed disgust back at him.

"Anomalous," said Damien, rubbing his face, "I must apologize, this is—"

"Amazing!" The alchemist threw his arms up, the parchment he'd been writing on unraveling. "I've been too busy to experiment with that box, but clearly I should have. If you look closely, that broken lumbar joint is mending itself!" Floating past where he pointed, a small shadow was indeed knitting together in the darkness of the goo.

Damien turned instead to Mudryth. "Truly, we've made a mess."

"Oh, please, sweetie, we've had livelier inventory days around here." She patted at her frizzed-out hair and wiped off a last bit of shadow from her shoulder.

Damien's gaze fell back on Amma. He was out of his armor, the skin of his face and hands clean if his black tunic and pants were still stained. His look had dissolved from the rage he'd been wearing, but she still straightened when he strode over to her. "You," he said, "don't touch anything else."

Amma was prepared to protest that she hadn't actually touched anything to begin with, but Anomalous whirled back on them, voice booming, "You must spend the night! I've so much to do before we can possibly begin our grand experiment."

Damien grunted, Amma looking from one man to the other, and then the blood mage gave in, an exhausted slump to his shoulders.

A short while later, Amma was led along a raised walkway off the back of the tower and into cozier, if sideways, living chambers. Damien ushered her up a narrow staircase to a private room, closing the door behind him and then standing there, glowering at her.

She swallowed, unsure where to start, because the truth of it was, she *did* spill the table of body parts, and she even *sort of* turned on that whirring machine, but the rest of it, the start of it, was all that terrible, little imp, and it had been on purpose too. Yet Damien seemed determined to be angry with *her*, and gods did she hate to upset anyone, especially a blood mage who had threatened to kill her while they were in the perfect place to dispose of a body. Amma lifted her arms and opened her mouth.

"*Sanguinisui*, do not hurt yourself, do not hurt anyone else, and do not leave this room."

Amma snapped her mouth back shut despite that he hadn't ordered her quiet, the familiar, awful crawl of the spell working its way through her. His voice had been fairly flat, yet he still stood there, glaring, instead of sweeping out of the room and leaving her alone.

She glared back. "Is there anything else?" she asked, surprised by the cut of her own voice, but suddenly overwhelmed with anger herself. "Something you want me to do for you?"

"What? No," he spat back at her.

"Really? You're not even going to force me to tell you the truth about what happened? You're just going to assume it was all my fault, and—"

"I know that wasn't your doing." He cut her off, and she straightened, the shock of both his words and sudden shift in demeanor chasing away her own anger. Damien sighed, settling into his usual irritation. "Kaz clearly has it out for you, but I didn't expect him to be so hostile. Risky when he's of so little use to me. I'm thinking of killing him off again."

Amma gasped at the nonchalance of his words. "Again? You've...you've killed him before?"

"Well, there was an accident—he fell off the parapet at the keep, and it's quite a long way down."

"But he has wings."

"He does now, I suppose because his new body thought it needed protection from being kicked off something high this time around." The blood mage had forgotten all his ire, a wistful grin sliding up his face.

"That's awful," she hissed.

He chuckled. "It certainly wasn't my proudest moment, but I was only eighteen or so. And he comes back, obviously, not that it's a great loss when he's gone. You certainly won't miss him, will you?"

"I..." Amma searched the ground, heart beginning to race. No, she wouldn't miss the imp who had done nothing but call her terrible things and cause her misery, but she didn't want him put to death because of her. "You're not really going to kill him, are you?" And then another familiar feeling began to crawl over the back of her throat and burn in her eyes.

He shrugged. "Why not?"

"It's just..." Amma took in a staggered breath. If it was so easy for him to kill off an infernal being, it was going to be even easier for him to do the same to her when the time came. She took a step back and sat on the bed with a whimper.

Any amusement Damien had at the thought of ending Kaz was wiped off his face. "What are you doing?"

"What do you think?" Amma coughed out, wetness spilling onto her cheeks.

"Oh, no, no, none of that again. Do *not* start crying."

"What do you care?" she muttered, wiping at her face, dirt coming away with the tears.

"I don't," he growled, turning from her. "I just can't possibly understand what would possess you to shed tears for that horrid, little imp."

"It's just that,"—she sniffled—"that..." Amma blinked through the blurriness, unable to find the words that it was just *everything*, and it was all really quite *a lot*.

Damien waited impatiently for her to compose herself, and then snarled, "Oh, for fuck's sake, *sanguinisui*, stop crying right this instant."

Amma inhaled sharply, breath hitching. The sting in her eyes was gone as was the stuffiness in her nose, yet the desire was still there, burning even deeper in her chest, as if on the verge of a sneeze yet incapable of letting it out. Her throat swelled with a sound that wouldn't come, and she looked around for help, anything to relieve the powerful ache buried inside, clawing to be free. When there was nothing, she stomped a foot and squealed. "Now I'm not even allowed to cry?"

He looked absolutely incredulous. "Do you *want* to?"

"No!" she spat back, her face so hot she knew tears would follow if they could, but instead there were only angry prickles running under her skin like talons clawing to get out.

"Well, then you are very welcome, though shouting at me is hardly appropriate gratitude."

"Gratitude?" Amma squeezed the edge of the bed until her knuckles went white. "By all the gods of light, you're just the absolute worst, you know that?"

Damien scoffed, but looked like she had struck him. "Me? I'm offering to put down the cause of your suffering."

"You think this is all because of Kaz?" She gestured to herself and the wreck she knew she looked.

"That *is* what you said, though I am unsurprised to misunderstand," he grumbled.

"Me too," she grumbled back.

"And what, pray tell, does *that* mean?" Damien took a few steps toward her, arms still crossed tightly over his chest.

She mimicked him by crossing her own arms and glared up from her spot on the bed, her anger only intensifying. "I don't know, what do *you* think it means?"

He narrowed his eyes even more, stepping a bit closer, but this time she did not relent and shrink away. This time she was mad, and if she was going to die, she may as well stay that way. "You know," he finally said, a mocking bite to his voice, "you were much more pleasant when we first met."

And that was all she needed. Amma saw red, jumping to her feet and pushing up onto her toes to get right into the blood mage's face. "Oh, you mean before you promised to kill me? When I wasn't your prisoner? When you couldn't control everything I do? When I could at least cry if I wanted to?"

Damien snarled at her then threw up his hands. "Fine, be miserable and sob yourself to sleep. *Sanguinisui*, cry your heart out for all I care."

Without her permission, the tears spilled down her face again, and sobs racked Amma's whole body as arcana rippled through it. She pressed a hand to her chest, unable to contain the sounds she was suddenly making, an awful wailing that felt childish and overwhelming. Vision blurred, she doubled over and fell back onto the bed, hands coming up to her face to keen into. "Make it stop," she managed to sputter.

Uncaring, he clicked his tongue. "Isn't this what you wanted?"

"Da...mi...en!" she wailed between sobs.

"*Sanguinisui*, get a hold of yourself."

Amma took a breath, deep and full, blinking away the last of the tears as they instantly dried up. She grabbed the excess fabric of her absolutely ruined tunic and smashed it against her face to wipe off the worst of it, and then let out one final whimper as the muscles in her shoulders and back relaxed with a deep ache.

"I imagine you feel better now, yes?" Damien asked, sarcasm heavy in his voice.

She stared down at his boots still standing very close to her. She thought to snap back at him, to take all of his satisfaction away, force on a smile and tell him, yes, she felt wonderful now, but that would achieve nothing. Instead, she just gazed up at his face. "Please don't kill Kaz, Damien. Not because of me. He would do anything for you, he loves you, just try being nice to him for once."

The blood mage's jaw clenched and brow furrowed, but none of it was with anger. He shifted violet eyes away from her, standing there a long moment as he studied the opposing wall. "First of all, love is an entirely foreign concept to infernal creatures. We do not feel anything of the sort. And second of all, he would most certainly not do *anything* for me. He wouldn't even mind you for me, and that should have been quite simple, you being...you."

Amma knew there was something to be offended about in what he had just said, but she had instead been struck by the first thing he had so easily glazed over. "You don't feel love?" Amma's voice sounded far away as she asked the question, too strange a concept to be real. Of course even creatures from the infernal plane felt love— everyone did.

Damien turned up a lip, but did not answer her right away. Instead, he just looked at her as if she should have known. "I'm demon spawn," he eventually said as if thinking on it very hard. "Evil incarnate, the Abyss brought up...here. All of that."

"Sure, but, like,"—she sniffled and rolled her hands over one another as if trying to work through the idea aloud—"even evil creatures must feel love. I mean, you must at least love being evil, otherwise why do it?"

"Why do—Amma, this is my *purpose*. There is no desire pushing me toward some malleable end based on a whim as fleeting as *love*. There is only duty and prophecy and revenge."

She scrunched up her face. "Gods, that sounds—" Amma cut herself off, gaze shifting past him to look on the stone wall beyond. *Awful*, she was going to say, as if she could judge what he had just

104

told her from some moral throne above him. It did sound awful, to exist solely to fulfill one's duty with no love behind one's purpose, but wasn't that exactly what she had been doing before all of this too? "Oh," she finally said, pulling her eyes back to him again. "I'm sorry."

"Sorry?" Damien looked as if the word were ash on his tongue, but his voice had lost all of its ire, only bitterness left behind. "If I did not think it would essentially render you mute, I would use the talisman to strike that word from your vocabulary."

With that, he swept from the room and left Amma there alone.

CHAPTER 12
TO LOATHE, HINDER, AND OBEY

Anomalous Craven was good for a number of things, but he was especially good for arcane cast offs. Damien had been left alone in Anomalous's study most of the morning and into the afternoon to go through a massive stack of books the alchemist had been keeping around just for him. He threw out nothing at first glance, but it was quite easy to get him to let go of things he deemed useless once Damien said they were magic in nature.

"Full of mumbo jumbo, take them, or I'll make them kindling," the man had said with a toothy grin, then went off to prepare for the day's experiment to remove the talisman from Amma. "So many calibrations to make," he said with a waggle of his fluffy, ginger brows.

Kaz was being punished for his mischief with the impossible task of finding Damien a sprig of yarrow out in the swamp. Yarrow required full sun to bloom, and the persistent clouds in Tarfail Quag wouldn't allow for such a thing, so he would at least be gone for the day if he returned at all and didn't get gobbled up by something hungry for a creature that smelled of brimstone and likely tasted even worse. Kaz was probably a delicacy in these parts, and if he just happened to end up dead that wouldn't count as Damien killing him. Probably not anyway, but it was impossible to know what conclusion Amma would come to.

The woman was with Mudryth, and that was meant to take the thought of her out of Damien's mind. If the hag were watching her, she would hopefully not get herself absorbed by a sentient blob of what Damien decided couldn't be luxerna but was mighty close. Still, as Damien thumbed through an ancient-looking tome that should have been even more absorbing than that ooze, he wondered what Amma might be doing.

Probably complaining to Mudryth about how awful he was—the *absolute worst*, she had said, and she hadn't even made it sound like the compliment it should have been—and how he had made her cry even though she had *asked*. That would be just like her, wouldn't it? Leaving out a pivotal detail, just like how she'd been carrying around a silver blade while they ran from werewolves or failed to explain why in the Abyss she was so upset about potentially getting rid of Kaz. Her anger was particularly frustrating seeing as he'd diverged from his own path and brought her all the way out here to—well, no, she had no idea why he brought her to Anomalous, and it was going to have to stay that way.

Damien slammed the book shut with a huff. "Stop letting her get under your skin," he said, sitting back and wishing the talisman were embedded in him instead—that would make ordering himself around much easier. But as it stood, he could only chastise himself every time her woeful face popped back into his mind, specifically the one she'd made when apologizing for yet another thing that wasn't her fault. She'd looked at him like it were such a pity, but didn't she know? To not feel love was a gift!

He tossed the old book atop the discard stack with the others, all full of vague earth arcana or homeopathic healing herbs and, indeed, only good for burning. It made tremendous claims about summoning evils and enthralling victims, but was full of spells meant to rebuff those things—all of which Damien could have shielded against when he was a teen. The scribe claimed to be a mage blessed by some dark god or other, but clearly didn't know the first thing about evil.

The last book was a smaller one, only the size of his palm, filled with a slanted handwriting. This was what Anomalous had wanted to give him the day prior. The alchemist felt it was very special, but Damien was unsure. The first few pages read like a journal, and he nearly tossed it atop the pile as well, until he came upon an intriguing line where the author questioned the source of noxscura. There were few who even knew of the infernal arcana that fueled demons and blood mages, let alone questioned it.

Chaos, it read, *so it is said, but where is this Chaos? And what makes the noxscura inherently evil? Could a force of destruction be used for anything else? And what of luxerna then?*

"Oh, lordling Abyss-spawn, we're nearly ready!"

Damien sat up with a start at the odd, crackling sound of Anomalous's voice. It came from a grate set high into the wall of the study. The alchemist was doing magic regardless of what he insisted on calling it, and hopefully it was strong enough to put an end to the deviation Damien's fate had been subjected to. He tucked the book into his hip pouch and headed up the stairs to the laboratory.

Anomalous had rearranged things, one of his largest tubes of glass pulled forward from the wall. It sat empty atop a dais, its hinged front open, and strung all along it was a length of thin metal with stones wrapped up within at equal intervals. The metal ran away from the tube to the machinery on the wall full of levers and switches. It was very much not subtle.

Beside it, the oozy, yellow stuff that had been the cause of so much grief was ebbing gently in its own tube, a dark shadow floating in its center, curled up and almost human. That had not been there the night before, but the goop seemed to be mending the parts that had been absorbed into it.

"My equations," Anomalous said, shoving a roll of parchment into Damien's face.

There were numbers and symbols alongside his scribbling in Key. Damien politely took the pages and flipped through them. He recognized most of the words, Key was the simplest of the languages he knew, but the true meaning of the diagrams and equations eluded him. "This would be like me handing you a book in Chthonic," he said, squinting at a crude drawing of a humanoid figure in a tube and squiggly lines radiating off of it. "I imagine Mudryth would be a better assistant."

"Oh, she will be assisting me, I just want you to know that I've run the numbers three times, and the whole experiment has a very low probability of going wrong."

He went to hand the pages back, but paused. "Wrong?"

"For the girl." Anomalous waved around a shining tool with a large, clipper-like end. "I know that's top priority for you, keeping her alive, and chances are she almost definitely will stay that way!"

Damien cleared his throat, standing straighter and shoving the papers at him. "I did not specify the order of priority—"

"Ah, well,"—Anomalous snatched away the parchment, 'trading off his strange tool before Damien could refuse to take it—"you didn't really have to."

Before he could protest further, Mudryth announced her arrival with a bright greeting as she came up the stairs, a shorter form just behind her.

It was Amma, but Damien did not recognize her at first, her hair even more flaxen than he imagined it could be, clean and falling in waves over her shoulders—not that he had been imagining such a thing. Amma had looked like an urchin in the back alleys of Aszath Koth, and being covered in swamp grime had done her no favors, but she was much improved now. Her ratty, ill-fitting clothing had been swapped for tight, leather breeches it seemed Mudryth had sewn her right into. They would have to be cut off to escape, perhaps by that silver dagger no longer hidden, the thin straps of its holster just pressing into her thigh as it flexed with every step she took.

She was cinched in tight at the waist by a protective leather bodice, hugging how her body curved, and her new, white tunic didn't dwarf her at all like the last. It perhaps had gone in the other direction, low enough in front to expose where the talisman had disappeared itself into her chest, but managed to just contain everything so long as the lace tying up its front wasn't pulled, which, Damien thought, looked dangerously easy to do. It would only take a simple tug.

He averted his gaze from that detail as quickly as he struck the thought from his mind, which was at least two moments slower than it should have been, but he couldn't really fault himself—there were very few humans in Aszath Koth, and humans were Damien's preferred bedchamber companion, so when he saw one who had been cleaned up with their best assets on display, he was bound to find them even marginally attractive.

Her face was a good distraction from the body she'd been hiding as, for reasons unfathomable, it had gone very pink. She looked as she had in the alley of Aszath Koth and yet not—a woman, his own age yet unhardened and naive, but then he saw something else behind the first look of nervousness in her eyes. She was staring right back at him, reading him, *seeing* him.

Anomalous bustled up to Amma then, ignoring how changed she was, and threw a huge, dwarfing arm around her shoulders to lead her deeper into the lab. He was saying something about metals and stones and conductivity as he gestured to the tube, but Damien refocused on the odd tool he'd been handed. There was no good damn way to hold the bloody thing, awkward as it was, but he'd been inexplicably hugging it to his chest. He had to have looked like an idiot holding the thing, and stashed it on the closest shelf.

"Wait, why do I need to get in the glass cage?" Amma's voice wasn't like how it had been the night before, neither the angry, strangled tone when she yelled nor the sad yet sweet lilt when she made another unnecessary apology. There was apprehension in it now, a taut quiver, but it had a friendliness to it too—that same voice some of the draekins and other servants at the keep used with Damien when asking something of him and fearing his response. He didn't like it.

Anomalous stuttered a moment. "Data! What is an alchemist without his data? You see, I extract a bit of information from every being who enters the tower, and now it's your turn!" Anomalous gave her shoulder a squeeze, eyeing Damien with a not-so-subtle wink. "It will only hurt a little."

Amma was struck still by the space between Anomalous's fingers when he held his hand up, likely meant to demonstrate something small, but with his huge hands it looked to be he was suggesting the interior of the tube was going to be extremely painful. She wasn't going to move without more coaxing, and Damien didn't want things to dissolve in that way.

"*Sanguinisui*, step into the tube," Damien said with a hefty sigh, and Amma strode right up onto the dais and into the glass container.

Anomalous looked after her. "Well, that was useful. Any chance you could engineer me one of those talismans?"

"It's one of a kind. And also magic, Anomalous."

"Sure it is," he said, swinging the door shut behind her. The click of its latch made Amma's form twitch, and she turned to look at them through the glass, the rosy color draining out of her cheeks. An uncomfortable feeling swam in Damien's stomach, and he would have realized it was guilt if he were more familiar with the sensation.

Anomalous skipped to the machinery the tube's wires were attached to. With a giddy giggle, he began flicking switches and knobs, only pulling out the parchment he'd shown Damien once to double check something, reset a few dials, and then dropped the pages. He turned to Mudryth. "You did the thing, right?"

She blinked at him slowly. "No, Louie, I just let you load the little human up into your contraption all defenseless-like."

Anomalous's brows raised all the way up to his ginger hairline. "I almost threw this switch! She would have been—oh, oh! Muddie, I see what you are saying. Very funny." He then smashed a lever upward with a resounding clang.

A blast of light like a divine spell filled up the chamber, and heat poured away from the tube. Damien shielded his eyes as Mudryth oohed and ahhed at the spectacle. When the brightness died down, Damien was sure the girl had been burnt to ash, but to his surprise—though he was unsure if it was a relief or an annoyance—she was intact, if glowing.

Mudryth crossed right up to the tube, handing Anomalous a pair of spectacles that he donned, making his eyeballs massive. Both pulled out parchment and scribbled down notes as they chatted to one another, but Damien held back. Amma's body had been illuminated so that her insides were on display. Damien had gutted enough beings to know the colors weren't right, but those were surely bones and organs exhibited in green and yellow and red. And just offset from the center of Amma's chest was a point that had an even brighter glow, a radiating light clearly arcane that had to be the talisman. How it could emanate such a light, he had no idea—nothing he made ever looked like that.

Anomalous gave the glass tube a tap with the hardened reed he used to scratch out notes. Amma didn't respond, her body, lit up in all the strange colors, unmoving.

Damien ventured a single step closer. "She can't hear us?"

"She's completely out," Mudryth said in a dreamy tone as she placed long, spindly fingers flat on the tube. "I put a fancy, little spell on her that Louie's metal gizmo triggers so she won't remember being in there. It ain't fun inside, I tell you what. But boy, that's a pretty glow, eh?"

Damien hummed in the back of his throat a sort of agreement.

Anomalous was rounding the tube, muttering to himself and scribbling. He poked his head around the edge of it, magnified eyes blinking behind the lenses. "That's a good job you did there, demon spawn. Couldn't have augmented her better myself, I don't think. It's like you grafted that right onto her heart—look, all those capillaries are connected."

Damien hesitated. Closer seemed dangerous, though he wasn't sure how. Anomalous's experiments were sometimes messy, but that wasn't it. Damien wasn't truly afraid of anything, though, and once he reminded himself of that, he strode up to where Amma was suspended on the other side of the glass.

The talisman was nestled under her ribs, shining brightly with a spiderweb of tiny veins running all around it as if holding it in a net. It thumped gently along with the beat of her heart, completely enmeshed.

"Death would do the trick," Anomalous announced, "but if we want to avoid that, and I attempt to cut this out—which I am willing to do, mind you—I would probably have to take the heart out along with it. I have some acceptable replacements in the function department." Anomalous gestured to a bin of organs that was frosted over. "But there might be a problem personality-wise."

Damien watched the talisman pulse, the rhythm so like the one in his own chest, beating harder the longer he looked. "What does that mean?"

"I've been finding that the squishy parts on the inside can really take a toll on how the outside acts, if not how it looks. Pieces seem to keep a little bit of their former owners. Sometimes it's a real problem."

Mudryth pursed her lips. "Made a man last moon who got up off the table and went right out to roll in the mud. Turns out it doesn't matter if hog parts are the same size as people ones, they don't always work so good."

"Didn't matter in the long run," Anomalous sighed, "he decayed in less than an hour like all the rest of them."

Damien paused for a moment, just long enough to acknowledge that was a tragedy. "So, you're saying all of your machinery and tools can't get Bloodthorne's Talisman of Enthrallment out of her without taking the parts she already has along with it?"

"Well, no, the scalpel will do it!" Anomalous produced a blade with a metallic gleam, tiny in his huge hand. "I could cut in and try to remove it while leaving the heart inside. Chances of death shoot up maybe thirty-seven and a half percent, but higher risk for a higher reward! I'd need to make an incision here and here and probably here." He poked at the tube with the sharpened tool, and with each tap on the glass, Damien winced a little more.

"No," he finally said, louder than he meant, and Anomalous looked back at him, eyes huge behind the magnifying lenses he wore. "No, Anomalous, I can't ask you to take on the burden of that risk."

"It would be no trouble." Anomalous loomed before him, holding up the scalpel as his light eyes twinkled behind the lenses. "And I've lost plenty of patients, I've learned not to get attached, so if she doesn't make it—"

There was a darkness that enveloped Anomalous's hand and plucked the scalpel away before letting the tool clatter to the floor at their feet.

"Ah, ha, right—guess maybe I don't have a steady enough hand for that right now, so *no* it is then." Anomalous chuckled lightly.

Damien blinked down at the tool and then picked it up, the noxscura faintly lingering on it before it totally dissipated. He hadn't even felt the arcana as it acted on its own again. He mumbled out an apology, laying the knife on a nearby table instead of giving it back to the alchemist, just in case, and Anomalous returned to the tube to take down a few more notes for his anatomy research.

With Anomalous and Mudryth engaged but no longer a threat,

Damien took a step back. Wanting a distraction, he went to pull the small journal he'd taken from the study from his hip pouch, but with it came a scrap of fabric. Damien turned over the handkerchief, a smear of dried blood across the embroidery in its center of a tree, its branches and roots entwined, coming around the trunk to form a circle. It was just another thing the woman nicked on her journey across the realm, he could only assume, for its high quality, yet it was something she'd selflessly given up, wrapping it around his hand when she thought he needed it.

"All right, she might be a little woozy," said Anomalous, pulling off the magnifying glasses and setting down his roll of parchment.

Damien stuffed the fabric back into his pouch and stepped up to the tube. As Anomalous bustled back to the machine and flipped the assortment of dials and levers, the lights inside the tube died, and the room returned to its blue glow. Mudryth clicked open the door, and Amma's pale form took a wobbly step forward.

Releasing a relieved breath, Damien ran a hand over his face. Amma took another step toward him, and then the third took her right off the platform as her eyelids fell down. Damien caught her as she collapsed forward, completely lax in his arms. Like a doll, her limbs were heavy, and her head slumped back. There was a jolt in his chest as he called for the alchemist.

Anomalous reached a big hand over Damien's shoulder and pulled open one of her eyelids. The blue iris roved up at them, and she mumbled something incomprehensible. "Just dazed, like I predicted," he said then bustled back to his notes.

Damien tried to set her on her feet, but she was like jelly in his hands. No longer radiating that intense glow, the talisman wasn't visible anymore, though her breasts were doing a good job of shielding where it would be anyway, pressed between the two of them and upward in her new, much lower-cut tunic. He shifted his arms and gave her a shake, but she only responded with a dreamy sort of moan, a noise he really preferred she not make when leaning against him so fully.

She was small enough to shift around, and he managed to scoop an arm under her knees and lift her into both arms. Amma turned her head inward and nestled her shoulder against his, a hand finding its way to his chest.

Damien nearly dropped her. He had been prepared for her to wake at the jostling, see his face so close and scream, flail and struggle to get away, but instead she'd once again utterly baffled him and—what was this? *Snuggling*? His stomach turned over. "What do I do with this?" he asked the room.

"She needs to sleep. Best just put her to bed."

Damien looked helplessly at the two who were still quite involved in discussing theories, the dreadful realization dawning that it was up to him.

He carried her to the room she was meant to be kept in, and she remained asleep even over the blustery walkway, only settling in a little deeper against his chest. She mumbled something, fingers tightening on his tunic, but he couldn't recoil from it, only wince and scowl. How dare she make him do this? He was meant to be marching on the realm's capital to bring about its ruin, not coddling some stranger and especially not feeling so flustered about doing it.

But he didn't just dump her onto the bed and leave her there, though he'd been envisioning doing just that the whole walk. "You are an incredible pain in the ass," he grumbled, setting her down gently.

Amma mumbled just as Damien turned to leave, something that sounded much too much like, "Wait until we're married."

He froze, looking back at her. "What was that?"

But she hadn't really spoken to him, still very clearly asleep. Amma's head lolled to the side, eyes closed but her brow pinched, and she groaned, twitching.

"Oh, of course." Damien blew out a breath, recognizing a nightmare when he saw one. Likely, he thought, because she had subconsciously perceived it had been his arms around her, and his dastardly presence had invaded her dream.

He waited a moment for her to settle, but instead things got worse. "No," she pleaded sleepily, "don't."

Damien took a quick glance around the chamber, but it was indeed empty save for the two. He clicked his tongue and leaned close to her ear, muttering out quickly, "*Sanguinisui*, forget this dream and sleep peacefully until morning."

When her body relaxed, and she fell quiet, he promptly left the chamber.

Up in his own room, Damien paced its length many times until he finally pulled the shielding satchel from his pocket and slipped out the shard of occlusion crystal. He was only a few days into his journey and already things had gone to shit. Trapped in the crystal, his father had no way of knowing, and it would be easy, perhaps even preferable, to keep him in the dark.

He hesitated and then sliced his thumb on the crystal's sharpest edge. Mumbling Chthonic, he called up infernal arcana into the shard, and an eye blinked to life under the surface.

"Kiddo!" Zagadoth's voice boomed louder than he was expecting.

"Father," he said through grit teeth after starting, "apologies, it has been days."

"Oh, ya know, time's a little weird in here. What are ya, like, halfway to Eirengaard by now?"

Damien raised his brows at the shard then looked out the window across the marshy scape of Tarfail Quag. "Not exactly."

"Master Bloodthorne!" Kaz's weathered voice exploded into the room from the doorway as the imp shuffled in, half flying with every other step, then landing and trying to run, get up the speed, and fly once again. In his grubby, little claw, he was holding a cluster of tiny, pink flowers sprouting off a long stem. He offered the sprig up as he landed at Damien's feet. "All I could find, Master."

"Is that an imp?" Zagadoth's pupil roved down to the corner of the crystal.

"It's Kaz, actually," said Damien, thankful for the distraction. "Reborn, a gift from The Brotherhood."

Kaz took a huge breath, bulbous, black eyes growing even wider. There was a tear in one of his ears, a scratch down his side, and he was limping when he took a step, but he froze under the red gaze of the crystal, then fell into complete supplication. The imp flattened himself to the ground, arms outstretched, the sprig still tight in a fist. "My Lord! Great Tyrant of the Abyss! Sitter of the Sanguine Throne! Overlord of all that is Infernal!"

"So, it is an imp," Zagadoth chuckled deep in his throat. "How are the old shaved-tops, eh?"

"Oh, you know, zealous, infatuated…bald." Damien reached down and plucked away the sprig as Kaz remained prostrate. He half expected it to be an illusion, but the herb felt real enough, and the smell confirmed it was yarrow as he'd requested.

"So, Champ, you must have something to tell me then. Defeated any Holy Knights? Caused a little chaos? Decapitated someone worth bragging about?"

Damien swallowed, tossing the yarrow onto the bed. "There has been some chaos, yes."

"Fabulous!" The eye squinted with a grin hidden in the other realm.

Kaz deigned to lift his head, and when he saw the crystal was no longer pointed at him, he pushed up onto hands and knees to watch Damien.

"The chaos, though," Damien began with a thoughtful breath, "is a little less...traditional."

"Even better!" Zagadoth's deep rumble couldn't be more pleased. "You're an innovator, kiddo."

"No, Dad, it's..." Damien rubbed his temple, squeezing his eyes shut, trying to figure out how to explain. "It's not good."

"Well, it's not supposed to be," said Zagadoth, "and do you think you can slow down? You're giving me the dizzies."

Damien pulled the shard away from his temple. "Right, sorry. What I mean is, I've run into a little hitch. It's a minor complication, a thing I could probably crush it's so small and fragile and...blonde, but the point is, I believe it will delay my plans."

At that, Kaz's eyes sharpened, and he pushed back up onto his feet. Damien spun away from him and stalked to the open window.

"Well, I didn't expect this trip to be all wasps and weeds, Kiddo, I know there will be hangups. Maybe I can help, brainstorm some ideas to fix things up?"

"No!" Damien put on a crooked smile. "I know how to fix it, the problem is just setting me back a little, and I..." He squinted over his shoulder. Kaz looked unhappy, remaining in his spot, arms crossed, but he almost always looked like that. Back to the window and the marshy waters outside, Damien took a breath of damp air. Why had he called? "I just wanted you to...to know."

The crystal took a moment to speak again, but Damien could practically hear his father thinking. It had been like this for almost as long as he could remember, the demon trapped behind a tiny wall of gemstone, easy to avoid when Damien felt less than or knew he had fucked up, yet something always compelled him to face the eye in the crystal and his own mistakes. "Son, have I told you the story of Valgormoth the Blind Fury?"

Damien's shoulders slumped. "Yes, you—"

"Valgormoth the Blind Fury was your great, great grandmother, a nigh invincible demon who ruled the realm in the age of beasts, thousands of years ago, before The Expulsion. She lorded over the frozen things, the frigid beings, the white dragons and frost giants and those chubby, little cats with all the fur and the really long teeth, you know, what're they called?"

"Jolakaturin."

"The jolakaturin, yes! Too bad they're extinct, you would have loved them. Anyway, all those creatures bowed to her whim. But there was a challenger to the Sanguine Throne. *Irromach*."

Damien mouthed the name along with his father, resting an elbow on the window ledge and his chin in his hand. It was difficult to imagine the soggy marsh outside covered in ice, but over thousands and thousands of years and twisting arcana and the rise of humans, the world was bound to change. It was not difficult, however, to imagine his great, great grandmother having a hated rival—Damien knew that all too well.

"Irromach believed he was the rightful heir to the Sanguine Throne. He declared war on earth, and he nearly defeated Valgormoth."

"But great, great grandmother was stronger, wiser, better learned and practiced, and, most importantly, the truer evil and rightful heir," Damien said, repeating what he had been told many times. The words were ingrained in him, difficult to echo without sounding totally put-upon, but they were only stories.

Zagadoth's rumble of a voice quieted. "That is all true, and she may have taken down Irromach herself, but Valgormoth did not defeat him and his armies alone." Typically, his father would laugh when Damien repeated things back to him, but this time he said something new. "I wish I could be there with you, kiddo, though I guess you wouldn't be doing this if I could. I just hate seeing you insist on struggling alone. If I've taught you anything, it is to not scorn those who are useful and loyal. Call in the loyalty of those you know and use them."

Damien stared out a moment longer at the marsh. Down on a mound of roots jutting up from the bog, a white bird had its wings outstretched. He blinked and squinted, but it was only a crane, not a dove like he had momentarily thought. Why would it be? That would be ridiculous.

He nodded, his gaze shifting back to the eye on the crystal. "You're right, Father. As always."

Zagadoth laughed heavily. "I never get tired of hearing that! Now, get some sleep, and don't waste all the power left in this crystal on me telling ya the same ole boring stories about your ancestors, all right?"

"Sure, Dad," said Damien, and he swiped over the crystal again, darkening the eye until Zagadoth's essence was locked back away inside.

Then, before he could think long on it, Damien pulled out his dagger, rolled up a sleeve, and cut a small slice into his forearm. He let the blood drip onto the sill and whistled sharply into the marshy air. The clouds above darkened, and a black speck fluttered out of them, diving down and coming to land just before him on the sill.

"Corben." Damien nodded to the raven who bowed back. When he muttered in Chthonic to the bird, its eyes shimmered violet and then he ran his hand through the feathers on the creature's back. When the message was conveyed, the raven took off again, disappearing into the clouded distance.

Kaz was still there when Damien turned around, the imp's eyes a little shrewder than when they'd been filled with awe at seeing the demon lord in the crystal.

"To bed," Damien demanded, pointing sharply away from him, and the imp scurried to the corner of the room. When Damien went to get into his bed, he saw the sprig of yarrow, no idea what to do with it. "Kaz?"

The imp whimpered from the corner.

"You've done an acceptable job fetching this today."

There was a long silence, and then a gurgly, delighted squeal from the imp. Damien rolled his eyes and turned over, determined to actually get some sleep.

CHAPTER 13
HOW TO FORCE COMPANIONSHIP AND MANIPULATE EVIL

Amma could not remember falling asleep the night before. In fact, she couldn't remember much at all from the previous day after bathing and being given new clothes.

It was probably for the best, the not remembering, because even if something awful had happened, she was still alive, and despite losing her temper with Damien in such an embarrassing way, he wasn't in nearly as grumpy a mood as she expected. Still grumpy, yes, just not *as* grumpy.

Kaz was also still alive, but sourer than ever, especially after Damien had announced they would be taking the "long way" to Eirengaard when they left Anomalous and Mudryth that morning.

"Master Bloodthorne," Kaz had cried out in his pinched, gurgly whine, "that is not what was planned!"

"Well, Master Bloodthorne has changed his mind," Damien had responded drolly. "Now, shut it."

After, the imp took to riding on the tail end of Damien's knoggelvi, glaring at the mage's back.

This was great news to Amma—the longer it took to get to Eirengaard, the longer she had to figure out how she might survive—and even though Kaz was absolutely miserable, he hadn't gone out of his way to antagonize her since he'd gotten the news, so it was twice the triumph.

But Amma was vexed with something else in the imp's stead: a vivid dream of being held in Damien's arms and carried off somewhere. Why she would dream such a thing and have it not end with being pitched off of a high tower was beyond her, especially since she'd yelled at him that she thought he was *the worst*, but instead of the dream culminating in her death, the ghosting of his fingers on her skin and the warmth of pressing into his chest just sort of dissolved into fuzzy sleep which, she supposed, was better than...*escalating*. Still, every time the dream slithered itself back into the forefront of her mind—and it did that morning, frequently—she had to focus on finding patterns in the clouds or in the knoggelvi's dark hide to avoid looking at Damien directly and giving herself either an attack of shivers, flushed skin, or, worse, both at once.

The swamp thinned as the day pulled on into afternoon, the ground hardening, the trees shifting from mangroves to pines. The smell improved as well, and like the short moment in the sun outside of Aszath Koth, Amma found her own mood lightening.

Her new garments helped, a much better fit, tighter and more practical for moving quickly, if not for being misidentified as a boy—that had been useful before, though it mattered a little less when she was traveling with someone so openly homicidal toward anyone who dared touch her.

Amma took a deep breath of piney air and worked up the courage to look at Damien again.

He wasn't scowling, for once, and that certainly helped. Astride his knoggelvi and donning clean, leather armor once more, Damien did not look as fearsome as when he had been irate with her in the tower or even when she first saw him in the alley of Aszath Koth. He held a small book open against the neck of his mount, reading, and then glanced up every so often to stare out at the way ahead. He was too lost in thought to look over at her, but if he had, the heat in her face would be easy enough to explain away with the warmth of the day.

It may have been the sunshine breaking through the pines or the softness to his features as he thought, but when Amma looked at him then, she didn't see any hint of infernal anything, even with those eyes that were strikingly violet in the light.

And after seeing him with the alchemist and the hag, she knew he was capable of being quite different. Dare she think even warm? Amma twisted up her lips—no, that may have been a thought too far, but Mudryth had spoken of him fondly, and Anomalous clearly adored him, so she reasoned Damien was capable of baseline amicability, and that was accessible to Amma, it just *had* to be, especially if she wanted to live. Not to mention, she was really getting tired of being cranky and mad all the time.

"What a nice day."

Damien did not look up from his book.

"I'm so glad I don't stink anymore." Amma stretched her arms over her head. "I'm not used to smelling like that."

This made his eyes flick up, if not at her, but then right back down.

"I didn't even know I *could* smell so bad, actually."

He turned a page. "Impressive bathhouse at the thieves' guild, is there?"

Amma sucked in a quiet breath. No, there probably wasn't, not that she would know. "Oh, I've had to rough it a lot, of course, I just mean that was really bad. Reminded me of a time I fell off a horse into a pile of manure, which I guess was sort of lucky because it's a long way down off a horse's back, but I couldn't get the smell out of my hair for weeks. My mother was so angry, maybe the angriest I've ever seen her because I was supposed to meet—" Amma cut herself off, and that was what actually interested Damien, of course. He looked over, a thin, dark brow rising. She swallowed. "Someone sort of important. I can't really remember who. Anyway, what are you reading?"

Damien's intense stare brought all the color back into her face, betraying her attempt to will it away. "A book," he finally said, and turned back down to it.

She leaned toward him over the gap between the knoggelvi. "What kind of book?"

"An interesting one," he said, completely disinterestedly.

"I mean, what's it about?"

His brow furrowed. "Things."

"Like, is there some treasure to be found or a curse to be broken or—"

"Nothing like that."

"Oh, okay, then…" She gave him a few moments to elaborate, wind whistling overhead in the spruces. He didn't. "So, is it about interesting *people*? Maybe a chosen one or a prince or—oh! Is it a love story? It's a love story, isn't it?"

"No," he scoffed, finally looking away from the pages to glare at her. She wasn't surprised, but she was amused by his irritated reaction. "This isn't fiction, this is research. Research you're interrupting."

"That doesn't sound interesting," she said, a challenge she hoped he would take up.

"I assure you, it is." He turned another page.

"I don't possibly see how without any dragons or sword fights

121

and *especially* without any romance."

"These pages are full of the arcane," he said, shaking the book. "And just because it doesn't feature two idiots who trick themselves into believing the other cares for them just so they can see one another naked, doesn't make it any less interesting."

"Okay, that's not what happens in a love story—well, that's not *all* that happens—but if you insist that book is interesting, maybe you could read it out loud?"

"Why would I do that?"

She threw her hands up and rocked her head back. "Because I'm bored!"

"I'm not here to entertain you," he growled, "and you wouldn't understand it anyway."

Amma gasped and then pouted. "Just because I like stories that end happily doesn't mean I'm stupid, Damien."

"I know you're not stupid," he grumbled back. "If you were, things would be immensely easier for me, but you are unfortunately *very* difficult. I simply mean you aren't a mage. Unless you're lying to me about that too?" At this, Damien finally closed the book and gave her his full attention.

Stuck under his waiting gaze, she drummed her fingers on the back of the knoggelvi and tipped her head, playing at being, as he would put it, easy. "What, uh…what do you mean?"

He only smirked, waiting on her to elaborate which she struggled to not oblige. She squeezed her lips together and managed to not fill the uneasy silence with more blathering. "I am not stupid either," he finally said and opened the book again. "And you talk in your sleep."

There was a hitch in Amma's chest—what had she said? From his self-satisfied smirk, she feared it might have been about the dream, thoughts of being wrapped in his arms again making her face bloom bright red, but as mortifying as that would be, it might be heaps better than accidentally divulging anything about herself.

Then again, if Damien really believed she were lying about something, he could order her at any time to tell him the truth of things—he had almost done exactly that in the Sanctum when she first absorbed his stupid talisman. Thankfully, what she'd said was specific to the moment, compelled to spill out of her against her will: she was only there to steal the scroll. If he were concerned about something, or even just curious, he could use that awful magic word and force her to tell him just about anything.

But he was already back to reading his oh-so-interesting book that didn't even have a title for her to peek at. Amma calmed the beating of her heart, looking for a distraction, and there was Kaz. The imp had done nothing but glare at the back of Damien since he found out their path to Eirengaard had been subject to yet another detour, but he might be willing to chat.

When she said his name, the imp's head twitched toward her in a horrifying way. Amma laughed nervously. "How are you?"

The imp bared all of his teeth, the crooked ones especially daunting in the sunlight.

"Thought so," she said, eyeing his ear and how it looked beaten up. "Didn't sleep well, hmm? Have a rough night?"

"I do not sleep," the imp growled back. "Not like you anyway, human."

Human. Well, that was better than *trollop*, she supposed. Amma pitched her voice higher, like she were speaking to a small child. "You don't ever get tired?"

Kaz grumbled something indiscernible, scrunching up his horrid face so his nostrils flared.

"Well, you sure act like you need a nap," she lilted. "So, what do you do while everyone else is asleep then?"

"Serve my master," he spat out.

Amma's eyes flicked to Damien, and she frowned.

He twitched as if feeling her look of disapproval, but he kept his long nose pointed down at the book. "He is not forced to remain awake out of cruelty; imps do not require sleep in the way you or I do. But Kaz should have rested last night as he was quite busy the day before. He had the opportunity to do so at least." Then he grunted. "And rest was certainly deserved after the impressive feat he completed at my request."

Kaz's terrible face changed then, eyes going watery, toothy mouth falling open, and ears perking up. His tail even unraveled from around his haunches and gave a little wag.

Amma grinned at him. "Good job, Kaz!"

The imp crumpled back into a sneer. "I do not require your praise."

"Well, you have it anyway." Amma continued to smile at him, and he only bared pointed teeth back, but he didn't call her something nasty or suggest she was only good for serving one or two base needs, so she considered it an improvement. "So, what else makes being an imp different?"

Kaz grunted, but his face seemed to say he didn't know what she meant.

"You can fly," she offered. "What's that like?"

123

"Terrifying." He shook his head, scrunching up his nose. "But it allows me to attack silently from above."

"That's true," she said, remembering. "You have some magic too, right? I bet that's fun."

The imp was glaring at her sidelong, but his arms uncrossed. "Minor infernal powers, yes. I can…I can do this." His tail flicked up, and the tip of it burst into a small, orange flame.

"Oh, wow!"

Kaz snickered, flicking the fire around so that he drew a circle in the air, then it went out with a single curl of smoke. "Beyond that, my powers are limited to what my master allows and requests."

"Geez." Amma tried to give him a pitiful look. "Is that why you couldn't protect yourself in the swamp? Because Damien wouldn't let you?"

"No!" Kaz shouted even as Damien opened his mouth. "Banishment and summoning strip an imp's powers, and they take time to restore."

She bit her lip, eyes shifting to Damien who was grinding his jaw. "Well, I still think he should have—"

"*The suggestion that arcana is wholly divine or wholly infernal is a fallacy. The existence of purely neutral arcana is proof enough of this*," Damien droned into the forest, voice heavy and put-upon as he turned a page in his book. "*For instance, in my work with the wise Maribel of the earth mages, we narrowed down the source of her powers to neither the Abyss nor Empyrea nor even the earth itself.*"

"Is that someone's journal?" Amma gasped. "It must be full of juicy details!"

"*Further research will need to be done to decipher the true source, if it ever can be.*"

"Eventually."

Damien continued to read aloud as they went on, putting a stop to Amma's attempted befriending of the imp, and proving her absolutely wrong: there weren't even any slightly-moist details on those pages let alone juicy ones. He kept right on reading until it got too dark to see, and they finally stopped for the night. The day on the road had been tiring, and after Damien ordered Amma to stay put as usual with that terrible arcane word, she soon found herself asleep, dreaming of a theology classroom she couldn't escape only to wake early, begin riding again, and for him to pick up right where he left off.

Finally, after reciting pages of ingredients and the uneventful reactions when mixed together in increasingly specific measurements, Amma reached her limit. "Damien, do you think you could take a little break?"

"Take a break? But I'm doing exactly as you requested." Bewildered, Damien gestured with the book, the first exciting thing that had happened with it yet.

"Well, maybe you could skip ahead."

Even Kaz made a small noise of agreement at that.

"To what, pray tell?"

"I don't know, something a little spicier? Local gossip, a run-in with an enemy? Maybe the author had a lover? You can't tell me there are no entries about at least *one* passionate night with that Maribel lady."

Damien grunted, flipping back through the pages with his brow narrowed. "I skipped that bit actually."

"What? Why would you do that?"

"Because the language is bloody, fucking vulgar. I mean, *I* don't even use *that* word." His eyes widened at the lines, then he clicked his tongue. "Look, you requested I read aloud, so I am reading aloud."

"Selectively," she said with a pout.

"I refuse to alter my actions further at your whim." He frowned down at the pages then, clamping his mouth shut.

"Oh, Damien, I just wanted you to talk to me," she admitted, knowing how pitiful she sounded. "You know, have a conversation?"

Damien pursed his lips, flipped another page, and then closed the book. "Fine. Converse."

"Oh!" She sat up straight. Of course, now her mind went blank— she never really expected to get so far. "What's um…your favorite color?" The question had come out as unsure as it possibly could, and she felt stupid for even having thought of it, much less asking it. She was twenty-five for goodness's sake, not eight, but she also knew it would be best to begin shallowly.

"My favorite color?"

Amma cringed at herself—too shallow, maybe—but doubled down. "I mean, if we're going to be stuck together for a while, we may as well get to know each other, right?"

"You want to get to know the man who's going to end your life?"

Amma's insides twisted—that was quite a bit deeper. "Sure, why not? What's your favorite color?"

He glanced down at himself, a solid shadow atop the knoggelvi, then back up. "Black."

"Right. Okay…" Amma breathed in and looked up at the trees, a red-winged bird flitting by and disappearing amongst the green. "What's your favorite animal?"

He scrunched up his nose then shrugged. "Raven."

"Food?" she asked quicker, feeling like it were a game.

"Meat."

"Moon?"

"Uh, Ero, I guess?"

"Hobby?"

"Spilling the blood of my enemies."

At that Amma clicked her tongue. "And I suppose your lifelong goal is realm domination or something?"

Damien tipped his head to the side. "Actually, yes."

"Whoa." She laughed. "How do you even...I mean, what makes you think you can control the entire realm?"

"I can control you, can't I?"

Amma gnawed on her bottom lip, making a noncommittal noise in the back of her throat.

"*Sanguinisui*, agree."

A tingle ran up the back of Amma's neck, compelling her head to nod, then she sat very straight and groused, "I'm just one person, hardly the whole realm. Why would you even *want* to have power over so many people? Doesn't it seem exhausting?"

"Why does anyone want to do anything?" Damien shrugged at the path ahead. "It is simply what I am meant to do."

"Oh, right, there's some prophecy you're following that you still haven't really told me about." She looked at him, brows raised, and he said nothing. "And I suppose it was some, what, blood seer in Aszath Koth that gave it to you?"

"It was the Denonfy Oracle, of course: blood seers aren't a thing."

Amma blinked, recognizing the name. "You've been to the Denonfy Oracle?"

"When I was about fifteen, yes." He shrugged again as if it were nothing.

The Denonfy Oracle couldn't be visited by just anyone. There were others who claimed to have the power of divination, but only one was blessed by the god of fortune and destiny, Denonfy, and there had yet to be anyone who claimed their visions untrue. But Denonfy was a god who had not been cast into the Abyss, and it was said the oracle only showed themselves to the worthy. Amma didn't know evil beings could be worthy, not that she was about to say something like that to Sir Self-Important. "What did you ask them? How many questions did you get? What's an oracle even *like* in person?"

Damien thought a moment. "My destiny, just one, and...strange."

"Well, that's only a little different than when I was fifteen." She laughed. "My friend Laurel and I would stay up late and talk about what we would ask the Denonfy Oracle, not that we could go traversing across the realm and hike Ashrein Ridge to find them like you, apparently. We almost always agreed discovering who we were going to marry was of the utmost importance, though I realize now that might be a huge waste of the oracle's time." Amma's wistful smile at thinking of Laurel fell away—now, she wouldn't want the answer to that question at all.

Damien snorted. "Honestly, they probably would be delighted for such frivolous conversation. I imagine answering *what is my fate* gets tiresome very quickly despite how many fathers insist their sons ask it."

Amma's interest pricked right back up at that. "Your father sent you to the oracle?"

He hesitated. "In a way."

"What *are* your parents like?"

At this Damien's jaw hardened. Uh oh, too deep. She wanted to take the question back, but before she could stammer for something else, he cut in, "What are *your* parents like?"

Hands on the knoggelvi's reins, Amma tightened her fists, chest filling up suddenly at the thought of them. "My mother is talented and charming and sort of perfect. And my father is warm and respected but he's always making jokes and laughing and, of course, telling my mother how much he loves her." She chuckled, seeing the two in her mind, arm-in-arm, strolling through the orchard.

Damien made a thoughtful noise in the back of his throat. "Interesting. I would have guessed they were awful to you. Or dead. Maybe both."

Amma's heart dropped to the bottom of her stomach, an imagined vision of the two with throats cut swimming through her mind for the hundredth time—a fear she was working hard to assuage. "Why?"

"You were wandering the streets of Aszath Koth all alone—most humans who do that have been quite unfortunate and typically orphaned. Even grown women can rely on their parents if they are truly as wonderful as you claim yours to be. And then there's your behavior." He scrunched his nose like the coming words were offensive to his senses. "You're quite docile considering your current situation, and you apologize at the slightest inconvenience like a beaten pet, so I can only assume someone has been quite cruel to you."

Amma's mouth fell open. She wasn't *docile*, she was *polite*, for goodness's sake, and hadn't she just yelled at him but a few days ago? She had *never* yelled at anyone like that. "That's not...I don't...you know, that's none of your business, and I asked you first anyway."

"And I prefer not to answer."

Damien opened his book again. She was thankful he had dropped the whole thing, not liking the thoughts it inspired. Damien didn't really know anything about her, but she did know one thing about him for certain. One thing that he didn't let her forget: one of his parents was a demon, and that meant *they* had to be awful.

She ventured a peek at him, his brow knit all over again in irritation that was significantly less amusing than the first time she'd purposefully annoyed him. "I'm sorry I asked," she said with as much care as she could muster.

"Do not—" Damien's voice raised, but then he cut himself off. Eyes flicking skyward, he took a breath and blew it out. "It is fine. Now, have you had your fill of conversing, so that I may go back to my research?"

She knew the question wasn't sincere—he would do his best to ignore her regardless, but at least he was feigning politeness, so she nodded and feigned giving him permission. "For now, I suppose."

As she found another lock of the knoggelvi's mane to detangle, she caught him giving her a look from the corner of her eye. There was irritation in it still, certainly, but his mouth was upturned, and not with the cavalier smirk he typically gave her. This was more like amusement, and even at her expense, she'd take it.

CHAPTER 14
KAREE ON, MAYK MARY, ADOOR TROOLY

The sun was hanging low in a cloudy sky by the time the pines gave way to flatter farmland. Damien eyed a low, stone fence, the first they'd seen cutting across the landscape, and then scanned the horizon where a hovel of a hut sat alone. Humans.

"We're probably going to run into some people up ahead." Amma's voice was quiet and careful, yet it always startled him just a little. "And I really doubt they'll have ever seen a knoggelvi or an imp before."

Damien gave her a look, wondering for a moment if he had said what he'd been thinking aloud, and then tugged on his reins and dismounted. The air was thicker as a threatening breeze blew across the fields on either side of the road. It wouldn't do to stop here, the cloaks The Brotherhood had given them would help but wouldn't keep them from getting soaked in the downpour that was coming, and so he walked to the side of the road where he could look back and appraise the rest of them. Amma sat atop her knoggelvi, a strange, bright patch of blonde and misplaced cheeriness amongst the gloom that settled persistently around their mounts and the ugliness that was Kaz.

"Come here," he commanded, gesturing to her.

She grumbled something about the difference between asking and telling as she scrambled down the side of the animal. He grinned at how she landed with little aplomb and then wiped the look off his face when she turned. Amma was hesitant to stand before him, though he had no idea why: she simply needed to be out of the way.

Damien turned his eyes to the knoggelvi. "Horses," he said, and immediately the infernal beasts' innate illusory magic took hold. Their rough skin began to shine as fur grew in, and though their size did not change, their skeletal limbs filled out with muscle, the red of their eyes muting to form dark irises, and sharpened teeth sliding back into much softer-looking muzzles.

"Oh, look at you, you're beautiful!" Excitement churned itself in Amma's voice as she went right back to the knoggelvi. So much for Damien's order. She attempted to pet one of them, but it pulled away, a dark eye roving toward her and narrowing ruefully. "Well, their personalities haven't changed," she chirped, "but they're very pretty now."

Her knoggelvi snorted with clear disagreement, pawing at the dirt.

"Oh, yes, you are," she teased back.

Then there was the sound of passing gas, loud and full-bellied, and the knoggelvi's tail whipped hard at its backside. A noxious, black fume dispersed around its rump and with it the distant sound of clashing swords. Amma looked as though she might be sick, backing away and covering her face.

"The shadows still have to come out somewhere." Damien tipped his head. "I suppose it can be explained away by some bad meat."

"Um, I don't think horses eat meat."

"Well, bad whatever-horses-eat then." Damien waved away the minor detail. "Kaz, you are strong enough to change now, yes?"

The imp propelled himself to the ground, gave his wings a stretch, rolled his knobby shoulders, and then his odd, little form twitched madly. His snout pulled in as did his ears, and his wings shriveled up and disintegrated away. Ruddy skin went tan as he fell forward onto four feet, and there was a terrible cracking as joints contorted. His already bulbous eyeballs mutated with a squishy snap and his tail curled up and fuzzed out until finally there was no longer an imp before them but a small dog.

At least, it should have been a dog, only it was much more like an over-sized rat. Short haired, and huge-eared, he stood very low to the ground with a thin, curling tail, a half-squashed muzzle, underbite intact, and eyes that looked in two different directions. Damien wondered if maybe Kaz had forgotten how earth-dwelling animals looked until he yapped, high-pitched and horrible, but clearly dog-like. And then ran right for Amma.

The woman shrieked and sprinted away despite Kaz's dog form being a tiny, pathetic thing, but the imp was just as fast on four legs, nipping at her ankles as she rounded the knoggelvi-turned-horses who both kicked up dirt and snorted. As the chaos erupted before him, Damien could not, at first, fathom what was going on, but then recalled Amma's story about the dog that had terrorized her as a child. Apparently, Kaz had also remembered.

She was still running, but changed course, bolting right toward Damien and ducking behind him. He felt her small hands press against his back, giving him the slightest shove, and she squeaked out, "Make it stop!"

Damien's boot connected with the dog's belly, scooping up under him and flinging him off. Kaz howled, flying through the air, and disappeared amongst the wheat of the nearest field with a far-off thump.

There was a sharp slap against Damien's arm, and he pulled away to see Amma glaring up at him. "Damien!"

There she went, saying his name again. The first time it had been on her tongue, she'd been sobbing, but even then it felt too visceral, too intimate, and shortly after she had repeated it as a soft plea, and that had—well, fuck, it had done a number of things to him, none of which he cared to think on too long. Very few called him by his given name, but even now as she chastised him, it was like she were whispering it directly into his chest, making the muscles there tighten around her voice and hold it still so it couldn't escape.

But she *was* chastising him, and she'd just slapped him too, for darkness's sake. Not hard, certainly, but no one was meant to be allowed to get away with striking a blood mage. And yet, all he seemed able to do was gesture to the field. "What? I made it stop."

"That was Kaz, though! I thought you were going to, like, freeze him with magic or something, but you just kicked him!"

What was with her misplaced concern for that cretin? "Yes, of course I kicked him—he was being a little bastard, and to you specifically, I might add. So, you are very welcome, Amma." He knew when he repeated her own name it carried none of the affection, false as it was, he felt when she spoke, but he did it all the same as if he could force some understanding onto her. The dismay on her face shifted to a quiet confusion, and her eyes darted down to the ground. Perhaps it had worked.

"Apologies, Master." Kaz's dog form came trotting out of the field. He sat at the road's edge and scratched with his back leg at an ear that had returned to leathery, red skin. The ear grew back its tan fur and conical shape with a pop.

Another heavy gust blew down the road as the clouds rolled over themselves in the sky. Damien gave them all a last look, the faux horses still rattled, the realm's ugliest dog, and a woman who was as flustered as she was belligerent. "Do you think the lot of you can cooperate so that we can get to town before dark, or would you like to sleep out in the rain?"

There was a grumbling that answered him back, eyes all turned down, and one long, low knoggelvi fart that echoed with thrumming bow strings and arrows aflame. He took it as concession, and they continued on.

A town so close to Tarfail Quag was bound to be small and backward, but this one, seemingly without a name, was smaller and backwarder than Damien expected. Cottages dotted the farmed fields at its outskirts, housing animals and people alike, and then the buildings were a bit sturdier, closer together, and though the smell wasn't better, it was appropriate.

They rode in on the masked knoggelvi, the single thoroughfare to the tiny village unpopulated enough to stay mounted so long as they proceeded slowly. In the early evening, villagers were returning to their homes or chatting on porches, but most stopped to stare at the newcomers, few bothering to whisper as they pointed.

Damien cleared his throat as he scanned for whatever would pass as an inn, doing his best to avoid the slack-jawed gaze of the locals. He shifted uncomfortably, and the animal beneath him pulled closer to its companion, his leg brushing up against Amma's.

"Kaz, are you all right?" Amma kept her voice low, but she was easy to hear so close, glancing back at the imp.

Kaz had curled into a circle with his snout tucked under a leg on Damien's knoggelvi's rump. Disguised as a dog, he was perhaps even scrawnier and more pathetic than as an imp, and the shivering didn't help.

"The infernal pits are quite a bit warmer than this place." With his muzzle buried into his own thigh, his gurgly voice was muffled, though that was likely for the best as Damien didn't believe most dogs spoke Key.

"Oh, you poor thing," she lilted. "Do you want to sit on my lap?"

"No!" Kaz was quick to snap back.

Damien blinked over at Amma, half expecting her to follow up the distress with a laugh, but her brows were knit with concern and lips pulled into a pout as she looked on the miserable, quivering creature.

"Are you sure?" Amma's voice went even sweeter, leaning a little closer and brushing Damien's leg again. "I can tuck you down in my tunic and share my body heat."

132

Damien was quick to avert his eyes from where she had pointed between her breasts. Her honeyed words, even if they were sarcastic and not meant to illicit deviant thoughts, had struck a tumultuous feeling in his stomach. He grit his teeth and glared at the road ahead—maybe there was something arcane about Amma after all if she could do such a thing with little more than words.

A set of village children scrambled out from behind a building, one running after the other, and the two fell out right into the roadway. They shrieked with what Damien could only assume was glee though it pierced the ear and chased away the odd yet captivating feeling Amma's words had inspired. The children's laughter, though, came to an abrupt halt when they saw him.

One hid behind the other, each with wide, terrified eyes, dirty faces drawn slack from their place so low to the ground, too stupid to move out of the knoggelvi's way. Even disguised as horses, they were imposing beasts, and Damien knew he was even more so. He tugged the reins to slow his mount as the children gathered enough sense to back off the way they'd come to huddle at the roadside.

Damien leaned toward them as they passed. "Boo." Both children exploded into shrieks and fled, and he sat back up, chuckling.

"Damien!" Amma's voice had lost all of its sweetness, a fact that perturbed him much more than it ought to have. She, apparently, did not approve, yet she would speak to Kaz as if he were some worthy thing even when he was consistently awful to her. Damien, at least, was being *inconsistently* awful to her. Perhaps she would prefer if the blood mage chased her about instead, threatening to bite when she was finally caught. He nearly suggested as much and then bristled at himself—it would be too difficult to make those words sound vicious, especially when the first places he thought to nip at absolutely weren't vicious at all.

"Don't you think you should make a little effort to blend in too?" Her voice shook him of the baffling contemplation. "Like the knoggelvi and Kaz?"

"And how do you propose I do that?"

Amma's eyes traveled over him slowly, and he stiffened under her appraisal. "Well, everything you're wearing is all black. It's a little ominous."

"My illusory powers do not last nearly as long as wholly infernal creatures." He snorted and continued disparagingly, "And I told you, black is my favorite color."

"Okay, fine, but you also don't have to have your face like that."

Damien's jaw tightened. "We've discussed this. If I could remove

133

this scar, don't you think I would have already?"

"I didn't mean that!" She threw her hands up so quickly he thought she might fall right off the knoggelvi.

"Of course you didn't."

"Truly! I forgot it was even there," Amma whined. "It's not even—that is, I mean, it's…it's actually kind of…"

He let her flounder until she was only mumbling incoherently, but her discomfort was far too entertaining. "Yes? Go on."

"I don't want to say." She was biting her lip so hard it looked as if she could have drawn blood, and then she let out a defeated sigh. "That's really not what I meant anyway, you just have to believe me."

"I absolutely do not *have* to do anything."

Amma grunted in her frustrated way. "I meant this," she said, gesturing to her own face as she narrowed her brow and pushed out her lips into a comically terrible frown. She crossed her arms and flared her nostrils, and then she even growled out what may have been the least-terrifying sound Damien had ever heard including Kaz's attempt to bark.

Damien had to bite the inside of his cheek to keep from laughing. "Surely, I don't look like that."

"It's close," she warned, features relaxing. "You have resting villain face."

"I *am* a villain."

And then Amma, the girl he had abducted, dragged across the realm, and threatened to murder, actually rolled her eyes at him.

Taken aback only a short moment, he grit his teeth. "You don't believe me? Behold."

Damien swept his gaze over the path ahead. There were two older men playing a game of dice outside a shop, a rotund woman trading goods at an elderly woman's stall, and just a few paces farther from all of that, a child sitting on an upturned pail, clutching something that looked sticky and sweet in both hands, mouth open, ready to shove an entire pastry down his eager gullet.

Damien flicked a hand through the air, a nothing gesture for a nothing spell, and a shadow that had been only casting itself languidly in the very last rays of the sun snapped to life. Barely perceptible to the untrained eye, of which all in this town certainly were, the tendrils of airy blackness shot across the road, smacking the child's hands. Even the stickiness of the disgusting morsel couldn't keep it in the child's grip, and into the dirt the pastry bounced once, then twice, and right into the road where Damien's knoggelvi took a slightly longer stride to smash it into the earth. Just as they passed, the child broke into a terrible yet sweet wail.

Amma's mouth fell open. "That was atrocious."

He scanned the road behind them, but the villagers were occupied with their own work, none even paying attention to the sobbing child. Kaz's body was still shaking, this time with laughter. Damien cracked a smile. "It really was, wasn't it?"

"You need to replace that," she said, twisting back to him.

Damien only scoffed, searching once again for the local inn.

"What if that's the only food he has?" she snapped.

He refused to look at her, perfectly capable of imagining what kind of face she might be making, but a restless sensation crawled into his gut anyway. He pushed it away, slightly harder to do this time than the times before. "Well, then I suppose he won't eat."

"Fine, I'll replace it myself." She tugged on the knoggelvi's reins to pull it to a stop, but predictably it kept right on going alongside Damien's.

"With what copper?" he asked.

She struggled a moment longer with the reins, ignoring him, then exhaled harshly, leaning forward and swinging a leg over the mount's side.

"Didn't you learn your lesson the last time you fell off that thing?"

Amma had no effort to spare for him, focused wholeheartedly on dismounting the still-moving animal. With a squeak, she let go and hit the ground, but managed to stay on her feet. She planted her hands on her hips and grinned as Damien and the knoggelvi continued down the road.

"Get back here," he called, a little less bored, and a little more incensed.

She acted as though she didn't hear him, though the scrunch to her nose told him she did, and headed for the child who had devolved into sniffling and rubbing at puffy eyes. Damien would have been impressed with how little she appeared to care if it hadn't been him she were defying, but it couldn't stand. Plus, what would she do to replace the pastry—steal another? That would only cause a whole heap of trouble he would have to get her out of which was completely unacceptable. He was already running everything off course for her: there was no way he was getting tied up in the scheme of a rotten, little thief who just happened to get in his way. Again.

"*Sanguinisui*, get back on your mount."

Amma's form stiffened so abruptly she nearly fell right over. She turned on a heel and marched back up to the moving knoggelvi's side, reached up to its back, and scrambled. It seemed for a moment she would never make it up, being jostled about by just the beast's slow stroll, but then she finally made purchase against its side with a hand tangled in its mane and pulled herself over like she were saving herself from rushing waters at her feet.

Damien watched her panicked toil with a quiet amusement until she was finally draped over the knoggelvi's back on her belly, falling lax with a sigh. She lay there for a moment, catching her breath, and he continued to stare at how she'd perched herself, hind end upward, the desire to bite her swiftly returning.

She pushed up onto her elbows and glared at him. "I hate when you do that." Damien opened his mouth to protest that he had not actually been staring at her ass, and how would she even know, she wasn't even looking, but then she flopped back down hard and moaned, "That word makes me feel awful."

The knoggelvi snorted from beneath her, giving her another jostle.

Damien swallowed, and the guilt, which he was still failing to properly identify, snaked around in his stomach. "Well, do what I say, and I won't have to use it."

"I'm not talking to you anymore," she grumbled into the knoggelvi's side.

"What a terrible loss for us both." He peeked over at her one last time. "And sit on that thing properly, you're drawing far too much attention like that."

The place that would serve as an inn was just ahead, so when Amma grumbled something pithy about how it wasn't her drawing all the attention and didn't actually sit up, he chose to ignore her tiny rebellion. Frankly, he might prefer her that way, and was at least a little disappointed when they were finally able to dismount.

Damien had the masked knoggelvi led to the stable at the building's back by a young boy who had been sweeping the front stoop. The boy retched when they knoggelvi passed gas around the corner, even the increasing breeze of the coming storm not enough to save him. The two went inside, Kaz trailing behind on four legs, tongue hanging out.

A tired woman with a load of greying hair bundled atop her head and an apron covered in overfilled pockets was wiping down a countertop just by the door. She brightened when he offered her coin for two rooms and bustled them over to a small table in the corner of the cramped front chamber.

It had been some time since Damien had been in a human tavern in the realm, though this barely qualified. A small fireplace lined one wall, its flame the only light, and stairs ran up another over a low doorway into the back. The walls were covered in drying herbs and little, hand-painted signs with laconic yet syrupy sayings in misspelled Key. *Karee on, mayk mary, adoor trooly,* one read, beside it another with an image of an hourglass that had run out and the words *tyme for wyne.*

The keep hustled away into the back room to fetch them meals as a quiet rumble of thunder let them know they had made it just in time. Amma stared down at the table, sitting with her limbs all scrunched up and her face drawn into a frown. Still angry—shocking. When the woman came back, she placed two bowls of lumpy stew before them, dug out spoons from one of her many apron pockets, and told them she would prepare the rooms upstairs, bustling off just as quickly.

"Even though you are not speaking to me," he said, pushing a bowl closer to her, "you should at least use your mouth to eat."

Amma remained focused on the wood grain, hands clasped in her lap. "I thought you preferred things this way," she said miserably. "No conversing."

Kaz snickered from the floor where he curled up before the fireplace.

Damien picked up his spoon. "Going back on your promise?" She still refused to look at him, mouth snapping shut, and all the fun was wrung out of his prodding at her. "Do not make me make you eat, Amma."

She took a long look at the bowl, then gently picked up her spoon. Amma's eyes searched the small tavern room as they sat, feeding herself slowly. Damien watched her, having already taken note of the drunken man in the corner, passed out, the rest of the place empty. He thought to ask her what she was looking for, but if she was going to be silent, then so was he.

When the keep came back downstairs, she stopped at their table like she'd just had a thought. "You two aren't coming from Elderpass, are ya?"

Damien shook his head.

"Then you must be headed there. You ought to be careful." She looked Damien over. "Well, I suppose you might be fine, but there's some mighty strange goings on in that place. People been going crazy down there, hacking one another up, even their own kin, telling all sorts of fanciful stories about what's made them do it. Say it's demons."

Amma sat back, casting a wary glance at Damien, but he

continued to stare at the keep, the woman's dark eyes, flanked by wrinkles, narrowing on him.

"You wouldn't know anything about that, would you?" She pursed her lips.

"Demons?" he repeated, never letting his gaze leave hers. Another rumble of thunder sounded, closer this time. "Not a thing."

"Well," she finally said, features shifting into a smile that was clearly only for customers, "your rooms are all ready, just up the stairs, the two on the left, can't miss 'em."

When the bowls had been emptied, they took the narrow, creaking flight upward to a short hall with a block of four rooms. Damien peeked into the two beside one another they'd been given, biding Amma follow him into the second. She was quick to look at him with a tight frown and expectant eyes from the threshold. "Don't hurt me or you or anybody else, and don't leave the room. I know, I know," she said then trudged inside.

Damien much preferred her goading him on or even being irrationally incensed to this sullen, hurt act she was putting on. She stood there, staring at the floor, arms crossed, and rain began to pelt at the roof, filling up the quiet between them. He nearly stalked from the room then before realizing he had almost believed that she would choose to follow his orders rather than be bound by the Chthonic words of the talisman.

She winced under the spell, then walked dreamily over to the cot and sat herself down, all pouty melancholy. Damien almost ordered the dejection right off her face until he decided, if she intended to be miserable, then he would just let her, and it didn't matter if it, for whatever unfathomable reason, made him miserable too—he was meant to be that way, after all, so what was the difference?

CHAPTER 15
UNHOLY OFFERINGS

Damien rose the next morning to the twittering of a whole flock of tiny-beaked, chubby-bodied, incessantly-annoying sparrows that had made the tree outside his window their home as if they knew exactly what they were doing. The rain had cleared, and the morning was foggy and wet, but there were still nagging words at the back of his mind that refused to be washed away. So, he stood, donned his armor, and ordered Kaz to pop back into his dog form and follow him downstairs.

It was nearly impossible to reach the common room without the staircase creaking, but Damien did his best, glancing back at Amma's door to ensure it remained shut. When he made it down to the innkeeper, he purchased the last, day-old pastry she had, then gave it and instructions to an incredulous Kaz. The imp would be cranky again, and not just because he'd be stuck all day looking like a dog, but Damien could better deal with Kaz's ire than the agitation in himself.

He returned upstairs to watch through the branches of the maddening birds' roost as the imp begrudgingly trotted along the street out front and came upon the wretched child from the evening before. He didn't look malnourished or even forlorn anymore, but when Kaz put his tiny paws on the boy's knee and dropped the food into his lap, the pastry was gobbled up in seconds. Disgusting, surely, but done, thank the basest beasts.

Then he rapped on Amma's door, calling through it to meet him downstairs, but it swung open before he could march off. Dressed and beaming up at him, she fluttered long lashes and chirped, "Good morning!"

Damien stepped back from the doorway she had somehow completely filled though her body was small. "Is it?"

She gave him a nod, bouncing on her toes. He wanted to be further vexed at the sourceless change in her attitude, but found himself only confused, grumbling as he walked away. Kaz waited at the foot of the stairs, a little ball of anger himself, growling at everything that passed including Damien until he gave him *a look.* Together, the three fetched the masked knoggelvi from a cloud of noxious shadows in the lean-to and set off for the day, the haze in the roadway parting and the sun rising into a cloudless sky.

Damien returned to his reading, but Amma was talkative again, pointing out what she deemed "pretty," "cute," "pretty cute," and perhaps too often than the sights deserved, "beautiful." It was distracting, but a welcome one from Kaz's quiet brooding. As they were now passing others on the road, he had to remain under his illusion, and the knoggelvi seemed restless as well, but Amma evened the complaints out with a diatribe no one asked for about how walnut and sumac trees were often confused but distinctly different.

They slept under a clear sky that night and by late afternoon of the following day had made it to the river that ran along the northern border of Elderpass. It was a proper town, falling on the crossroads between the road they traversed running south to Eirengaard and another that ran east and west, both wide and well-traveled, if Damien's memory served. The bridge over the river into the city was flanked by a gatehouse with a small watchtower, an archer sitting at its top beside a bell for warning if, Damien supposed, a hoard of werewolves made the multi-day journey south for fresh flesh.

A problem could perhaps come, though, from the guard on the ground. His surcoat was white and blue with a symbol Damien had to assume represented devotion to some god or another emblazoned across his chest. There was armor beneath that, a sword strapped to his side, and perhaps arcana lurking inside him as well. Truly divine arcana, the foil to Damien's infernal, was unlikely, but one could never be too careful.

The knoggelvi and imp gave off minor infernal auras, easy to shield with the enchantments already on Damien, and the blood mage himself was only detectable by someone much stronger who had to know just what they were looking for. But the talisman was altogether different and untested.

Still far enough off to not be heard, he looked to Amma. "Time to prove that virtue of yours."

Her eyes met his, wide and questioning. "What? Here?"

He gestured with his head to the watchtower, prepared to use the enchanted word, but then stopped himself. It would put a damper on things to make her uncomfortable rendering her mute with it again so soon. "You are aware that if you say anything to this guard about the talisman or our arrangement, it will not go well for you, yes?"

Her eyes darted toward the tower they were slowly approaching then back to him, voice low. "Not well? You mean like you might kill me a little sooner than you planned?"

Damien snorted. "No, but I will kill both of those good, gods-fearing men. And maybe maim Kaz a bit too, just for fun."

This made her sit straighter, mouth drawn down, eyes focused on the way ahead. If she acted up, he could send a shadow into the tower to knock the man there out of it, the fall enough to incapacitate him if not kill, and the guard on the ground could be dispatched with arcana or with bare hands if he really needed to—Damien was larger than him, he could see at the shorter distance, and his sword hung at an improper angle, easy to be missed or even snatched away.

But none of that was necessary. Amma kept her mouth shut, and Damien traded polite, short words with the guard, handed off a silver to cross the bridge, and the man so proudly boasting the symbol of some holy god never even noticed he'd allowed the spawn of a demon into his town. It was no wonder Elderpass was supposedly already plagued by the infernal.

But, most importantly, the talisman was completely undetected by virtue of Amma.

Once they crossed the water, however, there was an unease on the air. They dismounted, the streets too busy to stay astride the knoggelvi. Damien expected more suspicious, frightened looks from villagers, but many kept their heads down, traveling quickly in small packs.

Amma seemed to pick up on none of this though, her eyes lighting up as she walked on ahead of the knoggelvi. Elderpass rose up from the bank of the river at a gentle incline, its main road cobbled and meandering. The crossroad to the east and west ran along the river, and then the small city grew upward beyond it, built into stepped ledges in either direction and edged by stone fences that zigzagged along ascending walkways. It was like crossing through the mountain pass out of Aszath Koth if there had been shops and homes built into the stone.

Damien watched Amma, so different from the rest of the crowd with her chin up and shoulders back, but he was keenly aware of the disquiet hemming in around them. He let his vision soften as they continued on along the road, feeling for the familiar thrum of discord with a whisper of Chthonic. With so many bodies packed into the city, he struggled for a moment, his feelers distracted by so much of the same blood, human, human, human, and then a pop of something slightly different, a bit of elven blood, a particularly strong elemental mage, a cat, and then he found it.

It was an almost friendly feeling, discovering other infernal arcana that sliced so brutally through the ordinariness of the rest of the world. Prickling somewhere up ahead was a chaotic magic that danced on the edges of the comfortable, and as they moved deeper into Elderpass, it pulsed stronger. They were wandering right toward it.

And then a different aura hit Damien, the total converse of the discord and evil hiding in the city, slamming into his spell and knocking him back a step before he dropped the enchantment completely.

"Can I make a quick stop, please?" Amma was standing right in front of him, tapping his arm with a fast-paced intensity, breaking through the spell he'd been concentrating on.

Damien shook his head. "Did we not just make our hundredth stop of the day in the bushes outside of town? You haven't even had anything more to drink."

"Not that." She pointed to a shop across the way with a rack out front filled with skeins of yarn. "I just need a moment, I know exactly what I want, so I'll be fast."

Damien considered her, the way the tip of her tongue poked out from between her teeth and how her freckles bunched up as she grinned, and there was a moment, however brief and absolutely mad, he would have given her anything she asked for then.

Well, that's bloody dangerous, he thought, but realized their small caravan had already come to a stop under the eaves of an out-of-the-way building, and she had, in fact, behaved at the city's entrance. What was the harm in allowing her this small freedom? She would either continue to be obedient or give him a reason to threaten and manhandle her again, and he wasn't entirely sure which one he preferred.

When he waved her on, she darted between a cart carrying gourds and a man with bags of flour on both shoulders to slip into the shop. She was small and swift, the villagers barely noticing her, and she almost completely evaded his own gaze in the shadows of the place. He realized his mistake immediately—she was a thief, and he'd just

142

set her loose in a place of goods.

But Amma did not disappear, she did not grab and flee, she did not even skulk about. Through the grimy window, he could see her go directly to the young woman at the shop's counter. Amma looked to be speaking with her, and then he saw her exchange actual coin—and where in the bloody realm did she get that, he wondered, patting his own pockets—for a small bundle of fabric. She came running back out, skillfully evaded a donkey, and skipped back over to him.

Amma held up her purchase, a tunic stitched of a thick yarn, but very, very small. As much as he would have enjoyed watching her try to squeeze into such a thing, he knew she was too clever to believe it would fit. "What is that for?"

"A baby," she said with a delighted grin.

Damien's eyes jumped down to her completely flat stomach then back up to her face which revealed nothing but adoration for the tiny tunic. It was knitted with an emerald green yarn and buttery yellow flowers stitched along the trim.

Amma tipped her head. "But I'm certain it will fit anyway." She squinted at Damien's feet where Kaz had planted himself, rat-like tail wrapped around his haunches, shivering.

Big, black, bulbous eyes rolled from one of them to the other, the tongue that was constantly hanging out zipping into the dart of a mouth. The imp growled.

"Let me help you put it on." Amma was already kneeling, holding the tunic out, and Kaz backed right up into Damien's boots, his growl intensifying, and then he snapped.

Amma pulled back with a sharp inhale. Damien could see that same fear she'd had when the imp chased her, yet she held still.

"Let her," Damien commanded, voice heavy as he stared down at the disguised imp.

Amma was quick then, popping the tunic over his head with her nimble hands as he was distracted. Kaz made all sorts of grunty, pained noises, but went floppy and didn't help at all as Amma wrestled his scrawny front legs through the arms, her own tongue sticking out between her teeth as she worked. When she was done, she sat back, clapped once, and in a total surprise to both Damien and Kaz, grabbed him under the arms and lifted him up.

Kaz held aloft, the tunic dwarfed his tiny body, falling over his hind end as he hung from Amma's hands, back legs dangling out like sticks for kindling. He glared at her, and she beamed back. "Kaz, you look adorable!"

"This is degrading," he grumbled.

"But aren't you warmer?"

Kaz scrunched up his snout, bottom teeth shifting around in the grimace, and Damien couldn't hold back the grin cracking up the side of his own face.

"Oh, what a cute puppy!" A passing villager stopped beside Amma and reached out to give him a pat. Kaz nipped at her hand, just missing a finger.

"Sorry," Amma said quickly, "he's sort of a little demon."

The woman laughed warily, eyes bulging at the word *demon*, and she slipped into the crowd with a quickness.

"Master," Kaz choked out from Amma's arms, "I look ridiculous."

"Yes, but you've stopped shivering." Damien gave him a nod then turned, and they continued along the thoroughfare.

Nearing the market in the town square, Damien slowed. The discord was stronger there, and his senses were heightened as he covertly cast the spell to feel for other beings and magics once again. Though the day was not truly over, there was a rushed sense of completion in the air as many of the stalls were closing down. In a place like this, he would have suspected at least an hour or so more of regular work before a slow shut down after dark, but it seemed most of the villagers wanted to be home before the sun had disappeared. The keep in the nameless town outside of Tarfail Quag had mentioned demons, and most were ill-informed enough to believe it was only under nightfall that the infernally summoned prowled. Of course, demons did prefer the dark, it was often too warm dressed all in black out in the sun, but still.

"Stay here," he said absently, handing the reins of the masked knoggelvi off to Amma and stepping away. There was a shrine in the center of the square they'd entered, a pedestal with steps on every side, and a statue of a woman there, one of the goddesses the people of the realm worshiped. Though he didn't know which, he assumed she represented fertility or the harvest based on her scantily clad, generous breasts and the carvings into the base of her statue, wheat in a less-than-subtle, vessel-like shape.

He covertly sent his magic over the structure, feeling for that infernal arcana again. Around its base sat a number of small effigies meant to look like the goddess, and other trinkets and offerings, a bushel of dried flowers, a copper cup filled with spoiling milk, a small chunk of honeycomb. It was clearly cherished, yet the shrine was giving off an infernal aura, and not just any, but one he thought he might have known.

A jolt of alarm broke into the careful focus of Damien's spell. There were plenty of others in the square, shouting and banging around their stalls and carts, and blood was pumping hard in most of the bodies as they toiled, but this pulse was different, this was laced with fear, and it had cut right through all the others to tell him it belonged to Amma.

She hadn't appeared at his side again to hound him, and when he looked back, she was not where she'd been told to stay by the knoggelvi, Kaz sulking atop one of them in his new tunic, head down and not watching. Damien quickly scanned the crowd, sending the spell to chase after until he found her on the square's other side, the sun catching her golden bundle of hair only for a second before it disappeared down a shadowed alley.

Damien strode to where she'd gone, snarling. What an idiot he had been to extend her any good will at all—a thing he had so little to spare as it was—only for her to make such a poor attempt at escaping. It was insulting really, darting off the minute he turned his back, barely any creativity at all, and that only made him more incensed in the short moment it took him to get to where she'd fled. Didn't she at least respect him enough to come up with a more inventive plan of escape?

When he got his hands on her he was going to—well, he couldn't exactly come up with something right then. The thought of cutting off some appendage or even bruising her was distasteful, her body too nice to mar, but creativity on his own part turned out to be unnecessary as he rounded the corner to see she hadn't made the choice to run off at all.

There was a man, much larger than Amma, with a hand around her wrist, dragging her deeper into the alley and toward a darkened, empty cross street. She was trying to pull out of his grip but getting nowhere. Damien spat out Chthonic louder than he normally would have in a city full of humans and cast a bind at the man, hitting him squarely in the back and taking him down. Amma began to fall alongside him, but Damien caught her, yanking her out of his grip and into him as he unsheathed his dagger.

With Amma pulled safely up against his chest, Damien cut into his palm, already spitting out the Chthonic to slice through the man with enchanted blades of blood and bring him to a swift and deserved end.

"Wait! Don't hurt him!" Amma grabbed his wrists, and he stilled beneath her hands, the spell crackling at the edges of his fingertips as his blood pooled in his palm.

The man had been laid out, wrapped in black tendrils of infernal magic, making him an easy target. The blades that were itching to leave Damien's hand would sink into his flesh, bleeding him out in moments, and the urge to cast coursed through him, the desire to rip the bastard to shreds for trying to take what was his, but then, what the fuck was he thinking? Casting infernal arcana? Killing a man in the city center? Even in the shadows of this alley, there were others just beyond the corner that would hear his cry, find his body, and there was a door right ahead anyone could walk out at any moment.

And then there was Amma, fingers digging into his wrists, face turned up to him, pleading with her eyes.

Damien clenched his fist, the blood slick and eager on his palm. "He tried to abduct you," he growled through grit teeth.

"No, he didn't." She tugged on his arms again, feeble but insistent.

"I saw him dragging you away. You were frightened. I could feel how panicked you were. I still feel—" Damien's own heart was racing, infuriated, but Amma was still up against him, and he couldn't entirely discern from where every sensation was coming. He dropped his arms, stepping to the side. "Explain what you think is happening then."

Amma pulled her arms in around herself, like a replacement for his body. "He's confused. He was mumbling about…about his daughter," she said, head snapping down and back up like a nervous bird, eyes not settling on any one thing. "He just thinks I'm someone else."

Damien strode over to the stranger still covered in magicked tendrils, turning him over with a boot. He was slightly older with flecks of grey in his beard, and though he was well dressed and clean, his face was red, light eyes taking too long to focus, longer than if the spell had simply knocked him out. "He's drunk."

"Exactly. He's just confused." Amma pushed Damien toward the alley's opening. "Leave him. Let's go."

But Damien did not let her lead him away, staring a moment longer as the man slurred out incomprehensible words. He was built like he had worked his whole life, still strong and healthy despite the drinking. If he had gotten her alone—the urge to cast welled up in him again, but then Amma wasn't exactly helpless. He glanced back at her, the dagger still strapped to her thigh. She hadn't thought to pull it out and defend herself.

"Please, Damien." She tugged at him a bit harder.

No, he couldn't kill this man, but he still had him locked in a bind. Damien pressed his boot into his shoulder, eliciting a groan. He squeezed the blood in his palm and let it drip down onto the man's forehead. As he whispered Chthonic, the man's pupils dilated and found Damien's. "This woman is mine. Do not even think of touching her again. Return to your home. Remain there." Then he swiped over him, and the tendrils disintegrated into haze.

The man blinked and sat up, features slack, the drop of blood beading down his face. When he clambered back to his feet, Damien clenched his fist a little tighter and considered taking a swing but ultimately let him wander off down the alley and into the cross street. A mix of regret and satisfaction roiled in Damien's guts, but then he clicked his tongue and turned back to Amma.

Her eyes were wide, face flushed, and she was not moving.

"What's wrong?"

She blinked like she had just woken from a similar spell. "What did,"—her voice was hoarse, and she cleared it—"What did you do to him?"

"I didn't create that enthrallment talisman inside you without learning enchantments that work on simple, intoxicated minds along the way," he grumbled, still frustrated, then grabbed her by the arm and dragged her back into the square.

Amma stumbled, trying to keep up, and Damien brought his incensed marching to a stop. Still shaken, she was taking a deep, full breath, and it came in ragged. He swore under his breath, letting her go—he was no different, he suddenly realized, glancing out at the square. The vendors were concerned with their stalls and shops, half already closed, and the villagers kept to themselves. None of them were concerned with what happened to Amma, not a moment prior when she was being hauled off, nor now when he was doing the hauling.

The two made their way back over to the knoggelvi a bit slower. "How did this even happen?" Damien pointed at Kaz who was suddenly alert and shaking despite the thick tunic. "Why did you do nothing?"

"It's not his fault," Amma admitted. "I went over to a stall across the way to get these." She reached into the small pouch on her hip to pull out two cubes of brown sugar.

"For sweets?"

"Not for me," she said, offering a cube to each of their mounts. They pulled their heads back from her outstretched hands.

Damien groaned. "Just as horses do not eat meat, knoggelvi do not—"

Suddenly, they caught the smell, and the two nuzzled into her palms and gobbled the cubes up.

"They do not have any strong convictions, I suppose." Damien was beginning to wonder if anything infernal truly did, himself included. He snapped his fingers, the lot of them following, away from the small shrine giving off a fading infernal aura and deeper into Elderpass.

Perhaps the man who had tried to snatch Amma was affected by the strangeness settling in on the town, but he was gone now, and Damien was left with that familiar unease. There was a tavern and inn just up the way, a sign in Key above the door reading The Jealous Gentleman. Though it wasn't terribly late, and they could probably cross through the whole of Elderpass by nightfall to take up lodging on its outskirts and be that much closer to Eirengaard the next day, he chose instead to stop there.

When Damien brought Amma to her room, she remained quite unnerved, rubbing her arms like she still felt strange hands there, eyes unfocused and lost in thought. She would not have been that hard to find if she'd really gone missing, her blood's signature branded into his mind, but only if she were not far. As they continued to Eirengaard, streets would get busier, cities more dangerous, and the perils ahead would be nothing in comparison to drunkards and even werewolves.

Damien pulled a set of feathers from his pouch. He could feel the magic thrumming in them, waiting to be cast. It was extremely complex arcana, some of the most precious he had, and wasn't even entirely his work alone. With a moment of hesitation, he offered one to her.

Amma took it delicately, but then that was how she held most things. He watched her face, her eyes narrowing as she ran a finger up the feather's stem. Even if she didn't know it was magic, she would likely feel the arcana inside it. "It's beautiful," she said.

Well, that was a surprise. "Powerful," he corrected. "If we are separated, and, for whatever reason, I cannot find or summon you, you can use this to instead summon me."

"If we're separated?" Her gaze popped up to him, suddenly mischievous. "You mean, like, if I run away?"

"Well, no—"

Amma wrinkled up her nose. "Because, why would I want you to find me if I ran away?"

"I'm sure there are *some* things in this world worse than I am, and you have proven yourself incredibly abductable, but if you'd rather I take it back—"

She pulled the feather close to her heart when he reached out for it. "No, I want it. Just in case."

He smirked, holding up his own. "Of course you do. But remember: it's only got one use, so do not invoke its magic thoughtlessly. This is the only pair of its kind, and the spell took the arcana of two blood mages to craft. Not to mention, executing the spell on my end will take a great sacrifice, which does make Kaz seem a bit more useful now that I think of it, but I'd rather not shift my shape for something trivial like a bad sense of direction on your part."

"Shift your shape?"

Damien shrugged. "As they've not been used, I suppose their magic is only theory, but the quickest way between two points is as the raven flies. And for you to use it, you will also need to spill your blood."

"*I'll* have to do bloodcraft?" She shuddered.

"If you can endure debasing yourself."

"That's not what I mean." She clicked her tongue. "It's that I can't do *any* magic, you know that."

"It doesn't require you to *do magic*, it only needs your blood and perhaps a bit of your will to awaken. So, you will cut yourself, and you will need to want...uh, me."

Amma twirled the feather between her fingers. "That's all? That seems pretty easy for being so powerful."

"Yes, of course, that's all. I'm a very good blood mage, you know."

Amma then snapped her head up at him, eyes shrewd and no longer impressed. "Why are we here in Elderpass? And why were you acting so funny today?"

Damien scoffed—her reverence for the enchantment too short-lived for his liking. "We are between where we were and where we are headed."

"But we stopped early. And we could have gone around the gate, forded the river and skipped the city altogether. You don't like being around other people, I can tell, but you've been so interested in everything here. Are you worried about what's happening in this town?"

"Worried? About this place? Dark gods, of course not."

Amma twisted up her lips in thought. "But that innkeeper told you something funny was going on—she even said it was demons—and then you made sure we came into town, and you've been in half a daze all day."

"Amma, please, grant me a little more respect than that. I may be slightly intrigued, but I am *not* worried. Not about anyone. Ever."

She spun the feather between two fingers absently, giving him a long look that he could only stand under and feel too seen. Then she shrugged. "Well, thank you for, I guess, re-abducting me today, Damien."

There was a tickle in his chest, and like so many other strange pokes and prods, he shoved it down and held it beneath the waters of ignorance in his gut until it drowned. "As I said, losing the talisman would be extraordinarily inconvenient." Distracted, he nearly forgot the Chthonic word and commands to keep her in place, rushing through them on the threshold of her room before finally leaving.

CHAPTER 16
THE CORRELATION BETWEEN THE BUSTINESS OF GODDESSES AND THE FORTUNE OF THEIR FOLLOWERS

Amma lay on the small bed in her room inside The Jealous Gentleman, her hip pouch and silver dagger on the side table at arm's reach. Disrobed of her leather bodice, tunic, and breeches, she was left in just the thigh-length chemise she always wore beneath her clothes. She climbed out from under the woolen blanket for perhaps the fifth time since she'd tried to fall asleep, too warm one moment, too cold the next.

Staring up at the ceiling when she settled back down, her eyes adjusted to the darkness in the room, the inn beyond her door gone quiet. The previous day had begun with a strange if delightful surprise when she spied Kaz through the window in that rickety, little inn. There was no way the imp was bringing that bread to the child of his own accord—Damien had surely sent him to do that, but he hadn't said a word about it, so she didn't mention that she knew. On the road, he'd been easier to talk to, and she'd even seen him smile a few times, and not in that self-absorbed, knowing way, but with some genuine mirth.

And then when they reached Elderpass, Damien had extended trust to her. Yes, those chances were allowed under threat of some unspoken violence, but Amma was *pretty* sure he didn't even know what he was promising. But then—Robert. The blood mage would have killed him if she had been a second slower to still his hands, though she had been shocked to be able to stop him at all. It would have been terrible if he'd followed through, yes, but he would have been doing it to...protect her? No, to protect the talisman, but he hadn't mentioned that when he was attacking Robert, or when he had held her close, or even when he had said, quite pointedly, that she belonged to him—words that struck her deeply but not with the indignation she expected.

Amma reached for her pouch on the side table and slipped out the feather Damien had given her. She held it over her head in the gentle moonlight of Ero coming in through the window. It wasn't truly black, not under this light that was only just a reflection. Like this, she could see all the colors hidden in the feather—blue, green, purple. Sapphire, emerald, amethyst. Soft and smooth, she ran it between her fingers to watch the colors change, feeling a spark of magic along its stem, and then lay it on her chest under a hand.

It was strange: Damien had promised many times over to kill her, but when he touched her, that intent didn't even dance under the surface. There was something about his fingers on her skin, even when he was dragging her about, that was so measured. Amma had been caressed in much more carnal ways, but when Damien's cautious hands were on her, even for decidedly callous reasons, she could feel a neediness in them. And when he let go, it was like he took her skin with him, leaving her exposed and desolate.

Amma's fingers slid up the feather laying on her chest once more, soft and pliable, then shook her head. She was simply starved for affection herself, that was all. She was completely mad to read any kind of tenderness in his words or actions. He told her plainly, he was only concerned for that stupid talisman, and, for now, she just happened to be its vessel. And anyway, no matter how soft and pliable Damien himself might appear to become, she had to use that to stay alive, to steal the Scroll of the Army of the Undead, and to escape to her home.

She lay the feather atop her things on the side table again, eyes closing. A vision of his face when she had suggested he were reading some romance floated in her mind, making her laugh. He looked appalled, embarrassed even, and she wished she had prodded at him just a little more. *Oh, Damien, tell me about the lovers in your book*, she could have said. *I bet there's a broody, angry, so-called villain lusting after a coquettish baroness in disguise that he's taken captive. Come on, read it aloud, I want to hear what happens next.*

Amma woke much later in the morning the following day, surprised to have been allowed to sleep so long. Well rested and yet restless, she slipped out of bed and stretched, got dressed, and sat on the edge of the cot, waiting with the feather in her hands. The sunlight in the room was mild, and the feather was black again, but still soft in her fingers. When there was a rap on her door, she stood, stuffing it into the small pouch on her waist.

Damien was leaning against the wall, looking tired and grumpy when she opened the door. His normally pallid skin had a bluish tint under his eyes and his frown was a little deeper than normal. She frowned back sympathetically. "What's the matter?"

His brow narrowed, but he only grunted. At his feet, Kaz was padding up, ridiculous tongue sticking out of his ridiculous snout. Seeing the dog mask he wore still made her uneasy, but the blow was softened by the too-cute tunic he was still dutifully wearing.

"Kaz, why is Damien so cranky this morning?"

"I'm not *cranky*," he groused.

Kaz's bulbous eyes rolled up from one of them to the other. "Master expended much energy last night. He was up very late and with little success."

"What were you doing?" Amma stepped out of her room and pulled the door shut, eyebrows raising.

He had been standing there with his head bent, hair falling in his face as he grimaced at the imp, then realized all at once she was so close. He straightened and stepped back, bumping into the opposing door in the inn's narrow hall. "Nothing."

Amma clicked her tongue and inched toward him. "Doesn't sound like nothing. Kaz?"

"Master said he was seeking out the source of the infernal energy." The dog's head tilted, pointed ears twitching, and then he snarled, and added for good measure, "Whore."

Amma pouted at him, and Damien took a very put-upon breath, shuffling another few inches away from her. "It was only more research." As he raised up a hand to run through his hair, his elbow banged into the opposing door. "Shit." He pulled back and rubbed the spot.

The door behind him creaked open, and an elderly man stuck his wrinkled head out, eyebrows so large and fluffy he had to be blinded by them. "What? What is it?"

"So sorry," Amma began, waving at him from behind Damien.

"What's with this racket, what do you want?" he crowed, waving a fist at the blood mage who towered over him.

Damien's voice was as sweet as vinegar. "Go back inside."

"Damien," Amma hissed then smiled at the man. "We didn't mean to bother you, sir."

"Well, you did!" he pushed out into the already cramped hall.

Amma tried once more to placate him, but Damien cut her off, "Then what's done is done, old man. Or would you prefer to be further inconvenienced by death?"

"You sound like that mad son of a bitch who killed the Stormwings. Look like him too!" Unafraid, the slip of a man shook both of his fists now, sleeves falling back to reveal skinny, liver-spotted arms.

Amma laid a hand on Damien's forearm, sensing it was about to raise. "Again, so sorry. We'll be going."

"Stormwings?" Damien held fast to the spot. "What do you know of the Stormwings?"

"Nothing I'd tell you!" He was spitting mad now, and another door farther back in the hall opened. A woman popped her head out and shouted for everyone to keep it down.

"Tell me, or I'll have your head." With the cold precision that said he meant it, Damien leaned down and bore right into him.

"Bah! My tongue won't work if it's not connected to the rest of me, will it? Piss off, you moody, little shit!" Throwing a hand in his face, the old man stomped back through his door.

Damien went to go after him, but Amma still had a grip on his arm and pulled back just as the door was slammed in his face. "Hey, just because you're in a bad mood doesn't mean you have to make everyone else be in one too."

"But he has information I need." Damien whipped around to her, gesturing to the door.

The woman a few doors down had stepped out fully, hands on her hips. "Excuse me, but can you have your little spat downstairs?"

Damien raised his other hand, and Amma felt the familiar crackle of magic. "Oh, you stop that," she said, giving his arm a tug.

He ended up allowing her to pull him to the tavern below, quiet in the late morning and nearly empty of townsfolk. There were two men playing dice in the corner, and the keep was serving a single patron behind a long bar. They found a seat at the back of the room, away from the others. There, Damien explained, gruffly, that there was indeed something strange going on in Elderpass, and he had done some digging the night before, uncovering the name Stormwing. He wanted to know more, but that man upstairs—this he said loudly while grimacing at the ceiling—was being incredibly unhelpful.

Amma clicked her tongue. "Oh, you just want to find out some gossip?"

"No," he spat, poking the table. "I want to know what's going on in this town, so I can find the source of this infernal arcana."

Amma rolled her eyes. "Yeah, gossip. Wait here."

Damien was muttering something about proper research as she

154

got up and sauntered over to the bar. Taking a seat a few stools down from the single, drunken patron, she put her elbows on the counter and leaned forward with a cheery smile, greeting the young man who tended it. It took her only a few questions, complete with giggling and pointed *oohs* and *ahhs* to get exactly what she wanted out of him, including a cup of spicy cider, and then she sauntered back to Damien with her drink in hand.

Amma sat down, gave him a wide smile, and took a sip.

"Well?" He leaned toward her, jaw clenched. Still so cranky.

"So,"—she took a deep breath—"the Stormwings are one of the wealthiest families in Elderpass. They made all their gold on trade across the Cobalt Strait, mostly in spices and unique grains. The barkeep used to be on one of their boats when he was a kid, so he knows them pretty well. Or, knew them, I guess, right up until they all got axed to death by Morel, the middle son, about half a moon ago. Morel claims to not remember any of it, he just came to all bloody, wandering out in front of the estate, but the barkeep—his name's Branson by the way, father's name is Bran, used to own the tavern and bar which Branson swore he'd never take over, his heart actually belongs to the sea, he says, but then his dad got sick, and—"

"Amma, please."

"Right, so Branson says Morel's always been really strange. He's quiet, keeps to himself, all that, so nobody's *that* shocked he killed them, and there wasn't even a trial or anything since he admitted to it. Branson also says they would have hanged him already if there wasn't an argument about who's inheriting everything once he's gone. *Apparently* there's a distant cousin a town over who claims it should all be hers, but there's an illegitimate son in town who's made a stake at everything too, and, get this, there's even a mistress making a claim, but nobody's actually seen her, she's just sent letters. The Stormwing patriarch, Claude, left a will with *her* name on it, and she's not even the illegitimate son's mother. Sounds like Claude Stormwing was a bit of a cad, and frankly I'm surprised it was Morel that took him out and not one of the three ladies he was fooling around with." Amma took another sip, wiggling her brows at him.

Damien blinked back at her. "The barkeep just told you all that? He wouldn't say a damn thing to me last night."

She grinned. "Well, you probably didn't buy a drink. Or smile at him."

His eyes darted down to her chest then back up as he reached out and snatched her cup away. "I'm sure that's what I was missing." His eyebrow cocked over the cup as he took a swallow.

"Well..." Amma cast a glance across the tavern at the strapping man who was already gazing back. She waved her fingers at him, and a big grin cracked over his square jaw.

"All right, all right," Damien huffed, placing the cup back down with a thump. "So, the Stormwing boy says he doesn't remember any of it?"

Amma shrugged. "That's what Branson says he says, but Branson also says he's, um..."

"What?"

"I don't really want to say it, it wasn't very nice, but he called him some less-than-complimentary things." She cleared her throat. "So, there's probably more to it, but Branson was adamant he's always been...weird."

Damien's eyes shifted across the tavern, his usual, calculating look going sourer. "So, you two are on a first-name basis, eh?"

While he was looking away, Amma grabbed her cup back. "Well, I didn't give him mine. Anyway, Morel Stormwing is being held under house arrest up at the top of the southwest steps in the Garden District. It's easier, I guess, to keep him and the estate under watch together while they figure out the inheritance."

"Straight to the source then." Damien stood, and Amma did the same, quickly throwing back the rest of her cider. "Ah, no, no, you're staying here."

"Don't you need my help?"

"Your help?" Damien chuckled. "This could be dangerous, and you're more of a liability than anything."

"Well, what am I supposed to do here?"

He shrugged. "That's none of my concern, just don't leave the premises."

Amma placed her empty cup down then leaned a hip against the table. "Fine. I guess I can take Branson up on his offer."

Damien had turned but came to a stop, looking back. "What offer?"

She tapped her lips in thought, eyes wide and blinking and as innocent as she could playact. "Oh, something about showing me how they manage to get all those massive cider barrels crammed into the really tight back room. I bet it's fascinating."

Damien groaned, scratching at his smooth chin. "On second thought, your assistance may come in handy."

"Are you sure?" She bit her lip. "Because Branson seemed really interested in showing me how those barrels get filled."

He glared across the tavern at the man. "The only thing that barkeep is interested in filling, is you with Branson-son."

She gasped, too playful now to be convincing. "No! That can't be what he meant. It's got nothing to do with chickens."

"Chickens?"

"He said if I went back there with him, he'd show me his massive co—"

"*Sanguinisui*, go outside!"

Amma couldn't even be upset as the magic crawled over her, squealing with delight at convincing him and skipping ahead to the tavern door before he could change his mind. She'd brought the hooded cloak The Brotherhood had given her and covered herself with it when she stepped out into the sun of the day just in case Robert had not taken Damien's hint to head home.

They gathered the knoggelvi and walked through the market again and then to the merchant and scholar district of the small city. There, the busyness of villagers felt different, but was slightly more familiar to Amma, heads turned down to parchment as studious workers left their shadowy studies to squint into the brightness for a few moments and knock furiously on the door of someone else and complain about this or that. Amma sussed out directions from a nervous young man after Damien demanded them from an older mage and failed miserably. When she took the opportunity to point out how helpful she was—*again*—Damien and Kaz both growled at her, and she just grinned back.

Upward along the cobblestone ramps built into the stepped landscape brought them to the Garden District of Elderpass. Everything here was lush and green, and a breeze blew over the plateau, the view back down into the city beautiful while the noisiness of it was swept away. The homes were massive, surrounded by sprawling, stone-walled gardens in good order. Even as autumn closed in on Eiren, the roses climbing up trellises were in full bloom, and the maples that hung over gated entries were deep burgundy.

Amma pulled her hood back when they found themselves farther away from the edge of the plateau, the gardens sprawling higher between each house and the villagers few. Beyond the barred gates and hidden at the end of long pathways off the road, only fanciful gables of even bigger estates peeked out over hedges and trees. Eventually, they made it to the quiet road the Stormwing Estate was meant to be located along.

"Keep your sticky fingers to yourself," Damien warned, bringing them to a stop a few paces before the gate and ordering the knoggelvi, still disguised as horses, to stay put.

Amma looked down at her hand—it wasn't sticky—then tutted. He expected her to resort to thievery, especially in a place so opulent, but that hadn't even occurred to her. "I'll do my best," she said as she pat her mount before they left, and it, for once, did not pull away.

Damien led them to the Stormwing Estate gates where two guards were stationed just inside. Amma had pulled her hood back up and scooped up Kaz, tucking an arm under him so that his little head stuck out from her cloak, and he was so surprised, he didn't even growl when she used her other hand to scratch behind his ears.

"Your prisoner, Morel Stormwing, I'll be seeing him now." Of course, that was exactly how Damien intended to get inside. Amma sighed quietly.

"You will?" The lankier of the guards asked, looking to his companion on the other side of the gate.

Damien gave them a curt nod, but the larger guard stood abruptly. "The captain didn't tell us anyone would be coming by."

"Your captain does not know. Nor does he dictate what I do," said Damien in a tone Amma was beginning to become familiar with.

"The list of those allowed on the grounds is extremely short, and I'm sure you are not on it, sir." That *sir* had not been terribly authentic.

Damien's mouth turned down as his jaw clenched and arcana crackled in his hand. That was Amma's cue. "Excuse me, gentlemen?" She stepped up beside Damien and beamed at the guards between the bars. "Valeria Vermissia wouldn't happen to be on that list, would she?"

The lanky guard's eyes went wide. "You're the Voluptuous Valeria from the letters?" The other guard elbowed him, hard, and he coughed out an apology.

Amma took a deep breath, face going red as she made sure her cloak hid her body away. It was a perfectly fine body, but voluptuous might not be the first word someone would use to describe it. She sniffled and gave Kaz another scratch. "That would be me, yes. I just loved Claude so, and I can't imagine why Morel would do such a thing. I couldn't bear to stay in hiding any longer and just had to come down and see the boy."

"Ah, and this is your..." The guard looked dubiously at Damien.

"My steward. He's a bit aggressive, but you understand how that might be necessary considering all the unpleasantness," she said quickly and bounced Kaz in her arms. "And my little Fifi. She's been my constant companion since I lost Claude." At that, Kaz began to growl, but she planted a kiss on his cheek that silenced him.

158

The guards gave one another a look, and then the gates were opened. "Follow me," one instructed and led them down the long path lined with maples to the house.

Damien leaned down to Amma as they fell a few steps behind the guard. "Who the fuck is Valeria?"

"Didn't you listen to a word I said in the tavern?" she whispered back. "Valeria Vermissia is the mistress in the will. You know, the one that nobody's seen?"

His brows rose, and he grinned. "You tricky, little liar."

Amma grinned back. "Tricky, little *helper*," she corrected.

Another guard was posted outside the front doors of the Stormwing Estate. The house rose up before them, imposing and grand, but dark even in the brightness of late afternoon. The two wardens exchanged a few, quiet words, and they were allowed entry through an opulent if dim foyer and to the exterior of a drawing room, its double doors shut.

Amma requested a moment alone with Morel, who she was told was inside, biting her lip and blinking fake tears out of her eyes. The guards let them enter unattended, and Amma was sure to have the doors closed behind them.

They stepped into another dark but lavish room, curtains drawn, fireplace out, a single figure sitting alone in a chair that dwarfed him.

"Who are you?" Morel Stormwing was a slender young man, maybe twenty, with hollowed out eyes and thin cheeks. He got to his feet when they entered, but remained hunched, like the weight of his own hair pulled his lanky figure down. A dark eye roved between stringy strands over the two of them and then down to Kaz who had been placed onto a settee.

Amma opened her mouth to fall back into the accent she'd used for Valeria, but Damien held up his hand, stopping her. He crossed the room to a clean hearth, sweeping past Morel like he wasn't even there.

The boy stepped away from him as if he might be knocked over from the breeze off his cloak. "I asked who you *are*." He clenched a fist but cowered, sidling behind an armchair. "Did that bastard who calls himself my brother send you? Or my bitch cousin in Aufield?" He looked to Amma for an explanation as Damien was ignoring him, inspecting the fireplace instead.

"Neither," she said. "We're here to find out what really happened."

Morel's jaw quivered a moment, uncovered eye searching the room and then the ground as he grabbed the back of the chair.

Fingertips pressing into the overstuffed upholstery, he swallowed hard, thin throat bobbing. "What really happened," he stressed. "I killed them. With an axe."

Amma glanced back at the entryway. The guards were poised outside it, their forms visible through the opaque glass in the door. Looking back at Morel, she couldn't imagine him wielding any weapon, let alone an axe, and bringing it down on someone with any kind of force.

"No," said Damien, standing and glancing up at the ceiling. "What really happened."

Watery and dark, Morel's eyes looked past them both to the room's far side but not at anything in particular. "Demons," he said, voice a whispered breath.

Amma and Damien's eyes met from across the room.

"I did it," began Morel, "but it wasn't me, not really. I don't remember…don't remember getting the axe. Don't remember doing any of it, just being in the street after." He came around the chair, sliding into it like his legs couldn't hold him up any longer. "There was so much blood."

Damien finally went up to Morel, interested for the first time. "You claim to have been possessed?"

Morel sank deeper into the chair. "What does it matter? They don't believe me. They'll hang me as soon as someone can claim the inheritance."

Amma felt sick at his words. Clearly, something was going on, and there was truth in what he was saying. "It matters," she said, crossing the room to stand beside Damien. "We need to know what happened. We can make them believe you, if it's true, and—"

"We can't make anyone do anything." Damien glared at Amma, and she screwed up her face. He certainly could make her do just about anything he wanted. "But we do need to know. Everything." He turned his cold stare back on the boy.

Morel swallowed. "It started off different. Just dreams. I thought they were dreams anyway. But they felt so real. Then I saw her, in the flesh."

"Her?" Amma leaned in.

"She was beautiful. No, not just beautiful. Something more. Like a goddess. Shevyabu."

At this, Amma glanced up. Above the mantle was a tapestry, well-made and intricate, depicting the symbol of the goddess of beauty and the harvest, Shevyabu, a set of barrels overflowing with grain in an autumnal landscape. It would not have been an inexpensive piece, some of the threads gilded to give a golden glow to the leaves falling in its background.

"The being you people around here worship," Damien mumbled, his eyes finding the tapestry as well.

"But not her, just how I imagine her." Morel's hand came up to rub a pendant he wore around his neck with a simpler depiction of the same symbol.

"You're very pious, aren't you?" Damien sighed. "You've been to that shrine in the market?"

Morel nodded with fervor. "Yes, and our whole family worships at the temple...or, they did. We owe our good fortune to Shevyabu."

"And their bad fortune too, I imagine?" Damien said ruefully.

Amma tipped her head. She had always expected that neither good nor bad fortune had much to do with the gods. "You thought something was wrong with that shrine, didn't you?"

Damien turned to her. "How do you know a thing like that?"

"I saw you making this face." She gripped her own chin and grimaced with her best grouchy-son-of-a-demon impression.

"No, I wasn't. And how do you even know? You were off getting abducted."

She shrugged. "Not the whole time."

"Something's wrong with the shrine?" Morel cut in, somber voice going even colder. "But it's a holy place. I've only ever felt goodness and light coming from it."

Damien was still staring at Amma. He cocked a brow. "Anything can be corrupted."

She tore her gaze away from the look he was giving her to check on Kaz, still perched on the settee, head cocking and one big ear flopping over. Why her face was suddenly going warm, she didn't know, and she tried to rub the feeling out of her cheeks.

"Has there been anything new in the market recently?" the blood mage was asking, stepping closer to Morel. "A change to the shrine, or more likely someone you've never seen before offering goods?"

"No, I—" Morel's face stiffened. "Yes, actually. I purchased an idol at the shrine a moon or so ago. I'd never seen the seller before, but his wares—"

"Show it to me," said Damien.

Morel straightened. "I have to..." He gestured to the door where beyond a guard was laxly leaning against it.

"Now," Damien snapped.

The boy hesitated, then led the way to the glass doors. He rapped on them, and, startled, one of the guards pulled the door open, eyes roving over the lot of them. "What?"

"We need to go upstairs," he offered meekly.

"Why?"

Damien went up behind Morel and placed a hand on the door, pushing it open and knocking the guard off kilter. The man went for his sword reflexively, stopping to stare up at Damien, a few inches taller than him. Amma held her breath, watching.

"You know how to use that?" Damien's eyes flicked down to the weapon.

The guard sputtered back a confused answer, something between a question and a confirmation.

Damien grunted, unsatisfied, and leaned out. "You better come along too," he called to the other guard who had been thumbing through a book. Then he looked down at Morel, caught between the two of them. "Well?"

Morel slipped out into the hall, and the guard pulled back, allowing Damien to pass and waiting for Amma. She scooped up Kaz who had padded over, putting on a sweet smile to play the role of Valeria again. Kaz snapped at her fingers, and she inhaled sharply, just missing his gnarled tooth, then hurried up a wide set of stairs behind the other two, both guards bringing up the rear.

The Stormwing manor was large, with wide halls and ornate doors even in the private set of chambers Morel was leading them to. Amma had been in many fine places, and no expense was spared here, but the emptiness of it, without servants, of which they had clearly had at one time, or even family milling about, was stark. Drapes were pulled closed at the end of the hall, only a thin sliver of light trailing in on them. The heavy footsteps of Damien and the guards echoed in the high-ceilinged hall, and Amma found herself hugging Kaz a bit closer. He didn't attempt to nip at her this time.

Morel stopped before a closed door, steeling himself to go inside, though there was nothing odd about the room save for the shadows it was shrouded in, and that seemed to be the manor's standard. More heavy draperies were pulled to over the line of windows at the far side of the room, the only light coming in through a set of glass doors that led to a balcony.

In the room's center stood a lavish bed with a dark-colored duvet and a tapestry spread out over the back wall, too shadowed to see. A desk was beside the entrance, the wood dark in color, its straight grain and shaded streaks suggestive of walnut if Amma's eyes were seeing it right in the dim light. She stepped off to the side to allow the guards entrance behind her.

Damien made direct eye contact with her from across the room. "Be mindful." Then he glanced down to Kaz, still in her arms. "And keep a better eye this time."

He swept back around to watch Morel cross the room. The boy picked up a statuette from the nightstand beside the bed, looking down at it as he turned to the others. His fingers slid over the wooden piece, carved into a vaguely feminine shape, eyes locked onto it.

Amma watched as Damien covertly slipped his dagger from the sheath on his forearm. Her eyes widened, afraid of what he might do, but then his other hand came around behind him, and he slid a finger up the edge of the blade to nick his thumb before sliding it back into its sheath where it was concealed. Then he crossed the room in two long strides and ripped the idol away from Morel with the hand that had been cut.

Morel stared at his hands where it had been, shock on his face that quickly turned to malice, snapping his head toward Damien who had taken a step back. But Damien didn't notice, now appearing enthralled by the idol. His thumb moved over it, and Amma only saw the droplet of blood he smeared across it because she knew what he had done. Then he let out a low chuckle.

"What are we doing?" asked one of the guards, patience worn thin as the other one glanced warily around the room.

Damien gripped the idol fully in his hand, squeezing until there was a crack. "Taking care of your little pest problem."

CHAPTER 17
IDENTIFYING ARCANA AND ITS USES

I don't know exactly what's going to come out of this, but it's not going to be a bushel of grain." Damien tightened his grip on the idol, and a hazy smoke wafted up from his hand.

The surlier guard readied himself, gripping his hilt, and the other followed suit, though much shakier.

"What's happening?" The harsh look Morel Stormwing had been giving Damien melted off his face. His arms pulled in around him, hands clasped against his chest.

"Something fairly unpleasant, I imagine, but it should be short-lived." Damien gave the idol a final squeeze, and there was a louder crack. The wood splintered in his hand, and from it a shadow shot up into the air with a human screech.

Amma covered an ear, her other hand wrapped tight around a growling Kaz as she backed fully into the Morel boy's bedchamber corner. The noise stabbed through her mind painfully, but then the feeling was gone as the sound was sucked from the room. When she looked back up, the beam of light coming through the balcony door was falling squarely on Morel, but everything about him had changed. He held himself straighter, chin up, arms and stance wide. There was no expression on his face, drawn down pallidly, but his light eyes roved over to Damien, taking in the broken idol at his feet, and then his entire form sprang across the room.

In a bound larger than he should have been capable of, all limbs spread out like a spider, Morel threw himself at Damien, but the blood mage lifted the hand he had previously sliced on his dagger, and, fingers spread, allowed the boy to slam his chest against his open palm. Morel's body jerked around the hand, falling forward with a sharp breath. From his back, a dark shadow was thrown out of Morel's body. The shade flew backward to fall on the bed, and both guards pulled out their swords at the room's doorway. Amma pressed harder against the wall.

"The fuck is that?" the more brazen guard shouted as a mass of darkness tumbled over the sheets. It spread itself out, and three forms rose up from the odd, black haze. The guard straightened, tip of his sword rising.

On the edge of the bed were perched three creatures that, if Amma had to put a name to them, she would certainly call women, if an almost comical exaggeration on the idea. Skin in vastly different shades, they were otherwise identical with wide hips, tiny waists, and breasts that strained against the thin binding strap barely holding them in. The light from the door fell squarely on the center one. Her crimson skin and the set of black, spiraling horns jutting backward from her temples were monstrous, but her features were human. Lips drawn into a deep pout, she looked on Damien and heaved an ample chest, spreading her knees slightly, and she crooked a finger at him.

Damien dropped Morel into a heap on the floor. "Interesting choice," he said, unsheathing his dagger fully this time, "if predictable." He turned to the guards. "Well?"

Both men's sword arms fell, the fear and shock on their faces replaced with goofy grins. They each took a step forward as the other two women with blue and green skin in kind, stood, one waving to them, and the other licking full lips.

"Don't you recognize a succubus when you see one?" Damien growled, and he sliced into his palm, tightening a fist around the blood that oozed up. Amma watched him call up a spell, throwing some sort of violet energy at the three, and then their faces changed. The sultry, heavy-lidded eyes flew open, flashing a hateful yellow, and jaws unhinged with a hiss to reveal rows of sharpened fangs.

The guards cried out in unison, swords back up, and just in time. The standing succubi rushed them with a flap of wings that burst out from their backs with a bone-snapping crackle. One guard was knocked out into the hall and the other into the wall, splintering the wood paneling. Amma shrieked, pressing hard into the room's darkened corner, Kaz still growling in her arms.

The third, red-skinned creature finally stood, her wings slower to unfurl as she kept her sights set on Damien. She'd been unhappy with the spell he cast, but the other two appeared to have taken the brunt of it. She raised an arm, and Morel's body raised with it, limply lifted up as if on strings.

"Oh, please." Damien rolled his eyes, not even taking a step back from Morel. He held his dagger up to the body's throat but kept his sight set on the red succubus. "If you think I won't—" Then his eyes flicked to Amma, and he clamped his mouth shut.

There was a crash from the hall and a flurry by the door as a guard threw off the green succubus, slashing blindly through the air at her. She used her wings to slow herself as she was thrown back, cutting between Damien and the other succubus. Black blood squirted out of her arm where the blade had sliced across her. She screamed in that same piercing way, and with a flap, went toward the guard again. She grappled him off the wall and tossed him across the room like he was a sack of flour where he crashed through the glass of the balcony door.

In the distraction, Damien had called up another spell. Amma watched blades form from the blood he flicked into the room. They tore into the succubus's wing as she tried to dodge them, and she hissed, raking an arm through the air.

Morel's hands shot out to wrap around Damien's neck. Again, he rolled his eyes. "He has the grip of a—" Then his eyes widened, and even Amma saw the strain in Morel's forearms as he squeezed. The succubus cackled as Damien begrudgingly sheathed his dagger and went for the boy's hands. He choked out words in that sibilant tongue Amma didn't know, and another hazy black shadow crept up Morel's back.

There was more of a scuffle from the hall on the opposite wall that Amma had herself pressed against, and a scream from the guard as well as a cheerful laugh from the succubus. Amma quickly knelt and put Kaz on the ground. "Go help him," she said, but the dog only huffed back at her. "They don't care about me," she insisted. "And Damien might need their help in a minute."

Kaz glanced back, the guard on the balcony still up and taking slashes at the third succubus in the late afternoon light, Damien working some spell on Morel, and the red succubus willing her puppet on. Kaz skittered to the chamber door.

Amma stood back up, watching as the darkness left Morel once again, hands falling off Damien's neck, leaving it red. This time, Damien took him by the shoulders and angled him away as he fell, but the succubus was prepared to take his place. She was hovering off the ground without flapping her wings, bringing herself to his height. Shooting out a hand, she took him by the collar of his tunic and ripped him backward.

Damien's large frame was thrown onto the bed. Before he could

166

block her, the succubus was on him with a single flap of her wings. She planted a knee on either side of his hips, and clawed hands dug into his shoulders, pinning him down. He grabbed her arms, but instead of casting on her, he simply fell still.

Amma gasped, nothing she could do to stop the demon from sinking fangs into his neck or shredding him with her claws, but the succubus did neither. Instead, she dipped her face down to his chest and shifted to drag her body, breasts first, along his. Amma scrunched up her nose—somehow seeing that was much worse than watching him be sliced open.

The chaos of the rest of the room, the succubi screeching and clanging of weapons, fell away, but it all appeared lost on Damien, his grip on his attacker's arms loosening from a rough hold to something closer to a caress. The succubus had lost her frightening visage, replaced again with the sultry woman who had initially appeared before them, and she skimmed her lips up the side of Damien's face.

"Oh, gods, of course," Amma grumbled, and she pulled a small stack of books off the nearest shelf. "Hey! Stop that!" She chucked a book across the room and nailed the succubus in the horn.

With a hiss, the creature's head snapped up to Amma, eyes flashing yellow and piercing through her.

Amma swallowed nervously, but heaved another book, and it bounced off Damien's still-slack face. "Don't get distracted, those breasts are attached to a demon!"

Damien shook his head just as the succubus lunged off of him. Amma shrieked as the creature flew right at her, but the woman was stopped mid-flight with a tentacle of blackness that wrapped around her throat from behind and a second around her midsection. She flailed, screeching in that skull-piercing way, and then a crimson blade sliced up through her middle from behind. With a choking gasp, the succubus's body melted around it into a pile of sizzling sludge that smelled of cinnamon and burnt hair.

Damien stood with a brand-new weapon held out, a sword of dark metal Amma had never seen him wield or even carry, covered in the demon's oozy innards, but then it disappeared in a haze. He blinked twice, seeing Amma, then quickly looked away from her as the shadows that had strangled the succubus climbed back and disappeared around his form.

Pulling his dagger out once more, he sliced through his palm again, the first cut already healed, and threw bloody blades across the room and out onto the balcony nonchalantly, cutting through the

167

green succubus as she was climbing atop the guard there. Another screech, and then another pile of sludge. Damien strode to the doorway, there was a crack followed by a wet squelch, and the guard whimpered from the hall as Damien strode back in with a huff. He wiped his dagger off on the bedding, sheathed it, and retrieved the broken idol from the ground.

The guards staggered back into the room, dazed and blinking, hanging off the wall to keep upright. One of them pressed a hand to claw marks that went through his leather armor at the shoulder, blood smeared there. "What in the Abyss?"

"The Wastes," said Damien, holding the two pieces of the idol, one in each hand. "They came from the infernal plane by way of the Accursed Wastes. Here." He tossed one half of the idol to the guard who juggled it between his hands before throwing it toward the other who simply let it pelt him in the gut and bounce to the floor. Damien turned up a lip. "Take that to one of your priests. They can confirm its origin."

Morel was pulling himself up from the ground, just as dazed. He moved like his body was tender as he retrieved the half a relic. Instead of gazing at it lovingly as he had done before, he simply stared, bleak-eyed.

"That magic you did," said the meeker guard, pointing his sword at Damien, the tip of it shaking. "That was…"

The blood mage looked up from the other half of the idol he still held, then pocketed the piece inside his cloak. He gestured to Amma and strode past the others, out of the chamber.

"Wait. That was bloodcraft you did, wasn't it?" The guard appeared to suddenly be incensed. "Stop. Stop him!"

Amma could see the fear still on the man's face and disgust creeping just behind it. "He just saved your life," she insisted.

"Come along, Valeria," Damien called from the hall.

Amma hurried after, scooping up Kaz as she went. Damien was continuing out the way they had been led despite the guards shouting for him to come back.

"Will that clear Morel's name?" she asked, catching up.

"Does it matter?"

She paused on the top of the steps even as he went down them. "Of course it does."

"Well, I don't know if it will," he said harshly, "but nothing will clear mine."

She watched him continue on, the light from the front room falling on him as he turned for it. Even to someone untrained who had just heard stories, it was easy to put together what he was. But he *had* saved those guards lives, and they would be thankful, surely, with a little reasoning. "Damien, wait, I think—"

"*Sanguinisui*, come, now."

Amma was propelled down the stairs, nearly tripping over herself to keep up with him, flooded with the urge to flee the estate. In the setting sun of the day, Amma glanced back only once, seeing the broken balcony door, the house otherwise dark. She shuddered, though whether it was from the spell urging her onward or the memory of the attack, she was unsure. The third, lanky guard was jogging up to meet them, asking after what caused the crash he'd heard, but Damien simply told him the others would need help and went for the gate.

"How did you know?" Amma asked when they passed out onto the street again.

"Could you not tell what those things were at first glance? I thought it was fairly obvious, and you're much more clever than those men."

"Oh, thanks." She chuckled, placing Kaz on the ground and reaching out for her knoggelvi when they approached. She was pleased when it actually nuzzled into her hand.

"Infernal darkness, they were pathetic," he muttered. "Falling under the succubi's charm so easily."

She clicked her tongue against her teeth. "And you didn't?"

His brows arched inward, already leading the group away with fast steps. "You will *not* speak of that ever again."

"I didn't mean identifying what they were anyway. I was talking about that possessed idol being in the house. You knew that someone had sold Morel something at the shrine. How?"

Damien shifted a hand inside his cloak pocket. "It's an old tactic of an acquaintance."

She blew out a long breath, stretching overhead as they turned down another road amongst the estates, the knoggelvi and Kaz trailing after. It wasn't the exact way they had come, but the street was quiet and pleasant with a cool breeze sweeping down it, and the magic forcing Amma to follow him was abating. "Well, that was still an awfully nice thing you did. You probably cleared Morel's name, and you stopped him being tormented by those demons which is a big help."

"Succubi and incubi aren't demons—ubi are just infernal creatures, like Kaz." Damien slowed his pace for a moment, glancing upward.

169

"Oh, okay, well regardless, getting rid of those infernal creatures was still quite thoughtful of you. If they follow up with their priests, they can destroy any more of those idols, and everyone around here will be safe."

He scoffed.

"I mean, if you think about it, you're sort of a hero to these people, and—"

"Have you forgotten already that you're the vessel of a talisman that renders you helpless to me, and that I'll be killing you later to fetch it out?"

Amma's shoulders drooped, and it was her turn to knit her brow.

"If you would like that death to be swift and painless, I would suggest not insulting me with words like *thoughtful* and *hero*." He took another turn where the estates were even farther apart from one another. It didn't appear they were headed back into town, but they weren't headed for the road either, and evening was slowly falling all around them.

Amma huffed. It wasn't meant to be an insult, but the finality to his voice told her there would be no convincing him otherwise. "Where are we going?"

He took a few more long strides she had to hurry to keep up with, and then stopped. "Here, I suppose, is good enough."

Damien turned to face a garden with high walls of sandy-colored brick covered in thick ivy. It stood alone, the closest estate set far off from the quiet path they had taken away from the main road, and the entrance they faced looked disused. They hadn't passed a villager in some time, and the sounds of evening had come out, crickets chirping in competing tones and a loon somewhere far off called into the setting dusk.

Damien stepped forward through the arch in the garden wall, its gate falling open at an angle. Though the exterior was sprawling, it looked uncared for, a corner of some lord's too-lofty estate, tucked away and forgotten.

"Um, this looks private," Amma said, standing at the arch and peeking in, the knoggelvi mimicking her from behind.

The path that led inward was overgrown, flat stones for walking along were hemmed in at their edges with dainty, white flowers. They led to a tree with a thick trunk that spun around itself and branches crawling overhead, gnarled to look just like its roots.

"Whoa, that is one beautiful calpurnica." Amma knew the tree, from both the look of it and the scent of its early-autumn blossoms, a sage green flower that was only slightly lighter than its thick leaves, of which would last into early winter. The cover was thick and sprawling and cast the entrance to the garden even darker.

Damien eyed her for a moment then swept through, seeming to take no notice of the ancient tree or the wild lilac bushes fighting for dominance with the cornflowers and knapweeds that tried to choke them back. Equally, he seemed unconcerned that this was where neither of them belonged. Into the shadows he went, Kaz scurrying along at his heels, and Amma followed before she completely lost sight of him in the overgrown garden.

CHAPTER 18
TRADE DEALS, TARIFFS, AND TRANSLOCATION

Damien pulled the idol from his pocket again. It was maybe the third time since they'd left the Stormwing manor, but he knew himself well enough: his patience wouldn't hold up, not even long enough for them to get out of town first. He had to know for sure, and he had to know *now*.

The garden was deserted and walled. It wouldn't protect from infernal arcana, but he hadn't seen a single guard wandering amongst the estates, holy or otherwise. A mistake on their part, but then he had taken care of their Abyssal problem, even if they didn't know they had it. Amma was right about that at the least, though it was just an aftereffect of his true goal.

There was a sparse patch of ground ahead, and Damien took a look around. The walls were set far off but high; one would need to stand on the roof of the closest estate to see inside, and the place was so ill-kept he doubted anyone would. As the sky shifted to deeper blue, he placed the half of the idol on the ground, his smear of blood still across it. Spent blood lost its magic quickly, a lucky thing for blood mages who were so cavalier with the stuff. It was only through arcane means of preservation that their inherent magic could linger in a droplet or smear, and that needed to be done immediately.

Damien moved to slice his finger once again on his dagger, but stopped. No. This would take much more blood than that.

He tugged down his tunic and cut into his chest this time, cold metal against skin still hot from the succubus, both from fighting her and...the other thing she'd done. Perhaps it was foolish to cast now, after expending so much arcana already, but the thought was a moment too late into the commitment. And this was no time to show weakness, especially with that embarrassment back in the bedchamber.

Succubi weren't typically formidable, and had he just cut through that Stormwing boy, he could have taken down the one who had gotten to him, but spending the time to expel the possession allowed that infernal creature to see too deeply into him and exploit the thing he wanted.

Being too careful with that human also put him right in harm's way. That wasn't how Damien did things, but when he saw Amma there in the corner, watching him hold a dagger to such a weak and possessed man, he felt compelled to show mercy, like he was the one embedded with an enthrallment talisman.

And weakness always followed weakness. Pinned down under the succubus, Damien had fallen under its charm, briefly but dangerously, and when he looked up, he hadn't actually seen the infernal creature atop him. Ubi creatures showed their victims forms and faces they believed would entice them, and Damien was embarrassed to admit she had looked like Amma for a moment. It was because the woman was in the room, of course, an easy target for the succubus to copy, but that visage had stripped away any desire for him to hurt the thing. And that was disadvantageous.

Damien shook his head, placing a hand over the cut on his chest before it healed. Hot blood seeped up between his fingers, but this cast would be different, not fast, not defensive. This was ritualistic, this was searching, feeling, calling. The idol had told Damien almost everything he needed to know—it had been turned into a gateway for purely infernal creatures. Like Kaz, when a succubus was killed, she returned to the infernal plane and would have to be summoned again in order to pass into the realm. But they needed someone to do the summoning.

The bit of wood cracked, and a red glow emanated from it. Damien cocked his head. Typically it was only a sigil that would pass through, a marker that would tell him who cast the initial spell, writing itself across the vessel for a moment before being swept away for good. No sigil showed itself, but instead, the bits of wood broke away from one another as the ground rumbled and tore itself apart. Damien took one step back, hearing Amma gasp behind him.

From inside the newly-created hole, smoke rose up. The earth fell away from itself, the flicker of a flame inside and then pitch darkness below. This wasn't how gateways to the infernal typically worked, they were never two-way. But the telltale signs of noxscura were not flooding over the fissure to suggest it actually led to the infernal plane. As impossible as it seemed, it looked instead as if a direct portal to somewhere else on earth itself had just opened.

"...don't you dare move, I'll be right—Bloodthorne?"

Damien heard his name spoken with that mixture of elation and disgust unique to only one being in existence. The darkness inside the hole shifted, and a head of brilliantly white hair appeared over the edge of the ground followed by two dark eyes that narrowed on him.

The man pulled himself up from the hole in one, swift movement, body long and lithe and dressed as if he had not just climbed through dirt and fire. He was barely dressed at all, in fact, with only a short, satin robe to cover him, thankfully tied tight enough about the waist with a silky sash. His mouth fell open with a wide smile, and when he spoke, the words dripped from it with a delighted revulsion, "Well, well, well, if it isn't my favorite demon spawn."

The name ripped out of Damien like a curse: "Shadowhart."

"How in the Abyss are—hey! My portal! You destroyed it!" Xander Shadowhart's shift from excited pleasantries to astonished rage brought a grin to Damien's lips. "Do you have any idea how long that took to make?"

"If anyone could possibly understand—"

"Yes, of course, it would be you! I can't imagine anyone else could undo my most theoretical work yet anyway." Xander kicked with a bare foot at one of the bits of wood that had once been a possessed gateway, then he crossed his arms and put back on that smarmy grin. "Not that I'm complaining."

"What are you wearing?"

Xander glanced down at himself, the silky fabric in a deep violet sliding over his tanned skin to reveal more of his lightly muscled, bare chest beneath. "You like it? It's not mine, but I think she'll let me keep it if I ask. Or if I just tell her it's mine now."

"It's not armor."

"Oh, who wears armor to bed, Damien? It covers up some of the best bits."

"Bed?" Damien glanced at the hole again then to Xander, standing there as if he had not planned any of this at all. "That goes directly to the Wastes? To your tower? How did you—"

"Ah, ah, I don't give away tricks for free, and especially not before proper introductions." Xander strode past him, extending a hand, and Damien remembered quite suddenly he was not alone in the garden.

Damien cut Xander off with his body. Behind him, Amma shifted and stiffened, sensing the danger, and Xander put up both hands but didn't back away. Daring for a man half naked.

"From afar then," he said, and clasping his hands behind him, Xander gave the slightest of bows, coming that much closer to them both, head bent, eyes averted, too trusting. "Xander Sephiran Shadowhart, at your disservice."

"That's your name?" Amma ventured quietly, half obscured by Damien's arm.

Xander rose back up to his full height, just the same as Damien's, pointed chin jutting out. "The myth incarnate."

And then Amma, the brilliant creature she was, actually laughed. Damien could have kissed her.

The corners of Xander's mouth plunged, voice falling flat. "What?"

"It's just…a lot of name, that's all."

"Oh, and his is so much better? Maleficus sounds like some kind of angry fern, and Bloodthorne has absolutely no subtlety to it."

"They are both sort of ridiculous," Amma giggled out.

Damien's own grin deflated a bit, and as if he fed right off of it, Xander regained his composure, licking his lips. "And what do they call you, kitten?" There was a venom behind that pet name, the kind only Xander could inject, both absolutely meaning it and hating that he did so.

"I'm just Amma."

"Amma," he repeated, rolling the name around his mouth like he were tasting her, gaze traveling down her body. It wasn't terribly different than how he looked at almost everybody, but it made Damien's blood run a bit hotter, spells itching to be released from his veins. But Damien waited—if anyone could sense Bloodthorne's Talisman of Enthrallment, it would be Xander.

His dark eyes tracked back up Amma a second time, thin, white brows arching with intrigue, lips pursed in deep thought, but there wasn't the kind of recognition on his face that the talisman warranted. And, just like the thin material of his robe, Xander wasn't very good at shielding his excitement. Amma was human, not even arcane, and she was clearly with Damien, in some capacity. That's all Xander could glean, the talisman completely hidden, and it was bloody brilliant, if begging for some kind of explanation.

"And you've got an imp with you as well?" Xander's eyes flicked to Damien's feet where Kaz had come to sit still in his canine disguise, something another blood mage could easily see through. "Bloodthorne, what *are* you up to?"

Damien relaxed as Xander finally took a step back. "None of your business."

"Well, you've sort of made it my business by wrecking my trial, not to mention the very good time I was having watching my girls cause a bit of chaos." He paced a few steps, lifting long fingers to drum on his chin. "But I know you're not gallivanting around the heart of Eiren for something as petty as thwarting me. I thought you were just in the mines of Phandar not long ago, and when did we even see each other last? You've been so busy you haven't given me the opportunity to kill you in almost a year. Whatever you're doing, it must be grievous."

"I don't give away information for free either."

"You'd like to trade for how I made the rift, wouldn't you? To figure out how close I've gotten to mastering translocation, eh?" Xander's smile widened as he stepped up to the hole still smoking and flickering in the ground then hopped over it, easy enough with long limbs. "Hmm, no, your words levied against mine aren't an even enough bargain. I'd be willing to take something else though." He grinned over at Amma.

Damien felt Amma shift further behind him. Good instinct on her part, though he fought against his own to fully cover her. Letting Xander know how much he cared about her—or rather, cared about the talisman—would go over about as well as a dragon with its wings shorn off.

"How about I give you all my notes on this spell, including the parchment I lifted from the Grand Order, and you give me that little human who's inexplicably following you around. Fair?"

Damien's jaw tightened, and he swallowed. "The spell's experimental, you said so yourself."

Xander groaned. "Fine, you can throw in the imp too, if you insist. I'm flattered you don't want to cheat me considering the value you'll be getting."

"I've seen your writings," Damien said, keeping his voice taut. "You only spell phonetically in Chthonic."

"Oh, it's *literally* a dead language, Bloodthorne, no one cares how you spell it," he groused then inhaled sharply. "But, I'm happy to duel you for it instead then. Winner takes everything? The spell, the imp, the girl?" He slid a hand beneath his robe's lapel.

Shit, thought Damien. He only wanted to confirm Xander was behind the possession and that he had thwarted him, but he hadn't counted on coming face-to-face with a fellow blood mage. Reflexively, he unhitched his dagger and slid the hilt into his palm.

"Really?" he mustered as drolly as possible. "You want to play some childish game now?"

"If it's just a game, it should be easy enough to win." Xander revealed the vial that hung from an exceptionally long, leather cord around his neck. The slender tube was filled with a thick, crimson liquid—his blood—stored careless and cavalier with an enchantment to hold the arcana in it, as was Xander's way. As his other hand came up to uncork it, he paused, and then his lips came together in another exaggerated pout. "Unless...oh, Bloodthorne, you're not actually considering going after it, are you?"

Damien lifted one brow. Now, that was interesting. The two of them were on near identical paths in life, and if Xander had suddenly figured out that Damien was headed to Eirengaard to release his father, why would he be so disapproving?

Xander clicked his tongue and dropped the vial so that it hung against his tan chest. "Listen, I doubt very much it's worth it. You know Malcolm blew himself up with that book, and I'd just be an absolute wreck if you accidentally killed yourself, and I ended up having nothing to do with it."

"Malcolm's dead?" Damien cocked his head.

When he nodded, both men dropped their chins and drew Xs over their chests, eyes flicking to the ground.

"Rest in darkness," Damien muttered as Xander whispered the same.

"But seriously,"—Xander pulled the neckline of his robe a bit tighter, the vial hidden again—"that Lux Codex is a grimoire for good. It practically ate through his hands when he touched it."

"Well, Mal was more allergic than most to holy texts."

"Sure, sure, but the binding on it is said to be dipped in luxerna itself. And the spells in that thing, from what I understand, are the exact opposite of our brand of arcana. Trying to work them actually *turned* him a bit—that's what his imps say anyway—and then he just combusted, spontaneously. It sounds like a messy way to go, not even a head left to have mounted." His lip curled with disgust at the wastefulness. "And I'm sure you remember just how nice Mal managed to keep his face. No scars or anything."

Damien rolled his eyes, but put the dig out of his mind, replaced with the idea of this Lux Codex. The crickets had gotten louder as night fell around them, buzzing in his brain with the image of a book that held magic so contrary to a blood mage's that its pages couldn't be safely touched by his kind. A firefly blinked into existence out in the bushes and then disappeared. "If I did want the book, where would I find it?"

Xander snorted out a laugh, biting his tongue. "If I tell you, will you share it?"

"I thought it wasn't worth going after?"

"Well, if *you* want it, then *I* want it, that's how this has always worked, with the odd exception, if you remember."

Damien did remember, and despite nearing thirty, Xander still acted just like the spoiled child he had first met over two decades prior. Almost each memory Damien had of him involved being tricked or hurt or challenged, all but one, and he wasn't sure that memory was even real.

But with their history also came the knowledge of what actually got to the other blood mage. He set his gaze right in the center of Xander's forehead and imagined boring a hole through to his squirrely, little brain. He wiped all emotion off his face and just stared, waiting, giving him nothing.

"Oh, fine!" Xander threw up his hands, and they were all lucky the shadows were doing the work his short robe couldn't. "Some intrepid adventurers recovered the book in the mess Mal left behind—I may have bumped into them trying to recover it myself, infuriating bunch of bastards—and anyway, they brought it to this library they've got in a place called Faebarrow, you know, with the magical grass or whatever? Just west of here, maybe a week or two if you go all the way around the Gloomweald. The Faebarrowins call their library The Grand Athenaeum because, apparently, they think quite highly of themselves for putting a few books together all in one room, but,"—he leaned in, a hand to the side of his mouth to whisper as if there were anyone else around to hear—"apparently the Lux Codex isn't even that well-guarded because they think the thing can't be stolen by a set of evil hands what with the burning when we touch it and all." He wriggled his fingers and snickered. "Admittedly, I did *not* have a plan for that."

Damien tried to keep the look of interest off his face, but it was mostly pointless—he'd asked, and Xander already knew.

"I can help when you fetch it." Xander reached into a pocket, and Damien readied himself, but the tiny stone he pulled out didn't seem particularly threatening. He tossed it through the air, and Damien caught it. In his palm, it was no bigger than an acorn, inside a red mist swirling about like a bloody sandstorm.

"That's another of these." Xander stepped back into the crevasse in the ground and began to descend as if steps were built right into the earth. "If you use it, you'll have a much better idea of how the whole

178

thing works, and you get the added bonus of seeing me in my natural habitat on the other end. Now, don't get killed, that's my job, but do have a little fun on the way."

As he sauntered downward, Damien pocketed the tiny orb. "You're being exceptionally generous for such an asshole."

"Oh, no, I'm not." Xander laughed as he finished descending, sticking a hand up through the rift as it began to close. "Toodles, Bloodthorne. And kitten, it was a pleasure. Until we meet again." The earth swallowed itself up just as he pulled his fingers away leaving the smell of cinnamon and charred flesh behind.

Damien stared at the spot he had disappeared within, the ground upset and burnt in his wake, but otherwise there was only the faint flicker of the infernal left behind, like at the shrine but even weaker. The spell he'd concocted for translocation, the one Damien now had a copy of in his own pocket, might have been experimental, but it was...*adequate*.

"Who on earth was *that*?" Amma peeked out from around Damien's arm to stare down at where Xander had gone.

Damien inhaled fully, recomposing himself. "A total prick."

Amma made a quiet, surprised noise in the back of her throat. "He just climbed out of the ground, and you said he came from his home? That's...that's amazing."

"Yes, yes." Damien waved her awe away. "Xander is...*Xander*."

"I saw that vial around his neck. He's like you, isn't he? Another blood mage?" She came to stand in front of him, eyes huge and full of even more questions than the multitude that fell out of her mouth. "Are you brothers? You don't really look anything alike."

"He is a blood mage as well, yes, and his mother is another demonic lord, but we're of no relation." Damien scoffed at the thought of Birzuma languishing in her own occlusion crystal, taken by Archibald a decade or so after his own father. She had been wreaking some kind of havoc out on the shores of the realm before being imprisoned. Zagadoth only ever had the most unpleasant things to say about her, and Damien's own memories of the demonic lordess from his childhood were fuzzy, as if his mind were protecting him from fully remembering. Amma didn't need to know any of that, though—she didn't even know about Zagadoth's predicament, so there was no use.

"It seems like you've known each other for a long time." Amma rocked up onto her toes, tipping her head up. "Like you're good friends."

"Bloody Abyss, no!" Damien clenched a fist. "I hate the mere thought of him. He's a despicable, little rat, and someday I will crush him into the nothing he is, and blot out his entire infernal lineage."

Amma frowned. "Is this one of those times when you're exaggerating to seem scary, or do you really mean it?"

"Of course I mean it. He is vile and wretched, and I loathe the fact he exists at all."

She bit a full bottom lip, eyes glassy. "Oh, well, but…were you really considering trading me to him for that spell?"

"No, of course n—" Damien's answer caught in his throat, and he looked her over. She was giving him another variation on *that* face, the one that could pull out almost whatever she wanted from him. "I *did* consider it," he lied, "but my work is far superior to anything Xander could come up with, so I'll be keeping you and the talisman. For now."

When he whipped away from her to head back for the garden's entrance, she hurried to catch up. "Because I'm helpful, right?"

Damien snorted but grinned, an easy thing to hide with her behind him. "Yes, exactly."

CHAPTER 19
A VERY GOOD THIEF AND A VERY BAD VILLAIN

Amma hadn't thought this far ahead. That man, Xander, had mentioned Faebarrow which was enough to make her innards clench and mouth go dry, but when Damien changed their course to head for the barony, she actually broke out in a sweat and patches of itchy redness all along her neck. They couldn't go to Faebarrow, they just *couldn't*, not together, not at all.

But Damien wasn't keen on spending another night, not even another moment, in Elderpass, and so they left that evening after the run-in with the other blood mage. Damien seemed renewed by the experience and had them travel well after it had gotten dark, but he also seemed eager to put space between them and the town. Amma knew this was because of the guards who had seen him do magic with his blood. There were plenty of mages in the realm of Eiren, most in service to the crown and many even within the royal houses, but of course none of them did bloodcraft. Considered innately evil, just like demons and the dark gods they served, blood mages were rumored to have horns and hooves and intentions that would put an end to anything that got in their way.

But Damien wasn't like that, not really—at least he didn't have any body parts that looked terribly goat-like—and even as Amma sat astride a knoggelvi, creepy and dark though masked to look like an average horse, and plotted to get away from him, she knew Damien was different from all that.

But *how much* different was the question.

When they finally stopped for the night, Damien had Kaz build them a fire that he lit with the flick of his tail to fend off the chill, and then the imp curled into a ball and slept before his night watch began. The road from Elderpass toward the west was mostly flat, and even behind a copse and against a tree, there was a breeze. Amma pulled her cloak around her, sitting close to the fire, and across it sat Damien, knees splayed out, elbows propped up on them, staring deeply into the flames.

"Are you sure you want to do this?"

He looked up. "Do what?"

Amma swallowed, trying to sound as casual as she could. "Waste your time going to that Fae-whatever place instead of Eirengaard. It's not exactly on the way."

"You wish to shorten your time left here on earth? Eager to meet the gods in Empyrea?"

Oh, *of course* that's what he thought of first. She looked over to Kaz, knowing he would agree, but the imp was still asleep. "No, it's just that you said Xander isn't your friend, so why do you even trust him about that book? He said it killed your other friend, which I am sorry about, by the way."

"Malcolm wasn't my—listen, you don't need to worry about what or who I trust, all right? I know what I'm doing." His eyes dropped back to the fire, and he bit down on a rabbit bone from their dinner, gnawing it.

She sighed, wrapping her arms around her knees. "Well, I know it's hard losing someone you're close to, so if you want to talk about it—"

"I do not."

His words felt very final, and Amma frowned, heat in her face from the offer. She supposed it was sort of stupid, and she should have known better, but it cost her nothing to offer kind words, or at least she thought it would. She didn't expect to earn his scorn though.

"He was very skilled," Damien said then. When she looked up, he was still gnawing on the bone, but his features had changed, a little softer under the firelight.

Amma was careful not to spook the talkativeness out of him. "Was he a blood mage too?"

Damien nodded absently. "He was one hundred, maybe one hundred and fifty or so, hard to tell with all the enchantments he used on his face, but I suppose he lived a long and fulfilling life."

"Did you know each other well?"

"We were acquainted enough to share notes a time or two. He showed me a more efficient way to summon imps when I was quite a bit younger, not that I utilize them that often." He tipped his head. "I

182

think he may have had a lich cat. Or was it an undead raccoon? No…no, that was Everild, and I'm pretty sure it was actually a badger. Malcolm had a sort of moat filled with very bitey fish, could tear the flesh off the bone in seconds. He could somehow tell them apart, and they all had names. Maybe he was just fucking with me though."

She studied his face, how his brows knit and then the corner of his mouth turned up. He didn't seem particularly sad, but he was admitting to not being terribly friendly with this dead man. And then she was surprised when he went on.

"We would always speak at Yvlcon gatherings, but I suppose I didn't know much about his personal life, and what I did learn I wasn't…keen on. He always had a new bride, someone very pretty and very young, never would say what happened to the last one, and you know, it just gets distasteful when your wife could be your grandchild. And that's another thing—he didn't have any of those because he always came up with some frivolous excuse to kill off his own children. I never understood any of that. I mean, if someone is willing to marry you, to have your child, why would you throw it all away…" Damien shook his head. "Nevermind, that's not the point. It's just that, I didn't even know he died. I've been wrapped up in my work for a while—my whole life, really—but never as separate as I've been from the others for the last few years."

"Aren't you all working toward the same thing though? Realm domination? Seems like it could put you at odds."

"Perhaps, but there are other things that need doing, crystals that need breaking and all that."

"But you miss your…"—she squinted at him, testing the word—"your friends?"

"That's the *thing*," he said, pointing at her with the bone but staring hard into the fire. "I don't. I'm surprised I wasn't abreast of what happened, but not all that bothered. My colleague is gone, so I should be bothered, shouldn't I?" When Damien looked up at her, she read the deep confusion on his face.

Was he actually asking her? Truly looking for advice? Her chest tightened, but she tried not to show the anticipation on her face.

"Um, well? Sometimes we grow apart from people." He nodded back, really looking at her and listening, so she carefully went on. "Especially if our goals or the way we feel about the world no longer aligns. You said you didn't like how he handled his relationships, so maybe you're just not sorry *Malcolm* is gone. Is there another person you'd be upset about losing? Or someone you lost that made you feel…bothered?"

Damien thought a moment longer, the pinched confusion falling away as the flames jumped in his violet eyes. "My mother," he said so softly she almost didn't hear, but then he flicked away the bone and sat straighter. "Well, it hardly matters. A man got himself killed by being an idiot. Such is life. And death."

Amma so badly wanted to drag him back to what he'd whispered, to make him say *anything else* about that, but the change in his demeanor told her it wouldn't be welcome if she asked, so she did the kinder thing and narrowed her eyes at him. "And you want to go way off course and do the same thing that idiot was doing when he died?"

"Difference is, I have something he didn't." Damien grinned back at her slyly. "A good set of hands that will do exactly what I tell them to."

They woke early the next morning, and with less sleep than normal, Amma was especially tired. Thankful for the knoggelvi, who happily accepted another sugar cube and nuzzled her in repayment, she stared out at the westerly way with bleary eyes as they rode, undeterred from Faebarrow. Damien's mood had lightened, and he didn't snap at either of them even when they were slow to get moving or when Kaz badgered him with questions about heading so far off course yet again.

Once the sun was high in the sky and her mind got to working a bit harder, she considered if heading to Faebarrow might actually be beneficial. It was where she needed to end up, regardless, she just didn't expect to be there with a strange man, looking so much like a villain with his black armor and his mysterious scar and his knitted brows, not to mention all the spooky blood magic. It was almost too perfect, she suddenly realized, staring over at him from her spot on her mount.

As if the two moons had aligned and an arcane eclipse were gifting Amma with unimaginable luck, Damien's presence with her would bring credence to a claim that she had no idea previously how she might prove. If she just bade her time until they were deep in Faebarrow—but the *scroll*. She needed the Scroll of the Army of the Undead first.

"What?"

Amma blinked, pulling her gaze away. She'd been staring and lost herself as her mind worked, but she had no idea how he noticed: he had been studying the pages of that boring book he called research again. "Nothing, I was just thinking."

"About?" Damien turned a page.

Thankfully, he hadn't used that word that forced out the truth. Her eyes flicked to the road ahead and a line of trees there. "Poplar."

"Pop-what?"

"Poplar trees." She pointed at the row coming up on their right. "There are three different kinds, black ones, white ones, and greys like those." When he continued to look at her as if waiting for more, she figured she should go on despite that no one, except Laurel on rare occasion, ever really wanted to hear more when she was talking about trees. "The grey ones are superior. They're a hybrid of the other two kinds and have the best of them both, so they grow faster and taller than their parent plants."

"You know a lot about shrubs and things, don't you?"

"Sort of." She shrugged. "Trees, really."

"Then you should like where we're headed. They've got a very unique species there."

"I know," she mumbled, busying her hands with the braids she'd put into the knoggelvi's mane.

"Perhaps we will take the time to seek them out, if you wish."

Amma's eyes went wide, but before either of them could acknowledge the cordiality in that offer, Kaz began to complain about additional detours, and Damien grumbled back at him about who makes the decisions.

When Kaz was admonished and Damien went back to his book, Amma grit her teeth, the scroll jumping right back into her mind. How would she get that stupid roll of enchanted parchment without him noticing? He didn't carry much on him, so it had to be in one of his pockets, but how would she get close enough to pick it?

Get herself in trouble, that would almost certainly put her in position. Damien was nothing if not protective—of the talisman, of course, but that was inseparable from her body at the moment. If she were involved in some scuffle, there also might be just enough distraction that he wouldn't notice her lifting it off of him.

Yes, that could work, but it relied on an outside source, and it meant she had to put herself in harm's way. Enough of that happened on its own, but when she really needed it, she wasn't sure she could manifest another supposed abductor.

There *was* another way, though.

Amma slid her gaze over to Damien again, as covertly as possible. He had his head bent but back straight, a large hand turning another page, throat bobbing with a swallow, eyebrow arching in thought as those violet eyes took in the words of the book. Damien might have been a blood mage, and he might have had the upper hand in just about every instance with her, but he was still a man—the succubi had done nothing if not proven that—and even if Amma weren't as well endowed as those infernal creatures or capable of possession, she was still a woman.

She let her gaze travel down his long form sitting atop the horse, the rigid leather armor over a well-built body, one he didn't really need what with the power of his magic but still generously maintained, then back up to his face, black hair like a raven's wing brushed away so he could read. It really was an extraordinarily pleasant face, even with, or perhaps enhanced by, that scar, especially when it wasn't pinched in anger.

She could start by running her fingers through that hair and then down the back of his neck, tickle over his broad shoulders, undo the straps of his armor. It wouldn't even be a burden, really. In fact, she might even like it. And of course, at some point, she supposed, she would have to slip into a pocket and grab the scroll. But she'd have fun figuring out just which one it was in.

Violet and piercing, Damien's eyes found her again, and her heart sped up like her thoughts had been drawn out in vivid detail on her face. This time, Amma couldn't hide what her mouth did, turning up as her eyes darted down. She'd been caught, and she could feel him still staring even as she tried hard to empty her mind of what he might look like stripped of his tunic. As the image persisted, she felt her face redden, biting her lip and failing to keep the smile off of it.

Do not ask me what I'm thinking about, she insisted internally as if she could cast her own enthrallment over him, though if he had ordered the truth out of her, the desire to steal the scroll wouldn't have even been floating around in her mind to tell, eclipsed instead by much lewder thoughts.

"Amma," Damien said, his voice such a low rumble then, that she would be compelled to follow any command he gave with or without the enchanted word.

Amma's knoggelvi reared up with a whinny, and when it slammed its hooves back down, she was nearly jostled right off its back just as the image of Damien nearly undressed was jostled right out of her mind.

On the path, a creature had darted out, all gnashing teeth and swiping claws. It charged her knoggelvi, missing as it cantered backward, then moved in a green blur, little more than a hiss and a tail. There was a sizzle and a snap through the air, and arcana connected with the thing, sending it tumbling off of the road. It landed in a heap amongst the tall grass.

Damien dismounted in one quick movement and crossed before Amma's calming knoggelvi to where it had fallen. A groan emanated from the creature, small now that Amma could properly see it, and it rolled onto its back. Stout and covered with scales, she had never seen anything like it until she had been to Aszath Koth, shocked something so similar was in the realm of Eiren.

The creature tried to sit up, but fell back again, and that's when she could see the bruising. Older marks, not from Damien's attack, blossomed in purples and blues all up its side and along its jaw where its skin was pale.

"Don't hurt it," Amma called as Damien stood over it. "It's already badly injured."

He took a knee beside it. "I don't intend to."

Amma slid down off of her mount in a hurry, stumbling in the dirt. Damien had a hand over a new wound on the creature, likely the one he'd just given it. He said something sibilant, and from below his palm a dark smoke emanated, and the wound began to close itself up, though the skin did not stitch itself very neatly.

With its eyes closed and head lolling to the side, it would have looked dead if not for the rise and fall of its chest covered in a yellowed, thick skin and more of that old bruising. If it had been standing on two feet, it would have perhaps reached her hip, and she could tell it walked on two legs, clawed hands lax at its sides.

"What is it?" Amma asked quietly.

"A draekin," Damien told her, finishing the spell and looking it over. "But I've seen very few outside of Aszath Koth and never this far south in Eiren."

The draekin wore tattered but well-fitting breeches and a threadbare vest, so like a small human, but it had a thick tail covered in green scales and a long snout with slits for nostrils and many pointed teeth. It mumbled out something like words, turning its head to Damien. Then yellow eyes opened fully, and it hissed again, attempting to scramble to its feet, wincing, and only managing to push up onto an elbow and hold out a claw less than menacingly. Amma backed up and shrieked anyway.

"Calm yourself," Damien said, holding out a hand and never flinching, "unless you'd like me to reopen the wound I just closed. I'm admittedly much better at that."

The draekin's jaw remained opened, fangs on display, but it brought back its talons to feel around on its chest until it found the newly-healed wound. Its browless eyes narrowed with a second lid, features contorting.

Amma took a breath, hand on her chest. "He looks like a baby dragon," she said, tilting her head from the spot behind Damien she deemed safe enough. At least, he looked the way they were described except for the wings, though she had never seen one.

"I'm thirty-three, you idiot!" it spat in a scratchy voice and snapped again at Damien's hand.

"They are distantly related," Damien said.

"And I can call one down to burn the two of you to a crisp, if I want!"

Amma pulled back, even with the blood mage between them, though she doubted his claim very much. "Are they always so mean?"

"Yes, but usually only when you're smaller than they are." Damien glanced out at the line of thin trees and bushes off the roadway. "Where is the rest of your clan?"

The draekin hissed. "Like I would tell you, filthy humans!"

Damien sighed, standing, then snapped his fingers. Beside him, Kaz's canine form contorted suddenly, and the imp was returned to his crimson and terrible state, though still clad in the green sweater.

The draekin looked on Kaz with surprise, then it seemed to calm, pushing up onto its haunches with another wince.

"It's bad enough you're attacking things much bigger than you with those kinds of injuries, but why are you even out here in a field? And by the road?" Damien scanned the nearby tall grasses again.

Rolling over another grumble in its throat, the draekin looked from one of them to the other, and then back to Kaz. "We had a den, but it was destroyed. We don't have anywhere else." It moved its arm tenderly.

"Well, you are very lucky I found you and not one of those Holy Knights."

The draekin growled then, but not at them. His lipless mouth curled down into something like a frown over his fangs. "Those knights are the whole reason we're out here. They set fires in our den and cut down almost every one of us that wasn't burnt alive."

Amma covered her mouth. "What did you do to make them attack?"

"Nothing!" It lunged at her with the word, eyes sharp and full of pain.

Damien did not stand as defensively as Amma thought that reaction warranted, but the creature didn't really move from its spot. Instead, Damien leaned down just a little, looking at him closer. "Draekin raise livestock and forage, and they have songs and stories of their kind. They're almost exactly like dwarves but with scales.

188

Unless they were, I don't know, waging some sort of tiny war on the nearest town—and look at him, I doubt it—they probably warranted no such attack. Of course, they were *existing* which is quite a risky thing here in the realm from what I hear, so well protected by the Holy Knights of Osurehm." There was a heavy tinge of sarcasm in his voice.

"You speak like you know us," the draekin hissed.

"I was raised by your kind in the infernal mountains," said Damien.

The draekin's beady eyes appraised him dubiously then spoke again in a series of clicks and growls that Amma knew had to be a language but was completely incomprehensible to her.

Damien nodded. "And may the rock you rest on always be hot."

The draekin's tongue darted out, and he visibly relaxed. "There were a hundred of us, but now we're only eight." With some effort, he gestured over his shoulder to the thicket. There was a rustling, and two more draekin shuffled out, both injured and supporting one another. Behind followed an elderly one with a bit of a hunch, then another, younger and thinner, holding claws with an even tinier one, and a final draekin with a swath of cloth strapped around her and a speckled egg nestled inside.

Amma's eyes widened, stomach twisting at the blame she'd been so quick to lay at their clawed feet. The colors of their scales ranged from a greenish hue to a deeper blue, and though they were all short, she could clearly see now the difference between a child draekin and the adult who was struggling to stand before them.

The smallest one was most cautious, hiding half behind the others and peeking out, a thumb in its mouth. Amma could barely contain the urge to pick him up and give him a good cuddle. Even with the teeth, she couldn't imagine the sweet, little thing being a threat, so why would the Holy Knights chase the lot of them off? Though, he said there had been a hundred, so there was no chasing for the others, she supposed, only death, and this certainly hadn't been the only child.

"Aszath Koth, do you know it?" Damien was looking over all of them as they cautiously came to stand in a small huddle.

A few of the others nodded.

"You will be welcome there." He pulled a scrap of parchment from the pouch on his hip, and as Amma watched, she saw the rolled-up Scroll of the Army of the Undead hidden inside. Damien ran a hand over the blank parchment, and with a puff of smoke, a symbol drew itself in fire across it. "When you enter the city, find the Infernal

Brotherhood of The Tempest. They display this symbol on their temple near the city gates, but they are quite difficult to miss. Tell them Lord Bloodthorne sent you and that they are to help you find the other draekin clans in the city. And don't drink the wine."

The draekin looked over the bit of parchment for a long moment when he took it, then folded it away and nodded solemnly. With another strange click, he turned for the others and began to head back for the thicket.

"Wait!" Amma ran back to the knoggelvi and dug around in the satchel strapped to it for the rations they'd bought in Elderpass and returned, handing them off. Then she scrambled into her own pouch for the rest of her coins. The draekin passed the wrapped-up rations to one another, but eyed the coins she was thrusting at him suspiciously.

Damien waved his hand. "Coin won't be useful to them here— most of the humans in Eiren won't give them the chance to spend it."

"But what about in Aszath Koth? They will need something when they get there."

"Well, yes, I supposed when they reach the city that will be,"—he raised a brow as the draekin finally cupped his claws and received the sum from Amma—"well, that will certainly be a *very* helpful amount."

Amma pulled back as quickly as she could after giving over the last of her gold, silver, and copper. The draekin with the egg strapped to her chest stepped up to them. "We, uh…we're sorry we tried to eat you."

Damien shrugged. "Everyone must eat."

The littlest one started chomping on what he'd been handed immediately, and with a full snout croaked out, "You're the nicest humans we ever met."

Amma grinned over at Damien, and he snarled. "Well, I'm not really human."

With another round of gratitude, the draekins disappeared in the tall grasses, and Damien and Amma went back to their disguised mounts. Kaz, who had shifted back into a dog, began to complain that Amma had given away all of their food, but she was quick to correct him that there was still at least one hunk of bread in the bag, and they needn't worry since the apples in this part of the realm were in season. Once they were mounted back up and on their way, Kaz had not stopped complaining, but Damien insisted that if worse came to worst, imp would suffice for dinner, and that shut him up.

Amma found herself staring at Damien again, this time outwardly, and when he inquired what was on her mind, she did not look away. "You could have left them, or even killed them, but you helped them instead. That was very sweet of you."

"Oh, Amma, thank you."

She beamed at his sudden appreciation for the compliment, then her smile faltered. "Wait, really?"

He pressed a hand to his stomach. "Yes, of course—you've rectified the fact you've given away all of our food: I don't think I'll ever have an appetite again after being called *sweet*."

"Stop it—you know it was!"

"No, my actions were only prudent." He stared forward, jaw hardening. "Draekin are good warriors when they're in their prime. A few of them could be useful in the future, and new blood will be good for the existing clans up north, not to mention they now have a debt to me. I've simply grown my army, and it cost me next to nothing. You, on the other hand, have been holding out. Apparently you're a very good thief who has been letting me pay for everything."

Amma hadn't counted the gold she handed over, but then she hadn't really ever needed to keep track of a thing like that. "They needed it more," she said quickly, then shifted the subject right back to him. "I think you did it because you have a soft spot for draekin. You like them."

"Draekin are messy, combative, overly excitable, and the furthest from likeable as a thing can be."

"And yet you like them anyway!" She laughed lightly. "But did you tell that one you were raised by them? I thought your parents were demons?"

"One of them is."

"And the other's a draekin? Okay, you definitely have a tail—"

"My mother was a human, obviously." He gestured to his face.

And a nice-looking one, I bet, thought Amma. She smirked at herself, intrigued now that they were back on the subject. "So, where do the draekin come in?"

Damien rolled his head on his shoulders. "The ones in Aszath Koth are loyal to my father. Well, everything is, but he thought they, specifically, would make good caretakers in his stead. They very infrequently eat their young."

Amma mulled over the hesitancy in his voice. "Was he right?"

"I'm alive, aren't I?"

"Well, you said they aren't very nice to things smaller than them, and you might be huge now, but I doubt you were this big when you were born."

"Draekin are not terribly tender, and hatchlings are covered in scales, so they're quite a bit tougher, but I wasn't in their care until I was—" Damien stopped abruptly, turning to her. "No more questions."

Amma pursed her lips, but swallowed down the next thing she meant to say. She would have shared with him that she too had many different people who cared for her when she was small. But then her own parents at least tried to make time for her, and she wasn't sure that was the case for Damien.

She watched him from the corner of her eye a moment longer, vision sliding down to his hip pouch and where she now knew the scroll was. Instead of lewd plans to snatch it away, though, a ball of guilt rolled itself into her mind. Once she got the scroll and they made it into Faebarrow, she would have to get away from him. There was likely only one way to do that, and it would not go well for him in the end.

"Damien?" she finally ventured after a moment, afraid he would shout at her for so quickly asking another question when he'd told her no more.

"Yes?" he responded, perfectly pleasantly.

"Do you think the draekin will make it all the way to Aszath Koth?"

He glanced back the way they'd come, face creased with a frown. "I don't know."

CHAPTER 20
FEAR AND LONGING IN THE HAUNTED FOREST

Damien was loath to admit he much preferred Amma's praise of his deeds to her complaints about their direction. Her admiration lasted the rest of the day, which he insisted was unnecessary but less adamantly than before. By the next morning, however, she once again second-guessed his desire to go after the Lux Codex that Xander had challenged him with. She asked if he was sure multiple times, and he read aloud to her from the journal he'd gotten from Anomalous to put an end to the questions. That seemed to help until her obsession with countering him shifted the following day to a new topic: the Gloomweald.

"It is *not* haunted," Damien insisted. He had never been told such a ridiculous thing—who ever heard of a *haunted* forest? "I know you revere trees, but surely when they die, that's it. They don't come back to possess their fallen trunks."

"It's not the trees." She was sitting on her masked knoggelvi with shoulders pulled in but eyes held open wide as they turned off the main road toward the edge of the wood. "It's only a few extra days to go around," she bargained in a small voice. "And everybody does it, so the road is well-traveled."

"Master Bloodthorne has set the course, and so we shall follow it!" snapped Kaz, for once on his side about their direction despite that they were headed west. Then the imp, still in his dog form, turned to Damien from his spot on the knoggelvi's head. "Though it takes us even farther off the course to Eirengaard." Ah, there it was.

"This Lux Codex will prove useful. Now, shut it, both of you."

The path into the forest was disused, grown over but easy enough to eke out. It led away from the main road that would add an extra week to the journey into Faebarrow and the Grand Athenaeum where the book was held. Being untraveled made the Gloomweald that much more desirous to Damien—less chances to see others and a faster route. The barony they sought was just on the other side, a measly two days, well worth the supposed risk of…what was it even? Amma hadn't been terribly specific, just something about spirits and unfinished business, and he had a feeling the vagueness only heightened her anxieties.

A few gnarled and thorny bushes marked the edge of the wood. Autumn was fast approaching, lending itself to the dead-appearance of some of the trees, leaves fallen away and trunks drained of their vibrancy. Damien led the way in beneath bare branches that blotted out the midday sun. As they entered the wood, a hollower, windswept sound came up around them.

Damien took a deep breath, the smell slightly fungal and wet, but then this was a thick and old forest, after all. Shortly, the path was gone, and they had to pick their way across by glimpses of the sun when it peeked through the heavy tree cover. Damien had found his way many times in much more threatening places. Frankly, he couldn't see what all the fuss was about. There was no flow of lava running beside them, no evidence of cannibalistic tribes littering the forest floor, not even the distant sound of over-sized wings beating ever closer by the second. Yes, there were moments when, from the corner of his eye, he thought he saw movement, but the animals of any wood were fast to hide out of the site of a predator, and what could be more apex than a blood mage?

Amma, however, was clearly not having any of it. Her head snapped about at even the slightest sound, and she didn't blink for a very long time. If he had been a weaker man, he might have felt a little bad. "Amma," he began, and even his voice made her jump, the knoggelvi beneath her huffing. Damien groaned. "Look around at this place. You're surrounded by your favorite thing—trees. How can you be so afraid?"

"How can you *not* be afraid?" she asked, voice low but annoyance creeping into it, an amusing surprise.

He scoffed. "Because I can kill anything with a simple spell, or—oh." That was right, Amma was not a mage, and even if she were, she was still small with none of the claws or teeth of a draekin or goblin. Perhaps he had been too quick to be bothered by her reaction, and he felt himself weaken a bit. "Amma, what is that?"

She swiveled toward the direction he pointed. "What?" Her voice was a terrified, little squeak.

He grimaced, not what he meant to inspire. "That tree. What kind of tree is that?"

"Oh, it's just a maple."

He waited, but she didn't go on. "All right, and what about that one?"

"That's...another maple." She bit her lip. "Can't you tell?"

"No," he lied. "How can you?"

"The leaves."

If ever he wanted her to be chatty, now was it, yet for the first time, she wasn't delivering. "Interesting. And that's another, I suppose?"

"Well, no, that's a hemlock, and it looks totally different." She eyed him then instead of the gloomy wood. "They're not poisonous even though most people think they are because of the name. You can actually make tea out of the leaves; Laurel taught me how."

"And what does that taste like?"

She glanced upward, and then a little smile played on her lips. "Like winter, I think. Like the stillness in the trees when it's cold enough to see your breath and the crunch of snow under your boots."

Damien stared at the dreamy look that took her face, how the shadows of the forest fell over her features, taking away the seemingly unending supply of bright-eyed wonder and revealing a deeper contentment, something quiet yet still joyful. He almost asked her about this Laurel, about sharing tea in the cold, about all of the memories of winter she had buried in her mind, and autumn too for that matter, summer, spring, but then he swallowed it all back and stuttered out another shallow question about the local flora.

They went on similarly for some time until Amma's words became less stilted, and she even managed to laugh lightly at Damien's perhaps obvious questions. Soon she seemed to realize there was nothing to be frightened of, and even as they went deeper into the thicket, she remained relaxed. The forest darkened, though, to be expected, and eventually night fell, and with it, the sounds of the night fell on them as well.

Amma had managed to find them food from fruiting trees and bushes along the main road as she promised, but the apples and berries were gone now, and so when they dismounted and Damien said they would stop for the night, he set out to find them something heartier. Amma attempted to stay close, but caused too much noise keeping on his heel. "You need to stay put," he instructed, pointing back for the knoggelvi.

195

"What, over there? By myself?"

"Kaz will stay with you."

The imp, who had taken on his natural form again, stood there with spindly arms crossed, glaring back black eyes that shined menacingly in the dark.

"And you'll have the knoggelvi." He waved a hand and returned them to their natural states as well. Dark shadows immediately enveloped their black forms, and as the fur fell away to reveal the sinewy hide beneath, even Damien shuddered a bit.

Amma whimpered in the back of her throat. Perhaps they weren't ideal companions for the eerie wood, but surely he wasn't much better.

"I will only be gone a moment. Just...*sanguinisui*, sit here until I return."

Amma dropped down onto the leafy floor with a huff, crossed her arms, and pouted up at him. He groaned and hurried off before changing his mind.

It did not take Damien long to find and capture a hare, but he decided to dress and butcher it where Amma could not see: she'd seen him spill enough blood, and he thought to save her further discomfort in the wood she detested so much. But the entire decision had apparently been wrong, as when he returned, Amma immediately sprang to her feet and demanded to know what took so long.

He held up the dressed carcass and tossed it to Kaz for setting up on the fire the imp had made. This didn't please her, but then nothing would, he supposed, and he could only shrug at her tiny yet irate form.

After eating, they bedded down as normal across from one another, the fire between them falling into low embers. The trees kept the worst of the chilly wind at bay, but the cover made it darker too, blotting out the stars and moons. Kaz sprawled out on the back of one of the knoggelvi and fell immediately asleep to begin the few hours an imp required, and Damien was quick to close his eyes as well.

"Did you hear that?" Amma's sharp whisper cut into Damien's mind as it began to drift into sleep.

He groaned. "You mean that terrifying cry that sounded like a woman being gutted?"

"Yes!"

"No, I didn't. Go to sleep."

Amma whined pathetically again followed by the sounds of her flopping over in the dead leaves on the other side of the fire. There had been a noise, but it was just an owl, crying out low and long into the darkness, and they had certainly heard almost the exact same sound some previous night while lying out.

"You should have been more frightened when we stayed at the inns—there were actual, living beings there with sharp blades and worse intentions. I don't believe there are any squirrels about who are malicious enough to gnaw an acorn down for stabbing." Eyes still closed, he grinned at his own joke. Surely that would lighten her mood.

She moved about in the dark again with another whimper. "I'm sorry," she finally said with that infuriating but affecting tone. "We were just always warned to never come here, and sometimes people did and never came back, or worse, they would, but they were…changed."

Damien sighed, a hand behind his head, eyelids no longer heavy as he stared up at the outline of a branch, looking like a claw against the sky if he squinted just right. "You were told fairytales, yes? I can tell you, there don't seem to be any portals to the Everdarque here, so no need to worry about fae."

"Not fae," she said, a waver to her voice in the dark. "More frightening than fae."

Damien glanced over at where Kaz was still sleeping heavily, limbs hanging over the knoggelvi's back. Then he swallowed. "Look, if you are truly that frightened, you can come over here and—"

He'd never seen Amma move so fast. She was suddenly beside him with a skitter quicker than any rabbit through the underbrush. Wrapped in her cloak, she dropped down onto the leafy floor, breaths coming hard and fast, and fell onto her shoulder, her back pressing into his side.

"Oh, well, all right then," he mumbled, unable to lower his arm from behind his head with her nestled against him. Other hand on his chest, leather armor removed for the night, he could feel his own heartbeat thump harder and his body stiffen. He checked again to ensure Kaz was still asleep, but he hadn't moved, and even the knoggelvi had their heads down, not casting him disapproving glares.

Well, if everyone else were going to act as though this were normal, then he supposed it was. Yet he couldn't relax, the sudden urge pumping through him to get up and go for a sprint or take part in some other fatiguing activity. But then she wouldn't be touching him anymore, which would be quite the disappointment, and he couldn't just leave her there. No, that was the whole point—she was frightened, and he was *somehow* comforting her.

Damien forced his eyes shut again. In the darker darkness behind his lids, sleep was much further off than it had been before, though it should have been easier: Amma was warm in the chill of the night, warmer than the dying fire, and he thought briefly how much warmer and nicer it would be to roll onto his side, wrap arms about her middle, and pull her up against his chest.

Then he slashed through that idea like so much rabbit skin. She hadn't come over to him for that. Even after the looks she'd been giving him in the previous days, there had been something else on her mind, surely. He was misreading her longing glances, how her lips sometimes fell apart as if halfway through a thought she ought not be having, how her fingers slid over the knoggelvi's reins back and forth suggestively when she stared. Maybe he was just ruining her mind with the talisman—it hadn't been tested on anyone and perhaps his theories about it leaving the target unchanged were incorrect.

The arcana in the talisman was not meant to leech out into its vessel, but Damien was suddenly struck with the deep concern it was changing her, infecting her, and he did not want that. There was a way to check, he thought, and despite the wariness of his body, he had plenty of arcane energy left. Besides, reaching out with magic would be exceptionally easy when the one he wanted to touch was already touching him back.

He whispered the Chthonic as quietly as possible, opening his mind to the being nearest him and letting his magic creep over her. Amma's blood was racing like mad through her veins, heart pumping as if she fled through the forest at that very moment. It was a familiar reaction, fear, panic, terror. Those things could, of course, be confused for excitement under the right context, but that couldn't be the case now.

Past the coursing blood and intensely beating heart, everything remained the same as when he had first felt her this way in the swamp. No hint of Abyssal poison eating away at her, no noxscura lying in wait to choke out the goodness. There was, however, that familiarity again, that thing in her that was in him too that he so infrequently felt. Humanity.

He tarried about her aura a moment longer, and by all that was grim and unholy, it was truly *good*. No being could be purely good, of course, but everything that existed was tainted by its intent, and Amma's was such a comfort. Kindness floated through her and radiated out. It lulled him into a sort of bliss even as the intense beating of her heart began to have a reciprocal effect back on him— something that happened rarely and only when he spent too long focused on one other creature.

His own heartbeat quickened, pulse jumping in his throat. His body was mimicking what the spell attempted to deduce from her, but then he wasn't feeling the fear he expected. Not exactly. There was something, something that felt more frantic, more stimulating, and urged him to run a hand along the curve of her body, over her hip, around her thigh…

All at once, Damien went back into himself, snuffing out the spell. *Thank the basest beasts she's not arcanely adept and didn't feel that*, he thought. But then she stirred beside him, body shifting against his, and he knew at this rate he would never get any bloody sleep.

Damien pressed up onto the arm behind him and shifted onto his side to look down at the back of her head, hair golden even in the dark. "You're still not asleep yet, are you?"

Amma did not move. "No."

"Is it because you're staring out into the darkness and imagining all the terrifying things in it staring back?"

"Well, it is *now*," she hissed.

"For being so afraid of what you think is out there, you sure seem determined to see it."

"But,"—she swallowed—"the ghosts…"

"Is that what you were told live here?" He glanced out at the edge of the ring where the dying fire reached, a wall of pitch black beyond.

"They come in the dark, the souls who passed before their time, to drag you into a never-ending night. It's said if you lay eyes on one, your own spirit leaves your body so that they can trap it and keep it for their own."

"Well, you won't lay eyes on one if you just turn the other way."

Amma flipped over so quickly he had no time to readjust, and then she was facing him. Still propped up on his elbow, he looked down at her, an inch away. Her eyes were still open wide, staring hard at his chest, hands wrapped around the cloak she'd gathered under her chin. And then, as if just realizing what she'd done, her face tipped up toward his.

At first Damien had thought he only found Amma attractive because he was so infrequently exposed to humans, but it had become clear to him that the once dirty, little thief was genuinely beautiful, even with her face drenched in shadows and painted with fear. Though now the dread she wore was marring the face he'd become so inconveniently fond of. It was a look he had inspired so many times on others but had never before wanted to take away and replace with adoration. He'd seen the way she looked at the things she admired on the road, how she beamed back when she finally earned the knoggelvi's trust and nuzzling, the smile she'd given that lecherous barkeep, and suddenly he wanted very much to be the cause of that look instead, to see it now, for him.

Her knee shifted, inching over his leg, a thigh finding its way against his as if coaxing him closer. He had to remind himself that was not what she'd scrambled over the forest floor and cuddled up against him in the dark for, but dark gods, did it ever feel like she were asking him to take her. But then in Damien's experience, when someone desired him they simply stripped off their clothing and thrust his hand or length where they wanted it to go, making themselves very clear. Amma, regrettably, did none of that, but she did stare up at him with that apprehensive look that he still desperately wanted to take away.

"Listen to me," he said, setting his face stony. "I am the most frightening thing in this forest. Do you understand that?"

Amma's brows knit like she didn't quite believe him and began to glance warily over her shoulder.

Damien took his free hand to her chin and tugged her face back. "I asked if you understand. Do you?"

She nodded, and his thumb brushed up her jaw, skin soft under his fingers as he fought to keep from sliding his hand to the back of her neck and pulling her closer.

"Good. And since you have chosen to press yourself against the most frightening thing in this forest, you are either very brave," he said with a playful lilt and then dropped his voice to a heady rumble, "or you are already in the worst possible danger you could be."

His eyes drifted down to the slight part to her lips, feeling her gentle breath fall over his hand. She would be so easy to guide to his mouth, full lips ready to be devoured followed by the rest of her. That would surely take her mind off of the imaginary horrors out in the dark.

But then he glanced back up into her eyes. It had worked, a bit, the fear in them replaced like he wanted, but with something new, and for a moment, Damien was the one who was afraid. He'd never been looked at quite so longingly, had never felt someone want from him the things he suddenly felt Amma wanting. More than just a soulless, animalistic tumble and a traded favor, her gaze was looking right through him, searching for what he kept inside. She wasn't going to trade her body to him for arcane resources or militaristic forces—she only wanted to know him. And, for a brief moment, he wanted to know her too.

But then it occurred to him that, no matter how willing she

appeared, with the enthrallment talisman inside her and a countless number of his violent threats in her memory, Amma having an authentic choice in the matter was an illusion. In fact, Damien knew what it was to be enthralled himself, and even enthusiasm in the moment didn't make up for being at the total mercy of someone who didn't really need their victim's "yes." Damien knew he was evil, he had cut throats and set fires and reveled in the pain of others, but he wasn't a monster.

He pulled his hand away from her and shifted onto his back once more, eyes flicking up to the darkness of the trees overhead. "You said you were told stories about this place, so you must have grown up nearby, yes?"

When Amma tried to speak, her throat was hoarse and dry. "Yes. Sort of."

"All right, then you must have happy memories of your childhood too. Think of one of those, it should help you fall asleep."

He felt her nod, and though she shifted onto her own back, she didn't move away from him, still pressed shoulder to shoulder.

"You can tell it to me aloud, if you prefer," he said hesitantly, hoping she would.

Amma hummed, a sweet sound in the hollowness of the forest, and then she began, "When I was about sixteen, there was a festival in the spring just when the whole world seemed to be in bloom..."

Damien listened to her dulcet voice, closing his own eyes. He was normally very uninterested in the lives of others in such a way, but when Amma spoke of the vibrancy of color, the softness of flower petals, the flavor of mint and citrus, he could see it in his mind, feel it on his fingers, taste it on his tongue, and then it all fell away as sleep finally took her.

In the quiet left behind, Damien waited, momentarily relieved, and then huffed; now what was he to do?

He glanced at her once more, head on his shoulder and resting against his side. Infernal darkness, he should not under any circumstances like that, and yet there he was, enjoying not even the touch but the accidental brush of a woman who had probably never even set a fire that wasn't meant to be lit. It was cruel in the plainest sense, what she'd done to him, and Damien was no stranger to cruelty, both given and received. Though he could not recall the last time he had carved into someone for fun, even just the thought now repulsive.

But for badness's sake, he *was* evil, wasn't he? And she was just so timid and sweet, she was afraid of *ghosts* which didn't even bloody exist. No, it wasn't worth even considering the two of them somehow…entangled, not when all the effort it would take would surely lead to disappointment. He cut the thoughts off like an infected limb, and focused instead on the sound of Amma's steady and quiet breathing, eventually falling into welcome sleep himself.

How much longer after, he was unsure, but his eyes opened again. Amma had rolled toward him once more, her forehead pressed into his shoulder and her fingers resting on his arm. It was exceptionally nice, and he did not want to move and disturb her, but he became aware of a milky fog that had come crawling in from the darkness beyond.

Damien sat up carefully. He scanned the trees then looked quickly to one side as there was movement across the dead fire. Nothing was there.

Amma nuzzled her head into the space where his body had just been, hand grasping feebly and coming up empty. He cocked a brow at that, but then the knoggelvi snorted, waking. One pawed at the fallen leaves. "Steady," he commanded quietly from his spot on the ground, a hand out.

Damien opened his mind for the second time that night though he felt almost drunk, tired and strangely spent from Amma's touch. His messy cast passed over Amma and Kaz and the knoggelvi to feel for other creatures. The forest was full of them, as expected, and then he realized that no, this was not as expected. This was more. Much more.

CHAPTER 21
ESSENTIAL KNOTS FOR CAPTURE AND RELEASE

On his feet, dagger unsheathed, Damien turned in place to take the number of them in. There were far too many, and how he had not felt them before, he had no idea, but then that was the nature of ghosts, he supposed—they weren't exactly feelable.

"Master?" Kaz's quavering, groggy voice told him the imp had just woken and recognized that they were surrounded, though he was equally unsure by what.

A figure stepped forward from the mist directly across from where Damien stood, body white and glowing. Tall and slender, limbs thin as bones and floating at its sides, the waif-like being glided another step closer. Then there was another and another, popping in at Damien's peripherals and filling in all around them. These remained amongst the thickening fog that rung their small clearing, but their presence was pressing in on his wavering spell, overwhelming it. He knew this kind of blood, but the source leaked out of his grasp in his still bleary state.

Though it glowed, the one that stood nearest him had features obscured, eyes only hollow, black pits in its skull, and when it opened its wide mouth, there was a rattling, breathless sound that swept down over the small clearing, and all at once the dying fire went out.

The knoggelvi were broken of Damien's command to be calm, one rearing up to fall back with a flurry of leaves. Amma rustled at his feet with a sleepy word and curled into a ball. Of course she would remain asleep through *this*, though that may have been better: he hated that it was beginning to look like she was right, and if they survived, she'd never let him forget it.

All of the figures were advancing now, the distant silhouettes of more scattered throughout the forest. Each was thin, practically skeletal, emanating some arcane light that shimmered off of the gnarled branches and dead leaves coating the ground. His heartbeat quickened at the sheer number, and if he were honest, the way they looked. Paler than even he, and with missing eyes and craters for mouths as their jaws dropped open to hiss out words in some ancient tongue, the forms froze him.

But Damien was the son of a demon lord. He had seen far worse, he had summoned far worse, and wasn't he himself *the* worst? There were many of them, but what was an army of the spectral to a blood mage? They didn't even belong on this plane, and who better than Damien to send them elsewhere? Well, a divine mage, actually. One of those fucking imbeciles with a dominion for a parent would prove useful right about now, but Damien could banish displaced souls off to the infernal plane just as well as he could call them up.

Taking the dagger to his palm, he cut in quickly, squeezing his blood into a fist, and whispered the Chthonic words of banishment. If these were just dead spirits, they should be easy enough to send away. The bravest of the ghosts had gotten closer, and Damien, stalwart, strode right up to it and with the extension of his arm, released the palmful of blood. It rained across the figure, and the air about the form crackled, fissures drawing themselves in space to absorb away the apparition.

But then the portals fizzled out, closing up without pulling the incorporeal forms around them inside. Damien glanced to his palm to check he had done things correctly. He did feel quite spent, but the wound was already healing, and he had seen the rift in the planes, the silvery noxscura flickering inside, and he had even felt the infernal energy reaching out to take what didn't belong, yet the spirits persisted.

"Oh, that was *vile*," a lofty if quiet voice remarked from somewhere in the glowing, white crowd.

And another answered in kind, "Terribly distasteful."

The figure before him raised its thin arms, the spatter of blood leaving a dark trail across its front, blotting out its sheer form. Damien knew that if ghosts were real, they wouldn't be corporeal, yet he'd stained one. And, really, the blood should have transformed itself with the spell if it had worked, not remained a dripping mess down the front of its target.

The specter let out a disgusted sort of noise, its eyeless holes looking down and then back to him. "That is never going to come out."

And then there was a shriek, loud and piercing and right beside Damien's boot. Amma threw herself behind his legs, grabbing onto him and giving him a fright all his own. She attempted to use him to pull herself up, falling as she blindly grabbed at his thigh, his hip, his—Damien snatched her hand off of him, and with little effort pulled her to her feet. If anything would snap him out of whatever had struck him so dumb, it was Amma inadvertently grabbing him exactly where he'd wanted her to hours earlier.

Blood. He had felt the blood of these beings through his now-defunct spell, and ghosts should have none of that.

"What are you?" he called, pumping authority into his voice, a hand wrapped tight around Amma's wrist as she flailed about to try and hide behind him.

"They're ghosts, obviously! Oh, I *told* you, Damien!" Amma gathered herself just enough to slap his arm then shrieked again when she turned to see the ring of other lithe, shimmering bodies behind them.

Kaz had also run up, his little claws digging into Damien's leg, and the knoggelvi backed toward them too, the five in a circle and surrounded.

"Really? All of you believe this nonsense?" Damien mumbled, casting a glance at his cohorts then back to the *ghost* he had spattered with blood. "Out with it—what are you really?"

"You heard the girl!" The voice came raspy this time, so unlike it had been a second before. "We are the spirits of the slain, felled here in the Gloomweald thousands upon thousands of years ago."

"Well, then no wonder you came to greet us; this seems a bloody boring eternity to endure." Damien's grip on Amma relaxed. "That banishment spell had no effect on you. You're of this plane."

"No, we're ghosts," another watery voice called from the crowd behind.

"Yes. Boo!" cried another.

The figure before them craned its neck, twisting its head, black pit for a mouth lengthening as it hissed.

"Enough of this." Damien reached down and grabbed Kaz about the excess, leathery skin on the back of his neck, holding him up. "Give us some light."

The imp gurgled, flicking his tail to shoot a burst of flames at the being. Thin arms went up to protect itself as it jumped out of the way, the others parting, and the infernal flame caught on a bush. The light fell on a handful of faux-spirits to reveal actual eyes and lips and teeth and hair and, most interestingly, long, pointed ears.

"Goodness!" The being closest to him hopped and batted at the robe they wore, the edge of it set aflame. Two others flocked over, thinly-fingered hands slapping at the burnt edge to assist.

Amma had stopped her flailing, and so Damien released her. She'd given up cowering too, standing beside him, eyes narrowed, head tipped. "Elves?"

"No!" cried out a voice from the crowd. "Ghosts!"

"Oh, it's no use," said the original one miserably, holding up the tattered end of the silky fabric to examine the damage. "As if the blood stains weren't enough."

"What in the Abyss is going on?" Damien ground his jaw.

"You've absolutely wrecked rare, hexabian silk, that's what's going on," the elf mumbled.

Damien took a step closer. The elf's face still glowed somehow, and their limbs did as well, but it had become much fainter in the firelight, and there were boundaries about his eyes and lips—actual eyes and lips, not hollow pits—where the glow abruptly stopped.

Tapered and long, everything about an elf's body was pointed. They were even rarer than humans up in Aszath Koth, and it was much more likely to meet a halfbreed anywhere in the realm than a true elf, but these had to be full-blooded, so tall and thin. Elves kept largely to themselves or traveled in a group with others, often as their token elemental magic-wielder. Unlike humans, nearly all elves had a penchant for magic, born with certain abilities blessed by their god, but they were not terribly keen to travel beyond the forests they typically called home. Never had Damien seen so many in one place.

He glanced at the lot of them, the circle they had made shifting into more of a crescent, no longer standing menacingly but leaning against trees or upon one another, hips jutted out, sighing, rolling eyes. It was an odd sight to be sure.

"I can barely believe this, Lora'iel!" said the elf standing beside the one who was still babying his robe. "Now we are failing to run off but two humans and their pet goblin?"

Lora'iel clicked his tongue. "Well, I didn't expect them to be so...disgusting." He held out the silk to show the drying spatter of blood.

Damien groaned. "That was meant to banish you, but clearly you aren't haunting this place, you're just living here."

"And that's all we want to do! Unmolested and alone!" The one who had berated Lora'iel turned on him, an anger flaring up in her eyes. She looked strikingly similar to the other, both with tapered jaws and delicate features, but was notably angrier. She took a step toward him, one long finger and a spindly wrist pointing out of a gossamer, bell sleeve. "But then you and your ilk come into these hallowed woods, and you slaughter rabbits, and you set bushes ablaze!" She had come right up to him and pressed the tip of her finger to his chest.

Damien was a tall man, but this elf, despite her frailness, was standing just to his own height. He could have taken her wrist and bent it back with the simplest crack, but that seemed terribly unfair, even with her slight features knitted so irately.

"Oh, no, the bunny." Amma clasped her hands beside Damien. "We're so sorry, we didn't know he was yours."

"That creature belonged to no one but Dil'wator'wovl!" she snapped.

The woman had invoked the name of one of the few gods Damien was familiar with, if only because he was named exceptionally strangely, which was really saying something for gods. Elves tended to make their homes in the uncharted, forested places and could journey freely between them through magic, so Dil'wator'wovl was appropriate, but the god was also purported to have pointed ears, and the funny name probably gave them a sense of kinship.

Nearly two heads taller than Amma, the angriest elf turned to her and bore down. "And now you will pay with your own lives!"

Damien had his dagger under the elven woman's chin before she could make another move, her frailness be damned. She froze when she felt the blade, light eyes flicking to him in the dark.

"Cora'endei," called Lora'iel, "we need not resort to violence."

"Why not?" she asked, voice a harsh whisper, "that is all they know themselves."

"It is not our way." Lora'iel waved a hand, going to Damien, and to his complete and utter surprise, actually placed it on his arm. The touch was so light, he barely felt it, no threat behind it.

Damien edged Amma a step back from both elves and lowered his dagger halfway. He could call up a spell and set the area aflame, send blades at the lot of them, even summon a beast to do the work for him, but though their numbers were vast and he was hesitant to relax his guard, none of that seemed necessary.

"Is this fairyheart?" Amma's voice was quiet as she reached out to the woman who had threatened her life, pointing to her arm and how it glowed.

Cora'endei's lips twitched, the anger on them subsiding slightly.

"That is the common name for the fungi, yes. How are you familiar?" A thin trail of silvery blood wept from where Damien's blade had been, though he thought he hadn't pressed hard enough to pierce her.

Amma glanced at the others. "A friend of mine. She's half...elven," she said carefully. "She brought some to me once. They're beautiful, and I could never forget how they glowed when we shut ourselves up in a closet with them. Tasted really terrible though."

At that Cora'endei's lips twitched again. "Your friend tricked you. All elves know fairyheart is too bitter to be palatable."

"Yeah, and it makes the inside of your mouth light up for a couple days and gets you in a lot of trouble for not being presentable." Amma glanced at Damien then back to the elves. "But you're using it to cover your bodies and pretend to be ghosts?"

"We are ghosts!" one of the elves from the crowd called out.

"I think they've figured it out," Lora'iel called back with a sigh, crossing thin arms and head lolling on a wisp of a neck.

"Well, what do we do with them then?" Cora'endei huffed, holding her chin up a bit higher and not bothering to wipe away the trickle of blood.

"You don't *do* anything with us," Damien told them, resheathing his dagger. "We will continue on our way, unbothered, and be on the other side of the wood in a day's time."

"And we won't eat any more of your rabbits or squirrels or anything," Amma added. "Promise."

At this, a number of them looked uneasy, and Lora'iel put up a hand. "Oh, no, no, we can't allow that."

Damien cocked his head, half a smirk crawling up his face as he gazed over the impossibly thin limbs of the elves, the way they held themselves so casually, unprepared, and how simple it had been to draw blood, even accidentally, on their most brazen member. "I doubt very much it is up to you. We'll be on our way now."

There was a clattering through the wood, and then many, tiny glints in the flickering of the fire as crossbows were hauled up onto shoulders and leveled at the two of them.

"Fuck."

It wasn't lost on Damien how ridiculous his predicament was the next morning as he sat in the thing the elves considered a cell. He could have survived the arrows that would have managed to pierce him, dodging the majority, and then cut a clean path through the elves to leave. He wouldn't have even needed to make a terribly fast getaway. Amma, on the other hand, would not have fared terribly well with even one arrow bolt in her. He could heal a strike on her if it weren't immediately fatal, but it would have to be quick, and to avoid the elves reloading and perhaps shooting her again, he would have to actually leave much faster than if he were on his own.

No, the risk of her death had been far too high for him to enact any kind of plan, a hypocrisy which also wasn't lost on him—that would be a simple way to get the talisman back, and he wouldn't even have to feel guilty about it, granted it would be a slow and painful way for her to go: suffering on the end of a crossbow bolt aimed carelessly for her thigh, bleeding out on the back of his knoggelvi. And then what would he do with her body?

The thought of Amma's lifeless corpse had really cinched the decision. Damien struck it from his mind, not even a possibility, and gave himself—and the rest of them—up to the ridiculous elves.

So, there he sat. Knees splayed supporting his elbows, head bent, fingers pressing hard into his temples. Beside him sat Amma on the single, makeshift cot. She had her hands in her lap, back straight, and was chewing on her full bottom lip when he glanced over at her. There were nerves there, surely, but more a hefty confusion as she looked out at the forest all around beyond the bars of the cage they were locked up in.

Damien sat straight, slapping hands down onto his knees. "All right, I've had enough of this."

Kaz spun toward him from where he sat at the cell's bars, baring all his teeth in a grin. "Just give the word, Master, and I shall light them all ablaze."

Both guards who stood by the exterior of the cage turned over a shoulder, casting wary eyes on the imp and then up to Damien. These two were indeed larger, taller than even Damien, and their shoulders were wide, but they had about three visible muscles between the two. Even the spears they carried weren't formidable, adorned with twisting vines and flowering blooms, and their tipped ends were pointed but crystalline, looking so delicate that they might snap if there was an attempt at running through even his bare stomach.

Damien rubbed a hand over his face in frustration. He wasn't intending on getting them out of there through force, not until it was safest for Amma—even if they were weak, he didn't know how precise they might be—but there was something else. Damien didn't object much to theoretically cutting through an army for his own freedom, and even less so for Amma's, but when that army was just *so* frail, it felt...darkness, he supposed it felt *wrong*, but by whose moral standards he absolutely refused to ponder.

He had agreed with Amma the night before, stupidly he supposed now, that the conversation the elven leaders insisted on having about them in a separate hut high up in a tree would result in their simple release. She had shrugged, asked him to be patient, and the two eventually both fell asleep, propped up against one another's shoulders. But as dawn brightened the shaded forest, and he felt arcanely renewed, his patience proved to have worn to nothing overnight.

"I demand to speak to your lord," Damien said, stalking up to the bars made of thin, reedy wood and tied at cross sections with a hempen rope. He grabbed onto one, and when the whole cage wavered, he scoffed.

"We do not have those, but when the conclave is ready, you shall," said one of the guards, turning to him fully.

Damien's hand shot out and took the guard by the neck of his robe, dragging him right up against the thin bars. "Make them be ready *now*."

The second guard gasped, scrambling and nearly dropping her spear, and then managed to somewhat level it at Damien from the other side of the cage. "L-let him go!"

"Oh, Damien, don't hurt him," Amma said though only with a wary sigh and not her usual panicked concern.

Damien snarled at the elf he had captured. He had fully dropped his spear, face smashed against the reeds of the cage, palms up in surrender. The other guard's brandished weapon was just beside him. Using his free hand, Damien reached out and plucked the crystal spearhead right off. With a sigh, he dropped the guard who crumpled backward, and tossed the head of the spear between the bars, over the guards' shoulders, and into a thicket of ferns. "This is pathetic," he groaned, turning back to Amma.

She shrugged a bit, smiling with apology. "I know, but it's weird too, right? Why are they pretending to haunt this place?"

"Because they're utterly abysmal at everything else," Damien spat, glancing over his shoulder to see the guard he had grabbed straightening his robes. The other was down on all fours in the bushes, looking for her spearhead. "I mean, really, *this* is how you keep prisoners? In a flimsy box of wood and string?" He gave the so-called cage another shake.

The guard who had been manhandled clutched his spear, eyes going wider, but said nothing.

"And you've put us in here together so we can plot our way out in tandem?" Damien gestured back to Amma sitting on the single, narrow cot, which had been a complete waste of an only-one-bed situation and managed to somehow heighten the frustration he was feeling.

"Well,"—the elf glanced about— "we've only got the one cage."

Damien pinched the bridge of his nose and took a long, slow breath. "You didn't even take away our weapons," he grumbled then snapped his head up and paced. "You have naught but a few branches and sticks between you and a blood mage. You can't really expect this to hold me. You must be aware that I could burn through this sorry excuse for a cell and snap both of your necks before you even knew what was happening."

"Um, Damien?" Amma cleared her throat. "Are you really complaining they didn't put us in a sturdier cell?"

"I know you've likely become accustomed to this, Amma, but I find it ridiculous. Is it too much to ask to be treated like a threat? I mean, look at me." He held his hands out, turning to her and standing to his full height.

Amma's throat bobbed as her eyes trailed down him. "I am," she said in a slip of a voice, fingers grasping the edge of the cot. She bit her lip again.

Before his knees went inexplicably weak at the look she was suddenly giving him, he turned his vexation back on the guards. "We're not even tied up. Where are the manacles? Preferably enchanted, to suppress magic, and with a hex to cause just the slightest bit of pain to put the pressure on."

The guard cocked his head, eyes narrowing, and then he held up a length of rope.

"That will do," Damien grumbled and stuck a hand out through the cage. The elf passed it to him. "Amma, come here, please." Still eyeing the guard with annoyance, he turned to Amma as she eased herself up to the bars.

"What are we doing?" she asked in a little voice, blue eyes flicking out to the elves and back to him.

"Just showing these buffoons how to properly keep a prisoner. Stand here, yes, like that, and put your hands out."

She faced him, profile to the guards, and lifted her arms from the elbows before her, brows pinched in bewilderment.

"Now, look, and pay close attention," he began as the second elven guard came up, the crystal spearhead found though its tip was predictably snapped off. "Your instinct will tell you to do this." Damien looped the rope around Amma's wrists then tied a loose knot in the center. "But it can't be tightened, and is easy to break out of anyway." He slipped a finger into the knot's center and undid it before going on to more complexly tie her hands together. "You should instead loop around each wrist separately and then bind them together like so, knot on the bottom to make getting to it with teeth more difficult. You see?"

Damien held up her hands so the two guards could get a better look. He took a quick assessment of Amma, the confusion gone, but her eyes remained very wide.

"But," he said, again undoing the knot with a wiggle of a finger where he'd left it loose, "an enterprising prisoner can sever this much more easily if they can see it, and even if they can't find something sharp to rub against, they'll be at an advantage running with their hands in front of them—better balance and the ability to grip a weapon, so..." He lifted one of Amma's arms and spun her to face away from him. When he gathered her other wrist and pulled them together behind her, she inhaled sharply, standing straight. Worrying he'd hurt her, Damien loosened his grip. "Binding behind a prisoner's back is better, especially if they're in transport. You'll want to change the knot then, like so."

When he looped the rope over itself and tightened it to pull Amma's wrists together, her fingers flexed and then clenched, but he had been very gentle that time, determined not to cause any pain. He gave the rope a light tug, forcing her shoulders back a bit more, and leaned in. Another gasp escaped her lips. "Too tight?" he asked up against her ear.

She started then giggled nervously, voice hoarse, "No, no, it's okay."

Damien carefully lifted her arms a bit to show the guards. One had bent to see better, the other kneeling, face pressed against the reeds. "But neither of these are ideal, they leave far too much freedom." Damien again undid the knot but left the rope looped around one of her wrists. He spun her by the rope to face him again, and he didn't need to collect her free hand, she simply stuck it out to him.

He hesitated. Was that eagerness, or was she just being helpful? Her mouth had fallen slightly open, but her chest was still like she were holding a breath, and her eyes remained unblinking.

Taking her hands together, he walked her a few steps backward to the wall of the cage. From the other side of the bars, the elves scurried along with them.

"Ideally," he said, retying her hands, eyes locked onto hers, "you've got somewhere to keep them, and you can secure your captive to the spot." With a quick movement, Damien lifted both of

Amma's arms above her head and pressed them against the reed wall, looping the excess length of rope over a vertical bar and pulling down so her arms were taut. She sucked in another breath as he stepped closer to her and held the rope secure.

"When you've got someone bound up, they should believe they're truly in danger, like you might do anything to them, no matter how vile or loathsome, to get what you want." Damien tugged the excess length of the rope, and Amma inched up onto the balls of her feet. Her gaze never broke from his, eyes bright with, well, it wasn't *fear* this time, though it should have been. "But you can't leave them hopeless. You can't break them. You should instead push them right to the edge, to make them think if they only obey your commands, if they only relinquish control, that you won't actually be so cruel."

Watching her try to suppress the hitch in her breath with her arms pulled taut overhead urged Damien even closer. Her body arched toward him as he let the weight of his arm ever so slightly continue to inch her up onto her toes. Amma lifted a leg, her knee and thigh brushing along his.

"Let them believe if they only surrender to your will completely, you'll make it worth it, in the end."

Her hips finally pressed against his, eyes pleading, but not to be released.

"We're ready for the prisoner," a voice called from behind, and the elven guards scrambled to stand from where they had been leaning in, nearly losing their weapons. They turned and began trading words in their language with the elf who had come.

Damien released the rope, and Amma slid down the cage with a sigh. With her arms still bound behind her head, she wasn't quick to regain her balance, and Damien caught her about the waist. He pulled her to him up off the cage wall, pressing the rest of her body into his. Immediately, he knew it was a mistake, body reacting without his permission, but she was like liquid in his arms, demanding to be held up.

"I need both hands to untie you," he said, and with a noise like she'd suddenly woken from a dream, she planted her feet firmly on the ground. Amma held her hands out to him again, face flushed and looking everywhere but at him. With room to breathe, he could have undone the knot he'd made very simply, but instead leaned in. "You do want me to untie you, don't you?"

Amma swallowed, hesitating. Then she pushed her bound wrists closer to him, nodding.

With her between him and the bars, he cupped her hands and took his time carefully working in a finger, slipping the rope free of itself. Dropping the thin cord of hemp, he surveyed her wrists for damage. Only slightly red from the pressure, the markings would be gone in just a few moments, but he rubbed his thumbs over the soft flesh on the inside of her wrists anyway. "Apologies if I was too rough for your liking."

She shook her head, still averting her gaze as he tried to find it with his own.

"I see. Tighter next time, then," he whispered as the flimsy door on the cage opened with a creak. She finally looked up at him, shocked, and Damien reluctantly released her hands to turn toward the guard. "Has my presence finally been summoned?" he asked, raging with a confidence he'd forgotten he always had.

"Ah, no, sir," said a smaller elven woman who stood between the two guards. "The conclave wants to speak with her."

At that, Amma peeked around him and pointed at herself. The elven woman gestured to her, and all Damien could do was watch as Amma went for the door. "Wait, what?"

"It's all right," Amma told him quickly. "I'll take care of it." And then she was whisked away.

One of the guards scrambled to shut the door after realizing it was left open, and Damien scoffed. "Don't bother." He stalked over to the cot and threw himself down.

Kaz was in the cage's other corner, glaring at him, arms crossed, a foot tapping the ground.

"What?"

The imp growled, gesturing wildly to the space around him. "Master, what *was* that?"

Damien fell back and covered up his face with his hands. "Oh, shut up."

CHAPTER 22
NEGOTIATION TACTICS FOR
FOREIGN AND DOMESTIC SOIL

How Amma was meant to speak with the conclave of elves after *that*, she had no idea, but she told Damien with what little confidence she had left, negotiations would be taken care of because the alternative was turning into a mewling, pleading puddle, and holy gods, what would become of her then?

She tried to rub the redness out of her face as she was walked through the winding forest path the elves made their homes along, though more likely she was only successful at worsening it. Squeezing her eyes shut to still her heart, there was an image imprinted on her mind of Damien looming over her, the way his lip had curled up as he said things that should have been terrifying, how his eyes knew exactly what to look for, the recognition when they found it, and then the surprised pleasure at discovering what she couldn't hide.

An elf was saying something to her, and Amma blinked her eyes back open. She stuttered out an apology, and tried to listen, absently rubbing her wrists. Her senses were flooded again, every inch of skin too sensitive, sounds distant and muffled, but she'd been brought to an archway carved out of a tree completely foreign to her that was as wide across as a dining hall, and the wonder at that was enough to get her head back on straight.

She touched the bark as she was led beneath it, and then all at once remembered: quoteria. She must have read the name somewhere, seen a drawing of one, remembered some obscure fact, but that's what these massive trees were called, the name whispered in the back of her mind, and she nodded to herself, ready to face the conclave.

As if it had been some kind of joke played on her, the elves of the Gloomweald were perhaps the easiest negotiators Amma had ever dealt with. Intrigued by their circumstances, though, she couldn't stop asking questions once she was with the conclave, a group of seven apparently very important elves.

Without the fairyheart painted all over them to give off that brilliant glow, the elves had skin that varied widely from one another but were all shades that matched perfectly to tree bark. Some were as vibrant as cherry trees, others as pale as birch, and some deep as walnut. Each willowy and tall, they even moved smoothly, like branches bending in the breeze.

They were also rather talkative, answering Amma's questions about how long they'd been in the Gloomweald—apparently, forever—and what they were attempting to do. "So, you just decided to...stage a haunting?"

They sat at a round table that had been grown from the center of the trunk in the room carved out of the massive quoteria tree's insides. Lora'iel nodded, a pleased smirk on his pointed face. "Brilliant, I know."

Well, no, she thought, the plan had fallen right apart when Damien happened upon them, but then there were very few blood mages, and she herself and most of the people she knew had been afraid of the Gloomweald her whole life.

"We only wished for peace and quiet, and we've had exactly that for a few centuries," an elven woman called Sea'nestra said. "However, in the last moons, or, well, how long has it been again?"

The comparatively shorter elf who been the one to fetch Amma was standing just behind the woman and piped up, "Thirty-three years."

"Apparently that long," said Sea'nestra, "we've been pestered by the crown, of all things."

At that, Amma had made a thoughtful sound. The Gloomweald was purportedly haunted, but if this was the truth, it was largely harmless. Laurel, half-elven herself, had braved the very edge of the Gloomweald back when they were just thirteen and retrieved the fairyheart mushrooms. She had reported nothing happened to her at all, but there were others, people who disappeared, and then more who came back frightened to their very core, shaken for weeks, some never truly recovering.

"What do you mean, the crown?"

"Those useless Holy Knights," said Cora'endei, proving she had much more in common with Damien than either of them would like to admit. She attended the meeting but didn't sit on the council, glowering from the edge of the room. "Human men and women, casting stupid, human spells to rid this place of the spirits we're putting on."

"Giving them a fright largely does work," stressed Lora'iel, holding out his hands, the residue of the fairyhearts still on him and giving him a shimmer. "The mages who come try this and that, blessed by Turlecki or Qreefontoc or whichever god is the current favorite with you people."

Amma recognized the names of the gods, neither particularly nice ones, but at least they weren't of the twenty-five cast into the Abyss.

"And then the mages are followed by huntsmen and loggers," Sea'nestra told her, "who we also scare off until we, well...*don't*. We just need something *more*."

That was when Amma had an idea, something that might satisfy them all, and after a fair bit of bargaining, she was brought back to the makeshift cell.

"How did it go?" Damien asked miserably. He was sitting on the cot, head resting on a fist, and Kaz mimicked him at his side.

"Great!" Amma clasped her hands behind her and bounced up onto her toes, trying to cover the embarrassment that nagged at her at seeing him all over again. The guard who had escorted her back opened the cage.

Damien stood as if he weighed twice as much and dragged himself out, sneering at one of the original guards and making them wince. Kaz was right behind him, and mimed after the blood mage, and the second guard actually skittered back into the bushes.

"So," Amma told him, "we don't have to stay here forever or die or anything."

"We would have done none of those things under any circumstances anyway," he groused.

"I know, I know, but we agreed to very reasonable terms. The elves have graciously offered some food and to act as an escort to the edge of the Gloomweald—"

"—we do *not* need—"

"—using their elven journeying skills, so it should only take an hour or so instead of a full day and a half," she stressed.

Damien narrowed his eyes then nodded.

"And Vespa'riel, who—wait, where'd she go?" Amma looked around and then found the shorter elf hiding behind her. "Oh, here, Vespa'riel is their archivist, and she's actually familiar with that Lux

Codex book, so I secured her as our escort, and you can ask her any questions about it on the way."

Damien stared at her dumbly for a moment then screwed up his face. "You negotiated for *that*? Why?"

"I thought you would be pleased." Her heart sank a little.

"No, I...I am, I just don't understand—nevermind. What are our obligations in all of this?"

"All we have to do is enter into a sacred pact to never reveal the secrets of the Gloomweald," she said with a heaviness to suggest they should act as though that were a much bigger burden than it was, then she took a breath and told him quickly, "and also you gotta teach them how to be scary."

"I must *what*?"

"Oh, I dunno." Amma shrugged, looking up at the branches overhead. "I thought maybe acting lessons or something? Because you're so—" And then, at a loss, she just mimed claws and growled at him.

Damien raised a thin brow. "Amma, my father is a demon, not a thespian. And I'm—"

"Formidable and frightening and worthy of treating like a threat," she said with emphasis that didn't betray which parts she actually believed. "This is their home, and this is the only way they know how to protect it. They're having trouble with the crown and the Holy Knights of Osurehm, and—"

"The Knights?" Damien looked over Amma's shoulder where Vespa'riel was still cowering. "They're bothering you?"

When the small elf had gathered herself together to explain, in a stutter and with Amma's interjections, Damien warmed enough to the idea.

He met with the elves who headed up the illusions in the center of a clearing to look over the tricks they had up their silky, billowing sleeves. Largely they relied on the specter theatrics, much less impressive in the light, and some elemental arcana to shake the ground, make the trees look as if they were bleeding, and a wind that howled like a crying baby or an old woman dependent on the temperature. These were all fine and well, but Damien insisted they needed some kind of force to get their point across.

The elves were against it, and there was bickering. Amma watched from the edge of the clearing beside Kaz and the knoggelvi who had been very happily munching on a sweet, hardened tree sap thanks to their new penchant for sugar. Damien grew frustrated quickly, but he would cast a glance at Amma, take a breath, and then begin again from a new perspective.

They had those crossbows, perhaps consider flaming bolts? Oh, no, they said, half of the crossbows didn't even work properly anyway, and fire wasn't ideal when the forest was dry in the winter. Then spears—a different tip was necessary and one that could deliver a poison that paralyzed for which he could give them a recipe, but they were dubious of how that might affect the earth if spilled. Damien even suggested they consider weaponless combat with their long reaches and superior height, but attempts at getting them to do pull-ups on a tree limb to improve their strength proved fruitless. Damien tried to show them, but even the largest elves just hung there beside him and began to whine. Amma didn't mind watching Damien demonstrate though, disappointed when he gave up on that specifically.

Eventually Damien seemed to grow tired of arguing, and stalked up to Amma. "They are hopeless. If we cannot leave here until they are self sufficient, then you may as well pick out a tree to take up residence in for the rest of eternity."

She gave him the most sympathetic look she could. "They're just different. Come on, let's try thinking outside the crate." She walked back to the center of the clearing with him where Lora'iel and a few other elves were standing and looking frustrated. "How can we play to their strengths?"

Damien matched the elves' sour mood, taking a long, glowering look around the camp at the outskirts of the clearing. It was adorned with flowering plants, the archways of every entrance into the massive quoteria trees intricately carved, and he straightened with an idea. Damien reached into his hip pouch, and for a moment Amma feared he was going to use the Scroll of the Army of the Undead, but instead he pulled out a small, wooden box. Inside, there was a mound of red clay that he dumped out into his hand. "Listen, if you refuse to use force, I've something that can do it for you, in a way. Who amongst you is your most artistic?"

Lora'iel called over an elf who had been perched on a rock, barefoot, whittling a hunk of dead wood. He came over, long hair in many braids coiled around his head and dotted with flowers. Damien set the clay into his hand. "This is Skrimger's Amorphous Earthen Illusion. It will take some tactile skill as well as arcana to operate, but it may serve your people best. Imagine a beast that could protect your land, and form it out of this."

Amma stood close and watched the elf work the clay. In just a few moments it took on a shape she knew, if she wasn't personally familiar with.

"Well, that will certainly work," said Damien, taking the still-pliable figurine back. "Now, listen." He lowered his voice and spoke sibilant words directly to it. A black haze came up around the clay from his palm, enveloping it and then shooting upward for the sky. The trees at the edges of the clearing bent away, wind swept down on them all, and in a flash, a beast was hovering overhead, massive, scaled, and winged.

"Dragon!" cried an elf, and the assembled scattered, shrieking as they sprinted for the trees, but Damien simply stood beneath it, and though Amma started, she remained staring upward at its belly, wings flapping and disrupting the leaves, knocking one branch down and banging into a trunk. The last few spikes on the end of its tail flattened with the impact as if they were soft, and then bounced back.

"Not bad at all," he said, but when he glanced back down, the two were alone. "Oh, infernal darkness, really?" Damien brought his other hand down onto the clay figure, and the creature above them was squashed into nothingness simultaneously. "Come on, now," he called, "it's gone you great, lumbering infants!"

Lora'iel crept out first from behind a brambly bush. "I knew it," he laughed nervously. "I just…was that Chthonic you used to animate the illusion?"

Damien tipped the mound of clay back into the box. "Yes. I'll write the words down for you. It should be simple for your more skilled magic users, the arcana is in the clay mostly. They will need to work in tandem with the artistic one, wherever he ran off to." He was, in fact, hiding behind the most skilled magic user who was hiding behind a rock that was safely nestled behind another tree.

"You are suggesting we actually use infernal arcana?"

The disgust in the elf's voice visibly put Damien off, but the blood mage just crossed his arms.

"These are the tools of The One True Darkness."

Damien faltered. "The One True What Now?"

Lora'iel glanced at his companions who gave only wary looks and scratched at their skin like they could feel the discomfort in his words. "Darkness," the elf repeated. "It has been prophesied. We see it in the stars, feel it in the trees, hear it on the very whispers of the wind."

"The wind whispers it but is that vague about its name?" Damien frowned. "Perhaps you are translating incorrectly? Ask it to speak up next time."

Lora'iel clicked his tongue, head rolling on his shoulders. "No one speaks it for fear more power will be given to the chaos meant to consume the realm."

"Well,"—Damien held out the box with the bit of clay inside, and Amma could see in his stance his own discomfort, reminiscent of when they so quickly fled the Stormwing manor in Elderpass—"if you know this One True Darkness's form, I suppose you could mold it with this, but even then, I doubt any of you are capable of bringing about the end times with it. It is just an illusion, after all."

Lora'iel did not move to take it, leaving Damien there with his arm outstretched, almost as if he were pleading, and not for the trade, but for something else. Something like acceptance.

Amma grabbed the box from Damien and thrust it at Lora'iel. "Here."

The elf backed away. "But it's…it's…"

"It's no different than any other magic," she said, hearing the brusqueness in her words but not caring. "If it's infernal arcana or earth arcana or pretend-ghost arcana or *whatever*, you're using it to protect yourselves and this forest, so that must mean it's good, right? What's the big deal?"

Lora'iel was taken aback, but gingerly received the illusion. "Well, I'm just not sure what to say to that."

"You could say thank you." She planted her hands on her hips, scowling up at him. When the elf simply swallowed, she cocked her head. "Well, go on."

He mumbled out some very unimpressive gratitude. Amma was not yet pleased.

"And you know what else? You can apologize." She gestured to Damien, noting that he looked almost as afraid as the elf she was chastising. "I find your hasty judgment and your refusal to cooperate while Damien's been working so hard to help all of you completely unacceptable. It's bad enough you refuse everything he offers, but then to insult his heritage and his prowess? You should be ashamed."

"I, uh…" Lora'iel nodded in agreement and stuttered, "I am remorseful for my words and actions."

Amma gave him a contrite nod, arms crossed, standing with her chin jutting out, and then she cleared her throat and settled down, stepping away. She felt Damien watch her as she hurried back over to the knoggelvi where Kaz sat, glaring at her shrewdly, bundled in his sweater. After Damien taught them the Chthonic words and they made a few attempts at conjuring and squashing different possible beasts, they were finally free to be on their way.

Elves were rumored to have a quick way to step through forested lands, and this proved correct. They took a path that was lined with rocks, each of which their escort, Vespa'riel, knew by name. With just a few steps, they were traversing wide swaths of the wood, though it felt only like a simple stroll through the forest. During their walk, Damien asked Vespa'riel about the Lux Codex, and the elf had a number of stuttered out answers for him, mostly vague and overarching, but when he asked about its relation to infernal magics, she finally had a question for him instead.

"What do you intend to do with this book?"

"Nothing to the Gloomweald," he told her flatly, "so it is not your concern."

Vespa'riel cast a wary glance at Amma. "But you're solely interested in scholarly pursuits, yes?"

"Yes, of course," he said dryly. "Now, what is its physical effect on those who are touched by the Abyss?"

"Hives, burning, eventual necrosis, and death."

"And the spells contained within. Do they…that is, is it possible they…reverse certain effects of other magics?"

Vespa'riel tapped her nose in thought. "Well, um, I don't know exactly because it's not meant to be used that way. It's a book of goodness and light, like the name says."

"Sure, but that means it must have some mending or…say, healing spells within it? Maybe even, I don't know…curse removal? Artifact…purging?"

At this Amma looked a bit more sharply on the path ahead of them, the wood thinning and a brightness beyond the trees. Damien hadn't been clear what he wanted the book for, and Xander hadn't told him much about it except that it was deadly. Kaz seemed to notice too, and from his place where he rode on the head of one of the knoggelvi, he leaned forward between its ears to listen harder.

"I've never seen it, mind you, I just know about its history," said Vespa'riel, "but I imagine it must be heavy with clerical magics and thus arcane healing. I believe, in fact, it has the only proven resurrection spell in existence within its pages."

Damien nodded then, accepting this, and they reached the exit to the Gloomweald. Vespa'riel prepared to leave them, but hesitated a moment, fidgeting from foot to foot. "I feel as though I should say, if you do come in contact with this book, it should be preserved, not destroyed."

"Yes, of course, old words written down aren't just important to archivists," Damien said heedlessly.

"No, I mean, its use may be required and soon," Vespa'riel said, more courage to her words. "Lora'iel was not exaggerating about the whispers on the wind, but he was not entirely forthcoming either. There is a rot in the earth."

Damien appraised the small elf. "You've seen this rot?"

"Just as I've taken you to the edge of the Gloomweald so quickly, elves can travel to other forests in the same way. We've sought out the rot, and we've seen it in the Kvesari Wood, northeast of the realm. We believe it is a result of what the others call The One True Darkness. That isn't its name, obviously, but that is what it brings. Its intent is to blight out the entirety of existence. It is called E'nloc, and it is nearly as old as Dil'wator'wovl, though made up of things even older."

Amma's stomach twisted, watching the sincerity set in Vespa'riel's features, not even fear, but sadness.

Damien only appeared to be puzzled. "And you think it is wise to tell a blood mage, a demon spawn, that he should not destroy a book that could protect against this evil?"

Vespa'riel only frowned at him. "A demon spawn who helped us? Yes." And with that, she disappeared back into the thickness of the forest like a ghost.

They stood there for a moment at the edge of the wood, still under its shadows, looking after where she had gone. Then Damien turned and led them out of the Gloomweald.

"You still want the Lux Codex? After all that ominousness?" asked Amma as they stepped into the sun. The knoggelvi snorted as they followed, and Kaz squinted up at the sky and sneezed.

"Absolutely," said Damien though he looked less convinced. "Elves are just superstitious."

Across the scrubby moor before them, there was a rarely-traveled road that cut between farther off rolling hills and into the valley. The valley that was Amma's home. "So, we're still going to Faebarrow?"

"Despite your inexplicable hesitancy, yes."

But they couldn't make it to Faebarrow by sunset which gave Amma her last chance. It was also her first chance, of course, because she had yet to try and slip the Scroll of the Army of the Undead from Damien's pocket despite all of her wild plans to do so. And there would not be another chance after tonight, of that she was certain.

CHAPTER 23
A REBUTTAL TO THE USEFULNESS OF INTENT

Crickets trilled into the autumn evening as a cool wind blew over the plain that led into Faebarrow's outer fields and farmlands. They'd chosen to bed down behind a copse of brambles to shield from the chill, the fire crackling and popping lowly between them. They had eaten, and Kaz had fallen into a hard and deep slumber as he always did at the earliest part of the night in order to wake and keep watch when it was later.

Alone together, Amma glanced at Damien across the fire. He was nearly finished with his book, squinting down at the pages he had bent toward the light. The flames jumped over the severe angles of his face from below, sharpening his brow already arched in thought, thinning out his cheeks, and highlighting his scar. His eyes flicked over the lines quickly, then stopped, focused and bright in the firelight before continuing again.

It was going to be quite difficult to seduce him if he wouldn't even look at her.

"It's cold," she said into the quiet, rubbing her arms for effect.

He flicked his eyes up for only a moment. "Where is your cloak?"

It was balled up beneath her, and she gestured to it meekly. He only tipped his head as if she'd solved her own problem and returned to reading.

Amma sighed and gnawed on a nail as she thought. Maybe the whole idea was moronic. Damien might have been a blood mage, but he was undoubtedly handsome, and after how he'd spoken to and touched her in the Gloomweald, clearly not the stranger to intimacy she had thought. Looking on him, she realized he could have whoever he pleased, her included, but he had turned away when they were lying beside one another in the wood, and now he practically acted as though she didn't exist. It was foolish, reckless, dangerous even, but then she slid a hand over her own wrist, remembering sharply how he had looked at her with a hunger so feral she had forgotten everything else under his eyes.

Seducing Damien *was* possible, and not only could she do it, she would probably enjoy it.

Amma stood then, slow, deliberate. She reached arms overhead and stretched up onto her toes, squeaking out a quiet if suggestive moan as she arced her body and silently thanked Mudryth for insisting she wear the tightest things they could find. Amma caught Damien's eye only for a moment to be sure he was watching—he was—and turned away to pick up her cloak. She bent at the waist and tilted her hips just enough to reach the ground, then came up again slowly to shake the excess grass from the material.

Holding the cloak out, she considered it, the warmth of the fire falling over her body. Putting it on would be the exact opposite of what she wanted, so she lay it out flat with another bend, being sure to keep her best asset highlighted by the fire.

She lifted up again but only part way, working her fingers into her flaxen braid as it hung over her shoulder until her hair fell loose. Amma shook the strands out before flipping it all back, taking a breath that could only be described as heaving, eyes closed as she finally stood.

"A-Amma?" Damien's voice cracked, striking fear into her belly despite that it was borderline fearful itself.

Wide-eyed, she looked on him, frozen with her fingers in her hair. She'd barely done anything, but it was working, and that was…good?

"Would you come here, please?"

Please. He could magically order her about any time he wanted, but finally he was beginning to ask, and in a voice so soft and sincere, she couldn't help but comply. Amma went around the fire to sit carefully beside him on bent knees.

"I want to say," he began, putting the book down and angling toward her, though he didn't look her in the eye. "Well, for today…"

She leaned a bit closer. He was rarely at a loss for words—he usually chose to either use the most convoluted ones possible or none at all—but this was especially odd.

"You were very, well…how can I?" He rolled his hands over one another and blew out a breath before his shoulders drooped. "I think I mean to say thank you."

"To me?" She pointed at herself. "For?"

"You handled our predicament with the elves much better than I could have. I couldn't think of much else but slaying them all, but I'm…glad it didn't come to that."

Amma doubted that was high on the alternative plan list, but she smiled. "I'm glad too."

"Also, your negotiation to allow us to not just pass through the Gloomweald but do it quickly was brilliant." He was still thinking, quite hard. "And your request for information on the Lux Codex, for me, was…thoughtful." The word looked like it confused him, as if it came from some other language, and he wasn't sure if he were using it right, and, goodness, that was terribly endearing.

Amma bit her cheek to keep from smiling too broadly. Instead, she just shrugged.

"You were quite *thoughtful*," he said again with slightly more confidence. "Well, you are almost always that way, which can be incredibly inconvenient and irritating, but in this case it was useful."

At that, Amma actually did laugh. "I'm not sure if you're complimenting or criticizing me."

"No, I don't mean to…" Damien shook his head, grinning awkwardly, and there might have been color on his face, but the firelight made it hard to decipher. "What you said today, about infernal arcana and, in turn, about me—I would like to express my gratitude for it. Uh, that is, if that's what you meant."

"You mean about magic all being the same when it's used for good?" There was a hitch in her chest, and she brought her hand to her heart instinctively. "Yes, I meant that, and I meant it about you too."

Damien's features had softened, the firelight no longer severe but a gentle glow cast on the side of his face, the other half in shadows. His lips were parted, like he might say something else, but wasn't sure. She would have liked to kiss those lips, to kiss them and really mean it, and there was a pang in her stomach that told her not to, not like this, not with other intentions.

But he moved toward her, and the space was so narrow between them the decision was almost made for her. "Last night, before the unpleasantness with the elves," he said, voice throaty, "sharing body heat was wise. Are you still cold?"

Amma swallowed, nodding. He leaned back, holding an arm out, and she lay herself on her side into the hollow he carved out with his body. His hand rested on her back, and Amma held her breath. Damien, blood mage, son of a demon, was *cuddling* her.

It was strange, ridiculous, unbelievable, but it was also wonderful. Amma nestled her head onto his shoulder and lay a hand on his chest. Warm, even through the leather, she had the urge to feel his heartbeat, but the armor he hadn't yet taken off got in the way. She pressed her body against his side a little harder to try and sense it, and his hand around her waist tightened, sliding into the curve of her side. She pulled up a knee, dragging it slowly over his thigh, and for a moment when she closed her eyes, nothing else mattered. The world let her be, her duties back home ceased to exist, and the terrible past and future that waited for her evaporated into nothing, like a curse suddenly broken. All that was left was the night, the warmth, and Damien, who was just a man, after all, holding her.

She wasn't sure how much time passed, but his chest had begun to rise and fall a little heavier as if he had fallen asleep. She lifted her head to look on his face, turned toward her, eyes closed, black hair falling across it. She waited what felt like an interminable time, she wiggled a bit, testing his grip around her, steady but with the heaviness of a man asleep, and finally she let her gaze travel down his body.

Wasting this opportunity would be ludicrous, and he needn't know—not now, anyway—that she had taken the scroll. Amma lifted her hand from his chest leathers and moved it down to the small satchel tied to his belt. If she could just quickly wiggle her fingers inside, grab it, and tuck it away, she could settle back to sleep and act as if nothing had happened.

Until they got to Faebarrow.

Amma froze, hand hovering above the satchel. She looked back to his face, lax in the last embers of the firelight, peaceful, asleep. When they reached the city and she ran for it, he could just order her back to him, but if she sought out a guard, of which there were an inordinate amount, she knew they would protect her. They would do anything to see to her protection, in fact, including cutting Damien down where he stood. He spoke of himself as indestructible, and while she didn't necessarily disbelieve it under most circumstances, enough soldiers, in a strange place, when he wasn't expecting an attack would not turn out well for him. And in the unlikely event he was taken alive? Well, if certain people got a hold of him, living might be worse than a swift death.

But the whole point of running off to Aszath Koth, of traveling all this way and enduring so much, of leaving her home in the first place, was to steal the Scroll of the Army of the Undead. Yes, there was selfishness in fleeing Faebarrow, and she had considered briefly once she was gone to stay that way, nameless and free beyond the barony's borders. But there was duty in her quest too, one much greater that compelled her to return even if going back home meant possibly failing and facing retribution for what she had done.

Amma swallowed, arm beginning to ache as it hovered inches away from the thing she needed so desperately she was willing to pay for it with a man's life. A man on whom she was now lying, so warm, so comforting, so absolutely wonderful, and who had done none of the things to her that other men, men who were lauded as holy heroes, had.

Maybe...maybe there was another way. She could take the scroll and...what? Run? For the first time, he hadn't used the enchanted word on her before falling asleep. She blinked into the darkness—once she grabbed it, she could flee blindly toward home, to hope he never found her, never followed to Faebarrow and to his death.

That was the wisest and kindest thing to do, surely, but leaving him like this made her heart ache in a way it never had before, not when she had to turn away from what she wanted most years ago, and not even when she had realized her best efforts and her sacrifices had been for naught so recently. This was a deeper ache that made her eyes water and throat burn, but this was also the last opportunity she would get, and so she steadied her shaking hand and tugged on the string to loosen the pouch.

"What do you think you're doing?"

A hand clamped down on Amma's wrist, tight and painful. Fingers tensing, she lost the scroll she had just managed to touch, but it hardly mattered when Damien jerked her hand away.

Sitting up, he pulled her with him, and the firelight fell into his face again, highlighting the anger there. The betrayal. "I asked you a question."

Amma's mouth opened, but her throat had gone completely dry, no words coming out.

"*Sanguinisui*, tell me."

"Stealing from you," erupted from her chest, burning as it came out in exactly the way the truth should, so painful a tear escaped.

Damien exhaled through his nose, jaw tight, veins in his throat throbbing. He looked away from her into the fire, hand still clenched around her wrist.

"Damien, I'm sorry, I—"

"*Sanguinisui*, do *not* speak, I don't want to hear your excuses." He stood, pulling her up, and in two long strides, brought her to where she had laid out her cloak on the other side of the fire. "Stay here for the rest of the night," he said with a bite. "Do not move, do not hurt yourself or anyone else, and do *not* come to me pretending that you are cold or frightened or that you actually—" Damien cut himself off with a sharp inhale, a silhouette against the fire, but she could still see the anger, the disappointment, could feel it coming off of the shadow that loomed around him.

He turned from her and stalked back to where they had been a moment before, together. Amma slid down onto her knees as the spell commanded her to, body so heavy it would have dragged her down even without magic. Her chest heaved with the words he'd barred her from saying, the ones that would apologize, that would try to explain, that would tell him she hadn't meant to hurt him.

Except that it didn't matter what her intentions were, only what she had done.

Damien sat, back to the fire, and took up the book once more. He stayed like that for a long time, but did not turn the page. Amma fell onto her side, watching, cold. She could have wrapped the cloak around her but didn't, and instead just shivered until silent tears came.

CHAPTER 24
A MAN THAT STUDIES REVENGE, KEEPS HIS OWN WOUNDS GREEN

You're still angry."

"Angry? About what?" Damien did not look at her. It was easier that way. "That you're a dirty, rotten, little thief? Why would I be angry that you have turned out to be exactly the thing you've presented yourself as the entire history of our unfortunate affiliation?"

Amma said nothing. She was probably glowering or pouting or doing something else with her eyes and lips that was simultaneously alluring and annoying, and Damien refused to even acknowledge it just like he'd refused to speak with her that morning. She was right, of course, he *was* angry, but not with her. Not really. Because it was true, wasn't it? She was only being the person he already knew she was, and it was he himself who had tried to be someone else. And that had been very stupid.

But the trouble of it—all of it—would be gone soon enough. They would have the Lux Codex by the day's end, and he could be rid of her entirely with the right spell to purge the talisman from her heart. Then she could run off to whatever guild or slum she'd come from, and he could continue on to Eirengaard alone as it was meant to be to get on with things he had put off thinking of for far too long.

Morning had burned off into afternoon as they came upon the quaint barony of Faebarrow on knoggelvi masked as horses, Kaz disguised as a dog again though less upset than normal as the imp found a certain joy in Damien's willful cold shoulder.

Amma had swaddled herself in her cloak, hood up as if the full sun of the day were not warm enough. She had been opposed to going after the book from the moment Xander had told them of it, but perhaps it had not been the book she was against. He chanced a look over at her, sitting there with her shoulders slumped in, hood pulled all the way down—that was never how she rode, always with her back straight, face turned to the sky, sun dappling her cheeks and the tops of her breasts and—

Infernal darkness, why in the Abyss did his mind insist on casting her back in that light? Damien grit his teeth, remembering the night before and the subtle sense that had been tickled by her hand. He was briefly alarmed then that she had taken his invitation a step further, welcome, but not what he had meant by wrapping an arm around her, and then the deep disappointment when he realized what was actually going on.

After he had used her to demonstrate knots and seen her reaction, it was probably a good thing she'd been called away by the elven conclave, otherwise very little save for Amma's own protests could have stopped him ripping off her clothes right there—and she wouldn't have protested, of that he was sure. But after, when he was left riled up and stuck in that absurd cage, he was both gifted and tormented with the time to consider what any of it meant.

He had convinced himself that she was simply attractive, and he was simply an animal, and while it was frustrating, it was tolerable, until Amma had spoken to the elves. Simple as it was, her request for information on the Lux Codex, and then her defense of infernal arcana and, in turn, him, had complicated his—and of this he was not proud—but his *feelings*.

Of course, he'd still like to strip her, slowly and preferably with his teeth, but that festering desire had evolved, and he wasn't exactly sure when it had happened. Certainly he'd like to pin her hands above her head again, but he also wanted to pin her entire body against his own, and not just in some carnal entanglement. He wanted to press his flesh against hers to *feel* her, and for once not pull away, to bring her as close as possible, to touch her and to allow her to touch him back.

But that was asking quite a lot of himself, something he had been told he was incapable of, in fact. So, when he had risked putting an arm around her, inviting her to simply lay beside him, and things had gone so quickly to shit, he really should have known better. But perhaps there was a little room to make her pay for the annoyance she had caused him. Damien was evil, after all, and revenge was meant to be one of his specialties.

"Amma, you seem very nervous," he began in a drawn-out way,

glancing up the wide, pastoral street that led to the city proper of Faebarrow. "Is something wrong?" He knew very well there was.

"Let's just get to the library, take a look at that book, and get out," she mumbled.

"Oh, I intend to take the Lux Codex with me, so I believe we'll be spending at least one night in town."

She snapped her head up, catching her hood before it fell back. "We should camp outside the city," she said in a shaking voice, a terrible suggestion when they were already heading into it, one she had to have known.

"And why would we do that? I have plenty of coin, and look how nice it is here. Much better than Elderpass even." He gestured to a wagon headed toward the town, full of people and being pulled by a set of donkeys. Damien called out a greeting.

Amma dipped her head even lower. "Will you stop that?" she hissed.

He smirked, but allowed their small convoy to fall back so that the wagon pulled ahead. "Stop being friendly? Is that not the behavior you've been encouraging out of me all this time? Ah, good day, sir! How fare thee?"

"Oh, by Osurehm, you sound like an idiot—no one talks like that," she grumbled, hunching her shoulders even more and scowling at her knoggelvi's braided mane.

"Then maybe you should translate. Here's a good opportunity." A couple leaving the city was coming toward them, and he waved. Kaz even joined in, standing to balance on the knoggelvi's head and giving a friendly yap. The couple greeted them back, and he turned his smarmy grin on her when they'd passed.

She glared back from under the edge of her hood. "Damien, please." Ah, yes, so this was how his revenge would have to go. It wasn't as torturous as manacles and fiery pokers, but at the very least she was begging him to stop, so it would do.

Over the next hill, the city's official gates were laid out at its base, wide open but attached to a proper wall which made sense for a place that boasted both a scholarly bastion and the production of rare and expensive goods that was nestled into a valley with no other natural defenses. There were a dozen soldiers standing at the entrance in full plate armor, half carrying halberds, the others with long swords strapped to their sides.

The wagon pulled by donkeys had gotten well ahead, reaching the gate where the riders were being instructed to exit it for inspection, even an elderly man that had significant trouble getting down. When

Amma saw this, her whole body went rigid.

Damien's glee at her discomfort shifted to a brief pang of pity and then to the logical realization that, if there were trouble in Faebarrow for her, it meant trouble for him as well. He tugged the reins of his knoggelvi and dismounted, gesturing for her to do the same. Standing between the horses, he still couldn't quite keep the smirk off his face. "What's going to happen when we attempt to enter this city?"

Her eyes were searching the bottom of the hill where the guards were busy poking around the wagon and questioning the citizens. "They can't see my face," she said in one, frightened breath.

One of Damien's brows shot up. With the masked knoggelvi's reins in hand, he began to walk backward toward the gates down the gently sloping hill, eyes set on her. "You'd actually be recognized on sight? Sounds like quite the crime you've committed."

She didn't move to follow, gripping her own knoggelvi's reins tight as if that would somehow comfort her as she stood still.

"*Sanguinisui*, come along."

Amma's feet began to take her forward, and fear flooded her features.

He led her slowly for a moment, waiting for the magic to dissipate before his next question. "Now, tell me, what naughty thing have you done here, Amma?"

"It's…complicated." Her breaths were coming shallowly as her eyes pinged over his shoulder and back to his face.

Damien knew they were still too far off to be properly identified. "Let me guess: you've stolen something, but you're quite sorry about it, and perhaps you didn't even mean to, but you just *had* to, and when you're caught you'll be all quivering lips and fake tears to avoid whatever unjust punishment is levied against you."

"Something like that," she said, eyes glassy already.

"This doesn't seem the sort of place that would take your hands for your thievery, but what *do* you suppose they'll do to you?"

"To me?" She swallowed, and then her eyes found him, sharper and with a new kind of fear, one he was much less familiar with, tinged with something like compassion. "Awful things will happen, Damien."

His next step was hesitant, and then he brought them all to a stop. "As interested as I am in watching you pay for your crimes, I'm quite a bit less interested in being caught up in all that myself."

If she said the guards couldn't see her face, then so be it: he wouldn't let them.

Still with his back to the gates at the base of the hill and with the two of them hemmed in on either side by the knoggelvi, Damien slid his dagger from its bracer and sliced his thumb on the blade before sheathing it again. He dragged his bloodied finger over his bottom lip and began to feel the changes crawling over his own face as the spell took hold, then moved a step closer to Amma.

It occurred to him then, he had never cast this spell on anyone else. Illusion was difficult enough, innate to most infernal beasts, but something a blood mage had to learn. It could be quite draining, but for Amma he would of course do it.

He silently chastised himself for becoming so pathetic and stepped closer to her—she would need a smear of his blood as well for it to work. The cut on his finger was already healing, and the longer he contemplated how her lips would feel against his own if he chose to share his blood that way instead, the more likely he would have no choice but to find out, but then he came to his senses and pressed his sliced thumb to her bottom lip.

She didn't pull back, though her eyes, already doe-like and wide, went even wider. He let his finger drift to the soft edge of her mouth, whispering in Chthonic. He could feel the changes taking hold in himself, his hand cupping her chin for a moment until he saw the changes happening in Amma's face as well. Her hair darkened, her cheeks thinned out, eye shape elongated, and in a moment, she was the spitting image of a woman he'd seen in Elderpass.

"Branson?" she said in her true voice, strange coming from a wider mouth with thinner lips.

Though he wasn't any shorter and his clothes had not changed, he concluded he had accurately taken on the visage of that barkeep in Elderpass, the one Amma had flirted with to get them information. The slice on his thumb already healed, he took a hand to his face and briefly touched the scar still raised across it—as usual the magic worked on everything but that. "You can lose the hood," he said casually, turning from her and leading them to the gate.

They were predictably stopped and looked over by three of the most pompous soldiers Damien had ever laid eyes on, but at least they weren't Holy Knights. He smiled with Branson's face, odd forcing such a pleasantry on even with someone else's features, but when he thought about how easy it would be to arcanely kill these fools for daring to stop him at all, the smile was injected with an easier sort of sincerity.

They asked his business in Faebarrow while a third guard greeted Amma with a bit more politeness. She wasn't doing well to hide her fear, and so Damien put an arm around her shoulders and pulled her to him. "Just looking for a new place to settle down."

The two soldiers gave one another knowing looks while another rifled through the pack strapped to one of the knoggelvi. It was then he saw one of them had an extra marking across his chest. While they all wore the same sigil, a strange creature with the head of a lion and the body of a fish, the landlocked Faebarrow's inexplicable crest, he assumed, this one also had the holy mark of Osurehm on a patch on his arm. "And nothing to declare?"

Damien's eyes flicked to the man's pommel, and could see the faint, radiant glow about it. So, there was a mage amongst them. "Only our loyalty to the realm."

Two of the soldiers gave him a solemn nod, but the third narrowed dark eyes at him. Apparently serving one's god close enough afforded one the power to suss out sarcasm no matter how well it was disguised. Then there was a snap and a growl, and a fourth soldier pulled back after trying to pat Kaz. Up on all fours, back rounded, the rat-like dog was snarling from the knoggelvi's back.

"Ah, that too," said Damien, reaching up and grabbing him by the scruff of his neck to hand off to Amma. She clumsily took Kaz, and both were so surprised that neither could do anything too stupid in front of the guards. "My wife's. It's evil, but what can you do? She loves the thing."

At this, even the knight marked by his god cracked a grin, and the knoggelvi, the imp, the thief, and the blood mage were allowed to pass into Faebarrow.

Silently, they wandered into the town, and Damien turned them down the first open road away from the gate to find an unpopulated nook along an alley. The illusion that had been begging to dispel itself was dropped, and Damien breathed a hefty sigh. His skin went uncomfortably tight as his features shifted, and he had a moment of dizziness that quickly passed. Illusions were close to infernal arts, but they were a different kind of mage's game, and Damien had really only learned the spell to ultimately infiltrate the court at Eirengaard when the time came.

Amma prodded at herself as well, feeling the discomfort again but knowing what it was. She inhaled sharply then, like she'd been holding her breath the entire time, setting Kaz on the ground and pressing her own fingers to her lip where his blood had been but was now gone.

"You protected me," she said, eyes roving the ground and then up to his, big and bright and blue again.

"I protected myself," he half-lied. "And I need those hands of yours on the off chance some overzealous merchant or dignitary actually does want them as a trophy for stealing their...what was it?"

She shook her head. "It's not...I can't explain it."

Damien chuckled, leading them back toward the main road. "Can't or won't?"

Amma pulled her hood up again, looking shiftily over the street as they entered into it. "Don't want to."

"That's fine, I think I'll enjoy attempting to guess."

Faebarrow was bustling, but not overcrowded. The line of shops that marked the eastern entrance to the city were well-kept, and the displays out front were unmonitored, but the frequency of city guards likely played a role. They wore that same red lion-fish hybrid across their chests, though they were dressed more casually in the streets than at the gates.

"Let's see. Perhaps you took something of very high value. That would account for all that gold you had."

Amma said nothing, chewing on her lip, head still down under her hood as she led her horse.

"No, you didn't value those coins very much, did you? And I found you up in Aszath Koth attempting to steal that magicked scroll—twice now you tried to take it, actually—so it must have been something rare you took. Something *priceless*. And this is a good place for that, isn't it? Oh, of course, your mark must have had to do with the fancy, arcane trees."

"I took nothing from Faebarrow," she mumbled.

"Not thievery?" He snorted. "So, you went north with the intention of helming an army of the undead, but why? To clear a debt? Or maybe get a bit of revenge?" This thought sparked a certain excitement in Damien, and he hoped it was true.

Again, she said nothing, but the nothing this time was much louder.

"*Revenge*," he repeated, lips curling up at just the idea. "I can appreciate that. On whom?"

Amma's face was going the loveliest shade of pink.

"Is it a man? Oh, of course it is, it's *always* a man. But this scoundrel who's earned your vindictiveness—does he deserve the wrath of an entire army?" Damien watched her face for some hint of what she'd intended to do, delighted by the idea of her being so merciless, but it was quite impersonal, in his opinion. "You know, there are better and quieter ways to destroy a man than unleashing the literal Abyss on him. You're quite quick with your hands and I imagine good with that silver dagger. Why kill him when you could just cut off his favorite parts and make him wish he were dead?" Then he frowned—perhaps it wasn't wise to put those kinds of ideas into her head.

Amma clicked her tongue. "You know, you could just force me to tell you with the talisman."

Oh, he knew, he had always known the truth of her origin was one enchanted word away. At first he simply hadn't cared, but as time went on, he considered it a bit of fun to see what she might accidentally reveal, and then, more recently, he had begun to hope she would choose for herself to confide in him. It was only the night before when he realized how stupid that hope—like all hopes—had been. "I *could* do that, yes, but your suffering anticipation of *if* I actually will order you to tell me or not is much more satisfying, not to mention the struggle you're having with your morality."

Amma's mouth fell open, but predictably no words came out. Kaz snickered from their feet, hurrying along and tail wagging as Damien continued down the road, and Amma eventually caught up. She began complaining immediately, it was actually quite important, and she heaped on a bit more minotaurshit as if he should be much more interested than he was.

"You know, Amma," he said with a grin, interrupting her, "if I didn't know better, I would say you're getting a little too comfortable having your decisions taken away. You might even be enjoying that thing inside you."

"I am *not*," she said in a breathy protest that told him exactly what he wanted to hear.

"Well, the talisman isn't meant to help you overcome cowardice nor is it meant to give you undue attention." He sighed as if bored by the discussion. "So, when you decide to stop acting like a spoiled, little brat about whatever petty thing you think is so worthy of all this secrecy, you can just be a woman and tell me yourself."

Amma glared at him, the anger there more powerful than he'd ever seen it, and she actually stomped a foot. "It's not cowardice, it's—" And then her voice cut out again when they turned down another road.

Her face changed completely. The anger, the uncertainty, even the panicked anxiety had gone. She tipped her chin up, the light of the afternoon falling on her features as they softened. Her hood slipped back to reveal hair that glowed golden, and she dropped the knoggelvi's reins to walk a few paces ahead.

The road they'd taken led to a large, circular market interrupted in its center by a tree as wide at its base as one of the farmstead cabins outside of the city. Even larger than the trees in the Gloomweald, the trunk twisted as it rose up out of the ground, a rich, earthy brown, and its branches spread out over the cobbled street that encircled it, shading the stalls and carts set up beneath where villagers sold wares and foods. In the earliness of autumn, the leaves were beginning to change, or Damien thought they were, but it was difficult to tell as each one was a more intense shade of pink than the last until the few that had fallen to the ground were a deep, blood red.

Beyond the tree and through the thickness of its branches was a keep looming large and ornate in white stone. Though it was far off, it could look down and see this tree from the many stained-glass windows that caught the afternoon sun's rays, their colors shimmering between the branches as they swayed gently in the breeze.

Amma stood staring up at the tree with a reverence, a look that Damien knew, even if he couldn't feel, was love. A tinge of jealousy worked its way into his chest before he pushed it back out, pulling his eyes away to see a pair of heavy armor-clad guards making their rounds.

"Your hood," he said quietly, and she hastened to pull it back up, tucking her hair into the cloak. "This must be one of those...what are they called?"

"Liathau trees." She spoke the name like it was meant to come from her lips, a spell that only she knew, as if her tongue had coined it. "The oldest one in existence, born during The Expulsion. A gift left by the goddess Sestoth. It hasn't given up new seeds in years, but it still blooms every spring." Her eyes followed a leaf as it broke away in a strong gust, richly red as it drifted to the ground and fell like a drop of blood at her feet.

In Damien's experience, The Expulsion had left behind things like the Infernal Mountains and the knoggelvi, things made "wrong" by the thoughtless actions of the gods on earth, but he hadn't thought things like this tree, beautiful and so loved by Amma, could result from the same source. Sestoth—he didn't know this goddess, but it wasn't the first time he had heard her say the name with reverence.

Then Amma's face went harder, and Damien followed her gaze to find another guard who was speaking to a villager standing behind a market cart. The discussion was quickly growing heated, and then the guard swept his arm across the man's wares and knocked them to the ground. Pottery shattered, sharp pieces spilling out over the cobbled street, cries of surprise rising up from the scuffle that was breaking out. Two more guards hustled over, one pushing back a younger man

238

who attempted to intervene, and together, two of the crest-clad men dragged off the vendor. The younger one was swiftly punched in the gut, doubling him over, and he was left there on the ground.

Damien almost missed Amma stalking toward the tussle. She was walking with a purpose, chin raised, clenched fists at her sides. He shot an arm out and grabbed her. "What are you doing?"

"I can't let—" Amma's voice broke. She stood with all the momentum of an arrow pulled taught on a bow, then rocked back onto flat feet, and Damien released her.

The market had come to only a short halt as the villagers watched the seller be forcibly taken away, and then, slowly, a few of them tasked themselves with cleaning up the broken pottery and splintered cart. A couple picked up the younger man who had been injured and walked him into a tavern. The others returned to their business, but the voices in the square were quieter. Even the birdsong in the giant liathau seemed to dim.

Amma pulled her hood a bit farther forward, eyes falling to the ground, and then she more carefully waded close to where the scuffle had occurred to retrieve a small piece of the shattered pottery. Her fingers slid over it many times as she came back to him, and then she stuffed it into a pocket. "The Athenaeum is this way," she said sharply and turned away from the market, shielding her face from the crowd and from Damien.

Amma led them as Damien fell back a step, walking between the knoggelvi, a hand on each set of reins. They passed out of the center of town, away from the cleanest and widest roads heavily patrolled with guards in their red lion-fish branding.

Down a smaller road, Damien slowed to watch one of them talk with a young woman who was tending to the stall outside an herbal shop. The guard loomed over her while she organized hanging, dried bundles on a rack and replied with seemingly simple answers, her face clearly reading she wanted to be left alone—Damien knew because he made that face himself quite a bit if for different reasons. Someone older came out of the shop and called her in, but the guard stopped her, forcibly, to leave her with some other parting bit of information before she scurried inside.

Damien groaned at the odd discomfort that poked at him then, turning away before his mind would start telling him he was supposed to do something. Amma had come to a stop a few yards ahead, standing before a large board covered in tacked up parchment. "Have the forces here always been so involved with the people?"

Amma spun back to him, looking alarmed. "What?"

He glanced back to the guard who was wandering away, swiping an apple from another stall. "In Aszath Koth, I never have the troops bother with…whatever this is. Aren't they meant to be for outside obstacles and not harassing the civilians?"

Amma was suddenly right next to him, grabbing the reins of one of the knoggelvi and nudging all of them toward a different street. "I almost got eaten by a snake man in your city, so I wouldn't call Aszath Koth the pinnacle of safety in or outside the realm, but, no, things have not always been like this here."

"Not when you were young?" he ventured.

Amma shook her head. "Not even a year ago."

The sadness in her voice made him refrain from further questions, and they walked on in silence through Faebarrow. Eventually, they crossed over a bridge and came into a district with fewer shops and far more residences, larger and with many windows and entries to suggest shared housing. The streets were lined with benches and trees, though different than the town center's liathau. Damien assumed Amma could identify them, but she didn't need distracting, eyes casting about shrewdly from under her hood.

At the end of a row filled with more dense, residential buildings stood a squat but wide structure that rose up from the ground in white marble. It gleamed in the sun, columns along its face and a wide set of stone steps up its front to thick, wooden double doors.

"This is it," she said, not bringing them any closer, "the Grand Athenaeum." Guiding them off the main road where others were walking, noses frequently down in books or in deep discussion with others, Amma found a shady spot beneath a tree for them to stop. She dug in her pocket and pulled out more sweets, feeding them to the knoggelvi as she glanced around and spoke in hushed tones. "Anyone can go inside, but there are many books that are off limits without express permission from an academy or the crown. I'm sure the Lux Codex is one of those kinds of books."

"I imagine it's difficult to get this permission," Damien mused.

"Yes, but it's also unnecessary. For us."

Damien gave her a look, one he feared was more adoring than he would have liked to let on.

"I've been inside many times, places I wasn't supposed to go." She turned more fully to the building, her gaze roving over it, pinging from window to window as if pulling the path from her memory and watching what they would do unfold in her mind. "I can get us into the restricted section easily."

Damien swallowed. He was getting quite warm despite the fall

240

breeze that blew down the road. "Oh?"

She nodded. "But it has to be after dark, we have to sneak in unseen, and you have to cooperate with me."

Damien was shaken from his long, admiring stare at her when her eyes turned on him, still sharp. He cleared his throat and frowned. "You're making it very difficult to remain angry with you."

"Good," she said, the flicker of a smile there. "So, you'll actually listen to me for a change?"

"Of course. Is there some place you suggest we go in the meantime? This is your territory, after all."

"Um?" Amma pressed a finger to her lips, looking around. "Well, I don't really...I suppose this way."

He followed her again, and she took him out of the scholarly district, avoiding the main roads, though she did lead him into a few dead ends that made her grumble quietly to herself words that sounded like fluffy replacements for swears.

Eventually, they were in a much seedier place. Even Faebarrow had its dregs, and he assumed she was very familiar, yet she squinted and hemmed and hawed until stumbling upon a tavern and inn, the placard hanging over the door by one chain, the other broken. "Here. Here is probably good," she announced with all the confidence of a woman who was only half lost. She tipped her head to the side to read the broken sign. "The Too Deep Inn. Yeah, that's...that's the one."

They hadn't seen a guard in a bit, so Damien was amenable even if she seemed reticent. There was at least a makeshift stable for the knoggelvi to stink up with their infernal gases at the back. Inside, he paid for two rooms and food, and when they had found their lodgings, he told her he would be coming to get her after night had fallen, then cast the words on her to keep her in place in her room.

"Wait," she said just before he left.

He stopped on the threshold, glancing back.

"You're, um...you're staying too, right? You're not going wandering or anything outside? Leaving me alone?"

Damien looked over her small form squeezing the edge of the cot. She meant staying in the building, surely, and not there, in her room. "I don't intend to leave. I'll be across the hall if you...if you need me. *Sanguinisui*, you can cross the hall if need be."

She nodded, and then he left, torn with hoping she both would and would not knock on his door.

CHAPTER 25
ON THE DANGERS OF LIBRARIANS

Amma felt just about every kind of bad that she could. She hadn't been able to bring herself to eat, nausea roiling in her stomach every time she went to take a bite. She tried to distract herself by refreshing her clothing and scrubbing her face and body with the fresh water that ran from a tap in the room—at least Faebarrow had not yet lost the arcanely enhanced fixtures all throughout the city that the larger cities were abundant in—but then all she could do was lay on the cot, fail miserably at attempting to sleep, and feel awful. It was in her blood, the guilt, as profoundly as infernal arcana was in Damien's. And now she had so many more things to feel guilty for.

Foremost was Faebarrow. In the short time she'd been beyond its borders, she had forgotten the way things were here with so many soldiers siphoned in from Brineberth March, but that merchant was a grim reminder. What would become of him? Would he ever see his family again? See another day? She bit back tears at the thought, pulling out the shard of broken pottery she'd rescued from beneath the ancient liathau. There was half an image there, delicately laid into the red, hardened clay: the jaws of a lion pouncing on a tree branch. It was brave to have made this, braver still to sell it on the street, but costly, in the end.

And then there was the lying. Of course, she *could* just tell Damien why she had to hide her face in Faebarrow—and perhaps he was right that her own cowardice was why she kept her secrets all to herself, but they *were* hers, weren't they? If he knew, she couldn't imagine things would go much better. He may use the truth to what he would think would be his advantage but really turn out to be a danger. Not telling him was safest for both of them.

But did Damien need her protection? Did he even deserve it? He had abducted her, ordered her around through enchantments—which, for the archives, she was *not* enjoying—and who had threatened to *murder* her. Yet she still didn't want to see him hurt. Was she really that stupid? Or was it because she had stopped believing that he meant her ill will altogether?

Because why—*why*—did he want this Lux Codex so badly?

The book had nothing to do with his plans in Eirengaard and his mysterious prophecy, he was already on his quest before learning of it, so it was something new that encouraged him to go after it. Damien's questions for the elf in the Gloomweald were of artifact purging and curse removal. It was perhaps a little self-centered—well, no, it was almost certainly a *lot* self-centered when she truly thought about it—but there was a small chance he wanted the Lux Codex in order to get the talisman out of her without ending her life. And wouldn't that just be the luck of things if his decision to spare her led to the downfall of them both?

Amma sat up from the bed and went across the room to get a better look at the city from her third-story window. She struggled with its stiff hinges until it popped open so she could see past the grime. Darkness had fallen on Faebarrow, but the static moon glowed over the tops of buildings, and there was a faint smell of liathau even here, a bright twist of citrus with a floral undertone, and she was taken right back into every memory she had of toiling in the greenhouse, running through the orchard with Laurel, showing her parents her work, and simply being happy. Things had changed in the last few years, and then they'd gotten significantly worse after the soldiers' arrived, but there was still something here. Something worth saving.

Damien's knock on her door was too cheerful. She answered, and there he stood, leaning on the frame, much too confident for the danger all around him. Kaz was sitting at his feet, bundled in his knit tunic and still a dog, his tail unapologetically wagging. At least they were headed to the library, a place she would feel comfortable wagging her own tail and lounging against every door if there actually were time.

The tavern downstairs was busy and loud but easy enough to slip through and out into the darkened streets. Most had returned to their homes, and Amma told Damien of the curfew that had been imposed on the city as they made their way back to the Grand Athenaeum, keeping to the shadows and avoiding the guards that patrolled the empty roads.

The massive library stood in all its glory like a white copse of birches amongst a dark forest of housing for the students and scholars. They came up around its back this time, hiding in an alley as Amma took a breath, preparing herself. The Grand Athenaeum didn't call for much protection on its outside, just like most of Faebarrow, until it did. The yard at the sides and back of the building were rung with a stone wall with no breaks in it for even a gate.

"How are we going to—"

Amma cut Damien off, pulling out the key she never went anywhere without from her hip pouch and shoving it in his face.

"To the Athenaeum? Have I gotten things wrong? You've been a librarian all this time?"

Amma shook her head. "No, but I did steal this from one years ago."

"So, thief it is then."

She supposed, in a way, he was right. But he was very wrong too.

Scaling the wall behind the Athenaeum was easy—Amma already knew a place with good, natural footholds that had been worn in by time and messy masonry. She told him to watch, and with a quick check of the walkway for guards, she sprinted at full speed to the wall and used the momentum to propel herself to its top. She paused a short moment to gesture for him to follow, and then eased herself down the other side.

Damien landed beside her in the grass at just the same time as she did—*show off*, she thought—and Kaz flitted down with his wings just after, an imp again. Damien glanced back at the wall then to her, cocking a brow. "You scaled that wall much better than the knoggelvi."

"Knoggelvi don't have footholds, but they can get hurt if I dig my foot in wrong."

He thought on that a moment then tipped his head, sincere. "Regardless, I am impressed."

Amma looked away quickly, glad the dark would hide her face. Disturbingly, she found she liked impressing him with her worst behavior. It was nice to have someone to share it with, at least, but especially someone who appreciated it. And it was much nicer having him impressed with her than angry.

Her key could get them into one of the many doors running along the building's backside, and she chose the one she remembered didn't squeak when opened, but it did dump them into a pitch dark, back hall that required careful treading, the place used for storage and cleaning and often littered with old tomes needing mending.

"Now, be careful through here, it's easy to trip and—"

"Kaz, a little light."

Amma squeaked as Kaz's tail caught on fire. "The books!"

But Kaz did not shoot a blast of fire blindly into the hall. Instead, he became a lantern, riding on Damien's shoulder, tail hanging out to the side, its tip gently alight.

"Whoa, Kaz, very nice." She grinned at him.

The imp grinned back, then caught a look from Damien, and dropped back into a scowl. "I can set this whole place ablaze with a simple flick of my tail."

"You'll do no such thing," threatened Damien.

The warm glow of the infernal fire fell over the long corridor where books were stacked along the walls broken up by the many doorways, most closed and no light came from any of them, not rare, but useful. "There is a night shift who cleans up and tends to projects, but I know their usual rounds," Amma said, voice very low as she inched her way forward. "Less predictable are the keepers who stay late on a whim. They can pop up anywhere, and you don't want to get caught by them."

"What do either of us have to fear from a librarian?" Damien asked, voice similarly low as they came to the corridor's end.

"Many of them are mages, like you, blessed by one of the gods of knowledge or reading or whatever," she said, looking both ways in the dark and then scurrying down the path to the left and its end. "And almost all of them abhor rule breakers."

"Something we absolutely don't have in common." Damien's voice crawled up the back of her as he stood closer than her own shadow. She shivered in the dark like he had breathed right into her ear, having to take a moment before going on.

Peeking around the corner of the wide archway that led out into the main entry of the library, the place was as imposing as last she saw it. The main room off the Athenaeum's foyer was octagonal, its center an open, hollow space with tiled floors and mosaics laid into it, and near the ceiling there were long windows that let in the static moon's violet glow. Each wall was filled to the point of bursting with books to the height of the room itself, three stories, ladders set against them to reach higher tomes. The shelves were built from liathau wood, filling the air with a mixture of its soft, floral smell and the musky scent of old parchment and ink.

Amma associated that smell, however, not with reading, but

stalking. The many, many nights she had spent sneaking out, coming here, and learning all of the things she was never meant to, at first for fun, and then for knowledge, and finally with the singular goal of protection.

"This is odd," said Damien, reaching out to touch a small branch that was sprouting out of the bookcase closest to where they were hiding.

"It's their magic," she said, watching his fingers delicately run over a pink leaf. "Once liathau are harvested, they try to manifest their new purpose. This one understands it's too full of books, so I bet it's making new shelves." Amma's jaw hardened, eyes slicing down the room as she heard a sound. "Kaz, kill the light." The imp obliged her, the tone she used harsh enough for him to confuse it with Damien's voice.

Footsteps, soft but clacking on the marble came toward them as, from another archway, four figures emerged. Amma recognized one of them, an older night shift worker called Watchwoman Aretta who would cause them no trouble if they remained unseen, but with her was a man, face too shadowed for Amma to make out, though he held himself regally and dressed exceptionally well, and trailing behind them were two Brineberth soldiers with full armor and weapons. Now *that* was odd.

Damien raised a hand up beside Amma's face, his dagger in it, but she held up a finger for him to wait. The elder woman was speaking to the man, carrying a book, and beside her hovered a gentle, teal ball of light. It followed the small group instinctively as she brought them to one of the shelves. "I'm not sure this is exactly what you're looking for," she said in her soft, leathery voice, "but I've an idea that could act as a companion to the restricted tomes you've already taken out."

"Taken out?" Amma whispered almost inaudibly. The restricted tomes were not allowed to leave the library.

Watchwoman Aretta ran fingers over the spines that were lit up by the light she carried until she found what she wanted, plucking it off the shelf and handing it over.

The man opened the book with a displeased sigh. "That's it?" Amma recognized the voice and held her breath.

Folding her hands before her, the night shift worker showed no sign of being annoyed. "There are perhaps a few things in the head archivist's office, but you would need to speak with him. As I said, he is not in until the morning."

With another unsatisfied grunt, the man who Amma now knew

was Gilead snapped the book shut. "Take me there. I will leave him a message."

Returning the way they had come, the light disappeared with them. Amma tried to calm her nerves, hating that they were in the same building as a mage of Brineberth, and one so high up, but felt a little safer with a blood mage beside her.

Damien sheathed the dagger and made a quiet sound in the back of his throat, and Amma heard it almost too well with him so close. He had bent down to watch, leaning over her back to stay close to the wall. She almost regretted having to move on, but more night shift workers would be about, and it wasn't a good idea to stay in one place for long.

"There are two ways to the restricted section," she told Damien, turning her head just over her shoulder, "one is needlessly up those wide stairs right in the center of the library and then down again once you reach the offices up on the balcony. That's the public way you'd be taken if you were given permission to visit."

"And the private passage?"

"Is this way."

They crossed out into the main room, but only for a moment, Amma taking them to another alcove along the wall adjacent to them. There was a narrow door laid into the side that would be missed if one didn't know about it, and she flexed her fingers. Blowing out a steady breath, she turned the knob carefully, eyes squeezed shut, and there was that predictable squeak that made her cringe but pull the door the rest of the way open. She gestured for them to go in ahead of her, slipping inside herself, and pulling it closed behind, shutting out all of the light.

Stepping backward, she bumped right into Damien then stood straight. The hall there was narrow, and she was suddenly very warm. "Light would be good again," she said in a wavering voice.

Kaz's tail lit up once more. Here, the walls were a sand-colored stone, and the pathway curved downward. Amma looked up at Damien who was watching her very carefully, lips pressed together tight. "Hopefully no one heard that, and if they did, they'll just think it was Aretta," she said, squeezing past him. "Regardless, we need to get to the restricted section fast in case someone else comes."

Amma hurried along the corridor as it turned, heartbeat pounding in her ears. This was the worst part, the part where someone could be coming the other way, and there was nowhere to hide to avoid them. She had never run into that particular issue, but it always loomed over her. Thankfully, they got to the foot of the winding ramp where a single door stood, simple, arched, and made up of liathau, a keyhole set into the knob.

"Lucky you have that key," said Damien, still close in the cramped space.

"The key doesn't open this lock." She placed a hand on the door, spreading out her fingers. "There are keys that do, but we don't need them." Pushing her palm down flat, she felt the liathau under her hand, warm like it was alive. It tickled her palm and traced around the edges of each finger in turn, and read from her what she wanted. At least, that's how she assumed it worked, because what she wanted was for the door to open, and with a click, it did.

Amma grinned, satisfied anew every time, but especially after so long. She stepped through, but the light of Kaz's tail didn't follow, so she glanced back. Damien was standing in the open archway, ducking slightly, jaw slack. Up on his shoulder, Kaz's underbite was similarly hanging open.

"What?"

"You just,"—Damien flicked a hand in gesture to the open door and then to her—"You used arcana."

"No." She shook her head, chuckling lightly and scrunching up her face. "I just asked the door to let us inside. It's the wood that's magic, I told you that already."

Damien didn't seem to accept that, but she wasn't sure what to say—it was the truth. He simply continued to stare, not angry, but confused.

"Okay, get over it, someone else might take the passage behind us, and you can't be standing there. Kaz, you can put yourself out. And Damien, close the door, it knows to lock itself after because *the wood* is arcane," she stressed, hoping he would understand.

Amma turned back to the chamber, the space alight from glowing stones set into sconces on the walls. It was a warm, orangey hue, like candlelight, and it flickered similarly as well, but Amma was fairly certain that was added to give it a cozy effect without the danger of fire.

There was a click from the door as it was finally locked, Damien stepping up beside her. "There isn't time now, but we will *not* be glossing over what you just did like it didn't happen."

Amma shrugged, nothing more to say on the matter.

CHAPTER 26
THE PRIMEVAL ARCANA OF CURSING

Before Amma, hundreds of bookcases appeared to be packed in tightly together. There was no singular way forward, cases lined up with erratic spaces and hidden gaps, some reaching the ceiling, others just a foot or two over Amma's head. Labyrinthine, some were set facing the entrance, others perpendicular, and some on diagonals. The most direct route to the restricted section was from the main hall, but it was risky to climb up on that raised balcony with librarians and even guards shuffling about, so they would have to take the more difficult one.

"You know the way?" Damien asked.

"Sort of." Amma reached out for the bookcase right before her, made from more liathau. She walked along it to an opening, shook her head, and walked back, finding another. "This way. Stay close, they do move sometimes." And she slipped in.

Damien kept up with her, the heat off of him at her back. Swiftly, she twisted and turned through the walkways the bookcases created, trailing a hand along the shelves, feeling the smooth grain of the wood on her fingertips. They were getting close, she could tell from the way the floor dipped slightly and the way a sconce was hung askew, but she took a left instead of her normal right when the passageway came to a new end, and had to slip between a set of narrow, high shelves.

Damien squeezed in behind her, and down another row there was an opening that led to the room's center, a much bigger area with the entry to the restricted section against one wall, opposite it the exit to the stairs, leading back up to the main library. Amma nearly stepped out when the door into the library clicked and swung inward with none of the care or quiet Amma used when sneaking about. A rotund, robed figure swept in, Archivist Reinar, with his head down into a book and just enough distraction to miss Amma. She pushed herself back and knocked Damien around the shelf's corner.

Of all the possible librarians why *him*? Her heart pounded as she pressed into Damien's chest and caught his eyes, saying nothing, but apparently not needing to. Damien held up a hand, and she thought he would pull out his dagger, but instead just gestured for her to step back with him, retreating down the passageway of shelves.

The footsteps of the archivist were quick and loud, and the two hurried away as he came nearer. The corridor was narrow, and he was coming closer, but the shelves they'd slipped between had already closed up, and they continued on until they no longer could, ending at a stone wall.

Amma spun back to see a shadow moving toward the opening along the bookshelves. He would see them the moment he stepped into the row if he even so much as glanced to the side, nowhere for them to go. And then an arm swept around her middle and pulled her back, and a wall of hazy fog rose up from the floor. Amma inhaled sharply, Archivist Reinar turning into the row. He snapped his book shut and looked up, eyes falling on her.

"He can't see us." Damien was so quiet she thought he might have sent the words straight into her mind, but the vibration of his voice against her ear told her he had spoken aloud. His whisper, however, meant the archivist could still hear them if he were close enough.

Reinar strode forward a few paces and began to look through the shelves. She could see him, but his form was slightly muted, like the color had been sucked all out of it. Her eyes skimmed the row, everything in grey tones, and then when she looked to the shelf right beside them, she could read none of the spines, the words in a script that reminded her of the one scrawled on shop signs in Aszath Koth.

She felt odd too, lighter somehow, but also grounded, like she might not quite be in the Grand Athenaeum anymore but a hazy copy of the place that may or may not have been just as real. But there was Damien's arm around her, and that was definitely real.

Amma tipped her head up and back, and he was raising a finger to his lips to signal she needed to remain silent. Damien's hand pressed into her side with the deep, slow breath she took, and then his fingers inched up slightly, tickling at her ribs. She rocked her head back a bit more, pushing up onto her toes. Closer. She wanted to be closer to him, but what she would do when she got there, she didn't know, and she would never find out as a sound from along the row stole her momentum.

Archivist Reinar replaced his book on the shelf and continued toward where they were masked against the wall, and Amma froze, head still tipped up but eyes on the librarian. He followed his own finger, muttering to himself, blue light hovering at his shoulder as he looked for a title, bringing himself closer and closer to where they were hidden.

Amma pressed back into Damien's body, clutching onto his arm already around her waist. He tightened his grip, and she held her breath, but nothing could still her heart, thumping to be free from her chest.

The archivist stopped just before them, narrowed eyes behind metal-rimmed glasses that he pushed up his nose, and mumbled, "There you are, my dear. By Keluregn, which one of those goat-fucking imbeciles shelved you away here?"

Amma winced with a laugh that tried to escape—Archivist Reinar, swearing? As a tiny noise erupted from her lips, Damien clamped his free hand over her mouth, and her shoulders shook silently even as Reinar's brow furrowed in confusion, looking about for the sound.

Damien shifted behind Amma, and she saw from the corner of her eye a rat scurry down his arm and jump to the floor. It was a lucky thing Damien's hand was still over her mouth, the laughter stopping immediately, wanting to be replaced with a yelp as the rat scampered away from them and up a bookshelf.

Right into Reiner's line of sight, the rat poked its nose out, tiny underbite opening with a squeak, and Reiner gave a shout, swiping at it with the book he held. The rat ducked away, and the archivist turned on a heel, swearing some more about pests and poor upkeep and which of the apprentice librarians would be paying for this.

Once his footsteps fell away and the door into the library proper closed with a bang, the haziness wavered, color seeped back in around them, and Damien's hands released her. Amma remained against him for a too-long moment until the rat popped back out from the shelves and ran toward her. She jerked away as it sped past and jumped onto Damien's boot, scurried up to his shoulder, and was suddenly Kaz again.

"That bastard almost got me," the imp hissed.

Damien cast a wary glance at him. "Yes. Unfortunate." Then looked back to her. "Almost got you too."

Amma touched her chest, heart still beating hard. "That was

close."

"Much closer thanks to your giggling." Damien's hands were on his hips, and she frowned at them, wanting them on her instead.

"I didn't know Reinar talked like that." She shook her head. "But thank you—if Reinar caught me, he would have been thrilled to turn me in. He's always sniveling around the nobles any chance he gets." She carefully walked back to the opening that led to the exit of the shelving labyrinth.

Damien followed. "You're in trouble with the nobles?"

"Nope." Amma stepped warily out as if testing the emptiness of the chamber. But when she saw the double doors to the restricted section at the back wall, she walked up to them as if greeting an old friend.

Damien came to stand beside her. "Why do I feel like you're lying?"

"I think because you like it better when I do." She smirked to herself and pressed a hand to each liathau door, that familiar thrum of life coming out to touch her back, to read her as she did it.

Can I come in, please? she asked without a word.

Sure, the doors replied, and then opened.

"Seriously," said Damien, "we have *got* to talk about that."

The stairs leading downward were wide and dark, the wall on either side curving overhead like a stone tunnel into the earth. Chilly air rose up to meet them as they descended, footsteps echoing into the corridor below no matter how careful they were to be quiet. The sconces here were widely spread, illuminating only small patches of wall with pitch darkness between, but Kaz lit his tail once more.

At the foot of the stairs, the chamber opened into a wide room. There were rows of shelves here too, but these ones held far fewer tomes, many spread out from the others and set on angled stands so their titles could be read. Some were covered in chains, others under glass, while still others simply sat, able to be touched but only by hands that had been approved.

"So, this is the Grand Athenaeum of Faebarrow?" asked Damien as if he had not just been led through it already, eyes sweeping over the many cases.

"The restricted section, yes."

Less a labyrinth here, the shelves were laid out in clean rows and did not move about. Amma hurried forward. Typically when here, she would have to do much searching—the categorizing of things in the restricted section was always a mystery to her, especially as someone without arcana, and it seemed as soon as she began to learn it, the librarians would change everything about. She suspected it had something to do with fending off exactly what the two of them were attempting. However, there was a spot near the back of the large chamber where new things were always kept prior to fully cataloging them.

Damien kept up and cast an appreciating glance around as they turned down another row. "Is there anything else of particular interest to you here? Something you might want to liberate from this place?"

"Oh, lots," said Amma, knowing she had only read the smallest possible fraction of what the library had to offer from books on self-defense to magic out in the world beyond Eiren to fictional tales of adventure, love, and lust, but she knew that wasn't what Damien was actually asking. "But none of it's for you, so hands off."

He scoffed, and there was almost sincerity in his offense. "Now, that's where you're wrong—I can have anything I want."

She cocked a brow as she led them around the shelves that opened up into the uncategorized section, knowing their query would be close. "You're in Eiren now, Damien. The crown is all around, there are Holy Knights on every corner, and you had to sneak in here with *me*. We're here for one thing, and that's it."

He frowned when they came to a stop, glancing to the shelf beside him and reaching out. "Well, I think I'll take this too." The book he lifted suddenly jerked in his hand, snapping, and he dropped the newly animate thing to the ground.

"Damien!" she hissed, trying to pick it up, but it snapped at her as well, and she recoiled. The pages bent around a makeshift mouth, cover flapping, managing to thrash about on the stone floor, but it didn't get far.

Damien tried to retrieve it again, but it clamped down hard. "Oh, you bloody waste of parchment and ink!" He yanked an uninjured hand back—it was only paper and leather after all—but brought back a booted foot to kick it.

"Don't you dare!" Amma slapped at him to stop. "Kaz, do you think you can help?"

The imp looked to Damien, exacerbated, and the blood mage rubbed his hand, only shrugging and then gestured to the angry book. "Go on."

Kaz growled, fluttering down to it, and reached out his long, spindly arms. He threw himself at it all at once, rolled over the book to pin it to him, and flew back up to where it belonged to deposit the thing where it fell into stillness.

"That'll do," said Damien, brushing off some unseen dirt from his front. "But that's not what I was asking, Amma. Do *you* want something specific?"

She scoffed. "Do I want to *steal* something that I can't ever bring back? No, of course not!"

His features pinched. "But the opportunity is right here. What kind of thief are you?"

Amma wasn't sure how to respond, so she didn't.

Damien grimaced. "Fine, we're here for the Lux Codex anyway."

"And that should be just back here," she said, pointing.

In the carved-out space there was a table and chairs and a set of cases specifically for unknown things. Sometimes books would be left there for moons before they were properly researched and cataloged, and predictably there was a line of them, each unique but none clearly marked. In fact, not a single one had a name on its spine, which was typical for the restricted section, but would make this challenging. "Well, it should be amongst these, especially if it came here in the last moon or so, but I don't know how we're supposed to tell."

"We could just take them all?" Damien grinned.

"Sneaking back in the dark and avoiding the guards will be hard enough without a stack of books higher than your head to carry. Plus, the archivists will put out an alert immediately if something is missing, and they're much more likely to notice if it's multiple somethings and not just one."

"I guess you are a good thief, aren't you?" Damien sighed. "Well, I suppose we'll have to find it the hard way." He lifted a hand and set his gaze on the row.

She thought for a moment he was casting, and there was a brief flicker of fear he might damage the tomes, but instead, something damaged him. As he brought his hand right to the first spine, there was a light that pricked in his palm, the glow bluish, and then he swept his hand slowly down the row.

Damien's arm jerked, and he sucked in a breath between grit teeth, coming to a stop on a spine just in the center, sapphire with a silver filigree running down it. The book certainly looked the part. "That one," he said and took a step back from the shelf, cradling his hand.

Amma ignored the book, grabbing and pulling his palm to her face instead. "What did you do?" Under Kaz's flame, it looked gruesome just in the center, skin bubbling up, and it smelled worse. When she shifted her thumb closer to the blackened edge of the wound, he winced. "Sorry, sorry," she said in a hushed voice, making sure to be more tender.

His eyes flicked to her, and he smirked. "It will heal the same as everything else, just a bit slower."

She frowned up at him.

"But you see?" He nodded toward the Lux Codex. "This is why I need your nimble fingers."

She stared at the wound a second longer then released him, taking up the book. There was nothing special about it when it touched her skin, not even a warm blast of goodness. It simply felt like any other leather-bound book, though it was quite small. She levied it in her hand and flipped through the pages. In the very dim light, she could see it was filled with tiny lines of script—predictable—but nothing special.

"Impressive," he said, shaking his burnt palm and straightening. "Perhaps there truly is luxerna woven into its spine. Well, if you're sure there's nothing else—"

There was a click deep in the chamber, a key in a lock, and voices.

"Shoot," Amma hissed, head snapping in the direction of their exit. She'd been stuck in the restricted section before with an archivist, but by herself it was easy to hide and wait.

"You are more than welcome to check again." Watchwoman Aretta's voice was tighter than it had been in the main chamber. "Thank you for asking your guardsmen to stay behind. This chamber is sacred, and too many bodies within at once will disturb the enchantments on the tomes."

That didn't sound right to Amma, but then she didn't blame Aretta for wanting to be away from Brineberth soldiers—it was as if their training included entire courses on chauvinism. Still, why the woman had to bring anyone into the restricted section at all, *now*, was maddening, but she knew it had to be that Brineberth mage, Gilead, and that was even worse. If he spotted her, there would be *nothing* she could do.

Kaz instinctively put out his tail, and the small section fell into a deeper darkness.

"If there is anything new you've brought in, that would be best," said Gilead, arresting and pinched, and she cursed him again in her mind.

"They're coming this way." Amma tucked the Lux Codex into the small satchel she had strapped around her waist, lucky it fit. There was only one way in and out of the section. If they moved quickly enough, they could break off and head down a separate row, but footsteps were already coming toward them.

Damien grinned from the side of his mouth, once again holding up his dagger, and Kaz, on his shoulder, hunched his back and rubbed his clawed hands together. They didn't understand the meaning of stealth, obviously.

Amma didn't doubt they could get them out of there with violence, but she didn't want to leave death in their wake no matter how tempting Gilead's death might have been. If there were bodies, especially of a Brineberth dignitary, there would be an inquiry, and moving about Faebarrow would be almost impossible, nevermind leaving the city. But there wasn't enough time to explain any of that to Damien.

Amma shook her head, eyes darting around for a distraction, finding only more and more books and the shelves they stood on. But, of course—that was it.

"Sestoth, forgive me," she said quietly, then turned to Damien. "When I run, you follow me, no detours, and no attacking anyone, got it?"

"Are you really giving me an order to—"

She poked a finger against his chest. "Got it?"

He frowned, then smirked. "Yes, ma'am."

Amma blew out a sharp breath, the steps coming closer, just on the other side of the case from them. In a quick move, she scooped up the book that had so recently attempted eating the two of them. It immediately tried to snap, but she was ready for it, taking it by the binding and winding back. With as much effort as she had, she chucked it over the tall stack, it thumped to the ground on the other side, and then all at once began to thrash.

Aretta and Gilead shouted, feet scuffling. The watchwoman began cursing at the animate tome, and the two continued to shriek as it sounded like someone tried to lift it, and it snapped back. There was an even louder thump, a yelp, and the case just beside Amma and Damien began to wobble.

"Oh, no, no, no." Amma threw out her hands to push it back as it tipped toward them, but Damien hauled her out of the way as the case plummeted down where they had stood, the rest of the uncategorized books tumbling out as the shelving crashed into the table.

Amma ran, and Damien was right behind her. They skidded out from the row, catching a quick glimpse of Aretta and Gilead, still fighting with the book, more tomes having been knocked down and arcana lighting up the room, but the mage's eyes flicked up just as Amma and Damien bolted into the dark. Whether their features could be made out in the din and the chaos, she didn't know, but Gilead's voice called after them, "Who's there?"

Faster than she had perhaps ever run in her life, Amma guided them through the stacks, catching corners and knocking off rogue books as she went. Glass crashed behind them as it sounded like another animate tome was freed, and there was a cacophony as another stack was tipped over. They certainly weren't supposed to be this easy to knock down—liathau was heavy and sturdy and the wood should have known its only job was to stay upright—but Amma was thankful for the barrier falling between them and the others, exactly what they needed to reach the stairs as Gilead's arcana burst behind them.

At the head where the public entrance was, she only needed to tap the door's knob, and it swung open forcefully so she and Damien and Kaz could spill out onto the balcony above that rung the main library. The light of the moons filtered in around them, just enough to see but not be spotted, though they were making enough noise for anyone below to hear.

They turned, headed toward one of the curved staircases to the ground level, and there was another, significantly louder crash from below in the restricted section. Heavy steps of men in plate armor and the unsheathing of long swords filled the hollow room from the exact direction they were headed.

Amma skidded to a stop, panicked, feeling completely trapped. Her feet wouldn't move, heart wanting to explode from her chest, mind spinning and making her too dizzy to see straight. She was going to be caught, she'd be returned to where she belonged, she'd be made to pay for what she'd done, and Damien would be imprisoned and killed.

And then she completely lost her balance, yanked off her feet and into a shadowy alcove along the wall. She wasn't even breathing, eyes stuck open wide, the sounds gone from the library as blood rushed passed her ears. And then the Brineberth guards ran by in a flash, so quick she wasn't sure she had seen them at all.

"Idiots," Damien murmured, a satisfied chuckle in the back of his throat as he leaned out of the alcove to peer at where they'd gone. Their footsteps were just falling away, down the stairs to the restricted section. Damien stepped out, bringing Amma with him. Her balance was still off, and he steadied her. "Careful. You still have to get us out of here."

Amma remembered to breathe all at once, sucking in a lungful of air and taking off again, flying down the stairs with Damien just behind. She ran blindly across the open floor of the main library, fear of seeing anyone else overridden by the soldiers she knew were already there, and then they were in the darkened corridor again where Kaz's light brightened the messy space. They maneuvered to the door, and Amma threw herself into the frigid night air, straight for the exterior wall of the yard where she tried to scramble up without getting a good foothold.

"Amma, wait, you'll hurt yourself."

She already had, a scrape up her arm from where she'd slid against the wall, but she did take a moment, snapping her head back toward the door they'd gone through, left open in their dash. "Fuck!" she squeaked.

"Did you just say *fuck*?" Under the moonlight, Damien's smile was the most delighted she had ever seen, but she couldn't appreciate it, she could only debate with herself whether to run back and close off the door, hiding their route, or to just keep fleeing.

And then the decision was made for her.

"Come on, now." Damien was grabbing her leg, giving her a boost upward. Wobbly, she pulled herself over the wall with his help and clamored down the other side.

A moment later, he appeared at the top and dropped down beside her. He grinned. "You know, I've never really run away from anything before. That was surprisingly exhilar—"

"No time," Amma said and grabbed his arm, running off into the dark.

CHAPTER 27
THE PRACTICAL EFFECTS OF SLOWLY ADMINISTERED POISON

Damien thought he was in good shape, but the woman whose stride was much shorter than his own had nearly outpaced him through Faebarrow's alleys. Thankfully, Amma had slowed when it was obvious they were out of danger and back on unpatrolled roads where the curfew she had mentioned meant a bit less and those about were as interested in being unseen as the two of them.

They reached The Too Deep Inn without having exchanged any more words, but he already knew exactly what was on her mind, and it was only terror. When they stepped into the tavern downstairs, serving patrons even for the very late hour, she was breathing heavy and still shaking. Kaz grumbled about being exhausted, already reverted to his dog form, and Damien stuck his room key in the imp's canine mouth so he could retire. But instead of going to the stairs himself, he guided Amma to a table shrouded in shadows and tucked into the far back corner of the tavern and had her sit. She said nothing, only glanced up at him with weary eyes, and he had her wait as he retrieved two ales.

When he sat a drink before her, she looked at it then back up at him. "I'm going to need more than that."

Amma didn't speak while she drank, but she did so quickly. Too quickly, probably, for her small frame, but Damien found the pained face she made every time she pulled the tankard away from her mouth too amusing to stop her. She downed three large steins, one right after another, not appearing to enjoy a single second if it, and then finally asked for something stronger.

He obliged her—she had earned it, after all—and procured a copper cup full of a spirit that the bartender assured him would "get you right fucked." After sniffing it, Damien poured half of it out into an abandoned tankard on the way back to their table in the shadows. He took a seat on the short bench right beside her, their backs to the wall, and handed off the cup. "Take this slow—"

She immediately threw it back.

"Amma!" He easily freed the cup from her clumsy grasp, but she'd gotten most of it down. For a tense moment, she looked like she might be sick all over the table, but only wiped at her mouth and collapsed back, sliding down against the wall with a dopey grin on her face.

He finished off the last drops left in the cup, and it was predictably atrocious, but would surely get the job done. Still nursing his second ale, he was far from being impaired himself. "Feeling better?"

Amma's glassy eyes blinked back at him from the shadows. She nodded, but chewed on her lip in that way that said it was at least half a lie.

"Think you might be willing to talk about that magic you did?"

"I didn't do magic—that was just magic," she said with a slight slur.

Damien narrowed his eyes. "Want to try that again?"

She shook her head. "In the liathau trees, er…in the wood? That's where the magic is. Not in me. It's not like you with the,"—she mimicked slicing her hand with an imaginary knife and then swung her palm like she were throwing something, a clumsy move that almost made her fall off the bench. "Oh, boy. You coulda done that, huh? Thank you for not killing anybody in there. Aretta's actually nice. She deserves to live. Maybe not Gilead though, he's a bastard."

Damien laughed at her second swear of the night, realizing she wasn't in the right mind to discuss too deeply where and how arcana worked—he should have cut her off more than one ale ago for that. "I've other ways to get things done than just murder, you know."

"I do know," she said, a grin playing on her lips and then dropping off again. "I'm just glad I wasn't…I didn't want to be the cause of any more problems."

It was a bit late for that, what with the knocked over shelving and damaged, one-of-a-kind tomes, but he didn't think she deserved reminding since she had other things to worry about. "Ah, yes, the thief and the problem she caused, as of yet still unknown." He took a slow sip of his ale, eyeing her over the rim.

"You were right," she said quietly, head hanging. "I want revenge."

If only she hadn't said it in such a sorrowful tone, Damien would have been elated, but as it was, she looked like she might cry, and that didn't exactly inspire the wanton thoughts her words should have. "Well, that's a very good reason to call the dead back up to the land of the living with an enchanted scroll. And even if your target doesn't deserve it, it's great chaos." He chuckled, trying to lighten her mood.

But she only picked at the edge of the table and gnawed on that plump bottom lip of hers. "I think they do. It's someone who hurt...they hurt the people I care about."

"And this someone,"—his jaw tightened—"they hurt you as well?"

Eyes still cast down, shoulders hunched in, she simply nodded.

Infernal darkness, it would have felt good to choke the life out of *someone* right then.

"This someone is in Faebarrow still, yes?"

She nodded again.

"Where exactly?" When she looked up at him with confusion, he clarified, "I would like to pay them a visit."

"No, you can't, and it doesn't matter anyway," Amma said quickly. "It's not nice to hurt people back for what they did to *you*."

Damien's fist had gone painfully tight around the handle to his tankard. He concentrated to release it, the tiniest bit of noxscura slipping away from his palm. Flexing his fingers, he opened his mouth to disagree, but she continued with that slurred tone.

"The thing is, it's just...it's everyone else. I tried really hard to fix things already, I mean, I really, *really* did." She dragged in a ragged breath and squeezed both hands around an empty stein, staring up at him like she wanted more than anything to convince him. It wasn't the look of someone holding onto a lie, of someone who wanted to manipulate and steal, but of someone backed into a corner and desperate for a solution.

Damien lowered his voice, nodding. "I'm sure you did."

She frowned down into her empty cup, then she shrugged. "Maybe some things are impossible. Maybe it doesn't matter how much you want them or how much you're willing to give up to make them happen, they just won't. Or it's me who failed. I stopped trying, I looked for a quick fix, and I ran away, and I can't take that back now." She blinked up at him again, eyes big and baleful. "Not that I would take it back. In fact, I wish I could—"

There was a clatter as their table scuffed toward them. Two

people banged into it from the other side, falling over one another. There was a woman there suddenly, a man's hand climbing up her dress and exposing her thigh beside Damien's half-full tankard. He grabbed the table before it flipped over as the two slid off of it, laughing out a drunken apology between one another's mouths and then stumbling up the stairs to the bed chambers above.

Amma stared after them, mouth agape, and then was suddenly broken of her melancholy. She giggled, holding up her empty tankard in front of her face. Her cheeks had gone blotchy and red as she tried to take another sip and got nothing, then her glassy eyes fell on him.

"Damien?" Her voice echoed into the hollow cup, cloying with sweetness. "Can I ask you something?"

Already concerned with where her words were headed, he picked up his own flagon and brought it to his lips. "I'm sure you will whether I say yes or no, so, I suppose you may."

"Um, well?" Amma squinted up at the darkened ceiling, looking like she was thinking quite hard and having a very rough time, poor thing. "That night in the forest,"—she took a deep breath—"I mean, do you remember when we were,"—she squeezed her eyes shut and swallowed hard—"Actually, I'm just curious: have you ever kissed a girl?"

Struck dumb, Damien swallowed a too-full mouth of ale, throat burning as it forced its way down. "What kind of question is that?"

Amma gathered up some courage then, scooting a bit closer on the bench so her knee brushed his. "Oh, sorry, um, should I have said a boy?"

Damien clicked his tongue. "Look, just because I'm a villain—"

"Not because you're a *villain*," she said, tone mocking, and then hiccupped. "Laurel likes girls, I get it. I just mean because you haven't tried to..." She worried her lip with her fingers then shook her head. "Well, you know."

"Know what?"

Tipping her head, a blond curl fell over her scrunched-up-with-frustration face. "Just answer the question. Have you kissed somebody?"

"Yes, of course," he said slowly as if she were stupid which, judging by how much ale was inside her, she at least temporarily was. When she stared at him hard, waiting for him to clarify, he droned back as if it were the most boring thing in the world, "Both, at the same time, but don't ask my upper limit at once—it's difficult to keep count when you've just got a writhing pile of bodies underneath you." When her eyes widened and face went even redder, he couldn't help but smirk.

"Oh, you're lying to me," she groaned and slid back down against the wall, utterly dejected.

"Believe what you'd like, I've told you the truth."

With an annoyed grunt, she tipped her head back. "I bet you've never kissed anyone before, *ever*. No wonder you're so cranky all the time—you need to get laid."

Well, she was at least half right: he'd certainly felt like he needed to get laid since, darkness, how long had it been? And she wasn't helping matters, crawling up onto her knees and leaning on the table to peer out at the occupants in the tavern, ass wiggling right in his face.

"Maybe someone in here will do us both the favor and put you in a better mood. What about her?"

She was pointing out a fiery-haired woman serving drinks to a table of men playing cards. She had a toothy smile, tanned skin, and a slight point to her ears to suggest elven ancestry. He glanced over at Amma again, her blonde brows waggling at him. "Too ginger."

"Oh, more into the tall, dark, and handsome type? Makes sense since you're so into yourself. What about him, then?" She pointed out a well-built man standing at the bar, meeting the criteria she'd just listed with roguish stubble and a hilt he wasn't trying to hide on his hip.

Damien was too amused by her candor to be offended by it. "That one's too tall."

"Too tall? That's not a thing." As she spun back toward him, Amma knocked into one of her empty tankards, and it clattered across the floor. The patrons closest glared over at their table.

"I prefer someone smaller that I can pick up and throw around." Damien took her by the arm and guided her back onto the bench. "Aren't you trying to keep a low profile?"

The barkeep had come over, collecting the fallen stein. He made a pointed effort to glower at Amma before walking off.

"Sorry," Amma giggled, ducking back into the shadows. She grabbed another empty tankard to hold before her face like she could hide behind it then grinned over at him. "So, tell me what your ideal companion would be like then, Sir High Standards."

"I'm evil, Amma, I don't have *companions*." He took another sip, gazing out over the tavern goers, each table filled with multiple people, laughing, carrying on. "I'm not made for that."

"Oh, yeah, you said because of the demon thing you don't feel love, but I don't really believe that."

He scoffed. "You don't believe in the fundamental truth that infernal-born beings are incapable of love? The teachings of all your great and holy gods insist upon the same thing. The dark gods were cast into the Abyss *because* of their inability to love, and that gift was passed on to their servants, the demons."

"Wait, that's why? I thought the gods just got in a fight or whatever? Well, still, no, I think it's minotaurshit." The way she said it, so flippantly, stunned him. It was fact, one he'd grappled with his entire existence, and she had just so casually told him she refused to accept it. "And I also don't believe you've never had a girlfriend or boyfriend that you at least liked a whole bunch."

"Well, which is it—I've got no experience or am well versed in romance?"

"The second, obviously," she said with a put-upon sigh.

Damien wasn't sure what was so obvious about it when she'd been needling him earlier, but he knew it was the preferable option. "Well, uh, yes, I suppose I was once someone's boy...friend." He winced at the word. He had certainly belonged to someone else once, though he had tried very hard to forget.

She shifted back up onto her knees to face him, excited. "Wait, tell me about *that*."

"No."

"Yes," she insisted, nodding enthusiastically. "I won't give you the Lux Codex unless you do, and you can't even touch it anyway, so you have to tell me if you want more help from my, what'd you call 'em?"—she drummed her nails on the flagon—"my *nimble fingers*."

Though she'd conveniently forgotten about the talisman, he supposed it wouldn't hurt saying something to satisfy her: she wasn't likely to remember any of it anyway. "There was a woman once—"

"Was she pretty?"

Damien snorted. "Considering what she got away with, she had to be."

Her eyes flashed then, narrowing. "*How* pretty?"

"I've met prettier since," he said carefully.

Amma's mood shifted right back to being absolutely enthralled, overly dilated pupils unblinking. "How'd you meet?"

"There is a sort of...assemblage for people of my persuasion called Yvlcon—"

"She's a blood mage too?" Amma again tried drinking from the empty tankard, turning it upside down over her head.

"No, there are very few of us," he said. "The word for what she is...well, you wouldn't like to hear any of the ones I'd use to describe her."

"Didn't go so well, huh? What happened?"

"Misery, mayhem, murder." Damien grinned wistfully then frowned. "But then it went to the Abyss." He took a long drink, insides queasy. Even the good memories seemed to sit differently now.

Amma whined in that charming way of hers. "Those aren't very good details, Damien."

He chuckled. "There's very little else to tell. I was evil, she was evil, and for a little while we were evil together until her hostility was turned on me in a way that was no longer arousing. I wanted out, and she did not."

"You broke her heart?" Amma gasped as if offended on the woman's behalf. If she had any idea, she would have known it was not deserved.

"Impossible—the nox-touched don't have those. And she was not sad, she was angry. Angry enough to try and kill me, so I probably made the right choice. Anyway, it all went terribly, as expected."

"Aw, but are *you* sad about it? About losing your one, true love?"

"She was *not* that. And I told you, demons don't feel those things. Only the vile and loathsome are drawn to my aura."

"Are you kidding?" She almost missed the table this time, putting the tankard back down with a thunk and grabbing onto his shoulder to shake him. "When you're not being a grouch, you're very charming, and you've got this whole dangerous, dark thing going on. You could probably just walk up to anybody in here and get them to go up to your room with you."

Damien's mouth went dry, and he focused on his half-empty flagon and not the way her fingers dug into his arm. "Sounds like too much work."

She tried to roll her eyes, but with her coordination so off, she just managed a weird blink. Bringing her face even closer to his, she dropped her voice a little lower. "Too much work to wink at somebody? Because that's all you'd probably have to do, you know. You're a lot more handsome than you think. I know you're self-conscious about that scar, but you shouldn't be, your face is great, and the scar is actually kinda…" She made a sort of groaning giggle then, eyes closing.

"You think my disfigurement is attractive?" He chuckled at how ridiculous she was being—easier than allowing her to rile him up too much.

"Well, yeah, duh, it makes you mysterious and scary, but *good*

265

scary, ya know? Makes you wonder, like, *how'd he get that*? And *what's he gonna do to me once he gets me tied up*? And also, I can tell under that armor you're all muscle." She actually tugged at the collar of his tunic then, and he was too surprised to stop her from trying to get a peek. Instead, he just grinned, and when she looked back up at his face, she giggled madly. "Oh, and Damien, you have such a nice smile. You should do that more. It just makes me want to—" She hiccupped, and it was like someone had clamped a hand over her mouth, stopping her halfway through a thought she didn't mean to say out loud.

He watched her contemplate what seemed like her whole existence as she pulled her hands back to herself and stared down at the table. It was his turn to lean in, voice low. "Why would I bother with seducing someone when I can just command them into my bed with a little magic?"

Amma's eyes widened, then she glared at him. "Because that would be really evil."

He pressed his lips just to her ear. "What have I been telling you I am all this time, Amma?"

He could feel her body stiffen beside him, but she didn't shift away. She held her breath, and there was a jump in her throat as her heartbeat hitched. And then Amma scoffed, sticking out her tongue and blowing. "Oh, please."

Damien sat back, admonished, wiping her spittle from his face with a laugh. "Well, what about you?"

"Me?"

"If you want me to be so candid, I think some reciprocation is in order. Regale me with tales of the hearts you've broken."

Amma's face went even redder than it already was, and she eyed his half-filled flagon. Grabbing it much quicker and better coordinated than anything else she'd done since her first ale, she downed it.

"Amma, stop that, you'll be ill." Damien grabbed it back but only retrieved an empty tankard.

"I don't think I've ever broken anybody's heart." She sighed, sitting her chin on her palm, or at least trying before slipping off and nearly smacking into the table. "Well, maybe once, but that was years ago, and he got over it and married somebody else. And now, well, I guess, you and I are kinda the same. I can't really be in love with anybody either, and I certainly can't convince someone to fall in love with me that doesn't want to—believe me, I've tried, and it just does not work. But if I could?" She grinned wide, staring out at the tavern, then closed her eyes and sat back again with a long, yearning sigh.

Damien gazed at her as she sat with her head back, perhaps daydreaming or actually dreaming, knocked out from the ale. Even in the shadows, her hair found the candlelight to shimmer softly when she moved with full, deep breaths, and though there was a certain melancholy to her words, she managed a wistful smile. He couldn't believe it, not for a moment, even when she said it herself, that there was a single soul in the realm that she couldn't convince to fall in utter and unconditional love with her. Then she hiccupped again and sat up straight, roused from wherever her mind had gone.

"Come on," he said, pushing his empty tankard and any of his own, maudlin thoughts away. "You need to be taken to bed before you can get your hands on anyone else's ale."

"Oh, yes, take me to bed, Master Bloodthorne." She was giggling again and grabbed his arm, squeezing it against her so that it pressed between her breasts.

He froze under her touch. *Why* did she need to say *that* and *now*? Reluctant to pull away yet knowing he should, he allowed her to hang on as he stood. She followed, needing the extra balance to ascend the stairs anyway. He could have just picked her up, but she was determined enough, and, really, she didn't seem to need any extra attention—she was already holding him too tightly, leaning her head on his shoulder, squeezing his arm—for balance, of course, he reminded himself with every step upward and every soft caress of her hand.

With the door closed inside her small chamber upstairs, the sounds of the tavern were all blocked out. There was a slight draft through the window, cracked open at the back of the room. Damien sat Amma on the bed and escaped her grip to go shut it, surprised at how it had to be yanked. He struggled to close the pane completely, finally securing the inner lock, and tested it for safety.

When he turned back, Amma had stripped off her boots, tunic, and breeches, too quick with her hands like always, even drunk. She was sitting on the edge of the cot in just the short chemise she wore under her clothes, and he wondered if she had so quickly forgotten in her drunken state that he was still there. He held very still, unsure what to do.

"Damien," she said, clearing that question up as she stood, wobbling. The chemise only hit her mid thigh, and would have been sheer in a room lit by more than just moonlight, but there was more than enough of her bare skin on display to both satisfy him and not. "You remember when you got all mad at me for trying to steal from

267

you?" She went to take a step toward him and tripped right over her own feet, falling forward.

Damien rushed to her side, catching her. "You are very drunk, aren't you?"

"Oh, I don't think so." She was giggling again, face rosy, slapping him on the shoulder with no real force. He guided her back down to the cot, but she wouldn't let go this time, pulling him to sit beside her. "But you remember?"

"Do I remember yesterday?" He chuckled. "Yes. Do you?"

She nodded, an over-exaggerated move that appeared to make her dizzy. "Well, I really didn't want to do that. I mean, I *did* want the scroll, but I didn't want to *steal* it from you. I actually wanted to do something else, and I thought maybe we could do that now." Amma's hands slipped off of his arms, and she pawed at his chest. "Do you think we could kiss?"

Damien forgot how to breathe for a moment until he managed to choke out, "You must be exceptionally inebriated to suggest *that*."

"Please," she mewled. "It's my only chance."

Yes, *exceptionally* inebriated.

"You're not making sense. You said you had already—"

"With someone I...with someone *else*, I mean." Her fingers squeezed his arm. "With you."

That didn't really clear things up, but he just shook his head. "You, kissing the most evil blood mage in the realm? Don't be ridiculous."

Amma whined, a pitiful sound as she shifted closer to him. She slapped a hand on either side of his face and held him still. "Damien, I'm *serious*. Don't make jokes about being evil right now."

"I am not joking. I am—"

"Shh. Stop. You're not evil, I know it, it's okay, you don't have to pretend around me." One of her hands slid over his cheek and to the back of his neck. Amma's touch was soft, no longer clumsy as her fingers curled into his hair. She frowned with a slight pout in that way she did when she was being earnest, but then she looked sad too, like she already knew what he would say. "Do you wanna kiss me or not? Because I want to kiss you."

Damien took her hands into his own, and she let him. It was a relief to have them no longer caressing his face, sending tingles down his spine, making him want them everywhere else, but then a disappointment welled up in him too. Disappointment as he realized a truth he'd been pushing away and swallowing down for too long.

"I do," he admitted, then held his breath at the shock on her face.

Fuck it, he thought, if she wouldn't remember any of it, what would it hurt to tell her the truth? It would, at the very least, call her bluff and end this game she insisted on playing with him. "I want to kiss you endlessly, Amma, and never stop."

Her eyes widened, pupils huge. For a moment he recognized the look—fear. He'd seen it dozens of times, hundreds maybe, but before his heart could sink and wallow that he had beaten her at her own game and she'd never meant any of it, a wicked smile crawled over Amma's lips, and her tongue darted between her teeth.

Amma lunged. She was surprisingly strong when her intent was to sloppily plant her lips on his, but Damien was able to hold her in place. Well, that had backfired.

She whined again, breath heady with ale falling over his face. "What's wrong?"

Oh, so many things, chiefly among them her drunkenness, but reasoning with someone about their own state of inebriation was nigh impossible.

Damien's grip on her upper arms loosened slightly, and she leaned in closer. He wished he'd been able to finish that second ale himself, but even if he had, he would be just as in control, and she'd been woozy two tankards ago. But then, he did have control, didn't he? She was only asking him to take it, and that put a new idea in his head.

"I do want to kiss you, Amma," he said, dropping his voice lower so she had to shift her focus to what he was saying and not what she was still trying to do to him. He cautiously released her arms, sliding his hands to her back. "And I'm going to. Not just your lips, but every inch of you."

Her eyes searched, trying to suss out what he meant, and then she seemed to get it. She made a small, excited sound and sat up straighter.

"Lay back for me." When Amma collapsed into his arms at the simple command, he chuckled in the back of his throat, guiding her onto the cot. That had been easy, and she deserved something for it. "You really are a good girl, aren't you?"

Amma's face flushed even more, and like it was contagious, Damien's skin felt as though it were on fire. She managed to loop both of her hands around his neck, tugging at him to lay back with her, but he caught them. With her fully on her back, he shifted up onto his knees and trapped her wrists against the soft pillow on either side of her head. "Not so good," he mused, frowning. "Remember, *I* am going to kiss *you*, not the other way around."

She arched her back slightly, lips parted and eager, but there was no force under his hands to try and wriggle away. Of course there wasn't—he already knew she liked that.

Amma took shallow breaths, breasts straining against the thin material of her chemise. He tore his gaze up to her face, though that was nearly as inviting, heavily-lashed eyelids fluttering, biting her full, lower lip.

"Now, close your eyes." She did, and he waited a moment as her body settled into the bed, face softening, breaths coming a bit more deeply.

Damien waited, glancing down the length of her beneath him. Kissing every inch of her hadn't been some fabrication, and with only thin silk between her skin and his tongue, it would have been the exact kind of torture she actually deserved for putting him through this. And then she stirred again, straining slightly against his hands still holding her in place, urging him on with a mumble of muddied, sleepy pleas.

"Quiet," he whispered, dipping his lips beside her ear, the heat off her body radiating against him. "Patience is a virtue, and I know how virtuous you are. For now."

Only her throat bobbed with a heavy swallow as she settled down again. Her next breath was deep and long. Then she took another, and when her lips fell open, they weren't waiting and eager anymore.

Silently, Damien released her wrists and slipped off the bed, leaving her undisturbed. He pulled the thin blanket up from the cot's foot and covered her. "Goodnight, Amma."

She didn't respond, already deeply asleep.

And then Damien did, indeed, keep his word, and he kissed her. Not quite how she'd attempted to drunkenly do to him, sloppy and urgent and barely conscious, and not at all how he'd wanted to do to her, ardent yet tender, starting at her mouth and then trailing everywhere else. The kiss Damien actually gave Amma was only a gentle press of his lips to her forehead, barely a brush at all. An accident, really. She wouldn't know, thank the basest of infernal beasts, but he would, and that was good enough for now. Bad enough too.

And enough was enough—Damien swept out of the room, surpassed his own, and stalked down the stairs and out into the night.

CHAPTER 28
IN KNOWING NOTHING, LIFE IS MOST DELIGHTFUL, OR AT LEAST TOLERABLE

When Amma woke, she felt absolutely fantastic for about seven and a half seconds. In that short time, she blinked up at the ceiling, disorientation at her constantly changing location assuage by the last fragments of a dream, a *very good* dream. Damien was in it more vividly than ever, and she had been wrapped in his arms on the verge of what she knew was about to be the most passionate night of her life. And then she sat up and laid eyes on the actual blood mage, sitting on the far side of the room, scowling at her with absolute fury.

Pain seared through her skull, the light flooding in through the window over Damien's shoulder much too brightly. She squinted, shielding her eyes with an arm, and then that too hurt. All of her muscles ached, and her guts were roiling. That was right—she had a lot to drink the night before, and it had all been sort of a blur, just like her vision was now.

She blinked back at Damien who had sat forward in the lone chair in the room, still glaring, Kaz sitting at his feet, looking like a dog and still in his sweater but just as mad. Why was Damien so angry? Amma glanced down at herself wearing next to nothing then ripped the sheet up to her chin from where it had fallen into her lap. Oh, gods, had it not been a dream? And had it really been so bad that he was angry about it?

"Good morning, The Honorable Ammalie Avington, daughter of His Lordship Bartholomew Avington and Her Ladyship Constance Avington, Baron and Baroness of Faebarrow."

Amma's heart stopped beating, her lungs stopped inflating, blood stopped pumping. Every bit of her stopped working, in fact, brain included, and she simply sat there on the cot, stunned, seeing and hearing nothing until the stupidest words finally leaked out of her mouth. "That's not me."

Damien was holding up a piece of parchment, identical to the ones she had seen tacked up in the city's squares the day before, the ones she had so carefully distracted him from. "Not you?" he said, incredulous, pointing to her likeness painted out on it. "These aren't your blue eyes? And this isn't your tiny nose covered in your freckles? And these aren't your soft, round—you get the point!" He grunted, shaking the poster. "When, pray tell, were you going to share this minuscule detail about your life with me? Not to mention the fact that you are apparently *missing*?"

She worried the edge of the blanket, dragging aching knees up to her chest. "Maybe...never?"

Kaz growled from beside him, but he nudged the imp into silence with his boot.

"I should have known," said Damien, pulling out a square of fabric from his pocket. "I thought you had just nicked this on your way across the realm, but, oh, no, this was *yours*. Just like that fancy silver dagger and all those coins you gave away as if they meant nothing. Of course they meant nothing—you're a fucking baroness!"

Amma blinked, the pain in her head making it difficult to focus, but eventually she could see he was holding up the handkerchief she'd wrapped around his wounded palm when they'd first met in Aszath Koth, the one she had embroidered a tree onto, roots and branches indistinguishable as they grew around the trunk into a circle, Faebarrow's crest. "You...you kept that?"

Damien's furrowed, irate brow relaxed, eyes darting over the cloth. "Uh, well, yes..." Then he quickly tucked it back into a pocket and huffed. "Don't try to distract me. Tell me the truth."

Her breath hitched, and then all at once it came out with an embarrassed rush of anger. "Oh, fine, yes, I *am* Ammalie Avington, the baroness of Faebarrow who's gone *missing*. Are you happy?"

"Am I happy?" He dropped the first piece of parchment to reveal a second one behind it. This had a cruder drawing of a man with dark hair and a long, ugly mark across his face. "It's not the best likeness in the realm, they didn't even get the scar going the right direction, but it's got two rewards listed here: one for me, and one for just my head. I need that, you know! The rest of me doesn't work without it, not even the magic parts!"

Amma covered her mouth. "Robert," she whispered into her

hand, remembering the man who had tried to rescue her back in Elderpass. Damien had told him to go home, after all, and apparently he had. And he'd been talkative.

"If it's not clear, they think I'm the one who's abducted you." He balled up the decree and stood, throwing it into the room's corner.

"Well, Damien, not to get all literal or anything, but you sort of did…"

"Oh, don't you dare," he growled, pacing the room. "You got the talisman stuck in yourself in the first place, and if I abducted anyone, it wasn't a bloody baroness, it was just some little street urchin who no one cared about. Ammalie Avington, with an entire army looking for her, is an incredible liability to parade around the realm, not to mention ludicrous to kill to get the talisman out, unlike Amma the thief who doesn't matter to anyone."

Amma squeezed her knees to herself, throat clenching around the words as they came out. "You thought I didn't matter?"

Damien stopped his pacing, eyes focused hard on the wall. "Of course you matter, Amma." He sounded tired suddenly, as if the weight of the situation had been dropped on him all at once. "If you didn't, we wouldn't have even come here in the first place. I've been dragging you all across Eiren to—" Damien cut himself off when a growl from Kaz interrupted his thought, and then he threw his arms up, irate all over again. "None of it bloody matters now. This town is absolutely crawling with guards, and they're not even wearing the Faebarrow crest with the liathau on it—they're all wearing that ridiculous red catfish thing across their chests. What in the realm is going on here? Did Faebarrow hire a load of mercenaries? Do you have some sort of crime problem?"

Amma bit her lip and gestured to herself.

"Oh, for fuck's sake!" Damien raked a hand through his already mussed up hair.

"I know, I'm sorry, but that's not the only reason we're overrun with Brineberth soldiers, it's a lot more complicated, but I did try and keep you from coming here, if you remember." She leaned over the edge of the cot, swaying with a wave of nausea before pushing it back down, and pulled her wrinkled tunic out of the pile of clothes on the floor. "Look, you've got the book you wanted now, or I do, somewhere, so we can just leave, right?"

"You've made it back home," he stressed, gesturing to the window and the city outside. "And you want to leave?"

She pulled her tunic over her head, mumbling into it, "I told you, it's complicated."

"How did any of this even happen?"

She swung her legs over the edge of the cot as she shook out her breeches. "That man in Elderpass, the one who thought he knew me? Well, that was Robert, one of my father's most trusted knights from when they were younger. He was apparently out looking for me. He probably deserves a reward for finding me."

"Amma, I almost killed him."

"Maybe you should have."

"You told me not to!"

"I know, I know…" She worked her feet into the breeches from where she sat then looked over at him. "Can you turn around, please?"

Damien snorted at her and swung to face the wall.

"Kaz, you too."

The imp also huffed and turned.

"So, because that man saw the two of us together, he thinks I'm the one who stole you away from here?" She didn't have to see his face to know he was grimacing.

Amma stood, sliding the breeches up slowly over her bare legs, body aching from the night of heavy drinking. "Well, it probably doesn't help that I sort of staged a little bit of a kidnapping when I left…"

"You *what*?" Damien whipped back to her, throwing his arms out.

"I said, turn around!"

He dropped his head back to stare at the ceiling, absolutely fuming, fingers drumming on elbows and tapping a foot as he muttered to himself about timing and modesty.

"I know it was…not good," she said, finally getting the breeches up to her waist and tucking in the chemise.

"It is very, *very* not good. In fact, I'd be impressed if I weren't so angry."

"I didn't mean for anyone else to get wrapped up in all this, and I didn't mean for someone to *actually* abduct me, which you *did*," she said with a bite as she strapped the leather bodice about her midsection and cinched it in. Shoving her feet into her boots, she tried to explain, "After I got the scroll from Aszath Koth, I planned to come right back here and pretend like I escaped my imaginary abductor. It was the only way I could leave this place, Damien—it's not like baronesses are actually free to do whatever they please like blood mages are."

Damien let out a grumble at that, face twisting up with words he

274

ended up not saying.

"That's why I tried to steal the scroll from you the other night and flee—if I was recognized once we got to Faebarrow and you were with me, it would look, well, exactly like this! And I knew if they found us, that they would hurt you, and I can't let—" Amma's voice cracked, eyes burning at the thought of what might happen to him if they were caught, but she held back the tears, knowing they would just make him angrier.

Damien's arms fell from their crossed position, tapping toe coming to a halt as he looked away. "What were you even going to do with that scroll anyway? You're a baroness—you already have a retinue of soldiers at your command and I'm sure a hundred different means of revenge against whatever imbecile wronged you."

She sniffed, composing herself. "That's too much to explain right now—we need to focus on leaving. If my father finds you, he's only going to want the head." Just as she strapped on her belted pouch with the Lux Codex inside, there was a thunderous knock on the door that felt like it had been right up against her skull. She brought a hand to her temple, gasping with pain.

Kaz turned to the door, hackles raised and growling, eyes jolting up to Damien who had frozen.

"By order of the Brineberth Watch and the Lordship of Faebarrow, open up."

Amma's mouth had gone dry, eyes pinging to the window, much too small for either of them to escape through, and she croaked out, "W-who is it?"

That shook Damien of his paralysis, looking sharply at her and letting his mouth fall open. She could only shrug back.

"Ammalie, is that you?"

At the stinging, authoritative voice, she straightened, answering reflexively, "Tia?"

There was a slam against the door, and the center of it bowed in.

Amma covered her mouth and jumped. Damien unsheathed his dagger, and Kaz's canine tail alighted. "No!" she hissed, waving her hands at the two. "Don't look like a threat!"

There was another crack, and the door bowed once more.

"I can handle this," she said, heart racing like mad as the blood mage contemplated slicing his palm. "Damien, you have to trust me."

"Trust you?" he hissed. "I don't even know who you are."

"Yes, you do," she insisted in a whisper. "I just didn't tell you my title. Please, I don't want you to get hurt because of me."

There was a final bang, and Amma threw herself between where

Damien and Kaz stood and the slamming open door.

"Ammalie!" A muscled body came at her and pulled her in, and the familiar smell of Tia's oiled-up armor enveloped her along with the woman's warm embrace. Stiff beneath it, she was stunned as soldiers filed in behind the woman, not an unfamiliar sight for the bodyguard to command, but then she saw the Brineberth crest across their chests and heard many swords sliding against their scabbards.

As Tia tried to pull her toward the entry, door hanging half off its hinges and frame splintered, Amma pulled back much more violently than the guard had ever experienced. "No!" she pushed against her, loosing herself and turning. "Wait, stop! He's not—"

Damien stood, both hands up, and not swathed in the aura of a spell or drenched with his own blood for casting, though he was glowering darkly at the six men who had surrounded him, weapons drawn. At his feet was Kaz, donning his sweater and growling, but still no more than an annoying, little dog.

Amma breathed the heaviest sigh of relief, a hand to her chest, then she drew herself up to her full height. "Put your swords away," she said in her most authoritative tone which was little more than a wavering squeak.

A few of the guards looked at her, and one of them hesitated, but the blades were still levied at Damien's throat.

Amma squealed with an indignant huff. "I *said*, put them down!"

"Ammalie," said Tia gently from behind her, a hand falling on her shoulder, "you must—"

"No, *they* must." She swung back to Tia, her face going hot, blood rushing past her ears. "Tell them to stand down. Now."

Tia stared back at her, hard. Amma did not even blink. Then the guard's eyes' softened, her lips tightening into a flat line, and she nodded. "Sheath your weapons. Stand down."

Every muscle in Amma's body relaxed, and the dizziness hit her all at once. She stumbled, she swooned, and she fell forward into Tia's arms where she promptly threw up all over the woman.

An hour later, Amma could scarcely believe she was standing back in Faebarrow Hall. The only thing she could believe less was how well she had lied with such a hangover coursing through her body. This wasn't at all how she had planned to return, not being recognized by the barkeep to the seedy Too Deep Inn and garnering a whole troop of soldiers to break down the door to her rented room, and definitely not standing next to the man who had kidnapped her out of her bed in the middle of the night, especially since that man did not actually exist.

276

She had made it look like a struggle before she left a moon prior—she may have been small and meek, but she would have put up a fight if someone had come to take her. She fled in the night under cover of darkness, dressed in things she'd collected from Perry, one of only two people in the keep who had known her plan, and sneaked away with both his and Laurel's help, like they had helped her so many times in the previous years to sneak out and go to the Grand Athenaeum. Now, those wild adventures seemed like childish games in comparison.

But she had thought quickly even as a hangover pounded her brain. Before the guards moved to arrest Damien, and before the blood mage moved to destroy them all with infernal shadows, Amma announced that Damien had actually rescued her from the clutches of evil that had originally taken her, and he was being so kind as to escort her home. When she was asked what they were doing there, in the dodgy end of Faebarrow instead of coming straight to the keep, she feigned another swoon, and cried out that she needed to see her beloved parents and to bring her savior home to be properly rewarded.

Damien had gone mute for this, but Amma could see the discomfort crawling all over him. It didn't help that Kaz had been emanating a constant, low growl the entire time, but his appearance as a pet did manage to mitigate some of Damien's threatening aura. Abductors didn't tote around tiny dogs.

Then they'd marched through the streets and to the keep, its inside wide and welcoming and warm but a blur, through the receiving hall, and were finally herded into the ready room for privacy where only her parents stood.

Her father swept her into a too tight but loving embrace, crushing her to his barrel of a chest, whiskers tickling her face, and then it was her mother's turn to hug her, so much softer and more delicate with her thin limbs, but full of the warmth and love she had always known. Her mother whispered into her ear how terrified she had been, how she had no idea what she would have done without her, how much she missed and loved her, and by all the gods what a horrible state she'd come back in. Guilt washed over Amma so fully she nearly drowned right there, but instead she resorted to breaking down into fat, messy tears.

The sobbing dried up, however, when she heard her father thanking Damien who had, as of yet, not said a single word. The baron asked Damien's name.

Amma jerked out of her mother's embrace. "Father, this is

Da...Day," she said quickly, then swallowed back a lump in her throat. She looked at the blood mage whose violet eyes had been injected with true fear for perhaps the first time since she'd met him. "Day Raven...heart." It was almost as stupid as his actual name, but it would have to do.

Then the fear in his eyes adjusted to a withering look before quickly correcting into the charming smile she'd gotten so used to. The one that she liked.

"Day Ravenheart," her father repeated in his jovial baritone, clasping onto his arm and shaking it while clapping him on the opposing shoulder with the other. Her father had always been tactiley expressive and made no exception with strangers. "Apologies for nearly getting you killed, good sir. We had reports of our daughter being absconded with by someone with your particular visage. Little did we know, you were only returning her to us."

Damien anxiously glanced down to his hand still clasped in the man's, then back up. "Ah, yes, well, lots of that going round. But that is what we did. Return. Together."

"And thank the gods. I cannot even bear the thought, our fragile, little Ammalie, lost in the wild," her mother lilted, gracefully slipping her father's grasp away and pulling Damien into a hug under which he stood completely stiff. Then, because it was exactly what her mother always did and this situation would be no exception, she planted an elegant kiss on his cheek. "We owe you everything," she said, voice like a song and sincerity in her eyes as she stepped back to stand beside her husband.

"Oh, no, ah..." Damien swallowed. "It was luck that we met at all. She is more than capable, and I imagine would have made it back to her home even quicker had I not slowed her down."

At that, both her mother and father laughed, and not in the polite, public-facing way they'd been taught to, but actually, sincerely, guffawed.

"It would have been quicker," Tia cut in as she stepped into the room after having cleaned off Amma's vomit, "had you come straight home instead of resting so close last night."

"Last night?" Though her mother's smile did not falter, her laugh cut off abruptly, and her eyes took on *that* look.

"Sir Ravenheart is being too humble," Amma blurted out, grabbing onto his arm and squeezing it while grinning back with too many teeth at her parents, hoping they would forget Tia's interjection. "That's *so* like him. The countryside was *awful*. There were werewolves and draekins and we even had a run-in with a demon."

Her mother gasped, pressing delicate, long fingers to her chest, but her eyes flashed when they fell on Amma's hands still touching Damien. Amma quickly released him.

Her father noticed nothing though, and only gasped in his most intrigued way. "Demons, you say? Good sir, what prowess you must have shown."

"Sweetling, oh, darling, dear, come here." Her mother's eyes had gone watery again, and she tugged Amma to her chest once more.

"A banquet!" Her father announced. "To celebrate this man's great heroism and the return of our only child, safe and sound."

"Oh, father, no," Amma squealed as she again escaped her mother's grip. "We shouldn't. Not another one of those things. It's not proper to use coin like that, and—"

"Nonsense!" He clapped. "*This* is cause to celebrate. Tonight!"

"Tonight?" Amma choked on the word.

"No, you're right, dear, there isn't enough time. Tomorrow night!"

Amma pinched her nose.

"We shall see to it that you are taken care of," her mother said to Damien. "Accommodations and anything you might need will be brought to you."

"I will see to that personally," said Tia sharply from over their shoulders.

"And you." Her mother's eyes turned on her with that same overly-anxious and loving glow. She took up her daughter's hands and examined them. "You need rest, but first a bath. A very long one, I think. I'll have my ladies take care of these and your hair and…everything," she said as if already overwhelmed by the prospect of assigning each chore. "If there's to be a banquet, you'll need to put your best face forward."

"Oh, can't we *please* skip that? We could have a quiet dinner instead, just the four of us."

"But dear, don't you want to see—"

The door to the hall burst open. Standing in the entry was Marquis Cedric Caldor, golden-haired and statuesque as his bright eyes took in the ready room. He was wearing that dress armor of his, spotless and without a nick or scrape, a similarly shined up sword with an overly-decorative hilt at his side. When his eyes fell on her, she felt as if he had unsheathed it and pierced her right through the heart.

"Ammalie," he said, breathless, and rushed forward, no concern for who might have been in the way. He swept Amma to him, lifting

279

her up as he bent his head, and pressed his lips against hers with such pressure and quickness their teeth knocked. But he did nothing to pull away, and she didn't dare either, even as his tongue slid passed her mouth and over hers possessively.

When Cedric finally pulled back, though he did not let go, both gasped for air. Amma had forgotten what a kiss was like, even in just a short moon's time. She wished she could continue to forget.

"My love, you've returned." His voice shook slightly, and he swallowed back a lump of prudent emotions. "I had my men searching high and low across the realm to bring you back. I was terrified you would be lost to us forever. That the future of Faebarrow itself was lost."

At this her eyes narrowed, but she remained wrapped in his arms, staring back at that face, a perfectly calculated mixture of horror and relief.

"If you hadn't come home, I don't know what I would have done. Terrible things, surely." Cedric pulled her against him once more, and a shiver ran up Amma's spine. "But now you've been returned to us, and I'll never let you out of my sight again."

Fuck, thought Amma.

Then he released her, and her body wavered, free of the too-tight pressure of his embrace and finally able to take a full breath.

"This must be the man," he said, turning to Damien and taking his hand. "The one I have to thank for bringing my betrothed home."

"*Your* be—" Damien was tugged into another embrace, this one he simply stood lax under as Cedric slapped him on the back. Left dumb once released, Damien could only stare at the floor, bewildered.

Cedric turned back to Amma, falling to a knee and taking both of her hands into his own. "Ammalie, I swear to you, on my life and by Osurehm's holy light, whoever is at fault for your disappearance, I will find them, and they will pay by my own hand. Dearly."

Looking down into his eyes, she saw it, the steely flicker that had evolved into something monstrous since they had met, hidden away and saved only for when they were alone. His words echoed back into her mind—she had disappeared, returned, come home, but not been taken—and the cold dread of realization rose up in Amma then that Cedric, somehow, knew exactly what she had done.

CHAPTER 29
THE MANY FACETS OF TEMPERAMENT

"I don't trust you."

Good instinct, thought Damien as he stared back at the tall, muscled woman that Amma had called Tia. She was human, though he would wager there was a hint of giant somewhere in her ancestry, like Anomalous, which would account not just for her size but for the graceful way she'd aged.

Damien crossed his arms and tipped his head with a grin. "Your charge, the baroness, does."

"I don't trust her judgment either."

Much worse instinct. He frowned, liking her a little less. "That is unfortunate."

The guard had taken responsibility for Damien, and in turn his dog, Kaz, once the painful meeting with Amma's parents—her *noble* parents—had come to an end. Tia collected multiple guards, though notably only ones wearing the tree and root crest rather than that lion-fish, on her long march with him through the Faebarrow keep. He was brought to a set of rather nice quarters, preferable to a cell he had to remind himself, where she instructed the guards to remain posted outside, which wasn't quite so different from a cell after all.

The skin at the corners of her eyes crinkled. "You will not leave this set of rooms without an escort, you will not request permission to leave these rooms from anyone but myself, and you will *not* see Lady Ammalie without my presence."

Damien would have been amused by how ironic her commands were if he were not instead imagining the multitude of ways he could break each of her ridiculous rules, not to mention her bones, but then

281

shrugged. "Fine. But I can't control what Amma will do." Which was of course both a lie and not.

"And you will call her Lady Avington," Tia growled, a hand going to her hilt.

"Of course, my apologies." Damien turned his back to her, taking a few steps deeper into the room. It was a sizable parlor with stuffy, white furniture, an already roaring fire, and a wall of four stained-glass windows depicting a liathau tree during each season which of course meant quite a lot of pink. Kaz had already trotted in and jumped up on a couch, testing its bounciness. At least someone was having a good time. "So, I am your prisoner then?"

Tia clicked her tongue against her teeth. "You're no one's prisoner, I'm simply placing you under a short surveillance to keep the family, this keep, and Lady Ammalie safe, as is my duty."

That didn't *not* sound like imprisonment.

He glanced back over his shoulder. "Ah, so it's *your* job I've been doing then?"

A vein in Tia's forehead pulsed, a nerve so easily struck, but then with her charge missing for a whole moon or more, he supposed she almost certainly would be on edge. And it hadn't really been her failing Amma had slipped past her—the baroness was a very good trickster, after all.

Damien sighed. "Apologies, again. I do appreciate your and that of the Avington's hospitality. It has just been an...arduous journey."

"Obviously, if you were with Ammalie," said Tia quietly through grit teeth. "She is not always the paragon of virtue she plays at."

Damien knew there was nothing he could say to that which wouldn't get him into more trouble with the guard, so he kept his mouth shut.

"You will have meals, clothes, and anything else you request, within reason, brought to you. The Avingtons will insist upon your presence at this celebration of theirs as well, so if you would deign to stay here through at least tomorrow night, I would be appreciative. After that, if you prove yourself trustworthy, you will be free to move about the keep or take your leave of this place, if you so wish."

Damien nodded, and the guard went to depart, but then paused before opening the door.

"I must stress," she said, voice lower, "Lady Ammalie does not need...this." She gestured vaguely at where he stood.

Damien looked down at himself then back up. "And what *does* the baroness need?"

Tia snarled, jaw hardening. "Structure, theology, guidance." She took the door handle, but hesitated. "But she has a very, very soft heart, one unchanged since she was too young to even speak, and she would do anything for this place. She does not need that to be ruined."

Tia finally swung open the door, snapping at the guards outside to stand at attention.

Once alone, Damien threw back his head, let out a guttural sigh, and collapsed onto the nearest sofa. Raising his arms straight upward, he called on the arcana swirling inside him, the noxscura that had been prickling just beneath his skin and begging to be released. It clawed out of his fingertips in wisps of smoke, and he sent it across the room to its farthest corners, sweeping over everything until he was surrounded by a dark haze. The arcana pinged a handful of magicked objects, the fireplace, the glass of the windows, the washbasin and tub in an attached room, but there was nothing illicit here, nothing that posed a danger or could be used to watch him. The Avingtons were, apparently, more trusting than most. That was probably one of their biggest problems, though particularly odd that it didn't seem to extend to their daughter.

He dropped his hands back onto his chest, spent. The ceiling high above was covered in tiles, copper and golden leaves carved out on them, and as if he were staring up at the sky through tree branches, the small spaces between the leaves were painted a shade the slightest bit duller than the blue of Amma's eyes.

No, not Amma, Lady Ammalie Avington, Baroness of Faebarrow and betrothed to that ridiculous man emblazoned with that stupid lion-fish crest on his chest. *Betrothed.* And she'd been begging Damien to kiss her just the night before! He'd found so much out about her in such a short time, he realized he had really only known her for a few weeks, and the two had been at odds nearly the entire time. He scoffed, thinking of how innocent she had pretended to be, how sweet, how—

But she *was* those things, wasn't she? When she had chastised him for knocking the pastry from the hungry child's hand, when she had wanted to help the possessed, accused man in Elderpass, when she had negotiated their release from the elves. No matter how many libraries she broke into, how many secret titles she had, no matter how many mystery fiances—though hopefully it was just the one— she was still Amma, the woman who had given the draekins every copper in her purse, who had said infernal arcana was no different than any other kind, who had drunkenly told him she thought he was capable of love and begged for his lips. And she was still the girl who had bandaged his hand when they met because, as she said, it was just the right thing to do.

"What are we doing, Master?" Kaz's watery voice was even more urgent as it popped up just over Damien's head. When he opened his eyes, the imp was as demonic as ever, hovering above him, red, leathery wings flapping as he hung onto the arm of the couch.

"I'm thinking, I'm thinking." He waved the imp away, and the creature whined, zipping across the room to peer out a smaller window.

"This is scalable!"

"We're not sneaking out the window. And keep your voice down."

Kaz huffed more quietly and scurried back to sit in a ball and stare at him. Wonderful, an audience would certainly help him think.

But Damien did try. He lay there, staring intermittently at the blue on the ceiling that was so close to the color of Amma's eyes and then squeezed his lids shut, considering everything. He was here now, in her home, and he knew the truth. There couldn't be much else to know, except that there definitely was. Something was off here, in Faebarrow, and multiple people seemed to have small pieces of the puzzle. Normally, he would have no time or interest in the petty drama of a barony in Eiren, but when a baroness staged her own kidnapping, when she had ferreted away the Lux Codex, when she harbored Bloodthorne's Talisman of Enthrallment inside her...

"Darkest, basest beasts, the *talisman*." Damien slapped his hands onto his face and raked his fingers downward. How in the infernal Abyss had he forgotten? The bloody talisman was still inside her, the one he needed to free his father who, he hated to remind himself, he had not spoken to or even thought of in some time. That was the only reason he'd needed the Lux Codex to begin with, the only reason he was here, and now he was mixed up in whatever *this* was, and, worse than perhaps all of that, he actually cared.

Damien sat up with a start.

He *cared*.

He had seen the look on Amma's face, the quiet discomfort, the bating anxiety, the masked fear, and he heard the way these people spoke about her like she were too delicate, still a child, or worse, a commodity. They simply did not listen to her—and she had said it herself, baronesses didn't have the freedom blood mages did—and he hated it all.

"Oh, fuck me." He stood to pace across the room. How dare she make him feel like...like *this*. Damien had never once been so

284

concerned with another being that he would put his life's work on hold—that he would forget about it even—until now, and especially not for a creature that had manipulated him. Though that, at least, was the slightest bit admirable. Arousing too, but that hawking, hulk of a guard was going to do everything in her power to keep him from seeing Amma—and even if he could manage to sneak off and find her, she was promised to marry someone else, and why in the Abyss, at a time like this, was he even thinking with his—

"Master?" Kaz was cowering in the spot he'd sat himself.

"You're not going to like this, Kaz, but we've got to stay."

The imp fell backward into an exhausted, infernal puddle.

Damien spent what felt like an eternity simply pacing. It was broken by the occasional knock at the door, each time his expectation that it might be Amma lessening when it was some nameless guard with food or clothes or linens. He did eventually break up the monotony by bathing, and he understood then why Amma had said she wasn't used to being dirty. The facilities in this keep rivaled his at home.

He thought of Aszath Koth while he sat in the bath, the bleakness of its stone walls, the chill in the high halls, all a stark distinction to this wallpapered and wooden place. The floorboards were smooth and light, and the counters were chiseled from white and pink marble, and the furniture was painted in soft pastels with flower-embroidered fabric. It turned his stomach, yet settled it at the same time, reminding him of Amma—he had stopped trying to not think of her, especially when he was naked and submerged in hot water. Compared to his own home, the contrast was almost comical, their worlds so different it seemed impossible they had even met at all.

She came from this place with its enchanted liathau trees and its hard-working populace and those parents of hers. Her parents who didn't really seem to respect her, but had at least seemed to mean how much they loved her, pleased to have her back. That was the problem, though, the *having*, but that was his problem too, wasn't it? His desire to have her to himself was counter to…everything.

But the desire of a parent to keep their child, even a grown one, safe, was no failing. Meanwhile, his own father was trapped in an occlusion crystal by the king of Amma's realm because he was a demon, of all things, and his mother was dark gods knew where since abandoning him and Zagadoth over twenty years ago. Another difference between them, the chasm ever deepening.

A sharp tapping woke Damien from his thoughts. The window at the back of the bath chamber was made up of opaque glass, but there was the outline of a bird on the exterior sill. A dove, he thought, then scoffed at himself as he climbed out of the water—it was never a dove, and especially not with the darkness of that shadow.

"Surprised to find me here, Corben?" he asked, opening the window.

The raven perched outside cocked his head and gave him a squawk.

"As am I."

Damien slid his fingers through the raven's feathers, and an arcane message ran through his mind in a throaty, inviting voice. It would have been good news if he'd received it sooner, but there was nothing he could do with it now. After speaking with his father at Anomalous's tower, he'd made a vague request of some associates, and their response through Corben was an eager offer to help—they were always eager to help, for a price—but these particular associates were unfortunately on the other side of the realm.

"Well, fine job, regardless, as always," he murmured to the bird, scratched him under the chin, and released him.

Damien stared out after Corben as he disappeared into the sky, blue and bright like Amma's eyes. He raised a hand to his face, fingertips wrinkled from the water, palm smooth and free of dirt and scars. He could slice into it at any time and release the noxscura full force, the darkness his father warned him about, the one he suspected chased his own mother away. He'd never truly unlocked it, but knew if he did, awful things would happen.

Awful things will happen, Damien. Those had been Amma's words when he asked what would arise from the guards at the city gates seeing her face. But if the guards, Brineberth or Faebarrow, recognized her then, they would have protected her, surely. So, what had she meant by *awful*? And why, when she'd had the perfect opportunity surrounded by soldiers in her room at The Too Deep Inn, hadn't she simply thrown him under the cart to free herself from him? Instead, she'd made up some ridiculous lie, painted him as a savior rather than a villain, and brought him home with her. Didn't she know he could raze this place to the ground and destroy all within it?

He flexed his fingers again. He could use the noxscura to break free of his current predicament, of his duty to Zagadoth, of everything, and just go. But whatever had anchored him to this place instead, continued to hold him, and he clenched his fist again, deciding to stay.

CHAPTER 30
A FEW DROPPED EAVES

amien dressed in clothes that had been brought to him, none of them black, predictably, but the deeply forest green tunic would suffice even if it was stitched with delicate, golden vines along one arm and the collar. He paced a bit more until there was another knock at the door and Kaz miserably changed himself back into a dog, sitting up on an ottoman with his asymmetrical underbite quivering as he held back a growl.

A young man entered, tall and lanky under the thick, white robes he wore. One of the Faebarrow guards stood in the doorway behind the newcomer, eyeing Damien with arms crossed, doing his best to look intimidating.

Damien waited, standing there a few paces back, conversely doing his best to not look intimidating with hands clasped behind his back. "Yes?"

"Oh!" The robed boy turned back to the guard and held up a leather bag. "Lady Ammalie requested I give Sir the blessing of Osurehm. It may take a few moments."

"Carry on." The guard shut the door with himself out in the hall.

The young man turned back and blew out a breath. "Hello." He gave him a quick, friendly wave. Odd.

Damien just narrowed his eyes. With dark skin covered in even darker freckles and a tight cropping of coiled hair, he looked nervous just standing there, both hands wrapped tightly around the handle to a leather satchel, fidgeting. "Who are you?"

"Oh, right, um, I'm P-Perry, and, uh, Amma—I mean Lady Ammalie—sent me."

"You're a priest?" Damien looked over his robes, some god's symbol, Osurehm he guessed, hanging from a chain around his neck. "And Amma sent you here to *bless* me?" Did she want him dead?

"Actually, she just told me to say that to the guards," he whispered, hurrying away from the door. "She was pretty serious about not blessing you actually, says you follow some obscure, foreign god? I didn't even know there was another pantheon."

Damien frowned at him. "Ah, so you're not a very good priest then, are you?"

"Not really since I'm just an acolyte," he admitted with a nervous laugh, shoulders drooping. "But I want to be! And Lady Ammalie says to just keep working hard and eventually I'll get there."

"A bit cruel of her," he mumbled, but the priest-in-training didn't seem to notice, continuing his ramble.

"There's a temple in Eirengaard I want to study at, and Amma's going to help get me in. She wrote a letter for me and everything, I just have to pass the exams, but they only hold them once a year, and they're coming up soon—"

Damien cleared his throat. "Right, no blessing, so why are you here then?"

"Oh, yeah! She wanted to give you this." He placed the satchel on the ground and opened it, pulling out a flat package wrapped with a swath of grey cloth. He held it out, hesitating, and then walked up to Damien with a bit of a wobble.

Receiving it, Damien could feel the magic inside the package, stiff under the soft fabric. Though it was wrapped tightly and tucked in, he could see the pattern on it, stitched with silver thread to look like runes.

"She said be really careful opening it, and that it's the thing you wanted, but she wouldn't tell me what it was exactly, just said you'd know, but I do know there's some divine magic in there because she asked me to get her a shroud from our temple for masking holy auras, and I told her that's stealing, and she said it wasn't if she asked me to do it, and I said it still felt a lot like stealing, and she said it's really her stealing it through me, so I shouldn't feel bad, but I still do feel kinda bad about the whole thing, and…"

As the acolyte went on, Damien flipped the wrapped-up thing carefully in his hands. It was the Lux Codex, it had to be, wrapped in a binding so that he could touch it. Darkness, if she could just stop being thoughtful for a little bit, he could be properly angry with her.

"…a message, but she didn't want to write it down in case I dropped it or someone took it from me which is sort of likely because that happens a lot. Hey, that is one cute dog. I've never seen one so small except the queen's, and they're not terribly nice. How are you, fella?" The man called Perry leaned in and began toward Kaz. The imp immediately snapped at him, and he pulled back.

"A message?" Damien waved the book at Kaz to stop his snarling. "From Amma?"

"Yeah, she says, um, well I need to repeat it exactly, so"—he held his arms out, putting on a slightly higher voice—"first of all, I'm sorry—"

"Of course she is," Damien mumbled, but the corner of his mouth tugged upward.

"—and I'm going to fix things—"

"Ever the optimist."

"—and are you all right?"

Damien blinked back at him. "That's a question?"

"Yes. Are you? She was really concerned."

Damien glanced about and then nodded slowly. He supposed he was.

"Okay, good, and then she wanted me to figure out how mad you actually were as opposed to how mad you said you were by looking at you, but I'm not really the best at reading people, and she knows that, so I don't know why she asked me at all, but she said to at least try, and even though I can't really tell usually, you seem like you might secretly be really, really angry."

Damien put up a hand, stopping him. "This is just how I look. I'm told I have resting villain face. Let the baroness know I am appropriately displeased with the situation but eagerly awaiting some kind of resolution which I anticipate she will…succeed at."

Perry nodded vigorously. He muttered everything back to himself, eyes closed, then popped them open again, huge and deeply brown and full of more anxiety than Damien had even seen on torture victims. "Sure, yes, okay. I have to go tell her right away, she said come right back to her and say, so—"

"Wait. You must know Amma well, yes?"

His face changed, a little smile that was free of nerves playing there. "Since we were really young, yeah. When my mom died, I had to go live at the temple, and it turned out Osurehm had blessed me with arcana, so they started teaching me, and then my teacher came here, so I did too, and Amma would get bored during theology lessons, and even though I really actually liked class, she'd sometimes convince me to sneak out, and—"

"So, you're local then, to Faebarrow?"

"All my life."

Damien nodded, looking him over once more. Amma trusted this young man, so he supposed he could as well. "The soldiers here, the ones all over your city and this keep that aren't local, what the *fuck* is going on with them?"

The poor, little holy man looked absolutely scandalized, and Damien chuckled a bit, but then Perry swallowed, working out an answer that amounted to, "I'm not supposed to say anything bad about Brineberth March."

"But you do *want* to?"

Perry swallowed again, saying nothing.

"What about that man Amma is meant to marry? He's from that place too, yes?"

"The marquis?" Perry couldn't hide what his face did then, disgust crawling over it, and Damien knew he had an in.

"That man is a marquis?"

"Well, I'm not totally sure, but he calls himself one. His older brother is one too, and I think maybe they split Brineberth March when the title was handed down? It's confusing though, because the march is still one big piece between Faebarrow and the sea. It's on three sides of us, actually, and I guess that's supposed to be a good thing? Faebarrow's never really had to have an army before, thanks to them. But anyway, Cedric Caldor's the marquis who came here about a year ago, and it was just him and some of his people at first, advisers and his head mage, Gilead, but then some guards came for protection, I don't know from what, and then there were more, and then he proposed to Amma, and we all sort of expected it, but it was still weird because then even more soldiers came, and things changed *a lot*. So, that's why Amma went and—" He cut himself off, eyes wide.

Damien opened his mouth to coax him on, but it was too much, scaring him off.

"I have to go. I'll tell Am—Lady Ammalie what you said. Promise." He drew a symbol across his chest which Damien could only assume had to do with his god. Then he gave him a short bow, robes trailing behind as he went to the door and knocked with a quickness.

Damien tried to get him to wait, but the guards let him out and swiftly shut and locked the door once again. "Kaz, come here, quick."

There was a thump, and then the hurried clacking of nails on the floor as the dog paced up to his feet.

Damien squatted down. "Listen to me very closely: make yourself into something small and follow that acolyte until he reaches Amma, and then I want you to follow her. Do you understand?"

"Spy on the trollop. Yes."

"If I had more time, I would make you pay for that, but you need to go, now." He stood quickly and grabbed the bag the man had left, striding to the door as there was a cracking and a sizzle from behind him. The air smelt of passing brimstone, and when he looked back, a tiny, grey rat was climbing out of Kaz's sweater left abandoned on the floor.

Damien knocked, strangely not the first time he'd had to knock to get *out* of a room, and he scowled at the memory before pushing it away when the guard cracked open the door.

"Your priest forgot his things," he said, holding up the satchel with a forced grin.

The guard eyed him through the small opening and shouldered the door open to take it.

Damien glanced down long enough to see Kaz's new rat tail slip out into the hall. When the door was again closed, Damien shook his hand, the light warmth from the divine magic within the satchel uncomfortable, then fell with his back against the door and closed his eyes. He reached out with his mind, darkness swirling behind his lids, and he caught onto Kaz's aura just before the imp in rat form got to the hall's end where he would be too far for Damien's spell to reach.

Kaz's body jolted as Damien's conscience entered it, along for the ride as he continued on, and he saw through the rat's eyes as he flew down the hall, hugging the divot where the floor and wall met.

It was not a spell Damien used often, detesting imps for the most part, but using one as a conduit was handy for exactly this. It was also nauseating being jostled about every time Kaz juked away from a set of feet or climbed himself up and over a step.

But the rat that was really an imp found the acolyte again and did his best to keep pace being so small. Perry was also a scurrier, like a human mouse, trying to be unseen as he hurried through the keep. He was almost lost a number of times until finally the holy man came to a door where he was let in immediately. The door shut again just before Kaz could reach it.

"Master, I am sorry!" Kaz's tiny voice rolled inside Damien's mind.

It's fine, it's fine, just wait until he comes back out.

Kaz did wait, and eventually the door opened again, but instead of just the acolyte, there were three sets of feet, two of which moved in one direction and the third, belonging to Perry, went another way.

Kaz followed after.

Not that one, idiot, Damien told Kaz mentally.

The rat turned itself around, and there was Amma, rushing away down the hall with another young woman in tow. She was clad in a long dress, simple but elegant, that she kept tugging on to move quicker. It was strange to see her dressed so differently, but he supposed this was actually the baroness's typical guise. Her hair was falling long and loose down her back instead of in its normal braid or knot too, but there was a single bundle of it secured at the back of her head with what might have looked like a long, silver pin to anyone else who hadn't seen her dagger so many times. There, that was the Amma he knew, tucked away and hidden but ready to strike.

She was speaking in a rushed, hush of a tone to the other woman, much taller with a cascade of dark brown, pin-straight hair and a slight point to her ears. Laurel, Damien thought, the half-elven woman Amma had spoken of, surely.

Kaz did his best to keep them in his sight, but the two were whispering and keeping to the shadows. Then the two stepped into an alcove and fell into complete silence when a set of guards turned down the hall. Why in the Abyss was Amma hiding from the soldiers in her own home? Kaz was at least able to catch up then so he could hear their voices as they darted out through an archway to a side courtyard, doused in the shadows of early evening.

"You know Thomas is in town, right?" the other woman who he assumed was Laurel was saying.

"Who?" Amma's voice was riddled with weariness.

The half elven girl stopped short, looking at Amma dumbly. Kaz almost ran into her feet.

"Oh, Thomas, of course." Amma rubbed at a temple, her clean face paler than normal, and she continued on across the grass that ran along a hedge. Damien grunted to himself—another man? Who was this bloody Thomas?

"Yes, *Thomas*, only the man you had a torrid affair with. That Thomas," Laurel added helpfully yet unwelcomely.

"Laurel!" Amma hissed. "A few moons of flirting and a couple nights together years ago *isn't* an affair, and nothing about it was torrid."

"Well, you described it as swoon-worthy and the best kiss of your life, so I didn't think you'd forget."

Best kiss of her life? Damien regretted briefly not replacing that memory the night before.

"I had a very different idea of what was swoon-worthy then. I

292

haven't been interested in him in years anyway, and he's married now. Why are you bringing him up at all?"

"Oh, I just realized he's going to be invited to your parents' banquet, and with everything else going on, I just thought you should know. I'm sorry." The girl looped her arm in Amma's and pulled her close as they headed to the far side of the courtyard, staying in the hedge's darker shadow.

"It's all right, the whole thing is going to be a mess anyway. Everyone's going to want to hear about what happened to me, and how I got away, and what Damien did to help me."

So, Amma had told her friend his true name. Interesting.

Laurel nudged Amma. "Don't worry about the story. While you were gone, I was imagining all these different scenarios you might have been in, I even wrote some of them down—I plan to change all the names when I publish it, of course, but I'm more than happy to speak on your behalf when the nosiest start asking questions."

Amma laughed lightly. "Just be consistent, okay? No plot holes. And don't lay it on too thick."

"Me? Never. I'll leave out all the lewd parts I made up too." Laurel brought her to a stop beside a set of topiaries shaped like a rabbit and a deer. "But listen, I do have something important to ask you, and I've been waiting because I couldn't say it in front of Perry and damage his delicate sensibilities, but I just can't wait any longer."

Amma's eyes widened, frozen with fear as the other woman checked the empty courtyard.

"Please tell me you fucked Damien."

"Laurel!" Amma shook her off and began storming away.

The half-elf cackled wickedly, running after. "That's not a no!"

Kaz ran over the stony walkway they'd crossed to keep up. Amma slipped between the topiaries, and Laurel was right behind, Kaz keeping to her heels.

"Believe me, Laurel, I thought about it. A lot." At that, Damien almost accidentally knocked himself right out of Kaz's consciousness. "But it's a lot more complicated than that. I haven't told you everything. Not to mention I'm, you know…"

"Oh, as far as I'm concerned, that engagement is absolute rubbish!"

Finally, thought Damien, *someone in Faebarrow worthy of Amma's friendship.*

Amma groaned in the back of her throat but came to a stop. Before her, there was a building made up of glass tinged deeply green, its roof and doors included.

"Which reminds me, I haven't told you everything either. Guess what else I've been doing while you were away?"

Amma didn't take her eyes off the greenhouse. "Probably something sinister."

"No, just acquiring a fancy set of poisons."

That broke Amma of her long stare at the glass building. "No, you didn't."

The half-elven girl was grinning in a way that reminded Damien a bit too much of Anomalous. "It's just a backup plan, for you-know-who."

"Laurel, you absolutely *cannot* do that. Are you mad?"

"Of course I'm mad! You're my friend. Am I supposed to just let him get away with—"

A rapping right beside Damien's head severed his connection to Kaz, and he blinked, disoriented as his vision blurred, the voices of the women swallowed up into the empty hollowness of the chamber he actually stood within.

Damien pushed off of the door, swearing under his breath, too far off from the imp to reach him again with his spell. Hopefully, the creature would remember whatever else he heard and be able to find his way back, sneak through the halls, reach Damien's room—no, he would almost certainly die before accomplishing half of that. Well, Kaz had another good run, he supposed and he drew a quick X over his chest.

Damien answered the door to a new guard, one he had not seen before, this one with the Brineberth crest on his chest.

"His lordship requests your presence."

The blood mage scratched at his head. "Of course, if the baron—"

"No, the marquis. He would like to thank you, personally and privately, for returning his bride."

Damien moved to shut the door. "He doesn't need to do that."

"Correct, he does not." The guard's boot wedged into the doorway, stopping Damien from shutting it in his face. "But he wants to, so he shall. Now."

CHAPTER 31
THE FUTILITY OF FINDING HUMOR IN EVERY CHAPTER OF A ROMANTIC COMEDY

With everything he's done to you?" The look on Laurel's face had shifted from playful to a sincere desire for blood. But poison? *Really*? What was Laurel thinking? She didn't even serve Cedric any of his meals.

Amma steadied her breathing, and then slowly wrapped her arms around her oldest and best friend. "Please," she whispered, squeezing hard, "let me take care of things. Don't put yourself at risk like that. You've done too much for me already."

Laurel's thin lips twisted up as she pulled gently back from the embrace. "I'll hold off. For now. It'll give me more time to get the dose just right."

That warning was likely the best Amma would get, so she nodded and smiled. The comfort of Laurel's touch and the sound of her voice, even when it needled or proposed murder, made her want to linger in the familiar moment, but the greenhouse was just there, and she was eager to go inside after so long away.

"It's too bad you didn't just elope with Thomas years ago, would have made things easier."

Amma huffed. "Then it would look like the Avington's only child was favoring one of the seven merchant families, and we've sworn to treat them all equally."

"That's so silly, you would never be unfair. And you *were* favoring him, in fact I walked in on the two of you favoring each other once."

"Don't remind me." Amma felt her face redden, going for the greenhouse door. "But you know I mean in trade. A Treshi and an Avington together would have upset the balance."

"So," Laurel said, following behind her and drawing her words out in that lilt she always had when asking a not-so-innocent question, "this Damien person isn't the son of some important merchant, is he?"

"No, he's, um…the son of…" Amma's voice trailed off as they stepped into the warmth of the greenhouse. It was just as well that the sight pulled all the words from her brain: she hadn't planned on telling Laurel anything about Damien's demonic heritage anyway, but the vague description she was going to use instead was ripped right out of her mind as well.

Barren. Never had it looked this way, even after a planting.

"What in Sestoth's name has happened?" Amma breathed, feet taking her forward, but it felt like being dragged along, like the world around her was a dream, or more like a nightmare.

With darkness falling, the small, arcane stones running along the ground were beginning to give off their dim glow, and it wasn't much, but it was enough to see the nothingness. The shelves normally covered in clay pots filled with seedlings were bare, dry, crumbling dirt spilled in sad heaps in their places. Pots were stacked in a corner, shards of others littering about a toppled pile. Gardening tools were strewn about, left haphazardly, but the most important, silver tools weren't to be found anywhere.

Laurel's hand touched Amma's shoulder. "I told you that you weren't going to like it."

Tears should have come. If there were any time for her to cry, now was it, but instead a rage rose up in Amma so complete she could have set the entire Brineberth army on fire with a single look. And then that look fell on a faint flicker of green, and she ran.

Falling to her knees before a pile of dirt in the greenhouse corner, Amma dug in with clean nails, ripping the soil away and uncovering a stem. She rifled through her hair, pulling the dagger free and using it to more carefully push the soil away and reveal the lone liathau sapling that had survived.

Brilliantly green, its tiny trunk was twisted, three leaves jutting off of its curves and a nest of roots beneath. It was a sad one, but it was all that was left. "Bring me a pot," she called as with precision, she dug the sapling out. Laurel appeared at her side with a container and started shoveling in dirt for a base, and Amma slipped her dagger beneath the liathau, whispering to it a rush of encouraging pleas.

The white roots twitched and slithered out from the soil, coiling themselves around the dagger's blade, and once they were hanging on, Amma lifted it and gently placed it inside the pot. The roots unfurled and each worked their way into the loose dirt, and Amma and Laurel hand-placed more soil with the utmost care to pack the earth around its stem.

Amma sat back, eyes on the sapling, dagger in hand. The thing she had used as a weapon on her journey across Eiren was really meant for this. Well, no, for severing seeds from grown liathau and keeping them healthy and their magic intact, but the saplings were delicate, easy to bruise with bare hands or to become infected if touched with anything but silver.

Laurel was frowning down at the plant on the pot's other side, hands blackened. Amma looked down at herself, dirtied to her elbows in soil, the front of her dress covered. "How?"

"They took them back to Brineberth," Laurel said, tipping her head as she watched a leaf on the liathau twitch. "They think they can grow them there, as if anyone has ever been able to grow one outside of Faebarrow in a thousand years."

"Did any of our people go with them? So they at least have a chance?"

Laurel shook her head.

Amma looked around again at the vast, empty building in the quickly growing darkness. "Where is everyone? Juliana? Nicholas? All of them?"

"Well, Nicholas got in some trouble," Laurel began quickly, "but don't worry, we've been working on it, and Tia says he'll be out by the end of the week after everyone kinda forgets what happened."

"Out of where? Are you saying he's in prison?"

"Well, when the Brineberth guards take over the prison and then you punch a Brineberth guard in the nuts, yes, you go to prison." A nervous, wary laugh slipped out of her. "And most everyone else went to the orchards for a while, but some of them are out searching for wild liathau, as pointless as I assume that is, but it's sort of all they've got."

Amma stood. "We need to go to the orchards too, and then out to find the others, and maybe—"

Laurel was shaking her head, carefully coming to her feet as her eyes darted over Amma's shoulder. "Now isn't the best time, I don't think."

Amma turned, and at the door to the greenhouse stood Baroness Avington, somehow finding the only light in the place and standing beneath it. Clad in a different gown than she'd been wearing when she'd first seen her that morning, one appropriate for evening and thus more ornate and with a slightly lower neckline, her mother had her hands delicately clasped before her and kept her chin high. As she slipped through the greenhouse door, she managed to not get a speck of dirt on any of the layers of her dress.

"Laurel, please attend to your duties," her voice called, sweet but firm as she crossed the greenhouse toward the two of them.

Laurel came to her full height, grinning widely, hiding her dirty hands behind her back. "But I am. Lady Ammalie is right here."

"Do you not have duties elsewhere?"

"No, Your Ladyship, they are all complete."

Amma had a very strong feeling she was lying.

"Then go embroider something."

Laurel's shoulders fell. "I hate embroidery," she grumbled.

"I know. Go." Amma's mother's eyes flashed.

"Yes, My Lady." Laurel straightened, gave a perfect curtsy, and hurried off with her hands clasped politely and head down. When she got behind the baroness, though, she turned with fists balled at her sides and silently stuck out her tongue.

"I can see you in the glass's reflection, Laurel."

The half-elf gasped and ran off. Amma would have laughed if everything else didn't seem so bleak in the emptiness of the greenhouse that had once been her favorite place in the realm.

"That girl is lucky you adore her so much." The baroness gave a small smile, and then her eyes fell to Amma's front and the mess down it, brow pinching. "Oh, darling, what have you done?"

Amma held her hands before her, soil in the cracks of her skin and under her nails as if she hadn't spent half the day being picked at and scrubbed by other hands and hating every second of it. "Mother, what has been done *here*?"

The baroness did not even look around at the shelves, voice still, shoulders only shrugging a little. "It was an order by the crown, but it will be full again by next season, and you can have your fun in the dirt as normal then, I'm sure. Now, come on, back to the bath—"

"You can't really believe that," Amma spat, dagger still in her hand as she pointed out the empty shelves, hair loose and splaying around her. "This will take years to replenish if we even get the chance."

Hand raising slightly but delicately, the baroness eyed the dagger. "Please put that away, dear, you'll hurt yourself."

"I'm not going to hurt myself, Mother, I'm twenty-five!"

"Yes, you are aren't you?" she cut in, voice suddenly biting. "Twenty-five and still unwed, still free to pursue your hobbies here as we've let you like a wild animal for your entire life, free to run about the keep as if you haven't a care in the world, confident enough to lie in respect to your whereabouts and go sneaking off as if there are no consequences."

Amma's mouth clamped shut, unsure if her mother were referring to earlier that day when Amma had pretended to be ill, refusing to see anyone, including Cedric, so that she could come here with Laurel, or if she somehow knew that she had much more deviously pretended to be abducted a moon ago. Gods, did everyone know?

Her mother did not clarify, but her light blue eyes softened as they finally took a slow look around the greenhouse. The sharpness to her voice fell out of it as quickly as it had filled it up. "When I was your age, I had been your mother for three years. I was married at nineteen. Most noble women are, Ammalie."

Though she wanted to spit out that she wasn't grateful for a freedom that should be awarded everyone, Amma bit her cheek and kept it in. Her mother had never spoken ill of her station, and even now there wasn't disappointment in her words, but pride. It had been easy for Constance Avington, she always said, so it should have been easy for Amma too. "But you love Father."

"Eventually," the baroness reminded her, "yes, I did, and I still do. But when things were decided for us, we didn't even know one another. I've told you how painfully shy and awkward he was back then. And, to be quite honest, he wasn't even terribly interested in me which is just...I mean, look at me, Ammalie." She held her hands out, slightly cocking a hip and making the gown she wore sway. "Imagine this thirty years younger."

Amma stared back at her, stony, but then her mother gave her hips a wiggle, and that forced the flicker of a grin onto Amma's face.

Her mother tittered and then stood poised yet again. "And your father was nothing like how Marquis Caldor is with you. You've been lucky enough to be courted by him, to have the chance to get to know him. That man already adores you, and with time you will adore him as well."

Amma's grin fell. It was absolutely true Cedric was nothing like her father, but her mother had no idea just how true. Getting to know Cedric—really getting to know him—had *not* been a boon for their relationship. A tick in her chest urged her to lay everything at the baroness's feet just then, a squeezing in her throat to blurt out words she'd been too afraid to say. She'd wanted to tell her mother many times in the last six moons since her engagement that it was so much more complicated than simply not adoring someone, but then the only two possible outcomes always came back to her. A heart would be broken either way: her mother's if she were told how cruel the man she'd been pushing her daughter to marry truly was, or Amma's if, when her mother found out, she decided none of it mattered and Amma should marry him regardless.

Baroness Avington had taken a step closer, feet silent in the greenhouse, only the sound of her gown swishing slightly to pull Amma from her melancholic thoughts. "I assume you have had your fun and are finished wallowing in the mire now. Here." She offered her a small, satin pouch that Amma hadn't noticed had been in her hand all along.

When Amma's fingers crushed the sachet slightly as she accepted it, she recognized the smell of the herbs inside at once. Her stomach turned over at the memory of Laurel acquiring this specific blend for her years ago and then again more recently, but did her best to play at being completely oblivious. "What...what is this?"

Her mother raised one brow only slightly. "Even if you're wed in the next moon, I doubt you'll be able to pass that stranger's baby off as Cedric's. This will take care of that problem for you."

Amma thrust the sachet back at her mother. "I didn't sleep with him."

The baroness's eyes only flitted upward in disbelief.

"I didn't." Amma's arm and voice fell, watching her mother's face, but there was no faith there, as if nothing she could say would change her mind. Her fist tightened around the herb, getting another whiff of it and feeling a flood of guilt and pain, but vindication in her decision to not share any other truths. She stepped toward a bench and collapsed onto it, defeated.

"I know you have been through a great ordeal, Ammalie, but the timing...it just could not be worse." It was strange how Constance Avington could do that with her voice, how she could make it seem so kind, how she could very likely *intend* to be kind, and yet say something that felt completely bereft of thoughtfulness.

Of course there was no time for whatever this was going on with Amma—the baroness had only been saying so for over a year now.

"Darling, you know how deeply I love you," she said, and there was an earnestness in her strain as she picked up a discarded linen, wiped off the seat beside Amma, and actually sat. "And you know how deeply I love Faebarrow. I may not have been born here, but this place has been my home, and it has been so very good to me. It has given me comfort, your father, and it has given me you." She hesitated but then took Amma's dirty hand in both of her own. "Your father and I have done our best, but we have made some mistakes, I think, in following the decrees so closely all these years. We have considered discussing things with the council, perhaps taxing the liathau differently—"

"You mean taking it from the people?" Amma's heart sped up. She had never once heard her mother or father discuss that.

She faltered. "It does grow on Avington land, Ammalie."

"That *they* work."

"The consideration has weighed on us heavily, but coin is not what it used to be, and when the crown demands more, *we* must make up the difference, not the people of the barony."

"The crown's apparently getting what they want regardless. And Brineberth March too. You've been giving it away."

"The greenhouse will be replenished and the orchard reseeded next season," she said wearily, hands tightening on Amma's as she glanced around at the empty greenhouse as if seeing it for the first time. "This is just…just the result of an intense harvest. The crown needs the enchanted timber, and the Caldors have been ordered to deliver it on our behalf."

Heated rage bloomed in Amma's chest. "The crown *wants* the timber, they don't need it, just like you want your comfortable life. Marquis Cedric Caldor is already acting as though he and I are married and the two of you don't exist. You know he's functioning as the lord of this place, and you and father are letting him. You let him bring his forces here, you let him imprison our people, you let him—" She choked on the words, not even sure what they would have been, if she could have been brave enough to say more than the honesty she had already blurted out.

Her mother's eyes had gone glassy, but she didn't allow a tear to drop. "You said it yourself: we can't tax the people, so what are we to do other than allow this in return for his gold?"

That was it. That had always been it. Things in Faebarrow were different, it was always said. Amma worked in the greenhouse alongside the people, and so she knew it was true. But the crown never liked any of it, not the barony's reluctance to over harvest, not the way the noble family shared profits with the people, and not the fact the liathau could be so much more powerful if only they could get their hands on more of it. But coin—coin could change everything. It could even convince a set of parents to give away their daughter.

"So, that's it?" She heard herself speaking, the words easier now, though she would have never said them before. "You're selling me off like cattle?"

"It's not a sale, Ammalie, it's just what happens." Her mother tipped her head, brow knit as if she felt sorry that Amma was too dense to understand. "It's what happened to me and my sister and perhaps someday to your child too."

Amma sat staring at the single liathau sapling left in the greenhouse, its twisting stem doing its best to reach up out of the dirt it had been packed into. It was small and alone and had so much work to do, the odds against it almost impossible.

Her mother put an arm around her then and pulled her against her chest. Constance Avington was always thin with sharp joints and a hard ribcage, but when she hugged Amma to her like this, none of that discomfort mattered. She was still her mother, after all. "You *can* make the best of it, Ammalie. You are too bright for your own good, and you are beautiful and so well loved," she whispered into the top of her head. "Whatever the marquis says, whatever he does, don't blame his failings on cruelty—"

"—when ignorance is the much more likely cause," Amma replied, finishing what her mother always touted as a firmly-held truth.

It had been Amma's truth too until she had put it to use in trying to talk to Cedric. Unfortunately, she had learned that it wasn't ignorance that made Cedric tell her in private she had no business getting involved with how her home would be run, nor was it ignorance when he threatened her with the death of her loved ones if she didn't accept his proposal, and it certainly wasn't Cedric's ignorance when he forced her into his bed so she could not back out of their wedding without being publicly ruined. He must have wondered how she had not fallen pregnant yet. Her hand gripped the sachet of herbs tighter, the smell batting up against her memory like a moth singeing itself on a candle, and she wasn't sure if she should thank or curse the gods for oblivious men who needn't be aware such things even existed.

The baroness smoothed Amma's hair back away from her face. "And, darling, if you're cattle, you're the prettiest little cow out in the field."

"Mother," Amma groaned up against her, "that's not funny."

"Come now." She tipped her head up to meet her eyes, smiling and sincere. "It is a *little* funny, isn't it?"

Amma's jaw tightened, and then she gave in and nodded.

CHAPTER 32
A LESSON IN VILLAINY

D
amien did not like being told what to do. He liked even less being told what to do by some shiny-armor-wearing, holy-weapon-wielding, punchable-face-having fuck of a marquis. And to be told what to do by said fuck through the summons of an ignoble guard without an ounce of consideration for his station and an incredibly stupid mustache? Well, that just bloody pissed him off.

But Damien dutifully followed the brusque Brineberth guard through the halls of Faebarrow keep, compelled by both his desire to play along with Amma's charade and to get a bead on the man she was supposed to marry. He did not want to acknowledge the fact that he really had no other choice.

The sun no longer lit the halls, but free-standing candelabras placed in alcoves and arcane stones set into the walls gave off a warm glow on the creamy marble. The keep was still busy for early evening, another contrast to his in Aszath Koth, but the busyness here was full of militarized troops.

Through a number of wide corridors, Damien was led into a different wing of the keep where it was quieter, and he recognized a specific stained-glass window from Kaz's jaunt as a rat, passing the hall Amma's chamber had been down, knowing she was no longer there. Tia was posted at the hall's head, clearly unaware her charge had slipped away again. She caught Damien's eye as he went by, lifting her chin and narrowing her eyes, but rather than be disgusted, she seemed curious.

Damien gestured silently to the Brineberth guard leading him then shrugged, giving her a baffled look. The last thing he wanted was for that woman to think he was in league with these idiots.

Another hall took them to a set of double doors with carvings inlaid all along their wooden frame, liathau he would have to guess, at the way the wood appeared to still be growing. Damien took a quick glance down the crossing hall each way. There were only Brineberth soldiers here, and Brineberth banners hung on the walls. If not for the liathau wood, there would be no sign this were Faebarrow's keep at all.

But there was one man who was not a guard, robed and vaguely familiar. Their eyes met for a brief moment, and there was a slight recognition there. He carried a thick book down the hall, and then stepped into another room, and Damien recalled from where he knew him—the man who had been in the library and demanded access to the restricted section.

Damien did not have a moment to think on that, though, as his escort knocked. In the chamber he'd been brought to, Cedric Caldor stood before a desk, waiting. His eyes locked onto Damien, and the blood mage took note of the dead look he had been boring into the door before he had entered. It was wiped from his face in a fraction of an instant, replaced with a warm, welcoming grin, but Damien had seen the man's cold expectation for him to arrive, and the displeasure at whatever was about to happen.

There was a heavy thunk as the door closed after Damien stepped in, his escort shut out on the other side.

"Day Ravenheart," said Cedric as if they were old friends, holding a hand out in invitation. Damien had almost forgotten the silly name he'd been given, but it did make him grin at the memory of Amma coming up with it, and that injected some much-needed sincerity into the hateful meeting.

"Marquis Caldor." Damien nodded at him, taking a slow step forward and glancing about. The chamber was a makeshift receiving area and study, but there were doors at the back of it that would lead to more rooms. While the whole keep was well decorated—provided that by *well*, one meant in the style of too many flowers and pastels— this room felt more opulent. Faebarrow was coming to be known to Damien for its reverence for flora and the soft nature of things, but nothing here seemed very organic, instead with dark, heavy furniture and weaponry hung on the walls, so out of place. Except Cedric, of course, who had made himself right at home.

"I've called you here to extend my gratitude for your service to Faebarrow and to me, personally. The baroness has such a hold on so many hearts here, and losing her would have been difficult to weather."

Damien grunted as he watched the marquis bow his head, eyes closed and hands brought together as if in prayer, but the whole thing felt off. Damien's eyes darted about the chamber once more, waiting for him to be done with...whatever this was, and then he cleared his throat. "You are welcome?"

The marquis seemed to take his words as permission to stand fully again, the deferential look replaced with a smarmier grin, and he leaned back against the desk. "But I must tell you, my gratitude is not the only reason I requested a meeting."

Here it comes, thought Damien, taking the man in fully. Cedric clearly put effort into his appearance, and he would have been quite attractive if not for the...too much of everything. His blond hair swooped a bit too much in front, his satiny tunic glinted a bit too much in the candlelight of the room, and his shit-eating grin wrapped a bit too far around his stupid fucking head. They were of matched height, but Cedric had a thicker build with broader shoulders and less of a neck. He wouldn't be as fast or agile as Damien, but there would be more strength behind his blows if he could land them.

"I must know more about the man who rescued Lady Ammalie." Cedric's speech was even unlikable, too emphatic to be sincere. "From where do you hail? And from whom?"

"Elderpass. A bastard son of the Stormwing family, or so I'm told. Mother's dead." He lied as easily as Cedric did, but better.

"And your line of work? Are there so many damsels in distress that you find the pay steady?" Cedric laughed too loudly at his own, stupid joke, especially considering the distress his own damsel had just theoretically been in.

"Trouble finds me," Damien said, less of a lie this time before dipping back into the untruth, "and I profit from it when I can."

Cedric cocked a thick brow, grin widening on his boxy jaw. "So, you're a freelance do-gooder then? Not in the ranks of Elderpass's defenders?"

"I like to travel," said Damien flatly.

He pushed off the desk, voice lowering. "Been all over the realm, have you? A man of your profession must have quite a lot to tell! Or, rather, leads, as it were, on any evil that has yet to be flushed out. There is a bounty, you know, and I have King Archibald's ear—I'm one of his chosen." At this, he laughed a bit, and Damien wanted to carve the smug look off the marquis's face. "Any information that is provided to the crown and proves truthful on the whereabouts of undesirable creatures can be quite profitable. Any dangers or threats we should be looking into?"

Damien did know the exact location of about a hundred and a half undesirables. In fact, he had one in his pocket. "I come across very little that is threatening, actually. Nothing that I can't take care of myself."

Cedric stared at him a long moment, smile faltering, and then he broke into a single, loud laugh. "Well, of course you do!" He clasped a hand down on Damien's shoulder and gave him a shake. "But it does bring up the true crux of why I've brought you here, Sir Ravenheart. I must know what took Lady Ammalie and how you came to liberate my bride from that evil."

Behind his back, Damien flexed his fingers, noxscura swirling under his skin and crawling upward to where Cedric's hand still gripped him. "Surely your future wife would be the best source of information for the details of her abduction. I wasn't present for that."

"No, of course not. I know you had nothing to do with her disappearance; otherwise, why in the realm would you have brought her back?" Again he chuckled, as if it were all a joke. Damien knew Amma's abduction wasn't true, but if Cedric thought it was, he certainly was being quite cavalier about it. "But her rescue, that was all you, good sir, and I must know if what took her was struck down or if we must seek out yet another evil in our realm to be destroyed."

Damien searched Cedric's eyes, their light brown so steady staring back into his own. "The evil that took Amma?" Damien had a brief flash of the moment he had discovered the talisman had burrowed inside her and how angry he had been, how he had blamed her, and his promise to kill her. "That evil has been destroyed."

Cedric's fingers tightened on Damien's shoulder for just a moment, the noxscura inching toward them to wrap around and squeeze and sever, but then whatever god the marquis prayed to must have interceded because the man let him go. "Good."

As the noxscura seeped back into Damien's skin, there was an odd tickle, and he recognized something he hadn't at first: Cedric Caldor was an arcane user, and the noxscura wasn't trying to attack but to fend off whatever spell he'd been attempting to cast on Damien. It hadn't been strong, but it had been well enough shrouded for Damien not to notice, and the possible origin of the magic…concerning.

Cedric, however, did not act as though he'd attempted and failed anything, he just took to thoughtfully pacing the room. "Now let me ask, as a traveling protector, are you aware of a sort of rumor plaguing the realm? One of darkness and lurking evil?"

Damien's eyes narrowed, and he said nothing, instead stepping up to the desk and turning to watch the man pace.

"A bit nondescript, I know, but there has been talk of something darker. Something more chaotic and destructive out there." Cedric said these things with a certain excitement, the kind that a man who has either never seen such things or has survived them quite by accident might.

Damien did not want to act too intrigued, but it was mostly because that seemed to be exactly what Cedric wanted out of him. He casually glanced at the records over the desk, an open ledger with neat but minuscule scribbles in it, and a letter signed with a massive signature and the seal of the crown. King Archibald—this was the closest Damien had gotten to him yet, and it made his hackles raise. "I thought Eiren was largely considered a…safe space?"

"Oh, surely it is, it *is*. His Majesty King Archibald and the Holy Order of Osurehm have seen to the protection of the realm for decades, but there are whispers of a deeper evil. Something lurking, biding its time, waiting to be free."

Dad? Damien shook his head. "Does this evil have a name?"

"Oh, it likely has many." Cedric crossed the room to stand behind the desk, dropping his gaze to thoughtlessly flip through a number of pages there. "Or perhaps none at all. But it is said if you encounter it, you know. I would think a man that has been to the corners of the realm may have stumbled upon such a thing, a festering evil, a rot waiting to be cut out."

Damien's head cocked, lucky Cedric just missed it before he looked back up. He pulled the recognition of the words from the prophecy—*corners, rot*—off his face. A coincidence, surely. "Nothing like that."

"Well!" Cedric threw back on his smarmy grin. "Enough of that. Perhaps you could help me, though, as I am still trying to piece together my betrothed's ordeal. When, exactly, did you rescue her from this still as-of-yet undefined abductor?"

"Half a moon or so ago," Damien said carefully, watching to see if Cedric believed this were an inconsistency with whatever Amma had told him. Before the marquis could ask another question, Damien cut in, "But again, Amma would be a much better source for her tribulations. The two of you have surely spoken already, yes?"

The man sighed with a chuckle. "Oh, you know how women can be. Lady Ammalie's experience has exhausted her, and she has fallen ill, so we have not had the chance to speak nor will we tonight."

The fist that had been tightened around Damien's stomach since he'd entered the chamber loosened, and he bit the inside of his cheek to keep the satisfied look off his face. So, there was the reason Amma and her friend had been scurrying so covertly around the keep. Though why she *needed* to lie to avoid the marquis still vexed him.

"But, I assure you," said Cedric as he leaned forward, placing hands on the desk, corner of his lip curling up, "after tomorrow night's celebration, she and I will have a very long exchange regardless of her protests."

Damien imagined then that nothing would give him more pleasure than the feeling of Cedric's blood running down his arm, Damien's dagger plunged deep in his gut, twisting ever so slowly as he watched the fearful recognition cross over the marquis's face that he would die.

A metallic clang broke Damien of the fantastic vision of Cedric's body splayed out on the floor at his feet. The regrettably still-breathing man had dropped a purse of coins on the desk between them.

"No man does good deeds for free. For your service."

Damien cocked a brow; he could learn a thing or two about villainy from Cedric Caldor. He looked down at the sack of gold, but the parchment below it that had been shifted by the purse gripped his attention instead.

"Haven't seen more than this all at once, eh?" Cedric laughed, pushing the coin forward and moving the papers to cover what Damien had been staring at.

There was almost no possibility, but the word there on Cedric Caldor's personal notes, a name written by his own hand, had almost certainly been E'nloc, the evil the elves of the Gloomweald had spoken of, the so-called One True Darkness.

"I don't want that," Damien said, gesturing to the coin. "Seeing to Amma's safety is enough."

"There's that familiarity again," said Cedric, acid in his voice as his eyes found Damien's, openly hostile for the first time. "I know the baroness can be quite talkative; you must have become friendly on the road. I'll double the amount if you leave immediately and never return."

Damien knew somewhere in his mind that this would have made an awful lot of sense. Yes, the talisman was inside Amma, and yes, Damien was technically a prisoner no matter what anyone said, in an estate on the crown's land no less, and just because no one had pegged him as a blood mage yet—even a holy man—didn't mean someone wouldn't soon. Cedric, who had tried and failed to cast on him, might even figure it out, but for now, he was offering him freedom, and a shrewd villain should jump at that chance.

"Thank you," he said, "but no."

Damien turned and walked steadily to the chamber's door. He opened it and stepped out without a look back, all he could do to stop himself from gutting the marquis right then and there.

CHAPTER 33
BALL GOWNS AND BLOOD MAGES

B eing shunted into the role of hero at a banquet thrown by a noble family of the realm came whatever the exact opposite of naturally was to Damien. He stood nowhere that didn't seem like a corner, peered into no face that made him feel reassured, and Damien could say nothing that didn't sound like the sarcastic quipping of a villain. Even Amma's mother, a woman who he expected should have made him feel at ease only made him too aware of his own failings—failings he didn't think he actually had until just then.

Of course, that all should have been good! To still know one was evil when wrapped so forcefully in a linen of goodness was likely good—that is, good meaning useful, not good meaning virtuous— because then one knew deep down one was bad—that is, bad meaning evil, not bad meaning useless. Yet he felt a wholly different kind of bad, a conflicted clawing deep in his chest that left him at a loss both emotionally and linguistically.

There had been no opportunity to speak to Amma, not even to see her, the night before. When he had returned from Cedric's chamber, he was so furious with the marquis that the noxscura flooded out of him, searching for something to destroy. It went for the windows, glass an easy and satisfying thing to shatter, the smoke slamming into the colored panes and the room filling with a sharp splintering. But then he threw out his hands and stopped it, calling back the arcana just as bits of glass broke away in the center of the artful windows, saving them from being destroyed and himself from being discovered. He pulled the magic back bit by bit, setting the panes right again until they were firmly back in place, and then he collapsed on the couch, completely spent.

The following day had passed slowly with Damien doing little more than pacing, not even enough focus to read the journal he'd gotten from Anomalous or attempt to open the Lux Codex. He did bring the shard of occlusion crystal out from its shielding pouch and considered calling up the arcana to reach out to Zagadoth but couldn't seem to press hard enough to spill his blood over it.

What would he even say? *Yeah, Dad, I'm late to Eirengaard because I'm the guest of honor in one of the realm's baronies for saving a woman who pretended to be a thief but was actually the baron's daughter...Yes, yes, that was* saving, *not* slaying...*Well, no, I didn't* really *save her, but I'm only hanging around because I feel like I might actually need to soon...I* know *that's not what Bloodthornes do, but it is what I'm doing, and, look—I have to go and be fitted for a tunic that isn't even black, isn't that punishment enough?*

No, that would fly about as well as Kaz had done when being strangled in the quag.

Instead, Damien listened at the door for every sound and constantly sent out feelers for spells coming to peek in on him, but only Tia had come late in the day for the shortest of visits to remind him to behave that evening. And then, finally, it was time for the Avington's festivities.

He would have never chosen this dress coat, blue like the sky at dusk and speckled with silver to presumably look like stars, though he did have to admit he made it look much more threatening on than expected. He attempted polite talk with some merchant or dignitary or whomever—he hadn't remembered or perhaps even gotten their name and title.

Though he did bump into Robert, the man from Elderpass, who actually apologized to *him*, his memory of their altercation completely different but useful. Only one other man, Thomas Treshi, really stuck in Damien's mind. Amma's former lover was unendingly handsome with deeply rich skin and an accent to match the southwestern isles, but he seemed smitten enough with his own wife that Damien could let go of any ill will toward the man. Unfortunately, that just allowed him to focus back on his own anxieties as the baron stood beside him, chatting well and taking the pressure off so that Damien's eyes could dart out over the crowd in search of Amma.

He had yet to glimpse her in the throng of a few hundred wealthy, self-important fucks, a sea of glimmering precious metals and well-cut stones catching the arcane light of chandeliers in the high, domed ceiling of the ballroom. Faebarrow's celebratory room was drenched in more creamy marble, warm under the orange stones set into gold plates on pedestals to light the massive space. The sounds carried in the bowl-like room, joyous laughter and the din of strings and horns from a musical group on a dais in its center. An internal balcony ran along its upper edge with a few means of access, stairs spiraling in each of the corners and a wider, grand staircase at the room's head. Then there was Tia, headed down those stairs from the upper hall, and Damien kept his gaze locked there.

A moment, and then another, and finally there was Amma. It had been only a day since he'd seen her, but then it had been weeks since he hadn't had her arcanely chained to his side, and there was a lifting in his chest at her presence, as if he could finally take a full breath again.

She was on Cedric's arm, swathed in a fluffy, blue dress that was a little ridiculous, so many layers about her feet that she looked to be floating, but it did put a nice barrier between the two of them. Her hair was gathered at the back of her head in a spray of coils, but he noted no dagger hidden within. Sheer fabric was draped over her shoulders and billowed down her arms, covering everything but her collar and the slender line of her neck, head held high, face meant to be pulled into unreadable neutrality, but without her smile, he could tell there was disquiet beneath it all.

Damien watched from beside her parents as Amma stared dutifully out on the ballroom of the Faebarrow keep, eyes sweeping over the gathered who turned to applaud the two before they began their descent. Amma's eyes kept searching and then they found Damien, and that lifting in his chest twisted into a twinge. She stumbled on the next step, and Cedric buoyed her, but she never looked away, and the twinge in Damien's chest fluttered.

Baron Avington's booming voice filled the room. "Welcome all, and welcome home, my dear daughter, returned by the night's hero, Sir Day Ravenheart."

There was a thunderous applause, and Damien's innards went cold as the gathered parted for Cedric to lead her across the hall and to where they stood.

"The tireless, brave deeds of this man have made our home and our hearts whole again, and for this we could never thank him or the gods enough. And in this prospering time for the realm, the safe return of our Ammalie is a sign from the gods that all is as it should be. So, let the celebrations run long into the night!"

312

Music struck up from the dais, louder than before. Cedric bowed to the baron and baroness, Amma still on his arm, curtsying, but she didn't dip her head, eyes still on Damien, lips parted on the verge of saying something that just wouldn't come out. She was so close, an arm's length away, and he wanted little more than to close that gap, the arcane word itching at his throat to order her away from the marquis. But then Cedric shifted her about to her own surprise, tugging her out onto the dance floor and into the crowd.

She was spun in Cedric's arms, face flushing as she sucked in a breath, eyes wide. A quick pace took her away from him, blocked by the others on the floor, perhaps a good thing in that moment, seeing Cedric pull her about like a puppet inspiring more noxscura to scratch beneath his skin. The baron pulled Damien into another conversation then, and he endured more praise he neither wanted nor deserved, all the worse knowing Amma was so distraught and he was doing nothing about it.

This went on throughout the evening until the baron and baroness were distracted by two separate groups and had mingled away from him. Finally alone, Damien climbed one of the winding staircases to the balcony that ran the entirety of the ballroom. Both behind him and on the ringing balcony's far side, there were wide arches that led outdoors, the cool air of an early autumn evening wafting in.

It was quieter there, the music and voices rising up out of the bowl in a gentler din, and Damien leaned on the balcony's metal railing to gaze at the scene below, so many of them dancing, drinking, and then there was Amma being spun about, and he wondered if he had gotten it all wrong. Perhaps she *was* happy. This was her home, after all, and she'd spoken of it so passionately. The story of childhood festivals, of her friends, the comfort all around, the enchanted trees—was he only seeing what he'd hoped to see in her and not what was really there?

A knock at his boot made him look farther down. On the ground beside him was a little, grey rat waving tiny rat paws, crooked rat whiskers twitching over its underbite.

"Kaz!" he said, never before so pleased to see an imp as he bent to scoop him up. "You survived."

"Barely," he squeaked back, melting flat onto Damien's palm. "Boots should be outlawed. When do we leave this wretched place?"

Damien grunted back. He hadn't thought that far ahead. "I need the talisman..."

"I will help you take it!" Kaz popped back up onto his haunches. "We will decimate this place. Think of the chaos!"

313

"Let me guess." Damien wrapped his hand around the rat. "You want me to gut her right here in the middle of the ballroom."

"No!" squeaked Kaz, clawed paws gripping onto his fingers as he squeezed. "I was only going to suggest stealing her away in the night! Really!"

Damien glanced back over the balcony railing, spying Amma again. "Actually kidnap her out of her bed? The irony."

"Yes, Master, take her and flee."

Darkness, if that wasn't what he'd been fantasizing about, squirreling away details of the keep, blind spots of the guards, the arcana he could sabotage and sneak past, since the moment they'd come here. However difficult it might be, the greater difficulty was enacting it at all without knowing what she wanted, and damn if that wasn't completely counterintuitive to abduction and villainy. Kaz's suggestions, though, were typically a good measure of the bounds of evil, and the imp was suddenly holding back. Where exactly had he been in the last twenty-four hours anyway?

The blood mage brought the disguised imp closer to his face. "I find it odd you're not advocating for Amma's death. Especially after all of this."

Kaz's underbite wiggled about as he thought, then he went on hesitantly. "She *has* been deceiving you…and you *will* have to kill her eventually…but maybe the harlot doesn't deserve to die here…exactly."

Damien glared at the rat and his unreadable, black orbs for eyes, but footsteps at his back made him dump Kaz into the breast pocket of his coat. There was a presence behind him soon after, light-footed, quick, and familiar. "Slithered away, hmm?"

When the blood mage turned, Tia was standing there, arms crossed, eyes leveled right to his. Easier to read, he could tell she hadn't grown much fonder of him, but there was a newfound tolerance there. "Not far," he said.

"Ammalie is not telling me the truth about you."

"Or she is, and you just don't trust her."

"I trust her to lie to me when she must. She always has, and unfortunately she has gotten better at it with age." Tia took a step forward to stand beside him and glance down at the party as well. The guests were small below, but still easy to identify. "She thinks she can protect people that way."

"Noble."

Tia grunted in agreement. "I thought you might be a hired mercenary for Brineberth March," she said after a pause, "but it has

314

become clear to me that you are not."

The music was slowing, and Cedric pulled Amma closer to him.

"Definitely not."

"You wear no colors or sigils, and Lady Ammalie insists you are only a traveler. Your loyalty," she said a bit more carefully, "appears to be questionable."

"I have been questioning it myself as of late." Damien took in the number of guards with the red lion-fish emblazoned on them all around. "How would you fix this?"

Tia straightened, glaring at him again, then snorted. "Oh, you know, wave a hand and magically set it all right again."

"So, it *is* wrong now? I can't seem to get anyone to actually bloody say so." Damien ran a hand through his hair and leaned against the railing, dropping all decorum.

"I didn't say that either." Tia's eyes darted downward again as if anyone could hear them so far up. On the floor below, the song was ending, and Amma and Cedric actually took a step back from one another as Cedric engaged a small crowd who flocked around him.

Damien watched Amma backing away from the marquis. "None of you really have to say, but it does make things clearer."

"I would cut them down and drive the rest out," said Tia, her voice so low it was barely a whisper. She was watching Amma too. "Anything to return this place to what it once was, and to see her actually smile again."

Another set of footsteps came at them then, this one even quicker and lighter than Tia's. When they turned away from the balcony, Amma's friend Laurel was there, hair pulled back slick to her head, pointed ears sticking out as she wore a wide grin. "Tia!" she cried in a cheerful but sloshed way. "Oh, goodness, you look *so* pretty tonight."

The guard's face shifted from her typical slight annoyance to one of horror as the half elf bowled right up to them, stumbling over the hem of her dress and falling into the guard's arms. "Are you drunk?" she hissed. "Gods, this is terribly unbecoming of a lady-in-waiting."

Giggles erupted out of her as she climbed up the woman's arms. "Nah, it's fine! I only drank just the same amount as Sir Robert and Sir Terrance."

"They're three times your size," Tia insisted, doing her best to hold her up, casting Damien a short but withering look. "And Dil'wator'wovl knows elves don't hold their liquor well."

"Hmm, now that you mention it..." She rubbed her stomach, and with a dramatic sigh, flopped over the woman's arm. "Oh, Tia, I don't feel so good."

315

"Sestoth grant me the strength to help this woman and not drown her," she mumbled, hauling Laurel's long form up over her shoulder with ease. "Do excuse me," she said and turned from Damien.

Laurel's head popped up from where she had fallen lax, or at least pretended to, over the woman's back. The half elf winked at Damien and then started groaning, quite loudly, about how she needed Tia to bring her to bed, and it became a little clearer where Amma might have learned some of her own tricks.

Damien glanced down into the ballroom again, finding Cedric still surrounded and engaged, but no sign of Amma until the blue puffball of her dress caught his eye, climbing the winding stairs on the opposite side of the balcony, darting through an archway, and into the shadows outdoors.

Damien shoved a hand into his pocket to scoop out Kaz. "Keep an eye on the marquis, and alert me if he looks like he's headed upstairs."

"But, Master—"

"Just do it." Damien dumped the mouse off at the head of the stairs closest to him and hurried around the balcony ringing the room to where he had seen Amma go.

Through the archway, the balcony continued, jutting away from the keep with a stone railing at its edge some ten paces off, catching the static moon's light. It ran the length of the building and continued around a corner where she had to have gone. A guard stood just outside the arch he'd passed through, looking rather bored as he leaned against the wall. Damien stepped up to the man and politely greeted him with a hand on his shoulder. The arcana that had been begging to be used all night sank down into him easily. "Wouldn't it be nice to go inside and have a little break?"

Without a word, he did exactly that, and Damien frowned after him. Maybe this would be easier than he thought.

The sounds of the ballroom all fell back into a gentle murmur of music and the occasional voice that rose above the others the farther he got from the archway. The balcony continued on around the corner, the stone wall overrun with a thick ivy that had climbed its way up the entire side of the keep. Jutting out of the wall was a fountain, a round pool of water at its bottom in a raised basin and a stone figure of a woman pouring a jug into it. The gentle trickle of water plunking off the body into the pool filled the quiet left behind in the absence of the gathering's noise.

Amma sat on the pool's edge staring out into the darkness of the night beyond the balcony's railing. Moonlight on her face, tears glistened across her cheeks. There was that urge to kill again, and Damien clenched a fist around smoke in his palm, but it was easier to quell this time. And then he had a different urge, something confusing that he couldn't quite identify, but that made his chest twinge again and his voice go soft. "Amma?"

She started, jumping to her feet, and then she wiped at her face. "Oh, gods, I'm sorry, I know you don't like crying."

He crossed the balcony to stand before her. "Don't apologize, you don't need to."

She nodded, taking a deep breath. "I know. Sorry."

"Amma, don't—" It was Damien's turn to sigh deeply. He wanted to hold her, to crush her to him, but that would have been wildly unacceptable in this strange world they'd been thrust into, the part he was suddenly playing of powerless stranger, and her standing as baroness. Though he supposed even in their previous roles as captor and abductee it would have been inappropriate too. If only there were no guises to don.

He tried to catch her eye as she stared down at what would have been her feet if not for all that tulle. "It's not so bad," he said quietly, and she glanced up from under a pinched brow. "The dress, I mean. It would be much worse if it were, you know, maybe yellow?"

Amma pressed her lips together, but a weak laugh came out anyway. "It is awful, isn't it? I can barely move, and it's so itchy, you wouldn't believe." She actually dug down into the neckline then, scratching at her chest. "But it makes my mother happy, and she asks so little. At least that's what she always says when she's convincing me of something."

Damien raised his brows. "Your parents," he said, choosing his words carefully, "they are as you described them."

Amma bit her lip. "Are they? I sort of left out the part about them being nobles."

"You did."

"I should have told you before we got to Faebarrow."

They stood for a moment in a chilling breeze, and then Damien swallowed. "I don't think I've ever made telling me anything very easy for you, Amma." He flexed a hand, wanting to take hers. "But, please, you can tell me now. Everything. What in the Abyss is going on here?"

There was still hesitation in her, but she eventually pointed out over the balcony. "It's even worse now."

Damien turned and stepped up to the stone railing. A courtyard with a manicured lawn and hedges was directly below, shrouded in the shadows of night. Just past that and beyond the wall of the keep, there was an open field, though it hadn't always been that way, he could tell by the carnage left behind. There was still a swath of liathau, leaves changing and blood red even in the moonlight, ringing the edge of what was once an orchard, but the rest was simply rows and rows of hacked up stumps where liathau once stood.

"We would *never* harvest so many in a season," said Amma, voice turning to anger though still run through with sorrow. She gripped the railing, her delicate fingers pressing down hard. "They don't grow at a quick enough rate to replenish something like this, and cutting them before their time yields chaotic magic anyway. It's not healthy, it's not even safe. And you should see the greenhouse. Liathau don't grow anywhere else but here, but they'll all be dead and gone if the crown keeps at it like this."

"This has been ordered by that king of yours?"

Amma nodded. "Brineberth acts on his orders. It's why they came here in the first place. Why Cedric is here." When she said his name with a hatefulness Amma had never used before, Damien heard everything he needed to know.

"Then get rid of him," he was quick to tell her. "I know you have a difficult time saying no, but you—"

"It's not like that for me, Damien," she snapped, hand going to her face again and wiping away another tear. "I'm not a lord with any power and the arcana to back it up; I'm a bargaining chip. And there's no telling Cedric Caldor no anyway. He just takes whatever he wants—whatever he thinks he deserves."

Damien knew Cedric's actions were immoral, and he also knew they were meant to be admirable to a blood mage, but now they only made his stomach twist and his heart yearn for blood.

Amma sighed, blinking out at the orchard. "Brineberth March has stood between Faebarrow and the aggressors on the other side of the sea for centuries. They've always focused on military prowess, and we've relied on them for just as long, never bothering to grow our own forces. Even now, we've only got a small handful of city guards to keep the peace and an aging royal guard that drinks with my father more than it ever spars. We had an even trade with Brineberth though, we sell to them at cost an allotted amount of liathau, and we house and school their military officers. It has always been like this if you read about our history, but Cedric's parents hated the way my parents ran things. They always thought the citizens of the barony should work for half what they do and produce twice as much." This she said with a bite, snorting. "It doesn't help that my family isn't as old as the

Caldors. We can't map our heritage back to a blessed mage or a descendant of a dominion like so many other nobles. We just have Sestoth's gift of the land fertile enough for liathau to grow and the trees. Well, had."

Damien nodded, listening. Most of the nobles of the realm had some arcane lineage, but barons were at the bottom of the royal hierarchy.

"But the Caldors died a few years ago, suddenly in an accident, and their two sons took over. Cedric's got an older brother, Roman, who should have inherited the march, but Roman's always been a little dense. Cedric came here last year, and when he called himself a marquis, no one questioned it. He charmed everyone, especially my parents. When he asked to marry me, it felt like I had to say yes, but I knew something was wrong. And then more of his soldiers came, just for protection he said, but they were changing things, and I tried to stall, I tried to explain to him that we couldn't harvest like he wanted—like he said the crown wanted. He pretended to listen at first, but I think he got sick of playing nice with me, especially once he realized he could just..." She released the railing of the balcony and stepped back, eyes searching the orchard but not really seeing it.

"This is why you wanted the scroll."

Amma tipped her head down, something like embarrassment or guilt clouding her features in the dark. "He only wants to marry me to absorb the barony and make it his own. I understand my duty is to do what's right for this place, and I don't need him to love me, but I thought I could at least convince him to care for Faebarrow like I do, to understand how it needs to be tended to. I thought if I just gave him what he wanted...but it wasn't enough. I didn't want to use force—I didn't even have a force to use, but I ran out of options." She shook her head tightly, wrapping her arms around herself and looking so small, lost in the cloud of blue that was her dress. "He knows what I did. He knows I ran off on my own, that I staged the kidnapping. He's not stupid enough to think it was a coincidence I disappeared right before we were meant to be married. When he said someone would pay for this, he meant me."

Damien would never let that happen, he would cut Cedric's throat before he could order her condemnation, slice off his limbs before he could raise a hand to her, behead him before he even thought to hurt her, but the resigned look on Amma's face told him she wouldn't believe him if he said any of that. And what did words alone mean anyway?

"I gave you bad directions," he said, remembering when they'd met and he had deemed her too naive, too small, too *good* to take on the Ebon Sanctum Mallor. There was a pang in Damien's stomach, a feeling he had once thought completely foreign so easily identifiable as guilt now that he wondered how he had never understood it before.

"I gave myself bad directions," she whispered. "I was the stupid one, thinking there was anything I could do, researching in the Athenaeum. I realize now, after seeing the way Faebarrow is again, there's nothing I can do to fight it from the outside. The only hope is if I just go through with this marriage, I can actually teach him to be a better leader, like my mother did with my father. Maybe I can help him be better, kinder—"

"Kinder?" Damien grabbed Amma's shoulders then, propriety be damned. "Amma, do you hear yourself? You can't foster something that doesn't exist to begin with. There's no kindness in that man. He's bloody evil."

Her gaze swept over his hands still on her then up to his face, and she choked out a nervous laugh. "You…*you* think Cedric's evil?"

"Yes. And I think you need to be as far from him as possible."

"Damien, I can't leave the barony like *this*."

"Fuck the barony," he spat. "What about you?"

Amma only held out her hands. He stared back at her, but she said nothing. It was obvious wasn't it? If she stayed, she would be worse than miserable, even if she made some absurd headway with that bastard, it would never be enough. She *had* to go. But Amma only shook her head.

"You want to stay?"

"Well, no," she admitted meagerly, as if it were a thing to be ashamed of, "but it's my duty to stay. Plus, there are even more guards now than when I got out before, and that took a whole moon to plan."

"You're worried about guards?" Damien held up his arm to show her where the dagger was sheathed on his bracer beneath his tunic's sleeve. "Nameless soldiers are little more than sacks of blood waiting to be drained."

"No!" Her eyes flashed as everything in her face shifted from resignation to total alarm. She gripped onto his raised arm to pull it back down. "You'd reveal what you are. Cedric's just as devoted to Osurehm and cleansing the land of evil as he is to taking hold of Faebarrow. He even calls himself one of Archibald's *chosen*. It's bad enough you're here at all, but you can leave tonight. I made Tia promise that you would be able to leave, that you would be safe. You have to go."

Damien smirked—she thought he needed *her* protection? "I am flattered you are so concerned about me, Amma, but—"

"I know you think you're indestructible, Damien, but you aren't." She squeezed his arm, eyes pleading. "You *cannot* take on an entire army by yourself."

"Well, no, of course I wouldn't do it by myself." Damien reached into his pocket, pulling out the Scroll of the Army of the Undead, and her mouth fell open. "Wasn't this your original plan? The reason you went all the way up to Aszath Koth to begin with? You don't need to marry that idiot to fix things—you just need this."

"I can't *actually* raise an army to get myself out of a wedding," she hissed.

"Maybe you can't, but I can."

CHAPTER 34
A MORALITY PLAY IN ONE ACT

Damien, you absolutely cannot do this." Amma grabbed his arm again as he held up the Scroll of the Army of the Undead and let it unfurl before him. "Cedric intends to send my parents someplace quiet to abdicate the seat of the barony, but only if I cooperate. If I take this and stage a...a coup? An uprising? He'll have them killed." She swallowed. "And he'll keep me alive."

"Who said anything about you doing this? I'm not even sure you could. Can you read Chthonic?" Damien gestured with the unraveled parchment. Even in the darkness, the ink across it glinted in the moonlight with a smoky glow in a language she, indeed, could not read. That had been a slight oversight in her research, she had to admit. "I'm getting rid of this occupying force, Amma, and they'll be gone for good—you won't need to worry about retribution when I'm through."

Damien was always ridiculously confident, and the way the static light of Lo shined off of him now, how it highlighted his dark hair and made the clenching of his jaw seem so severe, she wished she had the arcana to freeze everything, to stop before she said what she would say next, and finally give in to the things she'd wanted to do to him. But she didn't—they'd already been missing from the banquet for too long, and now, as she stared at that smirk she wanted to ravage, she only delayed the inevitable longer. "You can't. There are too many Brineberth soldiers, and they're crawling all over every inch of this place."

He arched a brow at the parchment, eyes darting across the lines. "Amma, I, uh...I don't think either of us realized the scope of this spell. These numbers are massive."

322

"I don't care—I can't ask you to do this. You'll be going against the crown and brand yourself an enemy of the realm."

"You're not asking me, I'm just doing it." He took her hand gently, removing it from his arm but not letting it go. "Listen to me: go back inside and find that imbecile, pretend this conversation never happened, and let me unleash the Abyss, all right?"

She was shaking her head, tears welling up again. Damien opened his mouth, and she could feel the magic words before he even said them, the ones that would order her to do exactly as he said. "Damien, no!" She lunged forward, slapping a hand over his mouth to keep them inside. Stunned, he only stared back at her. "You're in the middle of Faebarrow Keep, and you're a stranger here. No one will know why you're doing this, even the people you're trying to protect."

He turned slightly to free the corner of his mouth, brows pinched. "But you'll know," he said softly against her palm. "What else could even matter?"

What Amma felt then, she was sure she had never actually felt before, not with this intensity and brightness. And even with Damien at its source, blood mage, demon spawn, dark lord, it indeed was *bright*.

With a shaking hand, she pulled back, pleading with her eyes that he not order her away. She slipped her fingers over his cheek and buried them into his hair. "They'll kill you, Damien."

"Kill me?" He lifted the scroll once more, grinning fully, as if it were a game he couldn't possibly lose. "They can certainly try."

"Gods, I'm telling you to stop," she said, pulling hands back, balling her fists, and snorting.

His head cocked. "And I'm telling you I'm doing it."

"No." She pushed his arm down.

Damien grunted, shaking her off again. "Yes."

They stood there, glaring at one another, the scroll between them.

"It seems we're at an impasse," he said. "And you forget which of us is technically enthralled."

Amma could feel her face scrunching up, her heart beating faster with the truth of what he said and also the fear of what would happen if he did exactly what he planned to do, without her. "At least let me help. Use me."

A flicker of the waxing moon Ero reflected in his violet eyes as they took her in. For a moment, he looked hungry, starved even, and like he might devour her right there. "Use you? How?"

Her mind worked, unsure. She had no arcana herself; she barely had any real power at all besides her name and her station, little more than a symbol that others swore to protect. "The thing I'm best at," she said suddenly, the idea practically coming up with itself.

He needed only a moment to understand what she meant. "You've certainly had a lot of practice being a damsel in distress. You want to play at being my kidnapping victim?"

Amma grinned and then narrowed her eyes at him. "If I do, it's got to look completely real. You can't just *pretend* to take me and run away—you have to *actually* take me when you escape."

Damien took in a deep breath through a clenched jaw. "It would be my pleasure."

Taking the scroll in both hands, Damien turned to the balcony and held it out before him. The Chthonic words were like music, a lilting but low hum that came from deep in his chest as he read them aloud. With each word, the ink lifted itself off the parchment into a smoky, swirling haze, each line a new wisp that coalesced together above the scroll, ever moving with arcana.

Amma felt the magic then, touching at places that hands couldn't, tickling behind her ribs and at the back of her throat. She'd been this close to him before when he cast but had never experienced arcana this way, and it was exhilarating. She watched how he stood even taller, eyes glinting amethyst and lids lowering like he no longer needed to see the words to know what to say.

As his voice grew, there was a rumbling, faint at first, and then a long, low crack like the falling of a tree from far off. The sky, dark but clear moments before, moved with a storm cloud sweeping in and over the moons. Amma's heart raced, unsure if it were for fear of the object he used, knowing from her research what it was supposed to do.

Meant to call on the spirits of those lost to war, the Scroll of the Army of the Undead was evil. It would animate bodies scattered and buried and forgotten, their sacrifices to be rekindled and their souls forced to again walk the earth and live how they perished. It was a cruel thing to do when it came right down to it, to force men and women who had been so brutally cut down at the whim of some king to be shunted back on this earth just to serve again with no will of their own. But as the ground split out in the heart of the orchard where the trees had been cleared and where death had already taken stake, Amma forgot all that and focused on the glint off something bone white as it caught the moonlight that peeked out from behind swirling clouds.

As Damien continued to read, Amma grabbed the edge of the

balcony, leaning over it to squint out into the defiled orchard. Those—those were fingers crawling out of the ground, and that was an arm, and then a skull, and a ribcage until an entire body had climbed out of the earth, devoid of flesh, of blood, of anything except the weapon strapped to its side. She should have been terrified to see it, to see the things meant to stay completely internal moving on their own, but something sparked within her, excitement and awe, as fog rose up around the skeletal soldier's feet.

Lightning crackled across the sky, the orchard bathed in daylight for a split second, a burst of thunder just on its heels, and then there was another form and another and another at the growing pit's edge, stumps cracking and falling into oblivion as the trembling of the earth continued. Skeletal forms of all shapes crawled out of the infernal pit. The stench of rot and burning filled the air as more bodies long gone from earth repieced themselves on the soil of where the liathau had been felled too soon. Some were massive and hulking, and some were small and stout, while others were four legged and even a few of those had human torsos, all carrying swords, axes, bows, halberds. They climbed from the ever-growing pit to stand in long, unending lines, multiplying faster than Amma could possibly count.

When Damien's words finally fell away, the clouds blotted out the moons completely. Darkness swallowed up the orchard where the undead army had convened. There was a wind whipping over them, freezing cold, clouds moving at an impossible rate overhead, shadows against an even deeper blackness.

Amma turned back to Damien in the dark, able to see him in the slight light that found its way out of the keep at their back, and she noted the ink had gone from the scroll, leaving it blank. Instead, a haze was hovering just before him, coming together to take the shape of a raven, its feathers made up of a transparent smoke. Damien held up a hand, and it landed on him.

"Strike down and clear out only those who wear the Brineberth crest. Chase them out of Faebarrow lands." Damien's voice was a searing heat, cutting through the newly-frigid air.

The raven took flight, its wispy body sailing over the balcony toward the orchard and disappearing into the dark. The last of the arcana Damien had expended hung heavily in the air like a blanket, encircling the two of them and keeping them safe from the impending horror that stalked silently toward the keep.

A sound from the distance, a rattling like many leaves crunching underfoot, was coming closer, followed by a more distinct scraping, and then in a sliver of moonlight from between the clouds, there was movement at the keep's wall. A shadow against the shadows dragged itself up to the top of the wall, and in the courtyard below, a lone Brineberth soldier was wandering toward it, lit from behind by the glow coming from inside the keep.

Atop the wall, the humanesque figure stood there in the dark, strange with its thinness and jerking movements, and then all at once it collapsed over the wall's edge to tumble to the ground of the courtyard some thirty feet below. With a clatter, the bones broke apart on the earth, scattering.

Amma's mouth opened, and a frail squeak of despair fell out. "They're skeletons, Damien," she said. "They're just bones. How are they supposed to hold up against actual soldiers?"

Damien placed a hand on the railing, eyes piercing into the dark. "Wait."

The guard was careful to head toward where it fell, stopping when he reached the first piece and picking it up from the ground. Like he were holding a dead thing, and to be sure it was, but in the dark he couldn't have known, he clasped the rounded skull by its top, turning the face toward him at arm's length. Too shocked to react, he stood there with a skull in hand that had, from his perspective, apparently just been chucked over the keep's wall, looking back at it like it might move on its own.

And then it did.

The jaw snapped, and the guard dropped it, jumping away from where it landed with a yelp. Unsheathing his sword, he stood ready, and from the shadow of the wall, a figure traipsed, slow and nearly whole again, the skeleton only missing its head. As it came closer, the guard took matched steps back, but didn't flee, nor did he scream, the horror of it seemingly too much, and the skeleton plucked its own skull from the courtyard's soft grass and sat it back up on its neck.

The guard had a moment of bravery then, which is, of course, quite similar to stupidity when all is said and done, and he rushed the stack of bones, thrusting wildly forward with his sword. The weapon pierced the skeleton, and the guard ran it through until he was right up against it, the blade fitting neatly between the ribs.

The undead warrior tipped its skull downward to assess and then back up to his challenger. There was a metallic clang as its own weapon was unsheathed, and with two bony hands, it was raised overhead and brought down across the man's shoulder to cleave his own head cleanly off. When the Brineberth guard's headless body fell back, his sword slid from between the skeleton's ribs, nothing to have pierced, and the warrior continued on as if nothing had touched it at all because, mostly, it really hadn't.

Amma tipped her head. "Huh. I guess just bones are good after all."

A clattering then filled the air as hundreds of other skeletal soldiers made their ungraceful fall over the keep's wall and reassembled themselves on the other side. Guards called from below, the sound too much to ignore, and there was chaos breaking out across the courtyard.

Damien's hand clasped Amma's. "We don't want to miss the fun." There was a smile on his face that made her want to throw herself at him, but he didn't give her the chance, pulling her along back inside.

In the ballroom below, no one had any idea the horror that was falling all around outside. The music was loud, the air heady with spiced meats and wine and sweets. Many hours into their cups, most of the guests would have perhaps not heeded a first warning if it had even come already.

Damien took careful stock of the room from above as his hand squeezed hers, the spiraling stairs downward, and the widest set at the end that headed back to the main hall. Amma searched for Cedric, eventually eyeing him in a group of Brineberth citizens who had taken up important posts in Faebarrow as well as a few merchants who were enjoying the deals they were getting now that Cedric had such a hold on the barony. She frowned and searched again for her parents. They were together, at least, if central to the room and vulnerable.

"Ammalie, where were you?" Tia's voice broke her of her long look over the edge. The guard had just ascended a flight of winding stairs, eyes finding Damien's hand on her and scowling even more deeply than she already had been.

Before Amma could say anything, Damien readjusted his hold of her, taking her by the wrist instead. "Take the baron and baroness to safety and then return. You'll be needed later."

"I don't take orders from you," she spat, looking him over before glaring back at Amma. "If there is a threat, she comes with me."

Damien hesitated, Amma could feel it in his hold on her, but she wasn't going to let him go back on their bargain. Amma stepped forward, loosing her hand from his hold and standing defiantly. "Then take an order from me for once. Get my parents somewhere safe, now." She winced at herself. "Please?"

The woman took a heavy set of breaths in through her nose and out, eyes flicking from one to the other, hand hovering over her hilt.

The tense moment was all too strange in the midst of everyone else carrying on, laughing, drinking, and dancing below.

"I'll be coming right back here, and I want you with me then," said Tia, eyes flicking once to Damien with a sneer. "And don't touch her."

When the guard stormed off down the stairs again, Amma swallowed, feeling lightheaded. There was a shout from the main hall, a guard calling to another, and someone else answered, clear the undead had breached the front of the keep. Voices were rising, and metal sang as it crashed against metal, echoing off the halls. From below, there was another disruption, an indiscriminate shout, a glass shattering, and it seemed the army they had called up had made it below as well. There was a sizzle of arcana through the air, both Faebarrow's and Brineberth's casters responding in kind.

"I suppose some theatrics are in order." Damien's dagger slid from his bracer into his hand, flipping around so that the blade caught the light streaming down from the chandeliers hanging out over the ballroom. He gripped the neck of his coat, pulling it to the side, and dragged the blade just under his collarbone, a long red line seeping upward, a deeper and longer cut than Amma had ever noticed him making before.

He placed his hand over the wound and muttered some arcane words, and the world around them devolved into shadows, darkness striking out the candles and dousing the magical lights. The last thing Amma saw before her vision went out were Damien's eyes glinting violet with delight.

Screams pierced the air as the rest of the guests fell into chaos in the new darkness of the hall. Damien and Amma stood silently, unmoving in the shadows while all manner of discord broke out below. As her eyes adjusted, she grabbed onto his coat and pulled him closer. A hand wrapped around her waist, and Damien's voice fell low amongst the growing noises. "I hope you are prepared to leave this place again."

She nodded, fingers finding their way to his collar and the warm blood dripping down him, sticky and wet on her palms as she held tight.

"Good, because I've decided to take you either way."

A shiver ran through her, be it from fear or excitement, she didn't know or care, and then movement on the far side of the balcony caught her attention. A line of skeletal soldiers was streaming in from the main hall and down the stairs toward the party. She hoped Tia had gotten her parents to safety.

Damien tugged her then, guiding her carefully along the ringing balcony toward the fray of skeletons. Easier to see now and so close, her heart hitched at how they looked, menacing with weapons drawn, but none even glanced at the two of them as they filed down the stairs. In their wake, not a single Brineberth soldier followed, and finally a line of the undead formed at the entry back into the main hall, standing at attention.

Damien continued forward with her to the stairs where they stood before the undead, looking down on the chaos below. From there, exits and escape seemed obvious, but within the mess of shadows and bodies, it was quite different for the rest, and they bumbled around like panicked field mice, shrieking as the undead closed in around them in the dark.

Arcana broke against arcana, some of the risen dead apparently casters in life, and even the assembled mages were having a hard time against the undead army. Damien was casting again, a hand pressing against the wound he'd made, still seeping, and something like a storm blew through the ballroom, wind whipping overhead, debris flying through it, and fissures opening above the crowd. Within the tears in space, silvery rivers ran, glinting with their own light, and Amma felt beckoned to them even as a pall of dread settled over everything. Crashes of broken glass, screaming guests, and the wet squelch of gutted soldiers filled the air.

The arcane lights in the hall flickered back on, casting the room in crimson, and Amma laid eyes on Cedric then. He was no different than the others, though perhaps stronger than most and using that strength to push people out of his way. Seeing him lost, trapped, terrified, Amma was inundated by a feeling she didn't quite know, a mixture of relief and anger, a sort of joyful righteousness at him finally feeling the fear she'd known for too long. Cedric managed to push himself closer to the stairs, and his eyes lifted to see her.

Amma's heart shot into her throat, and she pressed herself back against Damien at the head of the stairs. He gripped her and squeezed, her anchor to anything like safety in that moment.

"People of Eiren, I must thank you for your hospitality." Damien's voice rumbled from behind Amma, low but booming with arcana out over the sunken ballroom. She could feel the words as they left him, vibrating from his chest. "You are especially entertaining like this."

There was a glint of metal, and the blade Damien used to cut into himself was held to Amma's throat. Her eyes widened, fear flooding every part of her, hands slick with his blood as she gripped his wrist and choked on a scream.

A handful of Brineberth soldiers had reached the foot of the stairs, weapons drawn, but the undead met them, holding them back, though none moved to actually strike in the quiet unease that had fallen over the keep with Damien's words.

Taking a few slow steps down the staircase together, Damien and Amma were surrounded by a retinue of the undead, clad in bits of ancient armor, clearer who they had been in life, minotaurs, dwarves, even a centaur amongst them, swords and bows and halberds ready.

In the ballroom below, the guards had either been slain already or were being held at the end of a similarly deadly weapon, the few mages in attendance had been rendered useless, and if not for the red light illuminating everything, the streaks of blood on the ground would have been much more gruesome. The rest of the guests, dignitaries, merchants, and Faebarrow's wealthiest, were helpless.

"But I do grow tired of this charade," Damien announced to the assembled as they fell into terrified stillness, hemmed in by the undead who had covered every empty inch of the room. "It is time you knew me for who I truly am: Xander Sephiran Shadowhart."

Murmurs rose up from the crowd in response, and Amma glanced over her shoulder. "Oh, my gods, blaming Xander? What a good idea," she whispered.

"I know." He was already grinning slyly at those below them, but his brow ticked upward at her. "But don't forget, you're meant to be terrified of me, not impressed."

"Oh, right." Amma let out a scream and tried weakly to flail out of his grasp.

"Infernal darkness, Amma, not right in my ear," he groused under his breath, then chuckled deeply, laughter rising up in him and over the assembled, a dark sound that pulsed over Amma's back and made her shiver with delight even with the dagger still hovering near her throat.

Up the stairs from between the bony feet of the soldiers, a tiny ball of grey fluff zipped out, and it clamored itself up Amma's dress, hopping over her arm and onto her shoulder. The familiar rat perched there and addressed Damien, "Are we really doing this, Master?"

Damien's laughter died off. "If we are, you'll need to look a fair bit more frightening than that."

Kaz gave a squeak of elation and propelled himself off of Amma's shoulder, arcana sparking in the air as his body contorted, wings bursting forth so much bigger than she'd ever seen. With an explosion of smoke and sparks, Kaz was an imp once again, but the word did not do him justice, hovering with the beating of his wings and twice as big as any of the humans assembled. Clawed, horned, and horrible, Kaz's arms trailed the ground, wind off his beating, leathery wings hot and rancid-smelling, and the crowd screamed in horror at his appearance.

"Nice illusion," Damien said quietly, nodding to himself, then cleared his throat to address them all again. "It was a pleasure to abscond once with your pretty, little baroness, stealing her out of her bed in the middle of the night." Though he still held the dagger to her neck, his free hand came up and slipped under her jaw, tipping her head up and back. His fingers pressed into her skin as he took a moment to look down on her, grin intoxicating so that she had to bite her tongue to keep from returning it and, worse, to keep from pressing her lips against his and having him right there in front of the gods, the undead, and everyone. "And now, it seems, I'll be abducting her once again."

"Ravenheart!" Cedric's voice called out from the crowd. "You dare to steal the heart out of Faebarrow right before its people and lay waste to the land with your rotting army of undead?" He had pushed his way to the front and had that sword he always wore with the jewel-encrusted hilt in hand. "This shall not stand, villain!"

Damien made a questioning sound in the back of his throat, eyes lazily falling on the marquis. "Stealing the heart of Faebarrow? Laying waste to the land? Invading with an army?" He ripped his dagger away from Amma and pointed at Cedric instead. "Am I not only following in the footsteps of the villain who came before me, Caldor? It seems it takes one to know one. And it's Shadowhart, by the way."

Cedric was incensed, a look Amma had seen before and made her heart race faster than any weapon that could be brandished at her. He pushed against the line of skeletal soldiers that stood at the foot of the wide staircase. "You dare accuse me, accuse the *crown*, of acting in the interest of evil? Yet you...you abduct the baroness only to...to bring her back and abduct her again?"

"Right. I did do that." Damien brought the dagger back and tapped it against his chin in thought.

Cedric's pushing abated for a moment, brow pinched. "It just seems quite complex and roundabout and unnecessary." A low murmur of agreement rose up from the assembled, forgetting their fear. There was even a clattering of bones that seemed to suggest slight confusion.

Damien let out a growl, gesturing with the dagger flippantly.

331

"Well, you know, sometimes you just need to have some fucking fun, all right?"

Amma was spun off into Kaz's overlong arms then as Damien sheathed the dagger and stalked down the steps toward where Cedric stood. She reached out, but the overgrown imp squeezed her in place, surprisingly strong for what Damien had called an illusion, not to mention terrible smelling. She choked as she tried to call out and could only watch as Damien pulled a bloody hand through the air as a crimson sword appeared in it. The metal glinted like liquid under the low, red lights all around them, so similar to the time in Elderpass when he had slain the succubus.

The skeletal soldiers parted just enough to allow Cedric to charge him, and Amma finally worked out a scream as the two fell against one another. Matched, their weapons clanged together, loud with a searing sound, both urged on by magic. Cedric was a mage in his own right, something Amma had failed to mention to Damien, but it did nothing to stop the blood mage as he bore down on the marquis from a step above.

Cedric murmured some arcana then, and his blade pulsed, pushing Damien back. He reeled to the side, both standing staggered on the steps to face one another. Damien looked surprised, and then he grinned wickedly, hand flexing around his hilt, blood dripping off of it. "What *is* that, Caldor? Not of this realm, certainly."

"I've been blessed by Osurehm and Archibald himself," Cedric called back, raising his weapon overhead and swinging with a swiftness that a sword so heavy should not have had. "Not to mention the blood of a dominion runs through the Caldor line."

Damien threw up his own arcane weapon to block Cedric's as it came down, and a black mist enveloped the two as a yellow light sparked out from inside it.

Amma's gaze honed in on Tia then, the guard attempting to cut her way through the undead. With her crest of the twisted liathau across her chest, they only pushed her back, deflecting her blows and never swinging on her, so she was able to dodge and run through the ever-thinning crowd of shrieking bureaucrats, cowering merchants, and fallen Brineberth soldiers. The guard's eyes were on fire as she focused on her target, switching from Amma, trapped in what appeared to be a demon's grasp, to Damien, caught against Cedric with his blade.

There was an arcane blast as the men pushed off one another, staggering backward at least twenty paces apart. Cedric laughed then, a smile across his face. "You'll pay for the damage you've caused with your life!" His arm and weapon pulsed with an odd, grey aura, distorting both.

"Did you say dominion, Caldor?" Damien gestured with his sword, face screwed up, no longer standing defensively but intrigued. "That's rather vile to be divine, isn't it?"

Gripping his weapon two handed, the veins in Cedric's neck pulsed. "Vile? Your attempt at stealing my property,"—and at this he jerked his head toward Amma though never looked at her—"is the truly vile thing here."

Damien gave his eyes a hefty roll. "Well, if you're going to talk like that." With his free hand, he gripped the red blade and slid it upward, cutting into his palm. When the blood dripped down his arm and a violet sizzle rose up from the wound, Cedric's face fell.

"A blood mage?" he gasped. "Demon spawn?"

"Nice of you to finally catch on, but I'm getting bored now." Damien released the palmful of blood he'd collected, throwing it at Cedric to form thin, swirling blades in the air. Cedric threw his own forearm up, and a glint of golden light flashed, the blades breaking against it as he grunted in pain. One of them got through, slicing up Cedric's arm, his dress coat shredded, blood spattering, skin blackened from the arcana in the spell. Damien stood a bit straighter, and he grinned.

But then Amma noted Tia, even closer. A few more swings, and she would be thrusting her own sword at Damien too, sans arcana, but full of her unyielding rage. Amma didn't know if the undead would allow her to continue her onslaught without fighting back, or if they let her through, how Damien might juggle the two of them.

"Tia!" she shrieked, reaching out both arms and flailing in Kaz's grasp, the only distraction she could think of.

She slowed for a moment, eyes flashing in fear at the distress in Amma's voice, but her call did its job, alerting Damien of the guard's presence. He immediately pulled back up the steps as the undead fell between himself and Cedric once more, creating a barrier that Damien could turn his back on.

"Get back here, villain!" cried Cedric, swiping with his sword. A pulse of arcana cut into the soldiers before him and pushed them back up the stairs, one actually clattering to the ground in a heap of bones. "Fight me like a real man and discover what this power is for yourself."

Damien came to a stop, and Amma saw his eyes narrow, rage there, but intrigue too. There was still blood dripping from his hand, and he brought it up to his face as if he would cast again, but then his eyes flicked up to Amma. When she caught his gaze, she gave him a tight shake of her head. He clenched his jaw, and the crimson sword melted away from his other hand into nothingness.

Damien whistled sharply as he strode up the rest of the staircase, raising an arm overhead, and the smoky raven fluttered into existence to land on his hand. "Your new master," he said to the arcane bird, turning as he reached Amma and pointing to Tia who had broken through the ranks of the undead to finally reach the bottom of the stairs. The raven called out and took off toward the woman as Damien reached into one of his pockets.

The ballroom had erupted back into chaos under the crimson lights, smelling of rot and blood as the guests continued to scurry and scream. Damien threw what he had retrieved onto the ground at their feet, and the marble of the stairs cracked beneath it, revealing a pit of smoking heat and blackness.

"Again, Xander Sephiran Shadowhart thanks you," he called to those still assembled, taking Amma from Kaz and pulling her against him once more, not bothering with the dagger. "Son of Birzuma the Blasphemed, Ninth Lord of the Accursed Wastes and Nefarious Harbinger of the Chthonic Tower. Remember the name, for it was your downfall!" He took a step into the pit, pulling Amma along, a small shelf appearing below their feet and rocky stairs revealing themselves into the depth.

"What kind of harbinger?" a voice shouted back from the crowd.

Damien sighed, pausing. "Of the Chthonic Tower."

Tia had attempted to slash through the raven as it sailed toward her, but it only dispersed around her blade and reformed again to land on her shoulder. Distracted, the woman backed up, trying to bat it away, but then she began to blink and look about as if hearing something none of the rest of them did.

Cedric still fought against the undead at the foot of the stairs, pushing them off with blasts of arcana, and a bevy of Brineberth soldiers had broken through and made their way to him, Gilead, his mage, in the lead. "Foul blood mage Ravenheart, you will pay!" cried Cedric.

Absolutely incredulous, Damien's grip on Amma actually loosened as he stepped out of the pit. "Look, I know it's confusing because of the bird, but it's not Raven, it's Shadow—"

Amma grabbed his coat and yanked him backward.

"It's just Xander," he shouted, perturbed but stepping back again. "Xander, the blood mage from the Accursed Wastes will do. Remember *that* name." The ballroom had completely devolved into shrieks and clashing metal once again, and he squinted, looking unsure if anyone had heard him.

"Damien?" She nudged him.

"Oh, right." He grabbed her much more tightly then, dropping his voice. "Ready to go, my little prisoner?"

Amma almost giggled, tingling under his grip, but only cleared her throat, putting on her best wide-eyed, innocent look. "It's not really up to me, is it, Master Bloodthorne?"

Damien growled in her ear as he walked them down the steps into the earth that had opened up. "Careful talking like that, or I'll think you really are mine for the taking."

CHAPTER 35
THROWN IN THE DARK

The darkness was all consuming, the smell of rot gone, replaced with a burning in Amma's throat, and then a breeze. She took a deep breath but couldn't seem to completely fill her lungs, heartbeat in her ears, vision dancing as it came back. It was night, wherever they had descended to, and they stood out in the open, but not any place she recognized, flat, warm-toned, empty. Damien still had his arms around her like she might be pulled away from him despite that the sounds of frightened guests and clashing metal and rattling bones had been extinguished.

There was a thunk at the ground beside them, followed by a familiar, watery yelp. Kaz had, apparently, made it through as well, back into his much smaller imp form. Above them, the tear in the sky they'd passed through closed up.

Amma pressed her hands against Damien's chest. There was dried blood on his coat and her fingers, and she pulled his collar to the side. The lengthy slice he had given himself across his chest was nearly healed.

"That must have hurt," she said softly, running a finger along where it had been.

Damien gave a small, rueful laugh. "No, not at all."

She narrowed her eyes, letting a hand slide up to the back of his neck. "Liar."

"Well, maybe a little," he admitted, his own hands roving over her body slowly.

Amma tried to catch her breath, but with her front pressed against him it was nearly impossible. "What will happen in Faebarrow now?"

"Tia has been left in control of the undead. If she is as loyal to your family as she says, she will use them to drive the rest of the Brineberth soldiers out and protect the barony. Considering they're already expired, I can see them lasting quite a long time."

"You...you actually unleashed the Army of the Undead," she said, still a little in awe of the idea. "Thousands of them just came up out of the earth."

"It was quite exhilarating, wasn't it?"

"But you also attacked Cedric."

Damien's satisfied look deepened. "I know."

"You could have killed him," she said breathlessly.

The grin on his face faltered. "Ah, I'm...sorry?"

"No!" She curled her hands into the lapels of his jacket, pulling him closer. "That was amazing!"

"Amazing?" He dipped his head lower, all the satisfaction returning with his smirk.

"You were..." She pushed up onto her toes, fists tight but trembling. "You were wonderful." She wanted him closer still despite being right up against him. She wanted to be out of the dress, to have his hands on her skin, to tell him, to show him, what she really meant.

A shadow darted across the darkness they'd been thrown into.

"Master?" Kaz's voice was just a whisper. "We have company."

"Already?" Damien grumbled, hands releasing her and taking a step back. He slipped out of Amma's grasp, and a frigid gust swept through the space left between them.

There were figures in the dark, shifting against the dusky, warm colors of the plane they stood on. Hulking things moved hesitantly forward but kept their distance, forming a ring around the three, featureless even under the moonlight. Then a figure emerged, different from the others. This one stood tall, brighter than the rest, and both moons shone off his white hair.

"I am so very pleased you've taken me up on my offer, Bloodthorne," said the true Xander Sephiran Shadowhart, striding toward them, hands clasped behind his back. This time he was not clad in a silken robe, but in a tight-fitting suit of white and silver, a stark contrast to the deep reds and browns of the land all around him.

"Shadowhart." Damien's voice dropped deep, and he stepped toward the other blood mage, dagger sliding into his hand.

"What's this?" Xander gently lifted a single hand. "Not a social call? But you look hardly in a state to fight. And, well..." He gestured to the shadows surrounding them.

Damien took a deep breath. Amma had seen him expend quite a

lot of arcana at the keep, and there had been so much blood.

"No. You're not here for that. It's something else. You...you *need* me, don't you?" He smiled wickedly.

Damien reached into the small satchel on his hip and pulled out a flat package wrapped in linen. "You need me," he corrected, gesturing with the package and then thrusting it into Amma's hands. "And we both need her."

It was the Lux Codex, she recognized the shroud she'd had Perry wrap it in, and she pulled the divine linen off to hold up the book for Xander to see. There was a hiss from the creatures that surrounded them, and they backed away like she had run in a circle and smacked them each in the face with it.

But Xander only tipped his head. "You didn't actually fetch it..." His tongue ran over his lips, and he laughed. "But you *did*. And you came to *me*?"

Damien groaned. "That is the order of things, technically."

"What fun!" He clapped, face rearranging itself to show a gamut of emotions until it settled on pure delight. "And don't ruin it for me by saying you only came here because you *had* to—I know that already, you were never very good at sharing, so why start now? But no reason this can't be mutually beneficial, eh? Whatever you're hiding from, you can do it safely from the tower."

Relaxing just a bit, Damien straightened but still frowned at the other blood mage until Xander turned and began to walk off. Amma watched after him, confused—they'd just been offered safety, but Damien hadn't yet accepted. Then Xander came to a stop and whirled back. Damien didn't look the least bit surprised.

"Oh, I almost forgot my one condition. You'll have to let me in on the details of your other machinations. Don't get me wrong, I've had a think, and I'm fairly certain I've mostly figured out the whole reason you were headed south in the first place, but the minutia of what exactly you'll be doing when you get there—how you'll be doing it, to be precise—is something I'm just dying to hear all about."

Damien shifted with a different discomfort, his confidence wavering, eyes flicking to Amma. "Fine. We can talk later."

"Oh, can we?" He dragged the words out, bringing a long finger to his lips, dark eyes darting between the two. "Because I'd rather know now if I properly pieced together the visions of your travels I glimpsed through that translocation portal you used to get here."

"You were spying through that thing?"

"Barely! Seconds at a time! Some of the best seconds, admittedly." He winked. "Regardless, I know you've figured it out,

Bloodthorne—I don't know *how*, but you're planning to travel down to Eirengaard, take out that ridiculous King Archibald, and liberate dear old daddy from that occlusion crystal he's been sentenced to spend eternity inside so he can finally have his infernal vengeance on the realm and utterly destroy it."

Damien said nothing, but his fists clenched, and Amma silently worked out what the blood mage was saying. She'd never learned Damien's reason for heading to Eirengaard, never learned the prophecy he was following, but Damien wasn't denying a word of it. Was that what he truly intended to do? Travel to the capital, kill the king, and release his father, a *demon*, to wreak havoc on the realm?

She looked on him, but his eyes never flicked back to hers, caught instead in Xander's keen gaze. Damien's eyes were different then, pained and angry too, but there was something more, something…eager.

"That *is* it, I know it, no reason to play coy." Xander squinted up at the moons and sighed deeply. "So, whatever they are, you only need expand those plans to include yours truly since we've a shared interest, and I'll offer you asylum and a truce in trade. Do we have a bargain?"

Amma wanted to grab Damien, to beg him not to accept, somehow knowing without knowing it wasn't a good idea. But she held still, staying silent and hugging the Lux Codex to her chest instead of him.

"For asylum," Damien finally said. "We have a deal."

Amma and Damien's story will continue in:

VILLAINS & VIRTUES
BOOK 2

SUMMONED
TO THE
WILDS

Thank you, Dear Reader, I hope this book brought you joy.

Throne in the Dark is a self-published novel.
If you enjoyed this book, please leave a review!

ALSO BY A. K. CAGGIANO

STANDALONE NOVELS:
The Korinniad - An ancient Greek romcom
She's All Thaumaturgy - A sword and sorcery romcom
The Association - A supernatural murder mystery

VACANCY
A CONTEMPORARY (SUB)URBAN FANTASY TRILOGY:
Book One: The Weary Traveler
Book Two: The Wayward Deed
Book Three: The Willful Inheritor

VILLAINS & VIRTUES
A FANTASY ROMCOM TRILOGY:
Book One: Throne in the Dark
Book Two: Summoned to the Wilds
Book Three: Eclipse of the Crown

FOR MORE, PLEASE VISIT:
WWW.AKCAGGIANO.COM